PRAISE FOR
ROSARITO BEACH

"If you haven't read M. A. Lawson, start right now with *Rosarito Beach*! I loved this riveting thriller, which launches a new star in crime fiction, the tough-minded and tough-talking DEA agent Kay Hamilton."

> —*New York Times* bestselling author Lisa Scottoline

"M. A. Lawson's *Rosarito Beach* grabs you by the throat ten seconds after you've settled into your easy chair for a read. The writing's lyrical, the plot is breathtaking, and the characters, the good ones and bad, are utterly compelling and, most important, thoroughly believable. And then there's Agent Hamilton. I fell for her on the first page."

> —*New York Times* bestselling author Jeffery Deaver

"I love tough guys, even when they're gals, and Glock-toting, fast-thinking, wisecracking DEA agent Kay Hamilton is one of the toughest going."

> —*New York Times* bestselling author Stephen Hunter

"Mike 'M. A.' Lawson hits his stride in a big way with *Rosarito Beach*, featuring the impressive debut of DEA agent Kay Hamilton. . . . This is T. Jefferson Parker's brilliant Charlie Hood series on steroids with just enough Elmore Leonard thrown in for good measure. Flat-out great."

> —*The Providence Journal*

continued . . .

OTHER BOOKS BY THE AUTHOR

ROSARITO BEACH

A Kay Hamilton Novel

M. A. LAWSON

A SIGNET BOOK

SIGNET
Published by the Penguin Group
Penguin Group (USA) LLC, 375 Hudson Street,
New York, New York 10014

USA | Canada | UK | Ireland | Australia | New Zealand | India | South Africa | China
penguin.com
A Penguin Random House Company

Published by Signet, an imprint of New American Library, a division of Penguin
Group (USA) LLC. Previously published in a Blue Rider Press edition.

First Signet Printing, November 2014

Ⓢ REGISTERED TRADEMARK—MARCA REGISTRADA

ISBN 978-0-451-47251-9

Printed in the United States of America
10 9 8 7 6 5 4 3 2 1

To my wife, Gail

PART I

1

Kay checked the time. Again. María Delgato was forty minutes late. If María had decided to blow her off, Kay was going to invent a reason for arresting her tomorrow.

Kay was sitting alone at a splintery wooden picnic table near a taco stand that was closed for the day. Two middle-aged men in an unmarked Ford Crown Victoria were parked fifty yards away. If Kay hadn't been so pissed at María, it would have been pleasant sitting there, enjoying the view of the Coronado Bridge and the skyline of San Diego across the bay. Kay had just decided to give her five more minutes when María swung into the parking lot in her boyfriend's BMW convertible.

María stepped from the car, hesitated briefly, and started toward Kay, then stopped when she saw the two men in the sedan.

"Come on," Kay said. "Those guys are with me. They're okay."

María Delgato was eye candy: twenty-four years old, long black hair, a heart-shaped face, a coffee-and-cream complexion. She had an incredible body. They had surveillance photos of her sunbathing topless on Tito

Olivera's yacht, and there wasn't a DEA agent in San Diego who hadn't seen those photos. Kay was surprised they hadn't been posted on the Internet.

"Are you the one who called me?" María asked when she reached the table. She was probably surprised that Kay looked only a few years older than her.

"Yeah. I'm Kay Hamilton. Sit down."

"Let me see your ID." María's English had just a trace of a Spanish accent.

"Sure," Kay said. Kay was wearing a blazer, and she made sure María could see the .40 caliber Glock in the shoulder holster as she took her badge case from an inside pocket. The Glock intimidated most people, but probably not María. She was used to being around men who were armed. Kay flipped open the case and showed her credentials. "Now, sit down."

María sat. "Okay. What's this all about? What happened to my brother?"

"Did you tell Tito you were meeting me?" Kay said.

"No. Of course not. He'd kill me if he knew I was talking to a DEA agent."

She was probably right about that, Kay thought.

"So where did you tell Tito you were going?"

"I told him I had to go see my mother, that she's not feeling well. I see her three, four times a week."

"Good. After you leave here, make sure you go see your mother."

"Just tell me about my brother. You said he was in trouble."

"He is. I arrested him this morning," Kay said. "He

was carrying an unregistered weapon and four eight-balls of cocaine. Dealer's weight."

Miguel Delgato was a year younger than María and almost as pretty. He sold coke to college kids at San Diego State because he looked like a college kid himself. Kay didn't think he was a bad guy; he just didn't know any other way to make a living.

"Miguel's now looking at a minimum of five years in the federal pen at Victorville," Kay said.

"Ah, Jesus," María said.

"Yeah, that's right. When he gets out of jail, he'll be infected with AIDS and God knows what else, and he'll look like those washed-up hookers you see on El Cajon Boulevard. You know, María. The ones who look like zombies, all the life gone from their eyes."

"Why are you telling me this?"

Kay didn't answer the question. "To make matters worse, you, your brother, and your mother are all illegals. You're not U.S. citizens."

"Bullshit. I was born in Arizona and I got papers to prove it. Birth certificate, Social Security number, all that shit. So does Miguel and my mom."

Kay shook her head like she felt sorry for María. "You have forged papers, María, and they're bad forgeries. You were born in El Salvador, and you and your mother and your little brother snuck into the U.S. twelve years ago, right after your father died. María, I know more about you than I do about my own sister." Kay didn't have a sister, but she did know everything there was to know about María Delgato and her family.

It looked for a moment like María was going to continue to argue that she was a bona fide citizen, but she gave up. "What are you saying? You're gonna deport me?"

"That's right. Your mother, too. ICE is going to drag her out of her nice little apartment in National City, stick her on a plane with only the clothes on her back, and ship her back to El Salvador. You're going to be on the plane sitting next to her. Then I'm going to make sure you never get back into this country again."

"Why are you doing this? All the crime in this fucking country, and you've decided to destroy my family. Why?"

"Because you're sleeping with Tito Olivera."

"So what? That's not illegal. I don't have anything to do with the things he does."

"You're right. Fucking Tito isn't illegal, and I know you don't have anything to do with his business. But you see, María, my only reason for living is to put Tito Olivera in prison, and I've decided that you're the one who's going to help me do it."

"You want me to snitch on Tito? Do you know what the Olivera cartel does to snitches?"

"Yeah, I know what they do. So we need to make sure you don't get caught."

"I'm not gonna get caught, because I'm *not* gonna help you. That would be suicide."

Kay stared at her for a moment, then shrugged. "Okay. Have it your way."

Kay rose from the picnic table and made a *Come here* motion with her right hand. María turned to see who she was waving at, and saw it was the two guys in the Crown Vic. When they got out of the car, María could see they were two serious-looking white guys wearing suits and aviator sunglasses. They started walking toward the picnic table.

"Who are they?" María asked.

"ICE. They're taking you and your mother to a detention center tonight, and tomorrow you'll be on your way back home. As for your gorgeous brother . . . Well, there's no point repeating myself."

"Wait a minute!" María said.

Kay held up a hand and the two men stopped walking.

"My mother's got a heart condition," María said. "She could die if you send her back to El Salvador."

"Not my problem, María, but I'm sure they must have some kind of medical system down there."

"Look. I need some time to think about this."

"There's nothing to think about. You're either going to help me or I'm going to deport you and your mother, and I'm going to do it so fast that you're not going to have time to get a lawyer or anybody else to stop me."

"But I *can't* help you! I don't know anything about Tito's operation. He doesn't tell me what he's doing."

"María, we can't get recording devices into Tito's house. We've tried half a dozen times, but there's always someone there. I've got warrants to tap his phones, but even as dumb as Tito is, he knows better than to say something incriminating on the phone. What you're going to do is put a few bugs in the house for me. I have them with me. They're tiny. You're going to stick one under Tito's desk, one under that big black coffee table in the living room, and one under the bar by the pool."

"Tito has the house swept every week for listening devices."

"I know that, María. I also know the kind of equipment he uses, and Tito's equipment won't detect these bugs."

María was silent, probably trying to think of some other reason why she couldn't do what Kay wanted. Finally, she said, "And that's it? I put a couple bugs in the house and you leave my mother alone and you let Miguel go?"

Kay laughed. "Come on, María. You think all blondes are stupid? If I let Miguel go, you'll tell Tito about the bugs and Tito will help Miguel get into Mexico. Then Tito will get a hotshot immigration lawyer for you and your mama, and it'll take me years to deport you."

"So what happens to my brother?"

"Your brother is going to be arraigned for intent to distribute narcotics and for carrying a concealed weapon, and the judge will give him bail. We'll make sure he has enough cash to pay the bondsman. Then we're going to take Miguel into protective custody. It'll look like he skipped to keep from going to jail, but we'll have him. If you do what I want, as soon as Tito's arrested, we'll let your brother go and he won't serve any time. But if you don't do what I want, then Miguel goes to Victorville."

"This can't be legal."

"What do you know about legal, María? You're a wetback, not a lawyer."

"This isn't right."

"I don't have time for this," Kay said. She stood up again and motioned at the two men in suits, who were now leaning against their car. "Guys, she's all yours. Get her out of here."

"All right! I'll do it. I'll plant the bugs. But that's all I'll do."

"No, that's not all you'll do. I'm going to call you every once in a while from an untraceable phone. The number won't show up on your cell phone bill, and since we're watching Tito all the time, I'll call when he's not around. Then we'll just chat. You'll tell me what Tito's been up to, who he's been talking to, that sort of thing. You know, girl talk. If I think we need to meet, we'll meet."

"You're gonna get me killed."

Kay placed her right hand gently on María's forearm. "No, I'm going to take care of you, María. I'm going to take care of your brother and your mother, too. After this is all over, we'll put you into Witness Protection if we have to. We'll get you new identities. We'll relocate you. You want to become American citizens, we'll take care of that, too. And with your looks, I imagine it won't take you any time at all to find some rich guy to marry— it just won't be Tito Olivera. Now I'm going to tell the guys from ICE that you've decided to cooperate, and after they're gone I'm going to show you how to attach the bugs. They're real easy to attach."

María put her head in her hands and started crying. Kay gave her a pat on the shoulder and said, "Stop that. You're going to smear your mascara."

Kay walked over to the men leaning against the Crown Vic. One was a nurse at Scripps Mercy Hospital and the other was a yoga instructor. They lived together and were Kay's next-door neighbors. They were also wannabe actors. When Kay had told them she needed their help in a small sting operation and all they had to do was show up in suits and try to look tough, they were delighted to help.

"You guys can take off," she said to them. "And thanks."

"How we'd do?" one of them said.

"Perfect. You looked like two badass federal agents. The sunglasses were a nice touch."

Actually, the sunglasses were over the top.

"You want to come over for drinks tonight? Don will make up a pitcher of strawberry margaritas and you can tell us what's going on."

"Sorry," Kay said. "I can't tell you. But I will be over later for the 'ritas."

After what happened to Kay in Miami, she was going to limit the number of people who knew about María Delgato to only one other agent in the DEA—which was why she'd used her nice-guy neighbors to impersonate ICE agents. She was going to do everything she could to minimize the risk of María—or herself—being killed because people couldn't keep their mouths shut. There was not going to be another Miami.

2

"I think there's some kind of deal going down between Tito and Cadillac Washington," Gutiérrez said. Steve Gutiérrez had the shitty job of listening to the recordings produced by the bugs that Kay had forced María to plant in Tito Olivera's house. He had the job because he spoke Spanish.

The bugs, however, hadn't provided the smoking gun Kay had been hoping for. The problem was that they were *too* good. They picked up too much background noise, and half the time Gutiérrez would be trying to hear a conversation between Tito and his thugs over the blare of a Mexican TV game show, or if Tito was out by the pool, Gutiérrez could hear every plane landing at San Diego International. Still, between the bugs, the phone taps, and five months of watching Tito and his key people 24/7, Kay was making some headway.

She had a much better understanding of how the Olivera cartel was organized in the United States and who all the major players were. She also had the names of two bankers who were helping the cartel launder their money and, maybe the biggest thing, the names of three San Diego narcotics cops who were on Tito's payroll.

What she didn't have was anything to put Tito himself in jail for about twenty-five years—and she wasn't sure how much longer María was going to last before having a nervous breakdown.

"What do you mean you *think* there's a deal going down?" Kay said.

"I mean, I can't tell for sure," Gutiérrez said. "After Tito came back from Mexico the other day, he was in a rotten mood, yelling at his guys, yelling at his girlfriend, bitching about everything."

Tito would visit his big brother in Mexico every couple of months, and if he drove, Kay would tell the customs guys at the border to just rip his car apart when he came back to the U.S. She knew they wouldn't find anything, but she took an inordinate amount of pleasure in delaying Tito for as long as four hours at the border crossing.

"Anyway, last night he tells one of his guys to set up a meet with Cadillac, then right after that—and it sounded like Tito was snorting his own blow—he throws something at his television set. The girlfriend started crying, begging him to quit acting like a crazy man, and he says, 'Goddamn it, I'm not going to do it. I'm not going to settle with that fat bastard.'"

"And what do you think this means?"

"I think Caesar told him to quit trying to kill Cadillac and make peace, but Tito doesn't want to do it."

"Tito would never disobey an order from his brother," Kay said.

"Hey, what can I tell you," Gutiérrez said. "And

don't forget, I'm on leave next week, so you need to find somebody to replace me. I've told you about six times I'm taking my family to Disney World in Orlando and I've got nonrefundable tickets."

"Yeah, well, we'll see."

"Kay! Those tickets cost me—"

"I want to listen to the recordings myself, the ones where Tito is talking about Cadillac." She spoke Spanish as well as Gutiérrez. But she was thinking that what she really needed to do was set up a meeting with María. As for Gutiérrez and his nonrefundable tickets . . . why the hell didn't he just drive up to Anaheim if his kids wanted fucking mouse ears?

You know who this is?" Kay said when María answered the phone.

María paused, then said, "Oh, hi, Mama. What's going on?"

Kay knew Tito had left the house, but she figured one of his guys must be standing near María.

"Yeah, that's right," Kay said. "It's your mama. I want you to tell whoever you're with that Mama's having one of her bad days and you need to go see her."

"I can't, Mama," María said. "Not today."

"Yeah, you can," Kay said. "I know Tito's not home. He just teed off at Torrey Pines, and my guys tell me he's got a hell of a slice. He's not going to be back for at least five hours, and I want you to meet me in Balboa Park, by the El Cid statue."

"I'm sorry, Mama. I just can't do it."

"María, I'm not in the mood. Don't fuck with me. I'll see you in an hour."

Kay took a seat on a stone bench near ol' El Cid, up there on his big bronze horse, a spear clenched in his right hand. She'd bought an ice-cream cone to munch on while waiting for María but had forgotten to get a napkin and now had chocolate chip running down her fingers, making a sticky mess. She scanned the park as she ate the ice cream, trying to spot anyone who seemed out of place, but everyone she could see looked like typical tourists and city folk on their lunch hour out for a walk.

Kay loved San Diego. She liked it even better than Miami. While most of the country was experiencing a typical January with freezing temperatures and icy roads, here in San Diego it was a perfect seventy degrees and the air was perfumed by whatever flowers still bloomed at this time of year. Kay didn't know one flower from another. All she knew was that it felt good sitting with the sun on her face, and she couldn't remember the last time she'd taken a day off.

She was licking her fingers to remove the ice cream when this kid, who'd been giving her the eye, finally worked up the nerve to approach her. He was maybe twenty-two, a slim, dark-haired, good-looking kid dressed in cargo shorts and a Hard Rock Cafe T-shirt. Since she was thirty, Kay figured he had some kind of cougar fantasy. He flashed her a smile that must have cost his parents ten thousand bucks in orthodontist bills and said, "Hi. I just saw you sitting here looking kind of, you know, lonely, and—"

Kay rolled her eyes, then opened her blazer so he could see the Glock. "Cop. Go away."

Still, she was flattered.

María was only half an hour late, which María considered being right on time. She was wearing a white tank top without a bra, black jeans that hugged her butt, and red high heels, Jimmy Choos that sold for eight hundred bucks. Kay didn't know flowers, but she knew shoes.

"Why do you need to see me? This is dangerous for me," María said. She was speaking Spanish, talking a mile a minute, which is what she did when she was upset.

"It's not dangerous," Kay said. "I wouldn't meet with you if it put you at risk."

Actually, she would if it meant putting Tito in a cage, but why say that?

"So what do you want?" María asked.

"I want to know what's going on between Tito and Cadillac Washington."

"How the hell would I know?"

"María, we heard Tito the other day having a hissy fit about Cadillac, and I know you were in the room at the time. I could hear you telling him to calm down. So tell me what's going on."

"I'm telling you, I don't know. Tito doesn't tell me anything."

"María, the sooner you give me something I can use to put Tito in jail, the sooner you and your brother can get back on with your lives. Now quit saying you don't know, and tell me what's happening with Cadillac."

María looked away, as if she was searching for a doorway to some universe that didn't include Kay Hamilton. "Caesar told Tito to buy him out."

"Buy him out?"

"Yeah. He told Tito to give him twenty million."

"For what?"

"For Cadillac to just go away, and Tito will take over his operation."

That actually made good business sense, Kay thought. Cadillac was getting old, so maybe he wasn't averse to retiring if his severance package was big enough, and $20 million was practically pocket change to the Olivera cartel. The Olivera brothers would make back the money in less than a year. On the other hand, she could understand why Tito wasn't happy with the arrangement. He didn't care about the money. What he cared about was his pride. He hadn't been able to defeat Cadillac, and Cadillac would view this as a victory and rub it in Tito's face.

"When is this supposed to happen?"

"In a few days. Maybe this week. I don't know exactly. But Tito says he's not gonna do it."

"So what is he going to do?"

"He says he's gonna kill Cadillac."

"Do you believe him?"

Tito Olivera was a guy who often talked a better

game than he played. Like his golf game, come to think of it. Kay had heard him lie on the tapes about how he made birdie on a hole at Torrey Pines that the pros were lucky to par.

"I don't know," María said. "He's pissed. He's like a maniac about the whole thing."

And Kay thought that maybe, *finally*, she had what she wanted.

3

Kay sat there tapping her fingernails on her knee, looking at her watch about every two minutes. She was with an Assistant U.S. Attorney named Carol Maddox and they were waiting for a judge to finish reading their application for a warrant.

Two hours earlier, Kay had found out—via a cell phone call made by one of Tito's men—that Tito was meeting with Cadillac Washington at a bar in Logan Heights. The meeting was taking place at five p.m.—in just four hours—and Kay wanted to put video cameras in the bar.

Kay was worried about the judge—a pudgy guy named Wingate with white-blond hair, bushy white eyebrows, and a face that looked like a red candy apple. She and Maddox had never dealt with him before and they couldn't be sure he would grant them the warrant. It wasn't like in the movies, where the cagey prosecutor would go to his favorite judge, a guy he played poker with on Friday nights, to get a warrant approved. In the federal system, you couldn't cherry-pick your judges, and to make matters worse, it was Sunday. When you applied for a federal warrant, you ended up with whatever magistrate or district judge was on duty that day, and Kay and

Maddox didn't know if Wingate leaned to the left or the right when it came to the Fourth Amendment. Kay and Maddox preferred right leaners, as their primary objective was putting drug dealers in jail and they weren't all that concerned about privacy protections afforded to criminals by the U.S. Constitution.

As Wingate flipped back a couple of pages to reread something he'd already read twice, Kay looked over at Maddox and tapped the face of her wristwatch. The expression on her face said: *What the fuck is this guy doing?* Kay could have read the *Tribune* front to back in the time it was taking Wingate to finish the ten pages in his hand. Maddox gave her a look back that said: *Just settle down.*

Maddox was okay, though. Kay had worked with her to obtain previous warrants, like the ones she needed to monitor Tito's phones and install the listening devices in his house. Maddox, a frumpy-looking woman in her forties with a hairstyle Dorothy Hamill made popular in 1976, could weave her way through Fourth Amendment roadblocks like an Indy driver and she could quote the Patriot Act in her sleep. Kay *loved* the Patriot Act. It may have been designed to catch terrorists, but it was used ninety percent of the time to spy on drug dealers—legally.

The only problem with Maddox was that she had four kids and was constantly dealing with some problem her brats were having when Kay needed her. Kay just hoped that if they got enough evidence to convict Tito,

Maddox's kids wouldn't interfere with preparations for the trial. As far as Kay was concerned, women ought to make up their minds: Did they want a career or did they want to be mommies?

Taking off his reading glasses, Judge Wingate said, "So the gist of this is that you have probable cause, as stated in previous warrant applications, to believe Mr. Olivera and Mr. Washington are involved in narcotics distribution; you know, via an approved listening device, that Mr. Olivera is meeting with Mr. Washington; and you know, via a confidential informant, that money will change hands. Is that correct?"

Yes! What's so fucking hard to understand about that?

"Yes, Your Honor," Maddox said.

"Well, I don't see a problem with the warrant—"

Then sign the damn thing!

"—but I'm not familiar with the Olivera cartel. Tell me about these people."

Kay started to say that she didn't have time to give him a history lesson, but she knew that wasn't going to fly.

"Caesar Olivera," she said, "is the leader of the most powerful drug cartel in Mexico, Your Honor. He joined a small outfit in 1985 when he was seventeen years old, starting out as a simple soldier. In 1990, he wiped out his boss's entire family, including second and third cousins, and assumed command. Now, after almost twenty-five years in the business, the Olivera cartel is the Walmart of drugs south of the border, and we estimate Caesar moved $500 million worth of dope into the U.S.

last year. I don't know if they put Mexican drug lords on the Forbes 400 list, but if they do, Caesar would probably be on it. His net worth is about three billion, and that's dollars, not pesos."

This caused one of the judge's white eyebrows to elevate.

"Until five years ago, Caesar was primarily a wholesaler to U.S. drug dealers. His people in Mexico manufacture meth and grow marijuana, they bring in heroin from the Middle East and cocaine from Colombia and Peru. He ships the sh . . . the stuff north and lets gangs in the U.S. handle the street-level distribution. But five years ago, his little brother, Tito, moved up here.

"Caesar gave Tito two jobs. The first was to manage distribution of the cartel's products in the U.S. In other words, Caesar wanted to cut out all the middlemen between the supplier, meaning himself, and the street-level dealers. Tito's second job was to make sure everybody in the American Southwest buys their product only from the Olivera cartel, and to make that happen, Tito's had to eliminate a lot of people: dealers and their bosses, drug mules, security personnel, folks who make their own meth or grow their own grass. We estimate that Tito's thugs have killed about three hundred people in four states since he's been here. We're not sure of the exact number, because lots of times guys just disappear. Obviously, we can't tie Tito directly to these murders or to any other crime; if we could, he'd be in jail and we wouldn't be sitting here."

"Why haven't we deported him?" the judge asked.

"Tito Olivera is not an illegal alien, Your Honor. He's a U.S. citizen. His brother Caesar is Mexican, but Tito was born in L.A. and his mother is an American. Anyway, one of the people Tito's been trying to get rid of ever since he got here is Cadillac Washington. He's tried to kill him twice. Now it looks, as I've specified in my affidavit, like Caesar told Tito to cut a deal with Washington. You may have read that a couple weeks ago there was a drive-by in the Gaslamp Quarter, right in front of Jim Croce's bar? We ended up with four dead bangers and one old lady who just got in the way. Well, the bangers worked for Cadillac, and SDPD is about ninety percent certain that Tito's people did the shooting. We think that incident was the catalyst for Caesar telling Tito to make a deal with Cadillac. He's tired of all the headlines his idiot brother is generating, and he doesn't want more heat than he already has coming down on his U.S. operations."

"Which is why we need this warrant, Judge," Maddox said. "If Tito Olivera gives money to Cadillac Washington, it raises issues related to where the money came from and may allow us to get Tito for income-tax evasion. But what we're also hoping is that Olivera and Washington will make statements when they meet tying them to past murders and drug transactions."

"Well, okay," Wingate said. "Agent Hamilton, please raise your right hand."

Kay did.

"Do you swear that everything you told me and provided in your affidavit is true?"

"Yes, Judge," Kay said.

The truth was, Kay had lied to her boss, Maddox, and now a federal judge about what she really expected to happen when Tito met with Cadillac Washington. Well, it wasn't exactly a lie; it was more a sin of omission. She didn't tell them what María had told her: that Tito might kill Cadillac.

Fuck income-tax evasion.

I can't get the second camera to work."

"You *make* it work, goddamn it!" Kay said. "I need to be able to see the back of the bar."

"I'm telling you, the connector—"

"I don't want to hear it, Jackson. Fix it!"

It had been a real scramble to pull a team together on a Sunday, yanking guys out of church and away from family barbecues, getting weapons and surveillance vans, and then breaking into the bar without being obvious about it so Jackson could install the video cameras.

Kay and four other DEA agents were crammed into one surveillance van; Kay was the agent in charge. Everyone was wearing black combat fatigues and body armor. Helmets with face shields were sitting at their feet. They had enough assault rifles, shotguns, and pistols to invade Canada. Kay and her team had been inside the van for almost two hours, and although it was only sixty degrees outside, with the heat generated by five live bodies all the agents were sweating and the van smelled like the monkey house.

A block away was a second surveillance van containing five more DEA agents. When Kay gave the command, they would move into position and cover the small parking lot behind the bar and stop anyone from leaving by the back door. The two vans being used by Kay's team were long-body panel vans with no rear or side windows. One was identified as belonging to a plumber, the other to a catering service. Kay was in the plumber's van, and, because of the locale, it was old, beat to shit, and tagged with graffiti. A hostage negotiator was in his car two blocks away.

"Jackson!" she screamed into her mike. "It's almost five. What in the hell are you doing? I still don't have visual on camera two yet."

"I'm telling you, this connector—"

"Cadillac's here," an agent said. He was looking through a low-profile periscope that penetrated the roof of the van and was hidden by a battered ventilation scoop.

"Shit," Kay said. "Jackson, get out of there. Forget the second camera. We'll have to go with one."

"Copy that," Jackson said, sounding relieved. Officially, Jackson was an agent, but he was primarily Kay's go-to guy when it came to computers, cameras, and other high-tech gizmos. He was a geek. He wore a sidearm but barely knew how to fire the thing, and he was scared being inside the bar by himself. Kay could now visualize him scurrying out the back door like an oversized rodent, lugging all his equipment—equipment that obviously didn't work like it should.

"You should have had Jackson check his gear before he went inside," an agent said.

She looked over at the speaker: Wilson, her second-in-command on this operation and the guy who thought *he* was the one who should be in charge. He was the shortest man on Kay's team—even shorter than her—and he compensated for his lack of height by lifting weights two hours a day. He compensated for male-pattern baldness by shaving his head. As usual, he had this pissy look of disapproval on his face; he would have disapproved if Kay had given him a birthday cake. Or a blow job. Wilson was brave enough—she'd trust him with her back in a fight—but he was a stiff, by-the-book little prick, and he did everything he could to undermine her. She needed to get his ass transferred out of her unit.

"I did tell him to check his gear, Wilson," Kay said, "and when we're done here, I'm going to suspend him."

Before Wilson could say anything else, she said to the man on the periscope, "Donovan, move over so I can take a look."

Cadillac Washington—his mother had christened him Ronald—was just stepping out of what else, his Cadillac, when Kay looked through the periscope eyepiece. He was in his mid-fifties, which made him an elder in the drug business.

Cadillac was short—about five foot six—and weighed almost three hundred pounds. He wore glasses with heavy black frames. He looked like a nearsighted bowling ball with feet, and his appearance struck people as comical until they found out how many people he'd killed. This evening he was wearing a black hoody and black sweatpants with a gold stripe running down the legs. He almost always wore sweatpants, probably because he liked the elastic waistband.

Two other men stepped out of the vehicle: Cadillac's top guys, Tyrell Miller and Leon James. Tyrell and Leon, both about six foot four, had the kind of muscles you get when you spend all day at Pelican Bay lifting weights. Unlike their boss, they were also clotheshorses, wearing expensive suits and shirts. Leon had on pointy shoes made from the hide of a reptile whose species was almost extinct.

Cadillac looked around the street, and for a moment he focused on the plumber's van containing Kay and her four-man squad. Cadillac was paranoid—you didn't reach your fifth decade dealing drugs unless you were paranoid—and for a minute Kay was afraid that he was going to send one of his goons over to see if anyone was in the van. But he didn't—and she suspected the reason why was the tire.

Kay had deflated the left rear tire on the van when they'd arrived on the scene. She figured that if Tito or Cadillac saw the flat tire, they'd ignore the old van. Police vehicles on stakeouts don't have flat tires. Naturally, Wilson had argued with her, saying if they had to go mobile they'd be screwed, but she overrode him. She told him if they had to go mobile it meant the operation had failed and they'd have plenty of time to change the tire.

Finally, Cadillac and his guys walked toward the bar, Cadillac leading the way. Cadillac unlocked the front door and the three men disappeared inside.

* * *

The bar belonged to Cadillac. It was one of his first real estate acquisitions after he started making money selling crack to school kids. The walls were made of cinder blocks and all the windows were glass brick, like you see in old-fashioned bathrooms. You couldn't see through the windows—they barely let sunlight in—and it was like a cave inside the place when the lights were off.

There was a scarred mahogany-colored bar about twenty feet long, ten barstools covered with split red Naugahyde, and four wobbly tables with wobbly chairs in the space in front of the bar. There was a kitchen in the back the size of a walk-in closet, another small room that served as an office, and two bathrooms that were infrequently cleaned. The only hot food on the menu was sandwiches you could microwave.

Kay looked up at the monitor in the van. She could see Cadillac and his guys standing near the front of the bar; Cadillac had turned the lights on. The single DEA camera that was working showed the room from only one angle: looking toward the front door. She couldn't see the back of the bar, where the kitchen, office, and restrooms were.

Wilson, of course, had to point out the obvious. "If we have to go inside to get them and they go to the back, we're gonna be going in blind."

Kay just sighed and shook her head. She didn't bother to tell him—*again*—that she had no intention of sending men into the bar. Her plan was to trap Tito Olivera inside and then just sit there pointing weapons at the building until Tito realized he had no choice but to surrender.

Cadillac lowered his heavy body into a chair at the table closest to the door, and through the audio system on the functioning camera Kay heard him say, "Where is that spic bastard?"

Tyrell Miller ignored what he assumed was a rhetorical question and walked behind the bar. "Boss, you wanna drink?"

"No," Cadillac said.

"How 'bout you, Leon?"

Leon James shook his head.

"Well, fuck ya all," Tyrell muttered, and poured two fingers of Crown Royal into a tumbler.

K ay checked her watch: it was now five-fifteen p.m. and she was beginning to worry that Tito wasn't going to show. Two minutes later, she smiled when Tito Olivera's black Mercedes SUV rounded a corner and parked behind Cadillac Washington's car.

"Tito's here," Kay said into her mic. "Get ready to deploy on my command."

Tito's driver, a tattooed freak with a shaved head named Jesús Rodríguez, stepped out of the SUV first and looked around. He was wearing a wifebeater undershirt, so the full sleeves on his arms were visible. Like Cadillac, Jesús noticed the plumber's van with its flat tire and studied it for a moment before he decided it didn't pose a threat.

Ángel Gomez, Tito's other bodyguard, exited the SUV next. Ángel was dressed completely in black, like a Latino Johnny Cash. He was six foot one but weighed only about a hundred and forty pounds, and Kay didn't know if he was so skinny because of drugs or diet. Whatever the case, Ángel was the guy Tito used most often to kill the people he wanted killed.

Ángel opened the back door of the SUV and Tito Olivera—younger brother of Caesar Olivera—emerged from the vehicle. Tito was dressed in an Armani suit that cost more than Kay earned in a month. He was a handsome man in his late twenties with a narrow face and a dimpled chin, and he was not obviously Latino; his hair was light brown and had probably been blond when he was a child. His mother didn't have any Mexican blood in her. Tito reached his hand inside the SUV and helped María Delgato out.

María was wearing a low-cut black cocktail dress that stopped at midthigh and showed off every curve she had. Kay thought the woman was a little top-heavy but had perfect thighs. The way she and Tito were dressed, it appeared they might be planning to go out to a celebratory dinner after Tito finished with Cadillac.

But Kay couldn't understand why Tito had brought María to the meeting. Maybe it was a ploy on Tito's part to put Cadillac at ease. Or maybe he liked the idea of whacking Cadillac with her watching, thinking it would turn her on or make him a bigger man in her eyes. One thing Kay knew for sure: Tito wasn't worried about a witness testifying against him. No witness against the Olivera brothers had ever made it into a court of law. So Kay didn't know why María was there, but she was glad she was. If María was inside the bar when it went down, she'd not only have Tito on video but she'd have an eye-witness. That is, she'd have an eyewitness if she could keep María alive long enough to testify.

As soon as Tito's entourage entered the bar, Kay said into her mic, "Okay, they're in. Conroy, deploy your team."

"Roger that," Conroy said. Conroy was the leader of the five-man squad in the second DEA van. He and his men would take up positions behind the bar to keep Tito's and Washington's people trapped inside—or kill them if they came outside shooting.

"Saddle up," Kay said to the men in the van, and they checked their weapons for the hundredth time, adjusted their body armor, and put on their helmets. "Comm check," she said next, and spoke to each agent to make sure everybody's mics and earpieces were work-ing. Before she could tell her men to exit the van and take up their positions outside, Donovan, the guy who'd been watching through the periscope earlier, looked through the scope again.

"We got kids coming down the street," Donovan said.

Shit. It was Sunday evening and the bar was located in

an industrial area and surrounded by small manufacturers: scrap-metal recyclers, tire retreaders, and auto-body shops. All the businesses were closed for the day and the bar was also normally closed on Sunday. She had no idea why a bunch of kids would be in this part of town.

"How many and how old?" Kay asked Donovan.

"Four, teenagers, fifteen, sixteen, two boys, two girls, all Hispanic. They don't look like gangbangers. Just kids."

"Donovan, you and Jenkins get them off the street. Then, Donovan, you stay with them until it's safe to let them go."

"We should call in SDPD to handle them," Wilson said.

They'd had this discussion before. Wilson had wanted to alert SDPD to the operation before it started—and Kay had adamantly refused. She didn't trust the San Diego cops because she knew the Olivera cartel had penetrated the force. Her plan was to bring in SDPD *after* they had Tito Olivera trapped inside the bar—and then use them for crowd control and blocking off the streets. No way in hell was she going to alert the city cops until after Tito had killed Cadillac Washington.

"Wilson, for the tenth fucking time, I'm not bringing in SDPD until I need them. Donovan, Jenkins, why are you still here? I told you to get those kids off the street."

Donovan and Jenkins, who probably agreed with Wilson, left the van.

"Donovan might not be able to control four kids by himself," Wilson said. "And if Tito starts shooting, you're putting those kids at risk."

"Wilson, when this operation's over, I'm transferring your ass out of this unit."

Wilson made a snorting sound, and Kay felt like smacking him.

"Okay, the rest of you take up your positions. That means you, too, Wilson."

The men left the van and took cover behind vehicles and Dumpsters on the street, making sure they had clear lines of fire to the front door of the bar. Kay would remain in the van and monitor the video.

Kay was the only one who knew what was likely to happen next. Just like with Maddox and the judge, Kay hadn't told her men about the discussion she had with María Delgato and what Tito might do.

The first thing Tito did when he entered the bar was take off his suit coat and turn in a circle so Cadillac could see he was unarmed. Since Tito had tried to kill Cadillac twice, Kay figured Cadillac had only agreed to meet with Tito if Cadillac could choose the meeting place and if Tito agreed to come unarmed.

Ángel Gomez and Jesús Rodríguez were not wearing coats, but Cadillac gestured to Tyrell Miller and Tyrell frisked both men to confirm they weren't carrying weapons. Tyrell also looked inside a laptop case that Jesús Rodríguez was carrying.

"They're clean, boss," Tyrell said to Cadillac.

This wasn't good from Kay's perspective. If Tito and

his guys didn't have weapons, who was going to kill Cadillac?

"You want me to pat her down, too?" Tyrell said, looking over at María. Tyrell smiled when he said this; it was obvious María couldn't conceal a dime under the dress she was wearing.

"No," Cadillac said to Tyrell, but to Tito he said, "What's the bitch doing here?"

To Cadillac, every woman was a bitch.

"She needs to use the restroom," Tito said.

"No. She stays here where I can see her."

"What the hell do you think she's going to do?" Tito said.

And Kay thought: *Godfather I.* She'll go into the bathroom and come out with a gun like Michael Corleone.

"She stays here," Cadillac repeated.

"Hey, suit yourself," Tito said. To María he said, "You can hold it a minute, can't you, baby? This isn't going to take long."

Tyrell Miller had gone back behind the bar, and playing the host, he said, "Anybody wanna drink?"

Before Tito or any of his people could answer, Cadillac said, "Nobody needs a fuckin' drink. Let's get this over with."

Tito nodded to Jesús Rodríguez, and Jesús took the laptop out of its case and set it on the table in front of Cadillac. Tito sat down across from Cadillac and powered up the computer, saying, "This will take a minute, all the security programs on this thing."

When Tito turned on the laptop, Kay thought, God-damn it. Tito must have changed his mind.

If Tito had changed his mind, he was going to use the laptop to transfer $20 million to one of Cadillac's off-shore accounts, and after the transfer was complete, Cadillac would make a phone call to verify the deposit. But that wasn't supposed to happen—not according to María.

And it didn't.

Kay saw Leon James, Cadillac's second-in-command, take out his gun, a long-barreled Colt .45. Leon was standing behind Cadillac, so Cadillac didn't see the weapon, and neither Tito nor his two men reacted to the gun in Leon's hand—but Tyrell Miller, still standing be-hind the bar, did.

"Hey, man, what—"

Leon James shot his friend Tyrell—a man he'd worked with for more than a decade—twice in the chest, and Tyrell collapsed behind the bar.

From the microphone in the bar, Kay heard María scream, then immediately heard in her earpiece, "Shots fired inside the bar!"

"Everybody stay in position," Kay said. "Take no action. That's an order."

When Tyrell was shot, Cadillac jumped to his feet. Tito didn't move; he remained seated and smiled. He crossed his legs to show how relaxed he was. Cadillac looked behind him and said to Leon James: "What do you think you're doing?"

Leon pointed his gun at Cadillac and said, "Sorry, boss. Got a better offer from Tito."

"You ungrateful motherfucker," Cadillac muttered. Kay could tell by the expression on his face that Cadillac knew he was a dead man.

Tito rose and said to Leon, "Give me the gun." Leon handed the weapon to him and Tito pointed it at Cadillac's face. "Did you really think I was going to give you the money?"

"Does your brother know you're doing this?" Cadillac said. Before Tito could answer, he added, "Your brother gave me his *word*, and your brother's word means something to him, if not to you."

"Well, I guess I'm not my brother," Tito said.

Cadillac stood there for a moment, deflated and defeated, then he straightened. He wasn't going to beg a young punk like Tito Olivera. He'd die like a man—and he did. Tito pulled the trigger and the bullet entered through the right lens of Cadillac's glasses and exited out the back of his skull. The only one in the bar who reacted was María, who screamed again.

In Kay's earpiece, she heard, "Third shot fired!"

Then Wilson chimed in. "What the hell's going on inside the bar?" he said.

Kay ignored the question and said, "Wilson, use the bullhorn. Tell Tito and his guys to come out. Jackson, activate the wireless signal jammer and start monitoring the bar's landline." No way was Kay going to allow Tito to call in the cavalry. "I want no calls or e-mails going out of that place, Jackson. Do you hear me?" She didn't trust Jackson.

"Copy that," Jackson said.

"After the phones are taken care of, tell the hostage negotiator to move into position, then radio SDPD and tell them we need crowd control. I want every street around this bar blocked off."

Wilson said, "What were the shots?"

"Never mind the damn shots, Wilson," Kay said. "Make the announcement."

She heard Wilson curse in her earpiece, then heard his voice over the bullhorn: "Inside the bar. This is the DEA. You are surrounded by federal agents. Put down your weapons and come out with your hands on your heads."

Kay looked at the video monitor and heard Tito say, "What the hell?"

Since Tito couldn't see through the glass brick windows of the bar, he told Ángel Gomez to crack the front door open and look outside, and Jesús Rodríguez to look out the back. A moment later, both men came back and reported that cops were outside pointing assault rifles at the building.

Ángel Gomez went behind the bar and took a weapon off Tyrell Miller's corpse. Leon James disappeared from the picture for a moment, and Kay figured he must have gone into the office at the back of the bar, because when he returned he was holding a shotgun and a revolver. He tossed the shotgun to Jesús Rodríguez. Now everybody was armed but María; Tito was still holding the Colt he'd used to kill Cadillac.

"What are we going to do?" Ángel said to Tito.

Before Tito could answer, Leon James said, "I can't

believe you led the fuckin' cops here. How did they know this thing was going down?"

"I don't know. Shut up so I can think," Tito said.

"No way am I going back inside," Leon said.

"Shut up!" Tito screamed. He stood there for a moment with his eyes closed, then pulled out his cell phone. Kay didn't know who he was planning to call, maybe his big brother, but when he saw he didn't have a signal, he yelled, "Son of a bitch!" and flung the phone at the bottles behind the bar.

Kay laughed.

"Inside the bar," Wilson repeated, using the bull-horn. "You are surrounded. Come out with your hands on top of your heads."

Tito turned to his men and said, "You guys do what you want, but I'm getting out of here." Then he grabbed María Delgato by the arm and walked her toward the door.

"Tito, what are you doing?" she said.

"Shut up," Tito said. "You'll be all right."

He opened the bar's front door, and with María in front of him and his gun held against her head, he shouted, "I'm getting in my car and I'm leaving. If anyone tries to stop me, I'll kill this bitch."

Kay was thinking, *What an idiot,* when she heard in her earpiece, "I have a clear head shot on Olivera."

Kay screamed, "Stand down! Stand down! Do not shoot!" She pulled her Glock from its holster and stepped out of the van. She didn't bother to put on her helmet.

Tito saw Kay standing across the street, the gun in her hand, and said, "Did you hear what I said? I'll shoot her if you try to stop me." He began crab-walking toward his SUV with María, still using her as a shield, still holding the gun to her head.

Kay started walking toward him. "You're not going anywhere and you're not going to kill her. I have men pointing rifles at you. If you kill her, they'll kill you."

As she said this she continued to walk toward him, her gun pointed down at the ground.

"Back off, bitch," Tito said. "I'm not bluffing."

"I'm not bluffing, either," Kay said. "You kill her, we kill you."

She continued to walk toward Tito.

Then María Delgato sealed her own fate. She screamed, "Kay, what are you doing? He's going to kill me!" Kay heard Tito say, "What? You know this bitch?" Then to Kay he said, "Stay back. I'm telling you, I'm going to kill her."

Kay kept moving forward. When she was three feet from him, she raised her gun and pointed it at his head. Tito just stood there, not knowing what to do, then Kay took one more stride and placed the muzzle of her gun against the center of his forehead.

"Drop the gun, you moron."

5

Tito and María were both handcuffed. Tito was placed in the hostage negotiator's car and María in the front passenger seat of the surveillance van.

From this point forward, Kay didn't really care what happened to the three men inside the bar. They couldn't shoot through the glass brick windows, so if they wanted a fight, they'd have to come outside and her guys would kill them. She didn't think that would happen, however. She figured that after a couple of hours, Tito's men would give up—but whether they did or not didn't matter to her.

Kay already had what she wanted: She had Tito Olivera and a witness who'd seen him kill Cadillac Washington.

Kay had to do two things right away. First, she had to get Tito to a jail as fast as possible. The San Diego cops would arrive on the scene in a few minutes to provide crowd control, and Kay figured the TV guys would show up five minutes later. When the cameras arrived, it wouldn't be long before Caesar Olivera found out that his little brother had been arrested, and when he did, he just might order a hundred gangbangers into the area to try to free Tito. So Kay wanted Tito out of Logan Heights immediately, and she was personally going to make sure that he made it to jail.

The second thing she had to do was get María Delgato out of San Diego.

She told Jackson to turn off the cell phone jammer for exactly thirty seconds and made a call to one of the agents who would be transporting María. She then used her throat mic to call Conroy, the agent in charge of the team guarding the back of the bar, and told him he was coming with her to transport Tito to the Metropolitan Correctional Center. "Bring your M16," she said. Unlike Wilson, Conroy was a guy who followed her orders without questioning every decision she made.

Wilson immediately came running over to Kay. "Are you leaving the scene with those guys still in there?"

"Yeah, and until I get back you're in charge. That should make you happy. The San Diego cops will be here pretty soon, and they'll give you a hand if you need it."

"You shouldn't be leaving the scene," Wilson said.

"I don't have time to argue with you, Wilson. Just do what I tell you."

Kay walked over to the hostage negotiator. He was a tall man in his forties with narrow shoulders and thinning blond hair. He looked like a nice, easygoing, laid-back guy—probably a prerequisite to being a hostage negotiator. He'd made no attempt to contact the men inside the bar yet; he wanted to give them a little more time to think things over before he did.

"I'm taking your car," Kay told him. "I'm taking Tito to jail."

"Okay," the negotiator said.

Kay went to the surveillance van next, where María Delgato was waiting.

As soon as Kay opened the door, María began to curse at her in Spanish. Kay, who was completely fluent in Spanish, didn't think there was a Spanish swearword María didn't use. The gist of María's diatribe was: *You insane bitch, you could have gotten me killed. He was holding a gun to my head.*

"Aw, he wasn't going to kill you," Kay said. "He knew if he killed you, I would have killed him. You were never in any danger."

"Bullshit, you . . ." More swearwords.

"Oh, shut the hell up," Kay said. "You're alive."

"And why did you let them handcuff me?"

"I was trying to make it look like you were a prisoner and not my informant, but when you shot your mouth off and told Tito you knew me, that plan probably went out the window. Turn around and I'll take the cuffs off. Some of my guys are going to be here in a couple of minutes, and they're going to take you and your mother to see Miguel."

"Where is he?"

"A long way from here, María."

Kay figured she broke some sort of land-speed record getting from Logan Heights to the Metropolitan Correctional Center on Union Street in downtown San

Diego. MCC is the federal lockup where prisoners are often incarcerated until their trials; it's a towering, twenty-three-story monolith the color of wet sand, with windows so narrow it's surprising they allow light to enter. She and Conroy marched a handcuffed Tito Olivera into the building, and Kay told Conroy not to leave Tito's side until he was in a cell.

She walked over to a doughy-faced correctional officer and told him she needed to speak to the MCC warden. The officer informed her that as it was Sunday, the warden wasn't there. "Then get him on the phone," Kay said.

"This is Kay Hamilton, DEA," Kay said when Warden Clyde Taylor came to the phone.

"Why are you calling me at my home, Agent? You should be talking to the weekend duty supervisor."

"I'm calling because I just delivered Tito Olivera to your jail."

"So what?"

"So what is that you need to take special precautions with him. He should be placed in an isolation cell on one of the upper floors, and you need to make sure the people who come into contact with him—including your guards—don't give him a phone so he can call his big brother in Mexico."

"I resent you implying that my people would do something like that."

"You can resent it all you want, but I know that half your damn guards are on the take."

Half was an exaggeration, but Kay was correct in

principle. In the last year, five MCC correctional officers had been arrested or fired for passing contraband to inmates—drugs, cell phones, cash, and weapons.

"What did you say your name was?" Taylor shouted.

"Hamilton."

"Yeah, well, you listen to me, Hamilton. I'll decide how my prisoners should be guarded, and I'm going to be talking to your boss about your goddamn disrespectful attitude."

"Warden, you need to understand something. Tito Olivera is not your average prisoner. His big brother is richer than God, and he's going to do everything he can to get Tito out of your jail."

"I'll be talking to your boss," Taylor said again, and hung up.

Asshole.

Kay and Conroy drove back to Cadillac Washington's bar. Nothing had changed while they had been gone: Leon James, Ángel Gomez, and Jesús Rodríguez were still inside the bar, refusing to come out. They didn't realize there was a camera in the bar, and they sat there drinking, Ángel occasionally snorting a line of cocaine, cursing their luck and cursing Tito Olivera. They talked about trying to fight their way to one of the vehicles outside, knowing they didn't stand a chance. When the hostage negotiator got them on the landline in the bar, they taunted him, telling him to send the cops in after them. By this time, the SDPD had brought in banks of lights to illuminate the area around the bar, and there were TV cameras everywhere—on the street and in the sky in choppers—filming everything.

Kay sort of wished the cameras had been there when she arrested Tito.

She went to sit in the surveillance van with the hostage negotiator and was soon going out of her mind with boredom. There was nothing for her to do but twiddle her thumbs while the negotiator tried to talk the knuckleheads into surrendering. She finally found a piece of paper in the van's glove compartment—a flier advertising a pizza place—and she turned it over and made a sketch of her backyard. She was thinking about building a deck off the back door and maybe sticking in a hot tub, so she started fiddling around with the shape of the deck and where the hot tub would go.

When Kay was in Miami, she bought a place there—a real fixer-upper, in real estate lingo—and was able to flip the place for a decent profit when she moved to San Diego. She was hoping to do the same thing with the house she'd bought in California, a three-bedroom ranch-style home in Point Loma, about six miles from the submarine base. The houses in her neighborhood didn't have a view and went for about three hundred to six hundred grand, but she'd gotten hers for two-fifty because it had been foreclosed on and the owner was desperate to sell.

She didn't really have any hobbies—other than sports like surfing and skiing—so when she was at home she worked on the house, doing some of the work herself and using a Mexican illegal, who was a master carpenter, to do the hard stuff. She also didn't spend much on furnishings or pictures or anything else to make the place homey. She didn't care about homey; homey didn't increase the value of the house. She painted all the interior walls in neutral colors, because she'd been told that was best for selling. She installed the most energy-efficient heating and cooling system she could find, and got a tax break on that. The kitchen had been in pretty good shape when she bought the place—lots of cabinets and counter space, the appliances fairly new—so all she did in the kitchen was have the Mexican put in granite countertops because everybody went all gaga over granite.

Right now Kay didn't really care what sort of house she lived in; at this stage of her life, a house was only an investment and a place to sleep. But one of these days, after she retired—which was a long way off—she was going to own waterfront property in Southern California. She had this hazy vision of herself in her sixties: tanned, in good shape, playing eighteen holes every day, then going home to sit on the deck of her fabulous home to sip piña coladas and watch the sun set on the Pacific. There was a man in this hazy picture, too, but she didn't have anyone specific in mind, just that he had to have a little money, a sense of humor, and couldn't be a total slob.

The hostage negotiator interrupted her reverie. "Rodríguez and Gomez are coming out."

"What about James?" Kay asked.

The negotiator shook his head. "Just the two of them," he said.

Kay folded up the sketch, put it in her back pocket, and stepped outside the van. She didn't bother to pull her weapon.

Four hours after they had locked themselves inside the bar, Ángel and Jesús came out with their hands in the air and were immediately taken to the ground, handcuffed, and placed in a transport van. Both men were very drunk.

Leon James was a different matter. After Ángel and Jesús left the bar, he sat there, sipping whiskey slowly, then pulled out his cell phone and checked, for maybe the twentieth time, to see if he had a signal yet. When he saw he didn't, he disappeared from view for a couple of minutes, then returned to the table with some paper and spent fifteen minutes writing two short notes. Leon was faster with a pistol than he was with a pen.

Kay found out later that one of the notes was to his daughter and the other to his mother. In the note to his mother, he told her to go to their special place and pick up a package he'd left for her. Kay assumed it was cash he'd stashed away for a rainy day. Even men like Leon James loved their mothers.

Then Leon committed suicide by cop.

Kay watched on the monitor as he took out his gun and headed for the door of the bar, and she knew what was going to happen next: Leon came out and started shooting, even before he had acquired a target. After he'd fired no more than three shots, DEA agents and

SDPD cops opened up with automatic weapons and put—according to the coroner's report delivered two days later—twenty-one bullets into him. The TV cameras captured his execution, and the talking heads wondered aloud on the news the next day if it had really been necessary to shoot the man so many times.

After Leon shuffled off this mortal coil, Kay got into a screaming match with a patrol lieutenant from SDPD. The cameras recorded all the angry gestures and waving arms, but fortunately weren't close enough to pick up the dialogue, which consisted mostly of four-letter words. The SDPD lieutenant wanted to know why the San Diego police hadn't been notified in advance about the DEA raid; the screaming and swearing started when Kay said, "Telling you guys about the raid in advance would be like the SEALs telling the Pakistanis they were flying in to kill bin Laden." She clarified this statement by adding that SDPD leaked like a sieve, and if the San Diego cops had known what was going to happen, the television crews would have gotten there ahead of Kay's people. She didn't tell him that three SDPD narcotics detectives were on Olivera's payroll and her biggest fear had been a San Diego cop warning Tito. The lieutenant ended the discussion by calling her an arrogant bitch and saying that he would be talking to her boss.

"Well, you're gonna have to get in line," Kay said.

6

By the time Kay finished dealing with all the issues related to removing the corpses of Cadillac Washington, Tyrell Miller, and Leon James from Logan Heights, and processing Ángel Gomez and Jesús Rodríguez into the Metropolitan Correction Center, it was six a.m.—approximately thirteen hours after she arrested Tito Olivera. When she arrived at the DEA office on Viewridge Avenue, she saw that Wilson had gotten there ahead of her and the little prick was sitting in the boss's office, still dressed in fatigues, giving Davis his version of everything that had happened—and everything that he thought Kay had done wrong. Fuck him.

Kay went to her desk, dropped her sidearm into a drawer and locked it, then went to the restroom, washed her face, and made an attempt to comb her hair. She gave up on the hair after a couple of minutes, but looked into the mirror and smiled. She had just busted the brother of Caesar Olivera. This was even bigger than what she had done in Miami.

When she walked back into the bull pen, her boss yelled, "Hamilton, get your ass in here."

His office was where she'd been headed anyway.

Wilson was still sitting there, and the first thing she did was point at him and say, "I want this asshole transferred out of my unit."

"Shut up, Hamilton," Davis said. He made a motion with his head for Wilson to leave, which Wilson did after smirking at Kay.

"Close the door," Davis said.

Kay thought that Jim Davis was actually a pretty good guy and a decent boss. He was fifty-six and was planning on retiring next year. He was tall and had played guard at Wichita State; he hadn't been a superstar but a solid team player, a guy who made more assists than baskets—and the same could be said of his career at the DEA. His hair was short, thick, and white, and he wore a neatly trimmed white mustache. Kay thought he looked like the good town marshal in an old Western movie.

"Hamilton, I don't even know where to start," Davis said. "I received a call from the warden at MCC telling me that you called him at his home, accused his people of being corrupt, then—"

"They are corrupt. By now Caesar Olivera knows exactly how his brother's being guarded and probably everything else he needs to stage a jailbreak."

"I know that, Hamilton, but until we can make different arrangements we're going to have to trust Warden Taylor and we're going to have to work with him."

Kay just shook her head. It wasn't a matter of trusting Taylor, and Jim Davis knew that. It was going to be almost a year before Tito Olivera went to trial, and there was a very good possibility that Caesar Olivera would try to free his brother before the trial. Caesar had so much money he could bribe almost anyone—he could certainly bribe a few low-level correctional officers—and if he couldn't bribe them, he would kidnap members of their families and force them to do what he wanted.

"John Hernández also called me," Davis said.

John Hernández was the San Diego chief of police.

"He was appropriately outraged that we didn't notify him in advance of the operation and—"

"But you agreed we shouldn't notify him."

"I know that, Hamilton. But did you have to compare his department to the Pakistanis? I mean, couldn't you have been just a little bit diplomatic with his fuckin' guy?"

Kay shrugged. Diplomacy wasn't her strong suit.

"I also got a call from a lawyer representing some kid, some girl. The girl's mother said you traumatized her daughter when one of your guys, looking like Darth Vader dressed up in riot gear, ordered her into a building and wouldn't let her and three other kids leave for three hours."

"I couldn't let them leave," Kay said. "If one of Tito's guys had started shooting—which one of them eventually did—one of those kids could have been hurt."

"You could have had the San Diego cops escort them safely out of the area."

"Well, the truth is, boss, I actually forgot about them for a while."

"Jesus, Hamilton."

"Hey! They weren't hurt and they weren't trauma-tized. Donovan said they had a great time, drinking beer, listening to shit on a boom box."

Finally, Davis got to the real point of the meeting. "Hamilton, did you know Tito Olivera was going to kill Cadillac?"

Kay looked at him for a long moment, then said, "Do you really want to know if I knew?"

"What?" Davis said.

"You heard me," Kay said. "I got the warrant for putting cameras in that bar based on a confidential in-formant telling me a deal was going down between two major drug dealers. What do you think would have hap-pened if, hypothetically, I told the judge that I knew that Tito might execute Cadillac? Do you think, maybe, the judge would have told us we needed to do some-thing to protect poor Cadillac, a subhuman piece of shit who's been killing people for thirty years? I mean, do you really care that Cadillac's dead? I don't. What I do care about is that I have Tito on video shooting the guy, and I have a witness to back up the video. And Tito is either going to get the needle—assuming they ever exe-cute anyone in this fucking state—or he's going to give me information I can use against his brother. So I don't know why you're ragging my ass here. You ought to be congratulating me."

Davis sighed and shook his head.

"Hamilton, I don't know what to do with you. You just suck with people. You piss off everyone outside the agency and, as bad as that is, you piss off the guys who work for you, the guys who ought to be loyal to you."

"They don't like me because I got the supervisor's job instead of Wilson."

When Kay was transferred from Miami to San Diego two years earlier, she was immediately placed into a vacant supervisor's slot. And in spite of what she'd done in Miami—and there wasn't a person in the entire Drug Enforcement Administration who didn't know what she'd done in Miami—the people who worked for her, particularly Wilson, resented that she got the job. No one had the balls to say to her face that she'd slept her way into the position—although, in a way, she had.

"That's not true, Hamilton," Davis said. "Your guys don't even like Wilson. Wilson's a prick. But they don't like you either, and the reason why has nothing to do with Miami or the fact that you're a woman. They don't like you because you don't trust them and you don't include them when you're planning something. They don't like you because you refuse to recognize that they have wives and kids and can't work twenty-four hours a day. They don't like you because you're a constant hard-ass and you never cut them any slack when they don't measure up to your standards."

"That reminds me," Kay said. "I'm giving Jackson a two-day suspension."

"Jackson?"

"The geek. The one who was supposed to hook up the video cameras in the bar. He didn't check his equipment before he went in, and one of the cameras didn't work."

Davis shook his head again. "This is exactly what I'm talking about. Jackson's young. What you should do is take him out for a beer. Tell him you understand he was nervous and under a lot of pressure, but that what he did put people's lives in danger and how next time he needs to do better. You give him a suspension, he's going to find all kinds of reasons why you didn't give him enough time to do his job right and he's going to hate you for the rest of his career. And when you need geek help in the future, he's not going to give it to you."

The hell he wouldn't. She'd fire Jackson if he didn't do his job.

But she didn't say that. Instead she said, "So what are we going to do about Tito? You know we can't leave him in MCC, and we have to do something before they arraign him."

"Yeah, I know," Davis said, but she could tell he was irritated over the way she'd changed the subject from her management style to Tito. "I've got a meeting set up with the judge, SDPD, the warden at MCC, and the senior U.S. marshal in San Diego. It's scheduled for one p.m., so you have time to go home, get a couple hours' sleep, and take a shower and change."

"What time is the press conference?" Kay asked.

"Three."

"I want to be there."

"Yeah, I know you want to be there."

"Well, can I come?"

"Yeah, I guess."

Not exactly *I'd love to have you standing by my side*, but good enough.

Kay rose to leave.

"But, Hamilton—"

"Yes, boss?"

"I'll do all the talking at the meeting with the judge and at the press conference. Do you understand?"

"Yes, boss."

Just as long as I get credit for the bust.

As Kay was leaving to go home, she swung by Wilson's desk. He should have been on his way home, too, after having been up all night, but instead he was using two stubby fingers to type up a report—a report that would put Kay's actions in the worst possible light while still being accurate.

"Wilson, do you know who Colleen Brandon is?"

"No."

"Well, she's just been put in charge of the Far East Division and we're pals. You know how us girls stick together."

"Why are you telling me this?" Wilson said.

"Because Colleen needs a guy for Mongolia, and I told her you were the perfect man for the job. Colleen owes me."

Kay walked away, leaving Wilson sitting there with his mouth open.

Kay actually did know Colleen Brandon. The DEA

has eighty-five regional offices in sixty-five foreign countries, and Brandon was the newly appointed head of the Far East Division. Kay hated to admit it, but Brandon had risen through the ranks faster than her because she had the political skills to impress people in Washington. She was good at sucking up. What Wilson didn't know was that Colleen Brandon hated her and wouldn't piss on her if her head was on fire.

She figured Wilson would be in Jim Davis's office, wailing like a baby, before she left the building.

7

As Kay was driving to her house in Point Loma, she was thinking she should do what Jim Davis had said: take a shower and sleep for a couple of hours before their meeting with the judge. But she didn't feel like sleeping. She was still too energized from busting Tito. No, she didn't want sleep. She wanted sex.

She took out her cell phone and punched in a number.

"What are you doing this morning?"

"I have a meeting with Julian Montgomery's lawyer in an hour."

Kay knew who Julian Montgomery was: a guy worth a couple hundred million bucks who'd never worked a day in his life. He'd made his money the old-fashioned way: He inherited it. He was on San Diego's A-list, gave generously to the arts, was on the boards of several charities, and attended every exclusive social gala in the city. He was also a degenerate pervert, and he had just been arrested for having a computer full of child pornography.

Julian's gardener, who lived on Julian's estate, had caught Julian taking nude photographs of his nine-year-old son. The gardener—a normally gentle man from Honduras who barely spoke English—tried to split

Julian's head open with a machete. He missed Julian's head, but did manage to slice off part of one of his ears. When the police arrested the gardener for attempted murder, they didn't believe him at first, but eventually they obtained a warrant to look into Julian's computer and his camera's memory chip, where they found hundreds of pictures of children.

"Do you think Julian's lawyer would mind if you kept him waiting a bit?" Kay asked. "I need someone to wash my back."

"I'm sure he would mind. Your place?"

"Yes."

Kay lay there with her eyes closed, waiting for her heartbeat to slow down to something approaching normal. She finally opened her eyes and looked over at Robert Meyer. He smiled at her and said what he always said after they finished having sex: "Wow."

For a man who depended on his communication skills to make a living, Robert tended to be less than original when it came to postcoital pillow talk. He was, however, a beautiful human specimen. He was a muscular six foot two, had rugged features and a perfect profile—the kind you might see on old Grecian coins. He also had the same waist size he had in college, because he worked out four days a week to stay in shape. He was marvelous in bed; he wasn't the best lover Kay had ever had, but he was currently number three on her list.

Robert Meyer was an Assistant United States Attorney for the Southern District of California. One day,
and probably not that far in the future, he would be *the*
U.S. Attorney for the district, and Kay wouldn't be surprised if he ended up being the Attorney General of the
United States. He had money, looks, political connections, and brains.

He also had a beautiful wife and two beautiful daughters. A Meyer family portrait was the perfect campaign
poster.

"I gotta get going," Kay said, and rose from the bed.
She didn't bother to put on a robe; Robert Meyer had
seen her naked often enough.

"Me, too," Robert said. He didn't move, however.
He continued to lie there, his head propped against a
pillow, a small content smile on his face. If people still
smoked, he would have been having an after-sex cigarette.

Kay started to walk toward her bathroom, but Robert said, "Hold it a minute."

"What?" Kay said.

"Just stand there. I want to look at you."

"Oh, for Christ's sake," Kay muttered.

"You are definitely the best-looking woman I've ever
slept with."

What a bullshitter. Kay knew his wife was actually
better-looking than she was. Well, she wasn't as stacked
as Kay, but she was definitely a stunner.

When Kay came out of the shower—this one she
took by herself—Robert was still in bed.

"I thought you had a meeting with Julian Montgomery's lawyer," Kay said.

"I do. But he'll wait until I get there, and he'll charge Julian about seven hundred bucks for every hour he waits. What are you going to do about Tito Olivera?"

"We're meeting with Judge Foreman and a bunch of other bureaucrats to talk about that at one. We're going to try to impress upon the judge that Tito needs to be held someplace where his big brother can't get to him. I just hope he'll listen. If he doesn't, we're going to have blood running in the streets of San Diego."

She didn't need to explain why this was so to Robert Meyer. He knew about her yearlong investigation leading to Tito's arrest, and he knew the capabilities of the Olivera cartel. That was another thing she liked about Robert: They could talk shop when they weren't screwing, and he was the type of man who could keep what she told him to himself. Being a prosecutor, he was usually on her side of the game, although he tended to be a little persnickety about following the rules.

Kay met Robert when she first came to San Diego two years before. At the time he'd been working in the Narcotics Section in the U.S. Attorney's Office, and they met on one of Kay's first cases in the region. It didn't take long before he asked her out for a drink—she was hardly the first extramarital affair he'd had. He now ran the General Crimes Section of the Criminal Division. General Crimes was a catchall section dealing with bank fraud, organized crime, counterfeiting, weapons offenses, identity theft, computer crimes, and public corruption. And child pornography. Robert had asked for the job in General Crimes to round out his résumé—particularly as it related to computer crimes—and he was going to personally prosecute Julian Montgomery because it would be a high-profile case. Robert Meyer always prosecuted the high-profile cases.

In addition to being able to talk shop with Robert and his skills in bed, the other thing Kay liked about him was that she would never have to face the day when he came to her, a mopey expression on his face, and said he loved her so much that he was going to leave his wife and marry her. He would never do that. He was married to his career, and he knew divorcing his wife would be political suicide. He also knew that Kay Hamilton would never be the ideal mate for a politician.

And all of this was fine with Kay. She had no desire to get married again, or at least not anytime soon; she'd been married once, for almost a year, and didn't wish to repeat that experience in the near future. For that matter, she had no desire to have a live-in boyfriend right now. She liked her life the way it was. She liked living alone—at least most of the time—and she liked the fact that she wasn't tied to any person or place. If the DEA decided to reassign her, she had no emotional attachments to keep her from moving and advancing. Robert Meyer was the perfect lover, as far as she was concerned.

Kay normally dressed in pantsuits for meetings with other agencies or when she had to go to court, and she usually wore her hair in a practical ponytail. Today, however, she knew she was going to be on camera at the press conference—and she wanted the cameras on her. She let her long, sun-streaked blond hair fall to her shoulders and wore a dark blue suit with a white blouse and a skirt that clung to her ass and stopped just above her knees. She had good legs and she knew it. The cameras would be on her.

8

Sitting in the judge's conference room were Kay Hamilton and her boss, Jim Davis; Clyde Taylor, director/warden of the Metropolitan Correctional Center; John Hernández, chief of the San Diego Police Department; and U.S. Marshal Kevin Walker, head of the marshals' Southern District Office. The marshals were, among other things, responsible for security for the federal courts in San Diego. Also present was Carol Maddox, the Assistant U.S. Attorney who had obtained the warrant for Kay to put video cameras in Cadillac Washington's bar. Maddox would be prosecuting Tito Olivera for Cadillac's murder.

While they were waiting for the judge to arrive, Carol Maddox leaned over and whispered to Kay, "Did you know Tito was going to kill him?"

"How could I possibly know that?" Kay said. "We just got lucky."

"Hmm," Maddox said, giving her a look she probably used on her kids when she suspected one of them was lying. Which reminded Kay . . .

"Are you going to have time to handle Tito's trial? I mean, with your kids and all?"

"Don't worry about me doing my job, Hamilton."

Judge Benton Foreman of the United States District Court for the Southern District of California entered the conference room. He was dressed in a dark gray suit and maroon tie, and not the black robe he wore in court. Foreman would be the man presiding over Tito Olivera's arraignment and possibly his trial. He was sixty-three years old, six foot six, and weighed two hundred and seventy pounds. His black head was shaved, and gleamed as if he polished it with furniture wax, and Kay thought he looked like a retired NFL lineman. The judge hadn't played in the pros, but he had been a defensive tackle at Stanford. He'd also been number four in his class at Stanford Law and clerked for Supreme Court Justice Thurgood Marshall. He was a very bright man.

As he was taking his seat, he said, "I don't feel comfortable holding this meeting without Mr. Olivera's lawyer in attendance."

"Your Honor," Jim Davis said, "this meeting is only to discuss security for the court and actions necessary to ensure Tito Olivera remains in jail until his trial."

"You're assuming Mr. Olivera isn't going to be granted bail," the judge said.

"Your Honor, Tito was videotaped shooting a man in the head and he's the brother of Caesar Olivera, head of the most powerful drug cartel in Mexico. I can't imagine that he's going to be—"

"Stop!" Judge Foreman said. He turned and picked up the phone on the credenza behind his chair. "Martha, call Tito Olivera's attorney and tell him I want him in my conference room in half an hour." He hung up and said to the people in the room, "We'll resume this meeting when Mr. Olivera's lawyer is present."

Judge Foreman left the room, leaving the other attendees staring at each other. Or, to be accurate, glaring at Jim Davis.

"Shit," Davis said. "Prescott is going to turn this into a circus."

"Well, I think this entire meeting is bullshit," Clyde Taylor, the MCC warden, said.

Kay had only spoken to Taylor on the phone and never met the man in person. He turned out to be a short, round man with a double chin—and both his chins were quivering with outrage.

"It's not bullshit," Kay Hamilton said. "Your goddamn guards—"

"Shut up, Hamilton," Davis said. "Warden Taylor, we'll have this discussion when the judge returns, and you'll have a chance to present your case. I apologize for the delay."

Marshal Kevin Walker rose from his chair and said, "I'm gonna go get a cookie or something." Walker was in his early forties, and Kay thought he looked a bit like her boss, Jim Davis, although he wasn't as tall as Davis and his hair was dark instead of white. But like Davis he had a mustache, and Kay thought if he wore a cowboy hat, he'd look like the Marlboro Man. He was a hunk.

"Why don't you come with me, John," Walker said to Chief Hernández. "I'll buy you a donut. I know cops like donuts."

John Hernández, like Tito Olivera, didn't look Hispanic. Nor did he have a Spanish accent; he sounded like the Harvard Law School graduate that he was. Like Kay's lover, Robert Meyer, Hernández had political ambitions that went far beyond being the top cop in San Diego. Kay could hardly wait to tell him that three of his narcotics detectives were on the take.

"I don't eat donuts," the chief said, sounding both righteous and serious, the way some people sound when they say: *I don't smoke.* "But I'll come with you."

Kay figured the marshal and the chief were going off to see if they could agree on a position they could both support. They were probably going to gang up on her boss.

The meeting resumed with Lincoln Prescott in attendance. Lincoln Prescott may not have been the best criminal defense lawyer in San Diego, but he was definitely one of the richest. His full-time job was defending members of the Olivera cartel, and Caesar and Tito Olivera sent a lot of work his way and paid him well.

Prescott was dressed, as always, in a white three-piece suit. He wore the suits regardless of the time of year or the weather, to make sure no one would confuse him with any other lawyer. His hair was gray and long enough to touch his collar in the back and had wings sweeping out over his ears. He always looked like he needed a haircut—and he had his hair trimmed once a week to make it look that way. He was a devious, grandstanding, media-hogging asshole and was hated by every prosecutor who ever had the misfortune to go up against him.

"Okay," Judge Foreman said. "Mr. Davis, you can begin."

"Your Honor, as I stated earlier, the purpose of this meeting is to discuss security for you and your court and to make sure that Tito Olivera doesn't escape before his trial. I think it's a mistake having Mr. Prescott here, as he'll pass on everything he hears to Mr. Olivera's brother."

"I object, Your Honor," Prescott said. "In fact, I object on several grounds. I strongly resent Mr. Davis implying that I'd be a party to an escape attempt. I object to my client being treated differently than any other citizen who has been accused of a crime in this district. I also intend to show that the warrant obtained by the DEA to monitor a private meeting between my client and Mr. Washington was improper and unconstitutional and—"

"Mr. Prescott, you can save the warrant speech for later," the judge said. "Right now I want to hear why the DEA thinks extraordinary security precautions are necessary."

"Thank you, Your Honor," Davis said. "As I stated earlier, Tito Olivera is the brother of Caesar Olivera, head of the most powerful drug cartel in Mexico."

"I object again," Prescott said. "I also represent some of Mr. Caesar Olivera's interests in the United

States and I know he's never been arrested here or in Mexico, that there's absolutely no proof that he's involved with narcotics, and—"

"Oh, shut the fuck up," Kay muttered.

She didn't think she'd spoken loud enough for the judge to hear, but she was wrong. "What did you say, young lady?" the judge said.

"I apologize, Your Honor," Kay said, "but this isn't a courtroom and there's no jury here. If Olivera's mouthpiece keeps interrupting every time we say something, we'll never get through this meeting."

"Your Honor," Prescott said, "I will not stand for—"

"Be quiet, Mr. Prescott," the judge said. "Although I don't approve of Agent Hamilton's language, I want you to stop interrupting and let Mr. Davis speak."

It took Jim Davis about ten minutes to state his case. First, he said, the judge had to recognize Caesar Olivera's capabilities. He had thousands of people working for him in Mexico, had connections to every Hispanic gang in California, and, after twenty-seven years in the drug business, his net worth was estimated to be in the billions. But it wasn't just his money and his manpower that were frightening, Davis said.

"It's his *mind-set*. He's not intimidated by law enforcement. He's not like the old-time Mafia guys who were afraid to kill federal agents, and he knows as long as he stays down in Mexico we'll never get him."

In Mexico, Davis said, Olivera's men had killed cops,

lawyers, politicians, judges, and journalists who interfered with his operations. A year before, his people had attacked a Mexican jail with more than fifty men, using rocket-propelled grenades and automatic weapons to free a prisoner. Sixteen Mexican soldiers guarding the jail were killed.

"This isn't Mexico," the judge said.

Davis basically said *Not yet*. Since Tito Olivera had moved to San Diego five years before to manage his brother's affairs in the United States, the murder rate in the Southwest had tripled. Most of the victims had been criminals connected to the drug business, but a few had been innocent bystanders. One journalist had been killed, and although his murder was unsolved, the motive appeared to involve an article he wrote about Tito. Furthermore, Jim Davis said, the DEA had recently obtained evidence that Tito had three San Diego Police Department detectives on his payroll.

This statement had John Hernández leaping to his feet, demanding that Davis prove what he'd just said. "I'm sorry to blindside you with this, John, but the judge needs to know that Olivera has penetrated your department, because it's relevant to this discussion. I'll give you the names right after this meeting because you need to detain these men before Mr. Prescott can warn them."

Prescott opened his mouth to protest, but the judge said, "Not now, Mr. Prescott."

Davis continued. "What I'm saying, Your Honor, is Caesar Olivera has enough money to buy cops, and he's already bought some. We also know he's corrupted people at MCC in the past." Davis then recounted the five incidents in the past year where MCC correctional officers had been caught passing contraband to inmates, and three of those inmates worked for the Olivera cartel.

Now it was Warden Taylor's turn to sputter, saying that just because a few bad apples had been found in his bushel it didn't mean all his apples were rotten.

"I appreciate that, Warden," Davis said, "but the fact remains that Olivera has proven he can buy some of your people and he has an intelligence network capable of learning everything there is to know about how Tito is being guarded."

"Just cut to the chase here, Mr. Davis," the judge said. "What do you want?"

"The first thing I want is for everyone in this room to realize that Caesar Olivera will do *anything* to get his little brother out of prison. He will kill people. He will bribe people. He will kidnap family members of cops and prison guards. Even Your Honor's own family isn't safe, Judge.

"Furthermore, I think it's possible that Caesar may try to free Tito when he's being transported from the federal lockup to your court for the arraignment or during the arraignment itself, and Marshal Walker may not be able to stop him."

"Horseshit," Walker said, but Davis ignored him.

"I think Tito should be arraigned inside his cell at the Metropolitan Correctional Center, and I believe he should be arraigned as soon as possible. Like immediately after this meeting."

"This is absurd," Prescott muttered.

"I also believe federal marshals should be assigned to protect Your Honor, Your Honor's family, the federal prosecutor, and the federal prosecutor's family until after the arraignment. Now, I realize that you might decide to release Mr. Olivera on bail . . ."

There wasn't a person in the room, including Tito's lawyer, who believed that Tito would be released on bail.

". . . and if he is, I can't do anything about that. But if Mr. Olivera is remanded, I believe he should be placed in some facility that can literally fight off an army. I think if Tito is allowed to remain in the Metropolitan Correctional Center until his trial, the citizens of San Diego will be in grave danger and Caesar Olivera will eventually free his brother."

"My people can protect the citizens of San Diego," John Hernández said.

"John, how many cops do you have?" Before Hernández could answer, Davis said, "You have less than twenty-seven hundred people in your department and a third of those people are administrators, desk jockeys, and lab rats. Caesar Olivera could double the number of street cops you have with Mexican and California gangbangers. He'll pay them whatever they ask, and he'll arm them better than your police force."

"What's your point, Mr. Davis?" the judge asked.

"My point, Your Honor, is that with Caesar Olivera you might see something you've never seen before in this country: a group of thugs armed as well as U.S. Army soldiers, with no regard for human life, mounting an attack against the Metropolitan Correctional Center, blasting their way inside, and killing every correctional officer in the place to free Tito Olivera."

Before John Hernández or the MCC warden could object again, Judge Foreman said, "So what do you propose, Mr. Davis?"

"I propose that Tito Olivera be placed in the brig at Camp Pendleton until his trial and that his trial be held at Camp Pendleton as well."

Camp Pendleton, as every person in the room knew, was a Marine Corps base forty miles north of San Diego that covered one hundred and twenty-five thousand acres. It had a population of more than one hundred thousand people, of which forty thousand were active-duty marines. Camp Pendleton was the headquarters of the First Marine Division and the elite First Marine Expeditionary Force; there were M1 Abrams tanks and Cobra helicopters there. In other words, it was a place with considerably more manpower and firepower than the Metropolitan Correctional Center, and the marines were not overweight jailers armed with batons.

"I object, Your Honor!" Lincoln Prescott shrieked. The other attendees all responded with some variation of *You gotta be shittin' me!*

The meeting went on for another five minutes, Lincoln Prescott making a pointless speech about the rights of the accused, the warden of the Metropolitan Correctional Center voicing his umbrage about accusations that his officers couldn't keep criminals incarcerated in his jail, and the chief of police once again challenging Davis's "outlandish assumptions" about what Caesar Olivera might do. The only one who didn't protest was U.S. Marshal Kevin Walker. He just sat there rubbing his big chin, apparently mulling over everything Jim Davis had said.

Kay figured that Judge Foreman might take a little time to come to a conclusion, but he didn't. He said, "Although I believe Caesar Olivera may have the capability suggested by Mr. Davis, and may intend to take some drastic action to free his brother, I refuse to let the legal institutions of the United States cower in fear. As I said, this is not Mexico. Mr. Olivera will be arraigned tomorrow morning in my courtroom as scheduled, and you people will all do your jobs to make sure that happens."

As a result of Benton Foreman's refusal to cower, eighteen people would die.

T he press conference went about the way Kay had expected.

Jim Davis gave a very terse, very formal statement regarding how Tito Olivera had been arrested for killing one Ronald "Cadillac" Washington, how DEA agents arrested two of Mr. Olivera's men, and how Leon James was shot and killed. He stated that Mr. Olivera had been a "person of interest" for some time regarding his connections to narcotics trafficking in California. He made no mention of Tito's big brother.

The first question asked was: "Is it true that Kay Hamilton, the DEA agent who killed Marco Álvarez in Miami, was the agent who arrested Tito Olivera?"

This question may have surprised Davis, but it didn't surprise Kay. Half an hour earlier, she had called the reporter who asked the question—and told her that she should ask it. The reporter was a good-looking redhead who anchored the local news on Channel 8, and Kay had leaked information to her in the past when she thought it might do her career some good. She occasionally had drinks with the reporter as well.

Davis responded to the question by saying, "The DEA does not release the names of DEA personnel involved in arrests."

But the cameras focused on Kay, and she knew the following morning the papers would discuss her killing Marco Álvarez and three of his men in Miami, and how twenty-seven people were eventually convicted thanks to her efforts.

Kay figured that she'd had a pretty good day. Maybe she'd treat herself to a couple martinis and a steak at Morton's.

9

Raphael Mora watched as Caesar Olivera spoke quietly with Tito's lawyer.

They were in Caesar's home office at Caesar's Sinaloa estate; the desk Caesar sat behind had once belonged to Archduke Maximilian of Hapsburg, Emperor of Mexico from 1864 to 1867. The telephone was not an antique; it was encrypted. Caesar ended the conversation by saying, "Thank you, Mr. Prescott," and gently placed the phone handset back into its cradle.

Mora knew the calmness Caesar was displaying was a façade. He knew that Caesar was so angry about the idiotic thing his brother had done that he wanted to take the phone and beat it on his expensive desk until it shattered—but he also knew that Caesar would never do that.

Raphael Mora had worked for Caesar Olivera for almost twenty years, and he remembered how Caesar had been when he was younger. He watched him beat three cousins to death one time by smashing their faces with a claw hammer; when Caesar was finished, his face was so covered with blood it looked like he was wearing a wet, red mask.

Caesar had willed himself to become a different

person. Now he rarely raised his voice. He prided himself on remaining unemotional, logical, and coldly analytical no matter how he might feel about a situation. He had little formal education, but he read extensively; he particularly liked to read management books, because that's how he now thought of himself: as a CEO.

Caesar was forty-five years old. He was a handsome man, although not as handsome as Tito. And unlike his younger half brother, Caesar looked Hispanic; he and Tito had different mothers. His hair was thick and dark, his nose prominent, his chin blunt. His eyes were so dark they looked black. And where Tito was tall and slender, Caesar was five-ten, with a deep chest and the muscles of someone who might have spent a lifetime doing manual labor. Mora knew that Caesar Olivera had never done manual labor; the muscles were a genetic gift, further assisted by a personal trainer.

Caesar also no longer personally executed those who had disappointed him in some way. These days, he and his wife frequently dined with Mexican politicians and celebrities; he had a philanthropic organization in his wife's name; wings in hospitals and buildings at universities bore his name. People in the Mexican army, the federal police, local cops, politicians, and judges worked for him and protected his interests and his investments. And nobody—at least nobody in the Mexican media—called him a drug lord. He was simply a well-connected businessman with vast real estate holdings and controlling interests in many legitimate companies.

"Does Prescott have anything new?" Mora asked.

"No," Caesar said. "He just called to tell me that three San Diego detectives have been taken into custody but they never had any direct contact with Tito."

Caesar looked away for a moment, and again Mora had the impression he was struggling to control himself. "Do you think Juan knew what he was going to do?"

Juan Guzmán was nominally Tito's second-in-command, and when Tito went north to run Caesar's U.S. operations, Caesar had forced Tito to take Juan with him. Juan was older than Tito—about Caesar's age—and he was an experienced man and not a hothead. His job had been to mentor Tito, keep him out of trouble, and keep Caesar informed of what Tito was doing. Juan had obviously failed—and failed badly.

"No, sir," Mora said. "I spoke to him right after Tito was arrested. He knew Tito was upset about your order to buy out Washington. His pride was hurt, and he thought he'd failed you. But Juan had no idea he was going to do something so foolish."

"And the woman? Was she a DEA informant?"

"It would appear so," Mora said. "Tito told Prescott that she knew the DEA agent who arrested him. She called her Kay. He said only three people in his organization knew of his meeting with Washington: the woman, and the two men he brought with him to the meeting. He's certain the two men didn't talk to the DEA about the meeting. Juan vetted the woman, of course, when Tito started sleeping with her, and he saw nothing that gave him any cause for concern. She was who she appeared to be: a beautiful, not-too-bright party girl. Juan reviewed her cell phone records periodically and never saw any indication she was talking to anyone at the DEA."

"How did they get to her?"

"Juan doesn't know for sure, but he suspects it might have been through her brother. He was arrested five months ago, and when he was released on bail, he ran and it looked as though he'd fled to Canada. Phone records show that he called his mother periodically from Vancouver, and Juan thought he was hiding there, probably living off some woman, until he decided it was safe to come back to the U.S. But now . . . well, Juan doesn't know, but he suspects the DEA is hiding the brother and they used him to force the woman to cooperate."

"Where is she now?"

"I don't know. The DEA disappeared her right after Tito was arrested. I'll find her."

Caesar nodded. Of course Mora would find her.

An organizational chart of the Olivera cartel would show that Caesar had no second-in-command. His organization was relatively horizontal, with a number of men and women who would be considered senior vice presidents in a traditional company and all reported directly to him. Some were responsible for specific geographical areas in Mexico and South America and they managed drug trafficking, human trafficking, prostitution, and weapons. Others were specialists. A woman— a Harvard MBA—managed all of Caesar's financial affairs; she had more than a hundred people working for her in Mexico. One man was responsible for transporting Caesar's major products—people and drugs—both into and out of Mexico; another man was responsible for his physical security, the security of his homes, and his family. This person had technical personnel working for him who dealt with encryption, computer security, and electronic surveillance countermeasures.

Raphael Mora was, for lack of a better term, Caesar's intelligence officer and wartime consigliere. And Mora was more than a goon with a gun. He'd been in the Mexican army when he was younger, a graduate of Heroico Colegio Militar, Mexico's equivalent of West Point. He'd also received training at the United States Army War College, the Strategic Studies Institute in Carlisle, Pennsylvania, as well as training with U.S. Army Special Forces at Fort Bragg, North Carolina, before coming to work for Caesar Olivera.

"Well, do you have a plan for freeing my brother?"

"Yes, sir," Mora said. He had begun developing the plan an hour after Tito was arrested. He told Caesar what he had in mind.

"I leave for San Diego in half an hour," Mora said, "and I'm taking a couple specialists with me, but I'm going to have to rely on a local gang for manpower. The gang leader seems bright enough, but I'll have to trust his judgment to pick a decent crew. I don't have time to screen his personnel."

"Does Tito know what's going to happen?"

"Yes. We got to a guard quickly and he gave Tito a cell phone. I've told Tito what to expect, and he understands the risks." Mora hesitated. "Sir, I'm assuming you understand the risks as well."

"I do," Caesar said. He didn't bother with threats about what he would do if his brother was killed or seriously injured during the escape attempt.

"Is there anything we can do to force the judge to release Tito on bail?" Caesar asked.

"No. Marshals are protecting the judge and his immediate family, and we have less than sixteen hours."

"If you fail tomorrow, where will Tito be held pending trial?"

"As Prescott probably told you, the DEA wants to put him on a marine base, but he thinks that's unlikely to happen and he'll be held at MCC, San Diego. Obviously, it's going to be extremely difficult to get him out of there, but we'll have at least a year before his trial to work out a plan. Prescott will make sure we have at least a year."

"And if there is a trial?"

This was typical of Caesar Olivera. He had a Plan A—free Tito before his arraignment. He had a possible Plan B—free him from the Metropolitan Correctional Center before his trial. But he wanted a Plan C.

"The video is the problem," Mora said. "Prescott hasn't seen it yet, so we don't know exactly what it shows, but once Prescott sees it, he'll decide if it can be impugned. I will, of course, investigate methods for destroying it and any copies that are made. However, and as I'm sure you know, that may not be possible. The evidence against Tito will be well protected; they're not going to leave it sitting in a cardboard box in an evidence locker. There are also three witnesses to the killing: Tito's whore and his two men. They'll all be dead before the trial. Once a judge is assigned and a jury is impaneled, we'll start looking at those people to see who can be influenced. But, sir, we don't want this to go to trial. So, shall I proceed?"

"Yes," Caesar said.

"You realize that the reaction from the media and American politicians is going to be enormous, much bigger than anything we have ever seen in the past. The financial impact on our operations will also be significant."

"I understand. Proceed," Caesar said.

After Mora left, Caesar walked outside and took a seat in a wicker rocking chair on the large porch that ran along the west side of the house.

Caesar had several magnificent homes in Mexico: an urban palace in the Bosques de las Lomas area of Mexico City; an oceanside mansion in Playas de Rosarito that was close to the U.S. border; and condos in Manzanillo, Cozumel, and Tehuantepec. His primary residence was in the Mexican state of Sinaloa, where he had been raised, and he spent as much time there as possible.

The estate in Sinaloa was east of San Ignacio, on the western edge of the Sierra Madre Occidental mountains, and covered more than ten thousand acres. It was cool in the summer and there were miles of forest trails where his wife and daughters could ride their horses. He had orchards, stables, tennis courts, indoor and outdoor swimming pools, and several cottages for visitors. The cottages were nicer than the homes of ninety percent of the people who lived in Mexico.

Caesar lit a cigar; he permitted himself two a day. He had stopped smoking cigarettes ten years before. As he smoked—and thought about his brother—he watched his eldest daughter ride her horse in the exercise yard near the stables. Katrina, only fourteen, was an excellent rider and her coach said she could be an Olympic-caliber equestrienne. She was also going to be as beautiful as her mother. Caesar was almost sorry his wife and daughters were leaving tomorrow for Mexico City; well, he was sorry his daughters were leaving, not quite so sorry his wife was going.

Caesar knew he should never have sent Tito to the United States. He knew it was a mistake the day he made the decision.

Tito was twenty years younger than Caesar. Caesar's mother was his father's first wife, a Mexican national, and when she died, his father married a woman from L.A. who was almost Caesar's age. Caesar's father also allowed Tito to be born in California so he could claim U.S. citizenship.

All his life Caesar had spoiled his baby brother, and when Tito was twenty, he began to pester Caesar to give him a larger role in his business, and in particular to be allowed to expand Caesar's operations in the United States. Caesar initially resisted Tito's pleas; he didn't need to expand. He certainly didn't need more money. Furthermore, doing business in the United States was much more dangerous than doing business in Mexico, because law enforcement, for the most part, actually functioned in the United States. In Mexico, no one would ever dare to arrest Tito Olivera; north of the border, cops and judges were much harder to buy and intimidate.

But Tito continued to beg, saying that if anything should ever happen to Caesar—God forbid—he needed to have the experience. Also, taking control of distribution in the southwestern United States made good business sense—and Tito knew that a solid business argument would appeal to Caesar. So he eventually gave in, knowing when he did that Tito didn't have the maturity, the discipline—or the intelligence—to run his empire. He had hedged his bet by sending Juan Guzmán to San Diego with Tito, but for whatever reason, Juan had failed him when it came to Tito's decision to kill Cadillac Washington. Caesar hadn't yet decided what to do about Juan.

"Papa! Papa!"

Caesar looked out at his daughter; she looked so small sitting on the chestnut mare she favored.

"Watch me, Papa." And then, before Caesar could say anything to stop her, she ran the mare directly at the enclosure surrounding the exercise yard and jumped the fence.

"Katrina, are you crazy!" Caesar shouted. "Get off that horse right now."

But he was smiling.

Katrina was the right person to run his empire after he was gone. She had the courage, and she was definitely smarter than his brother.

10

U.S. Marshal Kevin Walker's job was to get Tito Olivera from the Metropolitan Correctional Center to the Federal Courthouse, to protect the court during Tito's arraignment, then get Tito back to the correctional center. And although he thought that Jim Davis was overstating what Caesar Olivera might do to free his brother, Walker decided he couldn't take the chance that Davis might be right. Kevin Walker was not going to allow the Olivera cartel to keep him from doing his job.

The Metropolitan Correctional Center in downtown San Diego is connected to the Federal Courthouse by a tunnel through which prisoners are taken for court appearances. Mother Nature, however, had caused the normal transport process to be changed. About a year before, an earthquake registering 5.9 on the Richter scale struck San Diego. There had been no fatalities, but cracks were found in the courthouse transport tunnel, and city engineers decided it needed to be reinforced. Then, as is often the case with construction work, a job that should have taken three months managed to expand to a year and triple in cost.

What this all meant was that for the last twelve

months, it had been necessary to drive prisoners from the jail to the courthouse. Typically, they were transported in groups in a van with a couple of marshals for escorts. The van had benches in the back and metal rings in the floor that prisoners could be chained to; the van wasn't armored. The good news was that the door-to-door distance from the correctional center to the courthouse was only a quarter mile and it took only a few minutes to transport the prisoners.

Walker also figured that Caesar Olivera's people knew everything there was to know about the prisoner-transfer process because a lot of cartel people had spent time in the jail. Furthermore, he suspected that Jim Davis had probably been right when he said at the meeting that Olivera had MCC jailers on his payroll.

The first thing Walker did was call the city bureaucrat in charge of the tunnel work and tell him that no workers would be allowed back into the construction zone until after Tito's arraignment. Walker said he didn't want to deal with potential security problems posed by the workers. When the bureaucrat asked Walker who was going to pay for the delay, Walker told him to send a memo to his boss, the Attorney General of the United States. This was Walker's way of saying *I could give a shit*.

To transport Tito, Walker scrapped the van that was normally used and obtained an armored truck, like the type used to move money from bank to bank. He also told the MCC guards that Tito would be transported alone, not as part of any group. In addition to the armored truck, he arranged for an SUV containing four heavily armed marshals to escort the vehicle holding Tito. He suspected that everything he told the guards would eventually be relayed to somebody in Olivera's organization.

To get from the jail to the courthouse, the transport vehicle would drive up a loading ramp on the north side of the correctional center, take a left onto F Street, travel two short blocks on F, turn left on First Avenue, cross E Street, turn left on Broadway, then left again on Front Street and drop Tito off at the back of the courthouse. About five short blocks, the distance made longer because of one-way streets. SDPD patrol cars would stop traffic while Tito was being transported, blocking the cross streets: where First Avenue intersected F Street, E Street, and Broadway. Total elapsed time to get Tito from the jail to the court should be just over a minute.

Inside the courthouse, additional U.S. marshals brought in from L.A. would stand guard near the metal detectors and provide security for the court during the arraignment. These men would be armed with assault rifles as well as sidearms. The courtroom would be swept by bomb-sniffing dogs half an hour before the arraignment.

The correctional officers at MCC, a liaison from the San Diego Police Department, and Walker's men were all briefed on the plan. At six in the morning, Walker did a dry run from the jail to the courthouse to see how long it would take to get Tito from his cell to a chair in front of the judge's bench.

* * *

At eight-thirty a.m., Tito, dressed in an orange jail jumpsuit, was led down to the transport holding area by two MCC jailers and two federal marshals. Tito's hands and ankles were manacled. As soon as Tito was in the holding area, one of Walker's men—a man who was the same height and weight as Tito and had the same light brown hair—put on a jumpsuit. Manacles were placed on his hands and legs, but the manacles weren't locked.

"What the hell's going on?" Tito said.

"Shut your mouth," Walker said.

Moving rapidly—so rapidly that anyone outside the jail would get just the briefest glimpse of the man—marshals surrounded the Tito impostor and hustled him into the back of the armored truck. One marshal then joined the impostor in the truck and four other marshals climbed into the SUV that would lead the armored truck to the courthouse. Walker told the driver of the SUV that he was to depart in exactly three minutes.

As the MCC guards stood there looking confused, Walker took the leg irons off Tito Olivera, then turned to one of his men, pointed at the MCC guards, and said, "You keep these guys here for five minutes and don't allow any of them to use a cell phone." Then Walker and four other marshals—one of whom was holding a large bolt-cutter—walked Tito in the direction of the tunnel that led to the courthouse.

"Hey! You can't go that way," an MCC guard called out. "The tunnel's closed."

Walker ignored the guard.

Because of the construction under way to repair the damage caused by the earthquake, the normal door and control point leading to the tunnel had been replaced with a temporary wall and a door large enough to bring materials and equipment into the tunnel. But because MCC was still a jail, the wall was made of half-inch steel plates and the door was also steel. The door had a padlock on it, and a guard watched that door twenty-four hours a day.

As the MCC guard asked him what the hell he was doing, Walker cut the padlock on the tunnel door. Then, with one big hand on Tito's upper left arm, and his men armed with Remington semiautomatic shotguns, Walker marched Tito past cement mixers, piles of rebar, and stacks of lumber, stepped over air hoses and electrical cords and jackhammers, and proceeded to the courthouse tunnel exit where another federal marshal was waiting.

So although Walker didn't believe that Caesar Olivera would be so bold as to attempt to free his brother, he decided to set up a diversion. He figured that if an attempt were made, it would happen while Tito was being transported, that being easier than Olivera's people trying to blast their way into the courthouse to free him during the arraignment. He let everybody think that Tito would be transported to the courthouse in a relatively normal manner—meaning that he would be more heavily guarded than other prisoners—but he never told anyone that he planned to use the tunnel.

Walker also figured his own people would be safe. They were heavily armed, the transport time would be just a couple of minutes, and the armored transport vehicle would be moving at a high rate of speed. How could anyone stop them?

Marshal Kevin Walker, like Judge Benton Foreman, turned out to be wrong.

The convoy containing the Tito Olivera impostor reached the intersection of F Street and First Avenue about thirty seconds after it departed the correctional center. An SDPD patrol car was in the middle of First, stopping traffic going north, and another patrol car was parked a block away, stopping traffic going east on E Street from crossing First Avenue. The truck containing the impostor made the turn onto First Avenue—and all hell broke loose.

From two different rooms in the Westin Hotel in Horton Plaza, three powerful rocket-propelled grenades were fired simultaneously. Two grenades hit the patrol cars blocking the cross streets and the third hit the SUV leading the armored truck. When the SUV was hit, the driver of the truck containing the Tito impostor slammed on the brakes, but not in time to avoid ramming the rear of the SUV. An instant later, a sniper fired a .50 caliber bullet through the bullet-resistant glass of the armored truck, instantly killing the driver. The sniper was one of the specialists Raphael Mora had brought with him from Mexico.

Two open-top Hummer H2s roared down F Street, moving at approximately fifty miles an hour. One went up a grass strip on the north side of the street and the other used the sidewalk on the south side. A woman walking on the sidewalk was killed instantly when she was hit by one of the Hummers and her body was thrown thirty-five yards through the window of a restaurant called the Athens Market Taverna.

The patrol car intended to stop traffic going north on First was on fire in the middle of the intersection of First and F. The cop driving the patrol car had luckily gotten out and been standing near it when the grenade hit; although he'd been knocked down by the blast and cut by shrapnel, he was still alive, trying to get to his feet. When the Hummers reached the intersection, the men inside shot the injured cop with M16 rifles on full automatic, then the Hummers came to a stop next to the armed truck.

At this point, the only U.S. marshal able to respond to the attack was the one sitting next to the dead driver in the armored truck. If he'd been a coward, he would have remained inside the cab of the armored truck, where he would have had some protection. But he wasn't a coward. He jumped out and began firing at the men inside the Hummers with a shotgun, and he was immediately killed by return fire.

One of the gangsters ran up to the back door of the armored truck, placed a shaped explosive charge on the door, and blew it open. The occupants inside the truck— a U.S marshal armed with a shotgun and the Tito impostor—were both knocked to the floor by the explosion. As soon as the door was blown off, the bomber tossed a flash bang grenade inside the truck, momentarily deafening and blinding the men inside. Then the bomber shot the U.S. marshal in the head. The Tito impostor, a man named John Newman, was lying on the floor with his hands over his ears, his eyes shut, dressed in an orange jail jumpsuit. The bomber didn't notice that Newman wasn't manacled; he didn't notice the sidearm lying on the floor of the truck near Newman's right hand.

The thing was, none of the attackers had ever seen Tito Olivera, and they naturally assumed the man in the jumpsuit was him. Two of the attackers grabbed John Newman, saying in Spanish, "We got you, man, we got you. You're going to be okay," then hustled him into a black Ford Explorer that had pulled up next to all the burning, damaged vehicles in the street.

The Explorer containing John Newman went barreling up First Avenue, made a right on E Street, and a block later turned into an underground parking lot beneath the North Island Credit Union on Broadway Circle. In the parking lot, the dazed man the gangsters thought was Tito was then transferred to an inconspicuous yellow taxicab.

By now a few SDPD cops had arrived on the scene and engaged in a brief gun battle with the men in the two Hummers. The cops were armed with sidearms and shotguns; the men in the Hummers were armed with M16s and Ingram MAC-10 machine pistols. The cops got off a few shots, one of the gangbangers was killed, and the rest of them piled into the Hummers and took off. The cops gave chase. They called in reinforcements.

When Mora developed his plan to free Tito Olivera, he told the bangers that once Tito Olivera was freed they were on their own getting away from the cops. One of the Hummers containing five men got away that morning. The other Hummer, containing four men, was boxed in by San Diego cops an hour after the attack and all four men were killed.

The cops were in no mood for taking prisoners.

Kevin Walker and the real Tito Olivera had just entered Judge Foreman's courtroom when the attack started. As the battle lasted less than four minutes, he was still standing there when he was called and told what had happened. His first instinct was to leave the courthouse and check on his men; but he didn't follow his instincts. Instead, he barged into Judge Foreman's chambers, told the judge what had happened, and demanded that Foreman immediately arraign Tito.

In one of the shortest arraignment hearings on record for a capital crime, Judge Foreman accepted Tito's not guilty plea and refused to give him bail. While the arraignment was taking place, Walker received an update on his cell phone regarding the attack and his face drained of color. Following the arraignment, he and his marshals escorted Tito back through the courthouse tunnel to a solitary confinement cell on the eighth floor of the Metropolitan Correctional Center.

Then Walker went to see for himself the carnage that had occurred on the corner of First Avenue and F Street. Who said this wasn't Mexico?

Eighteen people died in the attack: three San Diego cops, seven federal marshals, five of the attackers who were later identified as belonging to the MS-13 gang, and three private citizens. One of the private citizens was the woman struck by one of the Hummers. The other two citizens were men who had occupied the rooms in the Westin Hotel from which the rocket-propelled grenades had been fired. Both men were accountants attending a convention at the Westin. One federal marshal, one of the men in the escort SUV, survived the attack. He had burns on twenty percent of his body and had lost his left leg.

Another marshal who died was John Newman, the Tito impostor, but his body was not found until the day after the attack. He had been tortured before he was killed, and horribly mutilated. Walker refused to let John Newman's wife see his body; he told her that her husband had been shot in the face and, thankfully, had died instantly. It had actually taken several hours for John Newman to die.

Walker also offered his resignation. His boss told him he was thinking about accepting it.

* * *

The reaction of the American media and American politicians was as bad as Raphael Mora had predicted.

The day of the attack, cameras were at the Federal Courthouse hoping to catch a glimpse of handsome Tito Olivera doing the perp walk. When the shooting started, only a block from the courthouse, some of the faster cameramen were able to record part of the battle: the cops shooting it out with the gangbangers in the Hummers, the dead cops and marshals lying on the street, the burning police vehicles, citizens fleeing in terror, screaming and falling. The story instantly went international, with all the pundits rehashing everything previously said about drug cartels and how the savage violence in Mexico had clearly crept across the border.

The president made a speech standing in the Rose Garden, looking annoyed, saying he was going to be talking personally to the president of Mexico, demanding he do something to control the cartels. Like that was going to help. Congressmen made speeches about the need for sanctions against Mexico, and although the attack had nothing to do with illegal immigrants, politicians pounded on the podium about the need to boot out the aliens—as if the gardeners, pickers, maids, and busboys were all gang members in disguise. Glassy-eyed proponents for legalizing drugs made their pitch to whoever would listen, while gun-control advocates pointed out that all the weapons the gangsters used were manufactured in the United States; they asked once again if anything meaningful was ever going to be done to control the sale of such lethal hardware. The president of the NRA claimed that if a few of San Diego's citizens had been armed that day, they might have been able to help the cops; he said it wasn't the NRA's fault that criminals had more firepower than the police.

Of course, nothing changed after weeks of political posturing and heated rhetoric—except for the lives of seven U.S. marshals' families who would never be the same again.

11

When Jim Davis and Kay saw Kevin Walker the next day, he looked as if he'd aged ten years. Kay put her hand on his arm and said, "I'm so sorry, Marshal." He just nodded. He reminded her of pictures you see of survivors of suicide attacks in places like Baghdad—men wandering through smoking rubble, in shock, their eyes vacant, having no idea why they had been spared and their friends had not.

Clyde Taylor, warden of the Metropolitan Correctional Center, was also subdued. He'd been thinking about what Jim Davis had said, about how Caesar Olivera could raise an army to get Tito out of his jail. He now believed Davis, and he did *not* want to be responsible for guarding Tito for the ten or eleven months that would pass before his trial.

Warden Taylor was, in fact, the one who had called the meeting.

"That idea of yours about putting Tito in the brig at Camp Pendleton until the trial. Do you think you can make that happen?"

"Before the attack on the marshals, I wasn't sure," Davis said. "It was just an idea. But now, yeah, I think so. My boss in Washington is talking to the Attorney General and folks at the Pentagon. I've talked to the commanding officer at Pendleton, and he actually likes the idea. He's one of those guys who wants to be back in Afghanistan killing Taliban. It sounded to me like he would enjoy the opportunity to match his marines up against a bunch of Mexican hoodlums.

"The thing I like about Pendleton is the brig is miles from the main gate, and if Olivera tried to bust through the gate or the fence, the marines would have plenty of time to set up a defensive perimeter around the brig. This general at Pendleton will also run his guys through drills until they drop. But we can't rely totally on the military. Caesar Olivera can bribe marines just as easily as he can bribe cops and jailers."

Turning to Kevin Walker, Jim Davis said, "Marshal, technically, guarding Tito Olivera if we move him out of MCC is your job. I think we need your marshals inside the brig and living with Tito until his trial. The military will supply all the manpower to keep him in jail, but your people will be the ones running point."

Walker just nodded. Kay was really worried about him; he looked like he was barely able to function.

"What do I do with Tito until we can transfer him to the brig?" the warden said.

"You're just going to have to do your job," Davis said. "You need to handpick the guys you have guarding him and make sure they're people who can't be bought. If I were you, I'd also put a video camera in Tito's cell so you can see if anybody passes him a cell phone or anything else. You'll need to beef up your perimeter security, too. You should block off elevators, stairs, and doors that can be used to get to Tito. Ask SDPD to assist you outside the building. They lost people in the attack, and you know they'll help."

"What happens if Caesar Olivera kidnaps people in my family or the families of my guards?"

Davis shrugged. "I don't know what to tell you, Warden. Just do the best you can and I'll try to get Tito out of your jail as fast as possible. You also have another problem."

"What's that?" the warden said. He didn't want to hear about any more problems.

"You're holding two men who saw Tito kill Cadillac Washington: Jesús Rodríguez and Ángel Gomez. They're witnesses, but they're not going to testify against Tito, because they know if they do, Caesar Olivera will have them killed."

"Then what's the problem?" the warden asked.

"Olivera is going to kill them anyway. He's not going to take the chance of them cutting a deal and giving up information about the cartel. Their lives aren't worth the risk. So you need to put them in isolation and watch them like they're your own kids."

"Why not put them in Camp Pendleton, too?" the warden said.

"No. That's a silver bullet we're using for Tito. We can't put everyone who's connected to him on the base."

Before the warden could object, he said, "We also have to protect our informant, María Delgato, and her family. Caesar Olivera has probably figured out by now that María was the one who set up his brother, so he's going to do his best to cut her head off. And I mean *literally* cut her head off."

Normally, guarding a federal witness would be Kevin Walker's job, but Davis said, "If it's okay with you, Marshal Walker, my people will cover María. We've been hiding her brother for almost half a year, and right now we have her mother in custody, too. I know you're shorthanded with everything that's happened, so if you want to protect them, then maybe I can—"

"You can take care of your informant," Walker said. It was obvious Walker didn't really care about María Delgato. All he cared about was the seven dead men who had been his responsibility.

"Okay," Davis said. "I'll take the lead on getting D.C. to buy in on this plan." He nodded to Kay, and they left before anyone could change their minds.

As they were leaving Warden Taylor's office, Davis said, "Is María in Portland yet?"

"Yeah," Kay said. "I'm heading for the airport in an hour to fly up there. I'll be gone a couple of days."

12

The day Tito Olivera was arrested, Kay had two DEA agents pick up María Delgato's mother. Sofía Delgato thought they were immigration agents and went along peacefully, crying into a handkerchief nonstop for an hour. Kay had two other agents take María to meet up with her mother, then all four agents, two males and two females, headed north in a van. They were ordered to drive without stopping until they reached Portland, Oregon, and then wait for Kay at a safe house that she had rented for the month. Kay had no intention of flying María Delgato anywhere; she knew the Olivera cartel had the ability to check flight records. After she arrived in Portland, Kay was going to take María and her mother to see Miguel Delgato, María's younger brother.

For the last five months—while Kay had been trying to get enough evidence to put Tito Olivera in jail—Miguel Delgato had been staying with two DEA agents named Figgins and Patterson. The three men had been living together in an unimpressive, three-bedroom waterfront house that sat on two isolated acres ten miles from Neah Bay, Washington.

Neah Bay, Washington, is a bleak Makah Indian fishing village on the northwestern-most point of the continental United States; Canada's Vancouver Island is twenty miles away, just across the Strait of Juan de Fuca. The term *the end of nowhere* comes to mind, but Neah Bay is a premier place for catching salmon, halibut, and cod.

Miguel's minders, Mike Figgins and Ray Patterson, were both a year away from retirement. They were overweight, out of shape, probably alcoholics, and just coasting along until they could pull the plug on their careers—and the job of guarding Miguel Delgato was the best gig they ever had in twenty-five years with the Drug Enforcement Administration.

No one was hunting for Miguel; his friends and business associates all thought he'd fled to Canada. Once a month, Figgins and Patterson would let him make a call that was routed through a Vancouver exchange and allow him to talk to his mother so phone records would show he was living there. Miguel wasn't important enough for anyone to look for—and Figgins and Patterson weren't worried about his escaping, either. Miguel knew that if he escaped, his mother and sister would be deported.

So Figgins had borrowed a twenty-one-foot Trophy boat from the widow of a DEA agent who lived in Seattle, and for the past five months he, Patterson, and Miguel had done nothing but fish, play cribbage, golf, drink, and take an occasional trip to the casino near Port Angeles. The agents were both divorced—between them they had five ex-wives—and they were doing exactly the kind of things they planned to do after they retired. And not only were they getting their DEA salaries for babysitting Miguel Degato, they were also collecting per diem.

It turned out that Miguel actually liked to fish and golf. He didn't like being cooped up with two old boozers like Figgins and Patterson, but he knew it was either that or a cell in Victorville. So Miguel went along with the arrangement without bitching too much, and the three men actually became friends—or as friendly as a guy and his jailers can be. Figgins and Patterson were dreading the day the assignment ended.

Kay's plan was to stash María and her mother with Miguel at Neah Bay until Tito Olivera's trial—but there'd be no more golfing and fishing trips for Figgins and Patterson once María arrived.

Kay flew into Portland because she didn't want there to be a record of her being anywhere in Washington State. She rented a car at Portland Airport, then drove to the safe house where María and her mother were waiting with the four DEA agents who had transported them from San Diego.

Kay was going to drive María and Sofía to Neah Bay herself. She and her boss, Jim Davis, had made the decision that the best way to protect María until the trial was to hide her in the most remote place possible and minimize the number of people who knew where she was. And although Mike Figgins and Ray Patterson were both professional burnouts, Kay trusted them. She'd worked with them in Miami, and in spite of their many flaws, she was positive they wouldn't sell María to Caesar Olivera.

As soon as Kay walked into the Portland safe house, María began to bitch. Kay had ruined her life, and she wanted to know what was going to happen next. What was she going to do for money? Where were she and her mother supposed to live?

"Aw, Jesus, shut up for a minute, will you?" Kay said. "We'll talk about all that stuff later."

She didn't bother to remind María that if she hadn't shot off her mouth in front of Tito about knowing Kay, she wouldn't be in this predicament.

"First," Kay said, "I need to know more about your mother's heart condition so I can arrange for medical care."

"What heart condition?" Sofía Delgato said. "All I take is a high-blood-pressure pill."

Kay looked over at María, and María just shrugged.

María was no longer wearing the sexy, low-cut cocktail dress she had on when Tito was arrested. She was now wearing jeans—and not designer jeans—a bulky sweat-shirt, and tennis shoes. Neither María nor her mother had been allowed to pack before leaving San Diego, because Kay had wanted them out of the city as fast as possible. She'd instructed the agents who drove them to Portland to buy them clothes suitable for January in the North-west, where it was almost always raining and the temperature was twenty to thirty degrees cooler than San Diego.

Turning to one of the female DEA agents, Kay asked, "Did you get them enough clothes so they only have to wash once a week or so?"

"Yeah," the agent said. "And suitcases if you have to move them."

"Good," Kay said. Pointing at María's tennis shoes, she asked, "How 'bout waterproof boots?"

"Yeah. Rain gear, too."

"Why the hell do we need rain gear?" María asked.

"Have you noticed the weather outside, María?" Kay said.

"Yeah, but I'm not planning on going hiking or some shit like that. And these jeans she bought me make my ass look fat."

Kay thought her ass would have looked perfect even if she'd been wearing a burlap sack, but didn't say so. She also thought that María was really going to be a handful for Figgins and Patterson.

Kay thanked the four DEA agents for bringing María to Portland and told them they could head back to San Diego. She implied, without actually saying so, that María would be staying at the safe house in Portland until Tito's trial. She had no reason to distrust the agents; she just didn't want them to know where she was taking María. As soon as the agents left, Kay told María and her mother she was driving them to see Miguel. Sofía was delighted to hear this; she hadn't seen her son in almost half a year.

María asked where they were going, and Kay ignored her.

It was—or should have been—a six-hour drive from Portland, Oregon, to Neah Bay, Washington. The scenery, particularly along the Washington coast, was marvelous; the trip itself was a nightmare. They had to stop every hour so María's mother could use the restroom, and if they weren't stopping so Sofía could pee, they were stopping because María wanted to smoke, which she couldn't do in the rental car.

The six-hour trip to Neah Bay took eight hours.

Kay allowed María and her mother a few minutes for a tearful reunion with Miguel, then told everyone to sit down in the living room. Speaking in English so Figgins and Patterson could understand, Kay said, "Let's talk about what's going to happen next. Miguel, translate for your mom if she doesn't understand something."

Kay explained that it was going to be almost a year before Tito Olivera went to trial. It was a death-penalty case and Tito's lawyer was going to delay things as long as he could, and the reason he was going to delay was to give Caesar Olivera an opportunity to free his brother. More to the point, Caesar was also going to do everything he could to find María and kill her.

"If he can't find María, he'll try to find you two," Kay said, pointing at María's mother and brother. "And when he finds you, he'll kidnap you and threaten to kill you if María testifies, then he'll kill you anyway."

When Kay said this, María's mother began to wail in Spanish; it was obvious she spoke English better than Kay had thought.

"The three of you have to understand something," Kay said. "Caesar Olivera runs a large, sophisticated organization that has technical capability and contacts everywhere. The best chance of keeping you all alive is for you to stay here. This place is at the end of nowhere and Caesar has no reason to look here. But if you do something stupid, if you make a telephone call to anyone, send a letter, get on the Internet and send an e-mail, if you make contact with anyone from your past, Caesar Olivera will find you. Then he'll kill you.

"Now, María, I suppose I could put you in a maximum-security prison somewhere, but I don't think you'd like living in a prison for a year. Plus, there isn't a prison in this country that Caesar couldn't penetrate to have you killed. Your best bet is to stay here and be invisible."

"And these two fat old farts are going to protect me?" María said. She said this in English, and when she did, Figgins said, "Hey, we're not that old." And Patterson added, "But we are fat."

"Shut up," Kay said to the agents. "I'm not in the mood."

To María she said, "You still don't get it. I could put thirty agents up here and they wouldn't be able to protect you. Caesar Olivera could literally drop a bomb on this place if he wanted to. He could send in a hundred guys to kill you. So Mike and Ray aren't really here to protect you. They're here to make sure you follow the rules, and if you don't, you're gonna die."

"Jesus Christ," María muttered. "What the hell am I going to do in this shithole for a year?"

In Spanish, her brother said, "It's not so bad, sis. And you like to fish—at least, you used to."

"Fish!" María said. "Are you out of your fucking mind?"

"María, watch your language," her mother said.

"What happens after the trial?" María asked, switching back to English.

"The government is going to take care of you and your family, María. We're going to relocate you to someplace nice, someplace where Olivera would never think of looking for you. We'll get you a house. We'll get you new identities that are bulletproof. If you want plastic surgery to change your appearance—"

María made a little snorting sound that Kay interpreted as *Why in God's name would a woman who looks like me ever want to change her appearance?*

"Anyway," Kay said, "we've got a year to figure out where you should go after the trial. Right now, the main thing is, I have to make sure you understand that the only way to protect you is for you to stay here and stay out of sight."

Kay wasn't too worried about Miguel and his mother, but she knew María was going to be a problem. She was a spoiled glamour girl, and she was used to a lot of attention and a lot of action. She liked wearing nice clothes and going to nice places. She was used to being pampered at upscale spas. For her, a year in Neah Bay was going to be like being buried alive.

Thank God Kay had the video of Tito killing Cadillac Washington.

13

While Kay was moving María Delgato to Neah Bay, Tito Olivera was moved to the U.S. Marine Corps brig at Camp Pendleton.

Government agencies are not known for moving swiftly, particularly when there are issues involving the responsibilities and purview of those agencies. No bureaucrat likes any action that might result in a precedent for giving his work to some other bureaucrat. In the case of moving Tito Olivera into a military prison, several organizations had their fingers in the pie: the Metropolitan Correctional Center in San Diego, the U.S. Attorney in San Diego, the Justice Department in Washington, D.C., the U.S. Marshals Service, the DEA, and the Pentagon. For once—and most likely because of Caesar Olivera's attack in San Diego that resulted in the deaths of almost a score of people—all these entities moved at what, for them, was a blinding rate of speed.

In a long, formal document composed by various legal elves, it was agreed that Tito would be placed in the brig, and although the Marshals Service would be the primary agency responsible for guarding him, the marshals would be "augmented" by marines at Camp Pendleton.

In other words, if Caesar Olivera was dumb enough or arrogant enough to try to free his brother from the brig, he was going to have to deal with a battalion of superbly trained, armed-to-the-teeth marines.

Marshal Kevin Walker personally escorted Tito Olivera from San Diego to Camp Pendleton in a helicopter, but before they left, Walker made a phone call. He couldn't obtain a phone number for Caesar Olivera, so he called Tito's lawyer.

"Prescott," he said, "this is U.S. Marshal Kevin Walker. We met the other day in Judge Foreman's conference room."

"Yes, I remember you, Marshal. What can I do for you?"

"I want you to pass a message to Caesar Olivera. As you know, Tito is being transferred to the brig at Pendleton, and I want you to tell Caesar that I'm taking him there myself. Tell him that if any of his people try to free him while he's being transported, the first thing I'm going to do is shoot Tito in the head."

"That's an outrageous threat to make, Marshal. You're basically telling me you intend to murder Tito. I intend to report this phone call to—"

"Pass on the message, Prescott. I'm not bluffing," Walker said, and hung up.

14

There is a boxy, windowless, concrete structure on Caesar Olivera's estate in Sinaloa. It sits in a low spot so it can't be seen from the main house and spoil the view of the mountains. On the roof of the building are a number of antennae and small satellite dishes.

This building was where Caesar often held meetings, and almost all of his financial affairs were managed from there. It was guarded around the clock by armed men and was swept daily for electronic eavesdropping devices—although it was hard to imagine anyone having the nerve or the ability to penetrate Caesar's estate. The penalty for a guard found sleeping on duty was death.

Inside the building were state-of-the-art communications and computer systems—and state-of-the-art computer security. There was a conference room with a table large enough to seat twelve—the sort of table where a board of directors might sit—two standard offices with desks and file cabinets, a small kitchen, three bedrooms where people could stay overnight if necessary, and another room filled with racks of servers. Finally, there was one large room that had ten computer stations, half a dozen plasma screens mounted on the walls, and STU-III telephones for holding scrambled, encrypted conversations. It was the sort of room one might see at the Pentagon or the New York Stock Exchange, and normally this room was the domain of the Harvard MBA and some of her financial people who turned large amounts of Caesar's drug money into legitimate, profit-making investments.

This room was now occupied with different sorts of people: computer hackers and other Internet experts who were essentially electronic detectives. There were five men and three women, and they were pecking on keyboards and talking quietly on telephones. One of the women was in charge of coordinating their activities and maintaining an up-to-date spreadsheet of all intelligence acquired.

The room had become Raphael Mora's operations room—his war room—and the people in it were searching for María Delgato and helping Mora plan Tito Olivera's escape.

Mora was in the conference room by himself, studying a large paper contour map of Marine Corps Base Camp Pendleton. Most of the base was surrounded by a fence, and access points were manned by guards. Mora knew, however, that the fence and the guards were not the only barriers preventing people from reaching the brig where Tito was incarcerated.

Since 9/11, U.S. military installations had significantly upgraded their security measures, and Mora suspected, although he didn't know for sure, that there were cameras and motion detectors all along the perimeter of the large base. Most likely, roving patrols as well. One area that was not fenced in was the coastline that ran for several miles along the west side of the base. Mora laughed out loud at the thought of a horde of tattooed Mexican gangbangers making an amphibious assault against Camp Pendleton.

"What's so funny?" Caesar said. Mora hadn't heard him come into the conference room, and he was embarrassed by his laughter.

Caesar was wearing scuffed work boots, jeans, a wash-faded denim shirt, and a straw hat on his head. He looked like a strawberry picker you'd see north of the border. Mora figured he had probably been looking at the grapes he'd planted on a few acres on the north side of the estate; he'd hired a wine maker from the Napa Valley to help him produce his own wine.

"Uh, nothing, sir. I was just thinking—"

Caesar removed the straw hat, dropped it on the conference table, and took a seat. "Where do we stand?"

"If you don't mind, let's begin with the security at Camp Pendleton. Tito is being kept in an isolation cell on the ground floor of the brig, a two-story concrete structure. So far he hasn't been allowed outside his cell for meals or exercise. I don't know if they'll continue to keep him confined twenty-four hours a day until his trial, but I'll be informed if there's any change in his status.

"The brig is approximately seven miles from the

Camp Pendleton main gate off I-5, and is located in an area where there are a number of large warehouses and a few barracks where some marines are housed. To reach the brig, you have to pass through one of the perimeter gates, and guards do ID checks and random vehicle checks. A carful of men who look like they might work for us will certainly be given closer scrutiny.

"Just before one reaches the brig, there is a second gate. Until Tito was placed in the brig, this gate was not manned and was always left open. Now there are concrete vehicle barricades and guards stationed at this access point armed with heavy-caliber weapons. I've been further informed that Pendleton has over a thousand military policemen and if an attempt is made to breach the gates or the brig itself, these MPs will respond within minutes. The general in charge of the base is running drills to improve their response time."

"Who is providing this information?"

"A female staff sergeant who works in an administrative capacity associated with the brig."

Caesar didn't bother to ask if Mora was paying the sergeant or threatening to kill her family to force her to do what he wanted. Caesar didn't care.

"Sir, the bottom line is, I believe any sort of direct assault against the brig will fail. Within minutes, our people would be surrounded by marines and killed, and Tito might be killed as well. And there is something else you need to know.

"Inside the brig, there are no other inmates on the corridor where Tito is being held and two U.S. marshals are in the cell adjacent to Tito's at all times. Four marshals have been assigned to the base, and they are on twelve-hour shifts. The senior of these four marshals is the liaison with the marines, and he is constantly checking the procedures for guarding the brig. Personnel are not normally allowed to bring weapons into the brig, but an exception has been made for the marshals. I think this is very significant in that it means that Marshal Walker has the capability to follow through on his threat to kill Tito immediately if anyone attempts to break him out of jail."

"What do we know about the marshals guarding Tito?"

"Everything. They all have families: wives, children, mothers, siblings. The problem is that the marine guards at Pendleton, who are rotated frequently, all have standing orders that Tito will not be allowed outside the brig without an order signed by Judge Foreman, the man who placed him in the brig."

"Can we obtain a copy of Foreman's signature?"

"I already have it, and of course we can duplicate it. I also have a copy of the court's stationery and copies of similar court orders. The problem is that when they do decide to move Tito there will be a lot of . . . of fanfare. The brig will be notified days in advance. They'll use a team to execute the transfer, and he'll probably be moved by helicopter, as he was when he was taken to Camp Pendleton. In other words, it's not as simple as someone just showing up with a court order to move Tito."

"So as of right now," Caesar said, "you don't know how to free my brother."

"No, sir," Mora said.

Caesar glanced at his watch, said, "Excuse me," and left the conference room. He walked across the hall to the kitchen, removed a bottle of water from the refrigerator, and when he returned to the conference room, he pulled a vial from his shirt pocket, shook out two pills, and swallowed them. "My doctor says my cholesterol is too high and I need to take a little aspirin for my heart. More chicken, he says, less red meat, more exercise, fewer cigars. My father smokes two packs a day, has never taken a pill in his life, and he's seventy-nine years old."

"Uh, yes, sir," Mora said, not sure what else to say.

"What about the woman, the informant?"

"Once again, I'm sorry to report that I have no information regarding her at this time. She was taken away right after Tito was arrested, and right now I have no idea where she or her mother is. Her brother is supposed to be in Canada and I have people looking for him there, but I suspect Miguel Delgato is also in the DEA's custody. We're doing all the usual things: looking at telephone records of María Delgato's friends, checking credit-card charges, et cetera. But we have a year to find her, sir. I'll find her."

"And Tito's men, the ones who were arrested with him?"

"Rodríguez and Gomez. I already have people exploring ways to get to them in MCC. It won't be difficult, but I think we need to wait awhile. We need to let the administrators at the jail relax a bit before we move on them, and then I want to take out both men simultaneously. They'll be dead in less than two months."

"What about the video of Tito killing Washington?"

"That's our biggest problem if Tito goes to trial. Tito's lawyer has seen the video, and he says that even if all the witnesses are dead, the video alone is enough to convict him. It shows Tito very clearly killing Washington, and when Tito was arrested he had on his person the weapon he used. The DEA agent who arrested Tito, a woman named Hamilton, followed precisely all chain-of-evidence requirements regarding the video and Tito's weapon. She also had several duplicates of the video made, and she used video experts from L.A. to make the copies. Copies of the video have been given to the Assistant U.S. Attorney prosecuting Tito and to Tito's lawyer, and other copies have been put in other secure locations. The original is in a safe at the U.S. Attorney's Office. I don't think we'll be able to impugn the video, and I think destroying the original will be futile. Tito's attorney has filed motions claiming the warrant to videotape Washington's bar was flawed, but he doubts he'll be successful excluding the video evidence."

When Caesar didn't say anything for several seconds, Mora said, "Sir, I've only been working on this problem for a few days, and we have almost a year to come up with a solution. I need more time."

"Okay," Caesar finally said, and placed the straw hat back on his head and left the conference room. Mora knew he was disappointed—and he knew it was not good to disappoint his employer. He also couldn't help but wonder why Caesar was willing to spend so much money and manpower to free Tito. He knew Caesar had spoiled Tito as a child, and had been more like a father to him than an older brother, but when Tito became an adult Mora could tell that Caesar didn't have much respect for his brother's intelligence or his character. Did Caesar feel obligated to move heaven and earth to save Tito because they were related, or was it a matter of pride, showing the world, especially the Americans, that he couldn't be defeated? Whatever the case, Mora could tell that Caesar would never give up, and if Mora failed, Caesar would blame him.

Years before, Mora had developed a plan in case he had to run. He had a suitcase already packed with alternate identities and cash, a fast, untraceable method for leaving the country, and places picked out where he could hide. He'd always assumed, however, that he'd be running from the police and not his boss. If it appeared that freeing Tito might be impossible . . . Well, he was glad the suitcase was packed.

15

Kay Hamilton was dreading the year that lay ahead.

After she killed Marco Álvarez in Miami, she spent almost two years meeting with government lawyers, preparing for the trials of Álvarez's men that she'd arrested, and then appearing at trial after trial to testify. Kay liked catching crooks—everything that followed after she caught them was boring and irritating. It was rather like hunting: the *hunt* was the fun; skinning and butchering the critters after you shot them was just work.

She knew the same thing was going to happen now that she'd arrested Tito Olivera. She was going to have to work with the U.S. Attorney's Office to arrest the two bankers who were laundering money for the Olivera cartel. Then—and this was not going to be fun at all—she was going to have to work with the San Diego DA and the San Diego cops to prepare for the trials of the three detectives who'd been arrested for taking bribes and passing on information to Tito's people. Her relationship with the city cops had never been very good, but after cutting them out of Tito's arrest and Jim Davis embarrassing John Hernández at the meeting with the judge . . . well, things were chilly to say the least. On top of all that came preparations for the trials of Tito Olivera and his fellow felons: Ángel Gomez, Jesús Rodríguez, and a dozen other thugs they brought in after they arrested Tito—arrests made possible in part by the bugs she'd forced María to install in Tito's house. It was going to be an awful year.

She had to do something else in the year to come. Before Jim Davis retired she needed to suck up to the right people in Washington and make them believe that she was the one who should replace him. She knew, in spite of her performance in Miami and her role in bringing down Tito Olivera, that she was going to have a tough time convincing the powers that be to give her the job. For one thing, she was almost positive that Davis wasn't going to recommend her. He was going to say pretty much the same thing he'd told her the other day— that she was a great field agent but lousy at working with outside agencies, and her idea of leadership was kicking her employees in the ass. Somehow, if she was going to get his job, she had to go through a major makeover.

She also wondered if she really wanted Jim Davis's job. Davis spent most of his time dealing with budgets and personnel bullshit, feeding statistics to the bean counters back at headquarters, and coordinating with Justice Department lawyers and other law-enforcement agencies. Most days he didn't even leave the office, and she knew if she was chained to a desk it would drive her insane.

So did she really want the job?

Yeah, she did.

Maybe it was a matter of ego, but she also didn't want to end up like Figgins and Patterson, still doing grunt work when she was fifty, maybe taking orders from some dummy like Wilson. She had to polish up her image, maybe take a couple of management classes, learn to play the political games. But what she *really* needed were a couple of high-powered female politicians on her side. If she could get some senator like Barbara Boxer pushing for her . . . hell, who knows? Maybe she could end up *running* the DEA.

Okay, that was a stretch, but a GS-15 position before she retired wasn't totally out of reach.

She stopped fantasizing about Barbara Boxer becoming her political guardian angel and turned back to the computer to finish up a report that was a week overdue. Then she glanced up at the clock on the wall: five p.m. Fuck it. The report could wait until tomorrow. She took her sidearm out of her desk drawer, slipped it into her shoulder holster, and put on her blazer to hide the weapon.

She started toward her place in Point Loma, then realized she wasn't in the mood, quite yet, for going home to an empty house and decided to stop at a bar downtown on B Street that catered to law-enforcement types. She ordered a martini and soon began bullshitting with a deputy from the San Diego Sheriff's Department. He had a big bandage on his left forearm, and he told her how he'd responded to a domestic beef—and how the lady who'd been getting smacked around by her husband sicced a ninety-pound pit bull on him when he tried to arrest the guy. He had to shoot the dog, and the sheriffs were now getting sued for killing the mutt.

Kay, in turn, told him an I-can-top-that story about breaking into a trailer/meth lab in the Glades that was being protected by a six-foot alligator. "You ever tried to shoot a gun at a moving alligator while falling backward off the stairs of a double-wide?"

The deputy was a good-looking guy, a year or two younger than her, and doing his best to pick her up. But she didn't want him. She wanted Robert Meyer.

She glanced at her watch. It was only six. Assistant U.S. Attorney Meyer would certainly still be in his office, eager beaver, overachiever that he was. She excused herself from the deputy and called Robert.

"You have to go home right away?" she asked—meaning *Would you like to come over to my place and play with me?* She instantly regretted that she sounded needy.

"Aw, jeez," he said. "My youngest daughter's in a play at her school tonight. I, uh—"

"Yeah, I get it. I'll talk to you later."

She thought for a moment about taking the deputy home and playing with him, but then thought: *Aw, behave yourself.*

She knew she didn't have anything to eat in her refrigerator—she hardly ever cooked—so she stopped at a Ralph's and bought a microwave dinner and a bag of cinnamon rolls so she'd have something to eat in the morning. As she was driving, she thought that maybe she'd get started on installing the shelves in the laundry room.

The laundry room was her current home-improvement project. She'd put in a stacked washer and dryer to provide more space and had her guy—the Mexican illegal who did almost all the work on her house—put in a slate floor to replace the linoleum. But she was going to put in the new shelves herself, and maybe she'd do that tonight. You didn't have to be a master carpenter like the Mexican to put up shelves; all you needed was a drill, a screwdriver, and a level. Or maybe she'd just have another martini when she got home, put her feet up, and watch whatever mindless drivel was on the tube. Yeah, drivel and another martini sounded better than putting up shelves—but not as good as rolling around in a bed with Robert Meyer.

When she turned onto her street, she looked over as she always did at the house on the corner. The place was a mess, the lawn a field of dandelions and other knee-high weeds, the paint peeling off the siding. It was bringing down property values in the entire neighborhood, which might have been tolerable if an old lady who couldn't do the yard work lived there. But an old lady didn't live there. A young, skinny, scraggly-haired guy missing a few teeth, who didn't ever get up until about three in the afternoon, was the homeowner. He looked like a meth addict. Kay had been too busy with Tito Olivera in the past year to do anything about him, but now she thought she might make him her next home-improvement project, get his ass arrested and out of the neighborhood.

She turned into her driveway, and the first thing she saw was a girl sitting on her porch, and next to the girl was a small suitcase, the wheeled type you take on an airplane. The kid stood up when Kay stepped out of her car, and she looked apprehensive, as if she was afraid of Kay.

She was a pretty kid, maybe thirteen or fourteen, although Kay wasn't good at guessing kids' ages. She was slim, had short blond hair, and was maybe five foot four, four inches shorter than Kay. She was wearing a blue polo shirt, jeans, and hiking boots. Then Kay noticed there was a ski jacket on the porch next to her luggage, which was weird. Hardly anyone wore ski jackets in San Diego, not even in February.

"Who are you?" Kay asked.

The girl didn't answer. As Kay got closer, she could see that the girl had blue eyes and there was something familiar about her face, but Kay couldn't figure out what it was. She was sure she'd never seen the girl before.

The girl looked like she was about to cry and was making an effort not to. Then the look on her face changed to something else. Determination? Anger?

"Who are you?" Kay asked again. "And what are you doing here?"

"I'm your daughter," the kid finally said.

PART II

16

Kay Hamilton had done two really stupid things in her life.

One of those was marrying another DEA agent when she was twenty-three. Her husband, she realized later, was basically a male version of herself: a risk taker with a sense of humor who was good-looking and great in bed. Unfortunately, he thought that when Kay became his wife she was going to do all the things he saw his mom do for his dad: clean the house (by herself), cook, launder his clothes—basically, take care of him. He adjusted poorly to Kay's notion that being his wife wasn't the same thing as being his maid. She also learned that he wasn't like her dad, a guy who was always working on some project around the house, remodeling or fixing something. When her ex-husband wasn't at work, he primarily liked to sit on his ass and watch sports on TV, he'd never used a tool in his life, and he planned all his vacation time for hunting season. Shooting unarmed animals had no appeal for Kay.

She suspected he cheated on her the first time six months after they were married. She caught him cheating two days after their eight-month wedding anniversary—and that was that. She discovered she really didn't care that he'd slept with another woman—she just wasn't about to let him think that he could pull that kind of crap because he thought she was too dumb to catch him at it.

The most stupid thing she did, however, was not her eight-month marriage. It was getting pregnant when she was fifteen.

The father of her child had been a golden-haired, seventeen-year-old football star, and Kay thought at the time that he was the most gorgeous creature God ever created. Kay gave him her virginity; she could hardly wait to do it. She had no idea why the birth-control pills didn't work, and never trusted pills again after that.

She wanted to get an abortion, but her parents were Catholic—and her mother, unlike her father, was a true believer. She also went to a private Catholic school, and naturally there wasn't a kid in school who didn't find out that she'd been knocked up. Since her parents wouldn't let her get an abortion, she refused to leave the house— she said there was no way in hell she was going to let people see her with a belly the size of a watermelon— and her parents finally relented and sent her to live in Maryland with an aunt until the kid was born.

She had no idea what she was going to do with the baby when it came, but that turned out to be no problem at all. Her aunt had a daughter who lived in Nebraska, was almost forty, and who'd been trying to get pregnant for years. Kay had met the woman only twice. So Kay signed the kid over to her cousin. She agreed to give up all rights to the child and agreed never to contact her unless she received permission from her cousin. Maybe one day her cousin would tell Kay's daughter she was adopted and who her real mother was, or maybe not.

And that was all fine by Kay. She didn't want a baby at the age of fifteen; she didn't want to be a mother. She wanted to pretend the pregnancy had never happened and get on with her life. She saw her daughter for maybe ten minutes the day she was born and never again after that. She never *wanted* to see her again after that.

In the fifteen years that had transpired since she gave birth, she never—not ever—made any effort to get in touch with her daughter. When Kay's mother was alive, she tried a couple times to tell Kay how the kid was doing, but Kay made it clear that she didn't want to know. She didn't want to be reminded of what she'd done; she didn't even want to know the kid's name. When her mother tried to show her pictures of the little girl, she refused to look at them.

The child was a part of her life that she simply wanted to go away.

The last she'd heard, which was almost ten years earlier, the kid was doing fine with her adoptive parents.

It looked as if something had changed.

Not knowing what else to do, Kay invited the girl into her house and offered her a seat in the living room.

"Uh, would you like a glass of water or something?" Kay asked. "A Coke?"

"No."

"Okay. What, uh . . ." *Shit.* "Why are you here?"

"My parents are dead," the girl said. Again she looked like she was going to cry, but again she didn't.

Kay's family had never been a close bunch. They didn't hold family reunions or get together at Thanksgiving. Kay's aunt—the one she'd lived with while she was pregnant—had been her mother's much older sister and she was dead. Kay's parents had been killed ten years ago when a truck driver fell asleep at the wheel, and with her mom gone, Kay lost the only source she had for updates on her cousin and daughter.

"My dad died four years ago," the girl said. "He had a heart attack; he was only fifty. Mom died two weeks ago. Breast cancer." Then she added, "Thanks for coming to the funeral."

Sheesh. "I didn't know she'd died," Kay said. "I'm sorry." What she wanted to say was *But why are you here? What do you expect me to do?*

When the girl didn't say anything else, Kay finally said what she was thinking as diplomatically as she could. "What do you need from me, uh . . . I'm sorry. What's your name?" She knew her mother *must* have told her the kid's name, but she couldn't remember it to save her life; she wondered if she had subconsciously forced it out of her memory as a way of coping with an event she wanted to forget ever happened.

The girl shook her head and smiled—not a friendly smile, but one that made Kay feel like crawling under the couch. "My name's Jessica."

"So, Jessica, what do you need from me? How can I help?"

"I want to live with you for a little while."

"Oh," Kay said. She didn't know what else to say.

"I was told that because my folks are dead and because of my age and because I don't have any other relatives, I'll have to go live with someone, like a foster family. I told the social worker I didn't want that. I just want to live alone. I'm fifteen and—"

Kay knew that but thought she looked younger.

"—and I don't need someone to look out for me. I'm not a baby. I can take care of myself. But this social worker said I wouldn't be allowed to live alone and that I need a legal guardian until I'm eighteen."

"But don't you want to stay in your hometown until you graduate from high school?" Kay said, already thinking she *had* to find a way out of this. "I mean, you must have friends there."

"We just moved to Cleveland a year ago, and I hate it there. We had to move, because my mom got laid off and we had to relocate from Lincoln."

Jesus. It didn't sound like her cousin had had any luck at all. Her husband dies, she loses her job, she moves to a shithole like Cleveland, and then gets breast cancer. And now her kid—Kay couldn't think of the girl as *her* kid—was all alone. Except for Kay. *Her mother.*

"I'm not going to let them put me in a foster home or group home or whatever the hell it's called," Jessica said.

When she said this, her lips compressed into a thin, unyielding line—and Kay realized that Jessica looked exactly the way she herself did when she dug in her heels.

"I see," Kay said.

"Look, I know you don't give a shit about me. All I'm asking is that you let me live here for a little while. I need you to sign whatever you have to sign to become my guardian and then let me stay here until I sell my mom's house in Cleveland. I basically just need an address to give this social worker, and I'll pay you rent until I sell the house. I've got some money left over from my dad's life insurance, and as soon as I sell the place in Cleveland, I'll rent my own apartment."

The girl made her feel like a monster.

"Does anyone know you're here?" Kay asked.

"No. I split. The social worker's probably got some kinda missing-kid bulletin out on me by now." She smiled slightly—Kay had yet to see her really smile—then added, "I doubt I'm on a milk carton yet."

"How did you know about me?" Kay asked.

"You mean, how did I track you down? My mom told me about you before she died. I never knew I was adopted. I always thought Mom was my real mom. I even look a little bit like her. And she *was* my real mom. You were just a . . . an *incubator*."

Kay almost said *Will you knock off the attitude*—but didn't. The kid deserved some compassion, with everything that had happened to her. "Look," she said, "I know you've been through a lot, but I'm having just as hard a time as you are adjusting to all this."

"Anyway, Mom told me about you," Jessica said, sounding somewhat mollified. "She said you worked for the DEA and lived in San Diego, but I don't know how she got your address. So I bought a plane ticket and flew out here. Like I said, I have a little money. But I didn't know what I was going to do if you didn't show up today. I probably would have gotten a motel room and then found out where you worked and showed up there tomorrow."

Kay could imagine *that* scene: the daughter whose name she didn't know until five minutes ago showing up at the DEA office and asking if anyone knew where her *mommy* was. She could just see that little shit Wilson laughing his ass off.

"Uh, have you eaten?" Kay said, just to change the subject. She needed some time to think. The idea of having the girl living with her was overwhelming.

"No, not since this morning."

Then Kay realized the only thing she had in the house to eat was the Salisbury steak frozen dinner she had bought at Ralph's.

"Well, I don't have much food here in the house. Let's go someplace and get dinner."

"Are you going to let me stay here tonight?"

"Yeah, of course. What did you think I was going to do?"

"I don't know. You abandoned me once before."

They went to a place on Harbor Island. The sun had set, but there was still some light in the sky and they could see the soaring curve of the Coronado Bridge and the silhouettes of two big Navy ships in the harbor. The downtown area was blazing like electricity was free. It was about sixty degrees outside and it wasn't raining, so Kay asked for a seat on the outside deck, where they had propane heaters near the tables.

"God, it's gorgeous here," Jessica said, letting the shield around her drop for just a moment. "When I left Cleveland, it was twenty degrees and snowing."

"Yeah, it's pretty nice here most of the time," Kay said.

Talking about the weather beat talking about what she was going to do next.

Jessica ordered a cheeseburger and wolfed it down when it came; Kay had a Cobb salad she barely touched. She wanted to order a martini—if there was ever a time she needed a drink, this was it—but she ordered iced tea instead. For some reason, she didn't think it would be appropriate to have a drink, even if it was only one, then get into a car and drive home with her daughter. She couldn't remember the last time she was in a social setting and didn't do what she wanted because she was afraid of making the wrong impression.

Dinner was mostly silent, neither of them knowing what to say. All Kay could think about was that having a kid living with her was going to totally screw up her life. By the time they finished eating, she'd decided that she was going to have to do what the girl wanted and become her guardian. She really had no choice. But no way in hell was she going to let her move into a place of her own at the age of fifteen.

"Uh, I need to excuse myself," Kay said. "I need to call my boss."

Jessica looked at her for a moment with those eyes that were just like her eyes, and Kay wondered if the girl was thinking that Kay was going to ditch her. "I'll be right back," she said.

"Yeah, whatever. Take your time."

Jessica wondered—for about the hundredth time—if she'd made a mistake.

It was obvious this woman wanted nothing to do with her. Maybe she should have just stayed in Cleveland—but she hated Cleveland. She couldn't move back to Lincoln where her friends were, either—not if Hamilton became her guardian. She'd have to live in California, someplace near Hamilton in case the social services people ever checked up on her. And California, now that she'd seen the place, would probably be a great place to live— provided she didn't have to stay with Hamilton.

She had about twenty grand left from her dad's life insurance money—her mom had ended up spending most of the money when she got laid off and then spent more on her cancer meds—but even as bad as the real estate market was in Cleveland, Jessica was betting the small house there would sell for at least a hundred and fifty grand. So she'd get an apartment, maybe in San Diego, maybe someplace nearby, enroll in a school, and get on with her life. What else could she do?

At least for a little while, however, she'd have to live with her so-called mother. She knew she was emotionally blackmailing Hamilton—and she didn't care. She needed access to her own money and to be free of the social service dragon back in Cleveland, and if that meant laying a guilt trip on Hamilton, so be it. Hamilton deserved to feel guilty.

She couldn't imagine what it would be like living with Hamilton, though. She'd never met anyone like her before. Her parents—she couldn't think of them as her *adoptive* parents—had both been teachers. Her father taught physics at a junior college, and her mother lectured in political science at the University of Nebraska. After her mom got laid off in Lincoln due to budget cuts, they moved to Cleveland because her mom wanted to continue to teach at the university level and Case Western was the only place she could land a job. But her mom and dad had both been gentle, softhearted people; they were liberals who cared about social issues and fanatics when it came to gun control. They also read a lot and encouraged Jessica to read, and they took her with them all the time to listen to lectures by famous people.

Hamilton was no doubt a conservative, card-carrying member of the NRA, and when Jessica was sitting in her living room, the only books she saw were how-to books on home repairs. She suspected Kay Hamilton was about as liberal as George W. Bush. And she'd never met anyone before who carried a big black gun into a restaurant. She imagined cops and federal agents were expected to carry their weapons at all times, but . . . well, the gun just blew her away. The gun also made the stories she'd read online about what Hamilton had done in Miami and how she arrested that Tito guy seem more real. Hamilton had actually *killed* people in Miami—and Jessica had never met a killer before.

In person, Hamilton was even better-looking than she appeared in the pictures Jessica had seen on the Internet—she looked like a cop on a TV show with her blond hair, full lips, and the body she had. There was also an *edge* to her that Jessica hadn't seen in other people she'd known—an air of cockiness or confidence or something. Maybe you had to project that sort of attitude when you were a female cop going up against dangerous criminals, but whatever the case, Hamilton was . . . she was *intimidating*.

All of a sudden, she felt like crying again—it seemed as if she'd been crying almost constantly since her mom's funeral—and that had to *stop*. She was on her own now, and she was going to have to get used to that fact. It was time to quit acting like a kid. She could survive a month or two with Hamilton—it shouldn't take longer than that to get the legal stuff squared away—and then she'd move on with her life. Alone. She had no other choice.

Kay left the restaurant and went out into the parking lot and called Jim Davis at home. She thought for a minute about telling him about her daughter and then decided she didn't want to get into all that right now, and definitely not over the phone. She just told him she needed a few days off for something personal. Davis didn't object; she hardly ever took any time off.

Now what? Now what was she going to do?

And at just that moment, as if God had decided to give her a preview of her life to come, a woman and a girl about Jessica's age walked past her in the parking lot. The woman was saying, "I'm telling you, Heather, you're never going to see that boy again. Do you hear me?" To which the girl responded, "Oh, yeah. What the hell are you gonna do? Lock me in the fucking basement?"

Oh, Lord, help me.

She walked back into the restaurant and out to the table where Jessica was sitting, staring out at the bay. The kid looked so small and alone that for a moment Kay really felt sorry for her.

"Okay," she said. "The day after tomorrow, we'll fly to Cleveland and deal with this social worker and the guardianship stuff. We'll also get a real estate agent to get started on selling your mom's house."

"I already have the name of a real estate agent," Jessica said.

"Fine. Then after all the legal sh . . . stuff is squared away, we'll pack up your things and ship them out here. We'll let the real estate agent deal with the furniture in your house and anything else you don't want. When we get back, we'll enroll you in a school."

Kay sounded like she was taking charge, but the truth was that she didn't know what she was doing. She didn't know how one became a legal guardian; short of DNA testing, she wasn't even sure how she could prove that Jessica was her kid. She didn't have a clue about schools in San Diego.

"Anything else you think we need to do?" Kay asked.

"I have to get all my school records sent out here," Jessica said. "You know, transcripts and stuff. Probably my medical and dental records, too."

"What grade did you say you were in?"

"I didn't. I'm a sophomore."

A sophomore! It would be two and a half years before she graduated from high school. Two and a half years!

When they returned to her house, Kay showed Jessica the room where she'd be staying. Kay used one bedroom as a home office; the second bedroom, the one with the walk-in closet, was where she slept. The third bedroom would become Jessica's. The room had a queen-size bed she'd bought at a yard sale, a chest of drawers, a night table, and a bedside lamp, but nobody had ever slept in the bed. She and Jessica made up the bed together and then Kay showed her the second bathroom, which, she guessed, was going to become Jessica's.

Kay asked if she needed anything else—toothpaste, a snack, whatever. Jessica said no, and Kay said, "Well, uh, good night. I'll see you in the morning."

"Wait a minute. What do I call you?" Jessica asked.

"You can call me Agent Hamilton," Kay said with a straight face. When Jessica's blue eyes expanded, she said, "I'm kidding. Lighten up. I guess you should call me Kay. I don't think either one of us would be comfortable with *Mom*."

"You got that right," Jessica said. Then she said, "I've read about you, you know. There's a lot of stuff online about what you did here with that Tito guy and what happened in Miami."

Aw, Jesus. Miami. Kay had never been embarrassed about what she did in Miami—until this moment. She went into the kitchen, took a bottle of Stoli from the freezer, and poured straight vodka into a water glass.

17

MIAMI

Kay sat at the bar, sipping a virgin piña colada, watching Marco Álvarez out of the corner of her eye. In the three years she'd been with the DEA, this was definitely the best job she'd been given. She'd spent entire nights being bitten by mosquitoes and sand flies, watching through night vision goggles, until a cigarette boat filled with marijuana landed on a beach. She'd dressed up in grungy clothes that hadn't been washed in two weeks, her teeth blackened to give her that stinky, appealing meth-head look. Because she spoke Spanish, she spent mind-numbing hours listening to phone taps of some moron talking to his girlfriend, his mother, and his idiot buddies, just hoping to hear the moron say something that could land him in jail.

This assignment, however, it was . . . hell, it couldn't get any better than this. She'd used a government-issued credit card to buy the slinkiest dress she could find and a pair of high heels she'd only dreamed about; got a manicure, a pedicure, and her legs waxed all on Uncle Sam's dime; and was now drinking sixteen-buck drinks at the taxpayers' expense. It was just a basic surveillance job like others she'd been given, but what a place to do surveillance: The Blue Halo, the newest, hottest—and priciest—club in South Beach.

The DEA had learned from a confidential informant that Marco Álvarez might meet a new heroin connection tonight, and they wanted to know who it was. Marco liked meeting people in clubs because clubs were noisy and it was hard to record conversations, and because most federal agents would stick out like sunflowers in a rose garden. The other reasons he liked clubs was that they were typically filled with hot young women, and Kay Hamilton—twenty-five years old, tall, long blond hair, long shapely legs—was definitely hot. Her job—if you could call it a job—was to use her cell phone to take photos of everyone who sat with Marco in his regular booth. If it appeared that one of those people looked like he or she might be involved the heroin industry, Kay would e-mail the photos to agents outside the bar and tell them when the person was leaving so they could follow. There was nothing strange about a young woman sitting at the bar using her cell phone. So far, however, the only people who'd sat with Marco was the guy who owned the club, two girls who looked young enough to be freshmen at Miami Dade College, and a big-time real estate agent who was also one of Marco's customers.

Kay called the bartender over and said, "Give me another colada, but put the booze in it this time."

* * *

Kay's dad had been a New York City cop, and after he put in his twenty, he retired and became the chief of police in a little town in Connecticut. Kay grew up around cops, hearing their stories, and she decided in high school that she was going to be some kind of cop. After she had the baby, she finished high school in Maryland in her aunt's hometown, was accepted at the University of Maryland, and got a degree in criminal justice. Her dad wanted her to get a law degree, but she didn't want to be a lawyer.

She gave a lot of thought to what kind of cop she wanted to be. She considered being a big-city cop like her dad had been, but ultimately decided she wanted to go federal. She thought that's where the real action was— terrorism, drugs, organized crime—not wife beaters and kids killing each other for tennis shoes in the projects.

She didn't want to Protect and Serve. She wanted to arrest bad guys.

The FBI—and maybe her dad had made her prejudiced—just sounded too uptight and straitlaced to her. Dad always said the Feebs were like accountants with guns, spending more time looking at spreadsheets than anything else. As for the Secret Service, she had no desire to stand around being a human shield for a politician, and the U.S. Marshals Service—protecting witnesses and tracking down criminals who'd skipped—sounded monotonous to her.

The DEA was the one she wanted. She thought the war on drugs was a war that would never be won and that legalizing drugs would be the smartest thing to do, but until that happened the DEA was . . . well, it was the next-best thing to playing cowboys and Indians, except all the cowboys and Indians were armed to the teeth.

She was assigned to Miami right after she finished her training and had been there three years. She'd been involved in a number of small busts, operated as an undercover agent a dozen times because of her looks and her age, but never had the opportunity to do something really spectacular. Then along comes Marco Álvarez.

The DEA office in Miami had decided it was time to focus in earnest on Marco. He'd been getting bigger and bigger, running cocaine, heroin, meth, and marijuana— anything a junkie could inject, snort, or smoke. And as he got bigger, the body count increased as he dealt with his rivals. Then he made the mistake of killing a DEA snitch, and that's when the administration decided it had had enough.

A man and a woman, both in their forties, entered the club. They were well dressed, looked upscale, but were not the type you'd expect to see dancing the salsa. The man was balding, had a dark complexion and a big hooked nose. The woman looked just like him, except her nose wasn't so pronounced—and Kay wondered if they might be related. She found out later they were brother and sister, both originally from Lebanon. They walked over to Marco's table and sat down, and Kay took their picture a dozen times. They spent an hour with Marco, everybody looking serious, and when they left, Kay called the team outside.

Kay's orders were to stick around until Marco left, although she was pretty sure he'd just met his new connection. She thought about ordering another drink but figured a DUI might not look too good on her record. At that moment, Marco rose from his table and walked in her direction.

"I can't believe somebody would stand up a woman who looks like you," he said to her.

For the last two hours, she'd been beating away guys trying to pick her up. She was particularly rude to some of them—the ones who stood on her left and blocked her view of Marco's table.

"What makes you think I've been stood up?" Kay said. "Maybe I just like sitting here by myself."

He smiled at her—and he had a gorgeous smile. In fact, everything about Marco Álvarez was gorgeous: tall, well-built, curly dark hair, bedroom eyes. His eyes reminded her of the eyes of that actor Benicio Del Toro.

Kay laughed. "Okay. So I've been stood up, but by a girlfriend, not a guy."

But she was thinking, *Could this really be happening? Could this possibly be the chance of a lifetime?*

"Why don't you come sit with me?" he said. "I just ordered a few things to nibble on, and I hate to eat by myself."

Kay pretended to hesitate, then said, "Sure, why not?"

Two hours later, when Kay was drunk enough to know she'd have to take a cab home, her squad leader called her on her cell phone.

"Hamilton," he said, "what the fuck are you doing in there?"

"Oh, hi, Dad," she said.

"Dad? Hamilton, are you drunk?"

"Yeah, okay, Dad, I'll be right over. Just take it easy."

She explained to Marco that her mother had just had surgery and her father was the kind of guy who panicked every time she sneezed.

She could tell Marco was, as they say, smitten with her. He asked if she might be free this weekend. He said he was thinking about heading down to Key Largo on his yacht. "It's got two bedrooms," he added, maybe thinking she was worried about the sleeping arrangements.

"Why don't you give me a call," Kay said.

The next day, she met with her boss and her boss's boss and said she might have a chance to get close to Marco Álvarez—really close. Her boss, another pretty good guy like Jim Davis, said, "Are you sure you understand what this could mean, Hamilton? I mean, what you might have to do?"

"I understand," Kay said.

In a month she was Marco's live-in girlfriend. She reeled him in like a fish, playing a little hard to get but not too hard, making it clear she was the jealous type and not about to put up with him screwing around on her. One

night, after she walked out on him for flirting with a waitress and said she never wanted to see him again—Marco
was used to women who'd put up with anything to be
with him—he asked her to move in with him.

For the next seven months, she lived a life that only
movie stars and heiresses can imagine, eating in five-star
establishments, traveling with Marco to resorts all over
the world, dressing in designer clothes he bought for her,
staying on yachts and in palaces owned by other drug
merchants. And during those seven months, she collected
enough evidence to put Marco away for life and twenty-
seven of his people in jail for anywhere from five to twenty
years.

With a lot of help from electronic wizards hired by
the DEA, she bugged Marco's phones, installed GPS
devices on his cars, inserted spyware into his computers,
and downloaded copies of his banking transactions. She
personally heard Marco, in a very crude code, give the
order to murder two men.

Her biggest fear during the time she was living with
him was that too many people knew that the DEA had an
undercover in Marco's camp: other DEA agents, judges
who granted warrants, federal attorneys giving guidance
on the evidence needed to get convictions, technicians
contracted to help with the bugging equipment. And
somebody—right when they were about to arrest Marco—
gave her up. She didn't know if it had been a mistake or if
someone sold her out for a price.

Marco Álvarez was a man with poor impulse control,
and when he learned Kay was DEA, he went berserk. He

was naturally upset to learn that a woman he thought loved him had betrayed him, but more than that, he was enraged that he'd been played for a fool. He beat the shit out of her.

He broke two of her ribs, her nose, knocked out a tooth, and cracked one of the bones around her left eye. Then he told two of his thugs to grab her arms so he could cut out her tongue before he killed her.

Kay was saved only because one of the thugs wore a gun in an ankle holster for a backup piece and, when he bent down to pick her up off the floor, Kay grabbed the gun. She figured the only reason she lived was either that Marco and his men were lousy shots or that there was an angel in the room protecting her. She didn't know how many bullets were fired at her, but she fired five. She killed Marco, the two bodyguards with him, and then a third guy who heard all the gunfire and came in with an Uzi to see if he could help out.

Three things happened after she killed Marco, only one of which was good. First, after a short stay in the hospital and the care of a good dentist and a plastic surgeon, Kay got the commendation and the promotion she deserved for what she had done to bring down Marco Álvarez's drug empire. That was the good thing. The second thing that happened was that her name and her photograph were leaked to the media, which ended any chance of her being an undercover agent again.

The third thing was the reaction of the men she worked with.

If a man had done what she had done—penetrated a

criminal organization by having sex with the woman in charge—everybody would be patting the guy on the back. They would have approved of a man knocking off a good-looking piece of ass in the name of God and country. But when Kay did the same thing, her fellow agents looked upon her as some kind of slut and snickered—and not always behind her back—about how she'd spread her legs to bring down Marco. It wasn't fair—but that's the way it was. She was glad when she got the transfer to San Diego.

The other thing was, although Kay didn't tell anyone this, she had a great time being Marco Álvarez's girl-friend, living the high life, going to nice places—and spying on Marco. And Marco—other than the night he almost beat her to death—was actually a lot of fun to be with.

Regardless of what her fellow agents thought of her, Kay was proud of what she had done in Miami. That is, she was proud until she discovered that Jessica knew what she had done.

How do you explain something like that to your fifteen-year-old daughter?

18

Naturally, it took longer than Kay had expected to become Jessica's guardian and mother again. She ended up spending almost two weeks in Cleveland dealing with all the legal and financial crap, boxing stuff up to send back to San Diego, getting the process started for selling Jessica's house, and dealing with the social service "dragon." The dragon turned out to be a sweet, caring woman who only had Jessica's best interests at heart. Kay was also impressed with the real estate agent that Jessica selected, a blue-haired barracuda who had a jewel on her ring finger the size of a walnut. Judging by the bling, she'd sell Jessica's house in no time. She thought that Jim Davis might be upset with her taking so much time off, but once he understood what was going on, he told her to take all the time she needed. The guys who worked for her were delighted she was gone.

She learned more about her daughter from her bedroom in Cleveland than she did from talking to her. It seemed like the only time they talked was to deal with some practical matter, like whether to ship this or that back to San Diego or where to go for dinner. But the bedroom—that was enlightening.

Kay hadn't been around fifteen-year-old girls since she was fifteen, and the ones she encountered in shopping malls or on the street seemed incredibly dimwitted and shallow, saying *ya know* and *like* about every other word, cell phones glued to their ears, butterfly tattoos just above their butts. Jessica, as near as she could tell, was nothing like those girls.

There were no Justin Bieber posters on her walls or those of any other teeny-bopper heartthrob. There were a couple of nature photographs—waterfalls and forest scenes—and Kay thought that maybe she or her parents had taken them. Whoever took them, they were important to her, and she wanted them shipped to San Diego.

Even though she didn't have any boy-band posters, she did like music. She had a bunch of CDs, and her taste was pretty wide-ranging, from reggae to rock to hip-hop. She even had some classical piano and violin stuff—the kind of music that instantly put Kay to sleep when she heard it. When Kay asked if she wanted to keep the CDs, Jessica said no, that she now had everything on her iPod.

There were lots of books in the room, mostly fiction, but there were also some heavy-duty science textbooks. One was called *Beyond Genetics: The User's Guide to DNA*—and Kay thought *Whoa*. Jessica packed up almost all the books, and Kay was thinking she was going to have to buy a couple of IKEA bookcases for Jessica's bedroom back in San Diego. The kid had more books on one shelf in her room in Cleveland than Kay had probably read in her entire life.

Jessica didn't seem to have a whole lot of interest in clothes. She didn't have that many, and it appeared she mostly wore jeans and sweatshirts and T-shirts and shorts. Kay didn't see many dresses and skirts, and none that she saw were particularly sexy. Kay liked to shop for clothes when she had the time, and she got the impression her daughter didn't. In fact, she got the impression that they had absolutely zero in common.

She didn't see any sports equipment in the room—no soccer shoes in the closet, no little trophies for T-ball from when she was young. She did have a couple pairs of hiking boots and a decent backpack, the type with a lightweight frame you took when you went camping. Maybe the nature photos came from some camping-hiking trip.

One last thing Kay noticed was a picture of Jessica and a cute little curly-headed guy. They were dressed like they were going to a prom, and Jessica looked pretty and excited—and incredibly innocent. Kay wondered if she herself had ever looked that innocent. When she asked Jessica if she wanted to pack the photo, she looked embarrassed but said yes.

Finding a school for her daughter became a major problem. Kay didn't know anything about the school system in San Diego. She did know that she didn't want the girl going to a public school; public schools were combat zones. She looked online, found a Catholic high school a few miles from her house, and decided the place would be perfect. It was on a bus line, and Jessica would only have to walk a couple of blocks to catch the bus. It was also horrendously expensive. Nobody ever said that American Catholics weren't capitalists.

Kay and Jessica visited the school, both of them dressed like they were interviewing for jobs: conservative skirts and blouses, minimal makeup, hair neatly combed. Kay left her gun in the trunk of her car. As they were waiting to see the principal, Kay visited the girls' restroom—and the smell of marijuana was almost enough to give her a contact high. *Hmmm,* she thought.

The principal was a tall, gaunt woman in her fifties; her honey-colored hair looked as if it had been sprayed with something that would withstand a Force 5 hurricane. She was also a condescending, snooty bitch. When Kay explained that she wanted to enroll her daughter, the principal said, "I'm afraid you don't understand, dear. We don't accept just anyone here. We have a rigorous admissions process and all applicants have to be approved by the admissions board. We require references not only from the student's previous teachers but, well, references for the parents as well."

"Look," Kay said, "I've got kind of an emergency here. I work full-time and I don't have time to go school shopping. And Jessica's grades are fantastic. She has a three-point-nine-five GPA from her school in Cleveland. I have a copy of her transcript with me if you'd like to see it."

Kay had figured out that Jessica was bright—but she hadn't known that she was straight-A's, off-the-charts bright until she saw her transcript. The kid's intelligence both impressed and intimidated her.

The principal was less impressed. "Well, I'm not sure what a three-point-nine GPA means from a Cleveland high school," she said with a sniff—and Kay had to put a hand on Jessica's forearm to keep Jessica from coming out of her chair.

"Grade point isn't the only thing we look at, either," the principal continued. "Extracurricular activities, community service, all those things are taken into account. So what you need to do, Mrs. Hamilton—"

Kay didn't bother to correct her.

"—is fill out the application forms—my secretary will give them to you—and if Jessica meets our standards, maybe she can be admitted next year."

Her tone of voice said *Not a chance in hell*.

"I see," Kay said. "Jessica, would you mind waiting for me in the outer office? I need a private word with Principal Ford."

After Jessica left, Kay pulled out her DEA badge. "I'm a DEA agent, I'm busy, and I don't have time to fuck around here. You're going to admit my daughter into this school today."

"You can't speak to me that way," the principal said.

"Maybe not, but let me tell you what I can do. I smelled pot in the girls' head when I took a pee in there five minutes ago. I'll bet half the brats that go to this school smoke pot and use prescription meds they've stolen from Mama's medicine cabinet. They've got Oxy-Contin, Valium, and Vicodin squirreled away in their lockers and backpacks. So if my daughter isn't admitted, this place is gonna become the new front line for the war on drugs. I'm gonna get warrants for car and locker searches. I'm going to park agents on this campus looking for drug dealers, and follow kids to see if they hook up with any. I'm also going to leak every arrest to the media, and the people who send their kids to school here are going to think this place is a crack house in Chula Vista."

"This school is not—"

"I think it's time for you and this school to do a community service. Namely, a service for me. I'm a federal agent who spends her life protecting you, your students, and this country, and in return, I want my daughter enrolled here so I can get back to work."

The principal looked like she was going to explode—she was a minor demagogue and used to having people kiss her bony old ass—but she was also a pragmatist.

"Well, when you put it that way, that we need to pay you back for what you're doing for the public, I'm willing to make an exception in your daughter's case. But do you have any idea how much the tuition is here? I'm willing to enroll your daughter, but she's not getting a free ride."

The principal was thinking there was no way in hell Civil Servant Hamilton could afford to send her daughter to her posh school.

"Yeah, I know what it costs," Kay said, "and the tuition isn't a problem."

The reason why it wasn't a problem was that the late Marco Álvarez was going to pay for her daughter's high school education. When Kay was living with Marco, he lavished presents on her, and many of those presents had been in the form of jewelry: necklaces, tennis bracelets, rings, watches, and earrings. There was probably some rule that said she should have reported the gifts to her employer, but she never did. She figured she'd earned them, and estimated that she had almost fifty grand in stones. She'd been planning to use the money someday for something really extravagant—maybe a used Beemer convertible or a down payment on a beach place—and she was actually astounded with herself that she was willing to give up her treasure trove for her daughter. She had no idea, however, how she was going to pay for college.

Having a kid was a pain in the ass—particularly when the kid didn't like her or trust her or want anything to do with her.

19

In the three months following the attack on the marshals—as Kay was struggling to adjust to the concept of motherhood—the San Diego Police Department, the DEA, the FBI, and ICE went on a rampage, particularly the San Diego cops. John Hernández, chief of the SDPD, unleashed the dogs. He wanted to prove that just because three of his cops had been busted for being in cahoots with a drug cartel, *he* sure as hell wasn't in cahoots with anyone. Four gang members were killed in battles with San Diego cops, and hardly a day went by when a SWAT team wasn't seen on television, battering down a door in a Hispanic neighborhood. Drug dealers and users were rounded up in such numbers that the jails and courts were overwhelmed, and illegal immigrants were shipped out of the country by the busload. John Hernández waited until complaints against his department for violations of civil rights and police brutality reached a screaming crescendo before he told his boys to back off.

The Olivera cartel suffered in particular. Olivera's operations in California didn't exactly grind to a halt, but the cartel definitely lost significant revenues, and the gains Tito had made in taking over territories from other organizations were mostly lost.

But Caesar Olivera didn't care; all he cared about was getting his brother out of jail.

U.S. Marshal Kevin Walker was called back to Washington, and his handling of Tito Olivera's transfer to the courthouse was reviewed by a panel of bureaucrats. The Attorney General felt that *somebody* had to be held accountable for the seven marshals who were killed, and Walker was the obvious guy to hang.

Walker's biggest mistake, the panel said, was doing the dry run from the correctional center to the courthouse, as that gave Olivera's men time to study the route and plan the attack. Walker's defenders said that this was bullshit. The marshals had been taking the same route from the correctional center to the courthouse for almost a year as the courthouse tunnel was being repaired, and the only reason Walker had his people do a dry run was to reinforce the idea that Tito was going to be transported in the usual way. Walker's job, after all, had been to get Tito to court—and Walker did his job.

Walker's real mistake was that he, just like everybody else, including his bosses at the Justice Department, didn't believe Jim Davis when he warned them of the extremes Caesar Olivera might go to to free his brother.

Walker's supporters in Washington eventually won the day. They convinced the panel that the one who should be held accountable was Caesar Olivera and not a man who had devoted twenty years of his life to his country, first as a soldier and then as a federal marshal.

The AG finally relented, although Kevin Walker personally didn't care if he was fired or not. In the month after the attack, he attended the funerals of his men. He saw their widows sitting in graveside chairs, so numb with grief they were like statues, their kids sobbing, knowing they'd never see their fathers again. Every time he handed a widow an American flag, he went home and drank until he passed out. Kevin Walker's father had been an alcoholic. It appeared Kevin was becoming one as well.

Assistant U.S. Attorney Carol Maddox, the lawyer who would be prosecuting Tito Olivera, met three times with Jesús Rodríguez and Ángel Gomez, the men who had accompanied Tito to the bar on the day Tito executed Cadillac Washington. Maddox told them that if they didn't cooperate, she was going to prosecute them as accomplices to first-degree murder.

Maddox's case was weak, however, and she knew it. She could *say* they knew what was going to happen to Cadillac in advance, and the video showed them calmly standing by when Cadillac was shot, but she couldn't really prove they had conspired with Tito to kill Washington. Nonetheless, when Maddox was talking to Jesús, Ángel, and their lawyers, she made it sound as if a guilty verdict would be a slam dunk.

"You think there's a jury in this state that's going to let you two scumbags walk?" she said.

Carol Maddox didn't really want to convict the two men, however. What she wanted was for them to testify against Tito and give her all the information they had on the Olivera cartel. Their response to her generous offer of immunity in return for their cooperation was *Lady, go fuck yourself.* They knew they were dead men if they cooperated with the U.S. Attorney.

Two months after they were arrested, they were dead anyway.

It happened like this: Two psychopaths at MCC, each with double-digit IQs, who belonged in mental institutions instead of a jail, somehow managed to acquire knives. And these were *real* knives—hunting knives with five-inch blades—not the homemade shivs manufactured by prison inmates out of toothbrush handles and scraps of sheet metal. Then two men who were barely capable of rational thought, much less coordinating their actions, killed Ángel and Jesús less than five minutes apart, Ángel in the shower and Jesús while he was talking on the phone to his girlfriend.

Raphael Mora was pleased with the way the operation had gone.

Tito Olivera had settled into a routine at the Camp Pendleton brig. The only time he was allowed out of his cell was to exercise, and the exercise consisted of walking up and down the corridor outside his cell. He was served meals in his cell by the marshals guarding him, and before they served his meals, they poked their fingers into his food to make sure no one was sending him a message, drugs, a cell phone, or any other sort of contraband. They didn't give a shit if someone poisoned him.

The only visitor Tito was allowed was his attorney, Lincoln Prescott, who bitched mightily about having to drive to Camp Pendleton, being subjected to "draconian" security measures, and who was convinced that his conversations with Tito were being recorded, which they weren't.

Assistant U.S. Attorney Carol Maddox never met with Tito or his lawyer. Maddox had no intention of making Tito any kind of deal.

The Delgato family, up in Neah Bay, Washington, was driving soon-to-be-retired DEA agents Mike Figgins and Ray Patterson absolutely nuts.

Sofía Delgato wasn't too bad. She seemed fairly content to sit in the waterfront house and cook and read and watch TV. She missed her friends, but she liked to fry the oysters she could scoop up off the beach. She liked the ocean view. She also enjoyed the company of Figgins and Patterson, pretending to be shocked by their offers to warm her bed at night if she was cold.

The real problems were Miguel and María. Miguel had been at the Neah Bay house with the two agents for almost a year, and although he liked fishing and drinking with them, he'd had enough. And since María had arrived, Figgins and Patterson couldn't take Miguel fishing or to the golf course, nor could they visit the hookers in Forks. They knew the Olivera cartel was looking for María, so they had to play it completely straight and stay in the house at Neah Bay—and Miguel was sick of Neah Bay. He wanted to experience the bright lights of a big city again, and he wanted female companionship on a steady basis.

But María was the worst. She was a prima donna. She hated the rainy Northwest and she hated being cooped up in a house with Figgins, Patterson, and her mother. She complained the TV didn't get enough channels. She complained about the food, but never cooked. She complained about being bored, but showed no interest in doing anything to relieve her boredom. She had a full-blown temper tantrum about every other day.

Figgins called Kay Hamilton one day and said, "This broad's a fuckin' nightmare. I don't know how long we can keep her hidden up here before she decides to bolt. If you want to keep her alive until the trial, you might have to put her in a cage somewhere."

"Mike," Kay said, "you have to make her understand that her best chance for staying alive is to lie low up there. If I put her in a prison, anywhere in the U.S., Caesar Olivera will get to her."

"I've told her that! I've talked to her until I'm blue in the face. Maybe we can take her on a . . . I don't know, a *day trip* to settle her down. You know, take her over to Canada, Victoria, Vancouver, someplace where she can go shopping or something."

"No! She'll fuck up. She'll do some dumb thing and

Olivera will find her. Tell her if she doesn't stop being a little cunt, I *am* going to put her in a cell."

Raphael Mora was frustrated. He couldn't find María Delgato or her family, and he couldn't think of a way to get Tito Olivera out of Camp Pendleton. Mora's frustration was exceeded only by Caesar Olivera's, and Caesar was not a man you wanted to frustrate.

Mora had his people looking at everything. They continually checked the phone records of María's and her mother's friends, looking for out-of-area calls. They tried to locate María via her cell phone and checked daily to see if she had used her credit cards. They even tried to find María's mother through her medications. She took pills for high blood pressure and high cholesterol, and normally refilled the prescriptions at a pharmacy in National City, but the medications were so common they could be refilled anywhere, and Mrs. Delgato never contacted her doctor or her pharmacist after disappearing from San Diego.

Mora also looked at flights taken by DEA agents and by the U.S. Attorney who would be prosecuting Tito. The attorney never left San Diego, but one flight intrigued Mora. Two days after Tito was arrested, the DEA agent who arrested him took a flight to Portland, Oregon, and she rented a car at the airport. She put almost seven hundred miles on the rental car but didn't use a credit card to pay for gas or for anything else in the Northwest. On the rental car form, she put down Crescent City, California, as her destination, and a round-trip from Portland to Crescent City was about six hundred miles, so the mileage on the rental car was consistent with her driving to that location. But why would she go to Crescent City? And why would she fly into Portland to get there?

The other thing Agent Hamilton did was take a trip to Cleveland. The Cleveland trip appeared to be personal and not business related, as Hamilton used her own credit card to pay for the flight and a rental car in Cleveland. There were no motel or hotel charges in Cleveland, which meant she might have stayed with a friend. More inquiries showed that Hamilton was on annual leave from the DEA during this period, so maybe she went to Cleveland for a vacation. But who the hell went to Cleveland in the winter for a vacation?

After Hamilton's trip to Portland, Mora had people roaming the Northwest looking for any sign of María Delgato. He hired private detective agencies in Seattle, Portland, and Sacramento and had them scouring nightclubs, restaurants, expensive boutiques, and hair salons, showing employees María's photograph. The detectives from Sacramento spent almost a month in Crescent City trying to prove that María had been there. Mora also knew that María liked a little coke now and then. She wasn't an addict and took the drug only occasionally, but she took it. He put out the word to dealers—and the dealers' network was vast—to see if any of them had sold to María.

Nada.

20

This is Hamilton," Kay said when Carol Maddox answered the phone. "I was wondering if you could meet me for a drink when you get off work."

"What?" Maddox said. Kay had never socialized with Maddox in the past; she never had any interest in socializing with Maddox.

"Does this have to do with the case against Tito?" Maddox asked. "I mean, is this so urgent it can't wait until tomorrow?"

"Uh, it's not about the case. It's . . . it's personal."

"Personal?"

Aw, shit. She was going to have to tell Maddox why she wanted to meet; otherwise, Maddox would tell her that she had to go home to take care of her brood. "It's about my daughter."

"Your daughter? *You* have a daughter?"

"Yeah," Kay said. "It's a long story and I need to talk to someone—someone who has kids. I need some advice."

"You gotta be shittin' me," Maddox said, and started laughing.

* * *

Maddox surprised Kay by ordering A. H. Hirsch on the rocks. Maddox may have been a frumpy-looking mother of four with a goofy haircut, but she knew her bourbon.

Kay told her about getting pregnant when she was fifteen and Jessica showing up on her doorstep and how she was now her legal guardian. The whole time Kay was talking, Maddox had this amused expression on her face, as if the whole thing struck her as being incredibly funny. When Kay finished, however, she shook her head and said, "That poor girl."

"What do you mean *That poor girl*?"

"Hamilton, there are probably species of crocodile that are more maternal than you." Before Kay could object, Maddox said, "So what's the problem? Is she acting like a little bitch? I mean, I have a fourteen-year-old and girls can be a real handful at that age. They're worse than boys."

"No, she's not acting like a bitch. In fact, she's damn near perfect."

Kay explained how the girl was super bright and on top of that she was a serious student. "She's got almost a four-point-oh grade point. Not only that, she's really mature for her age, probably because of what happened to her mother—I mean, her adoptive mother. She got breast cancer, and the kid had to deal with that all by herself.

"Anyway, she's not really a problem. She doesn't leave crap all over the house and she takes care of her own clothes. When she comes home from school, she does about three hours of homework and then just diddles around on the Internet or reads. She reads a hell of a lot more than I ever did, or do, for that matter. And because she gets home before me, she usually makes her own dinner. She knows how to cook; I don't."

"Jesus," Maddox muttered—and Kay didn't know what that meant. "Has she made any friends since she's been here?" Maddox asked.

"Yeah, a couple of girls. She's actually pretty outgoing with everybody but me. Anyway, she hangs out with them on weekends and they go to the beach, the movies, that sort of thing. I checked them and their parents out; they don't have records. I followed them once when Jessica said they were going to the beach, and they behaved themselves."

"Good Lord," Maddox said.

"Hey! I had to make sure they weren't doing dope."

"So then what's the problem? I mean, if she's not dating some little shitbag, not doing drugs, not turning into a bulimic stick figure—"

"The problem is I don't know how to *act* around her. I haven't had sex since she's been living with me. I don't drink when I'm at home, because I don't want to set a bad example. I try to talk to her, but she doesn't want anything to do with me. She wants to move out and get her own place, but I won't let her."

"Of course you can't let her do that. She's fifteen."

"I know that. But she acts like she's doing *time* in my house, just serving out her sentence until she turns eighteen and can leave and have access to her own money. I mean, it's like living with a damn *cat*, this really smart, independent cat who looks down its nose at you."

Maddox took a sip of her bourbon, then sat for a moment like she was collecting her thoughts. "You have to do three things with kids. First, they have to know you love them, and that's kind of tough in your case. But they have to know that you're going to be there for them, no matter what. Second, you have to set some boundaries. They expect you to do that, and if you don't, as odd as it sounds, they think you don't care. More than anything else, though, you have to *talk* to them. You have to get inside their weird little heads so you can figure out if something's bothering them, and they have to know they can come to you when they have a problem."

"But she doesn't talk to me. I ask her how school's going, and she says *Fine*. That's it. Fine."

"You can't accept fine. She says fine, you ask what did you do in school today, how did your classes go, are any of your teachers giving you a hard time? You ask if there's a dance coming up or a game, or if she's met any cute boys. You *grill* her, Hamilton. That's your job now. You also tell her about what you did at work during the day, just to get a conversation started. Or you tell her about some experience you had when you were in high school so she can relate to you."

"Oh, yeah. Like getting knocked up at fifteen."

"As a matter of fact, you should talk to her about that. You *have* to talk to her about that. Tell her what it was like for you emotionally. How you dealt with the whole issue. How you came to terms with her adoption."

"Came to terms with her adoption? Are you kidding? I dumped her on my cousin two minutes after she was born."

"Whatever. You have talk to her about it. As for you not being able to act like yourself . . . well, you're not yourself anymore. You're a mother. You can't come home and start swilling martinis around the kid, but it's okay to have one once in a while. You can't drag some stud home and have noisy sex in the bedroom. I mean, you could, but that's probably not going to do much for your image or your relationship. So unless you want to be celibate for the next two years, you're going to have to sit down with her and tell her the truth, that you need a sex life and every once in a while you're going to be going out on a date and may not be back until the wee hours."

"I don't know," Kay said, shaking her head. "I just can't imagine having some kind of birds-and-the-bees talk with her."

"She's *fifteen*, Hamilton. She already knows about the birds and the bees. She's probably wondering if there's something wrong with you, never dating, not having a man in your life. The thing about kids is, you can't pretend to be somebody you're not. They can spot a phony from a mile away. You have to be honest with them if you expect them to be honest with you."

Maddox left not long after that, and Kay ordered one more drink and thought about everything Maddox had said. She knew Maddox was right. She had to make more of an effort to talk to the kid; she had to establish some sort of rapport with her. But Maddox had no idea how Jessica had this . . . this *force field* around her.

She tried to think how she could start a conversation with her daughter about sex—but soon found herself thinking about Robert Meyer. She thought about him about ten times a day. Two days after Jessica moved in with her, Robert called her at work and asked if she was busy that night—meaning his wife and daughters were out of town or otherwise engaged, and he wanted to come over to her place for a roll in the hay.

She met him for a drink that evening and told him about her daughter and that they were going to have to stop seeing each other. She couldn't articulate it very well—that having uncomplicated sex with a gorgeous married man had never bothered her before but it bothered her now that her daughter was living with her.

"We'll just go to a motel," Robert said. "The kid will never know."

"I can't do it, Robert. I'm sorry, I just can't."

Robert took their breakup amazingly well. In fact, he took it disappointingly well. He'd been seeing Kay for over a year and probably figured that he'd been pressing his luck both professionally and personally, and it was time to move on. For all she knew, he had some little honey ready to take her place in the lineup. Now she was thinking—since she was horny enough to screw a mountain goat—that maybe a visit to the nearest Holiday Inn with Robert might not be the worst thing in the world.

She'd call Jessica, tell her she was stuck on a stakeout, and . . .

Stop it! The whole point was that she had to be honest with the kid.

As she was paying her bar bill, she wondered if Jessica had made something for dinner.

21

Raphael Mora still had no idea how to get Tito out of Camp Pendleton. One day, after a so-called brainstorming session with some of his brighter people—a session that resulted in him losing his temper and calling them all idiots—he went to a movie. He just needed to clear his head, to think about something other than Tito.

The movie was one the critics had raved about, some ponderous drama about life and death and family, and he kept nodding off during the show. The third time his head hit his chest, he gave up on the picture and left, and on his way out he saw an older couple sleeping. He couldn't help but think that a theater full of sleeping people said all there was to say about the movie's quality.

And then he thought: *A theater full of sleeping people.*

Mora met Leonid Alekseyev at a café a mile from the Russian Embassy in Mexico City.

The Olivera cartel had connections in Russia that were particularly useful when it came to getting opium out of Afghanistan; Olivera's Mexican poppy fields were not large enough or fertile enough to keep up with demand. Leonid Alekseyev, while pretending to do whatever Russian diplomats did in Mexico, was often used by the Olivera cartel to liaise with Russian drug honchos overseas.

Leonid was an unimpressive-looking man—fat, bald, red-faced, triple-chinned—and the ultimate survivor. He'd lived through the political purges of the Soviet Union and flourished in the rampant corruption following the demise of the Soviet Union. Mora was convinced that if you dropped fat Leonid Alekseyev naked on a desert island with nine Olympic-caliber athletes, Leonid would be the last man standing.

After coffee and pastries were served, Mora said, "I wanted to ask about the incident that happened in Moscow in that theater in 2002. You know, where all those people were killed with that gas?"

"Not our finest moment," Leonid said.

In 2002, a group of Chechen nationalists, who claimed allegiance to an Islamic separatist movement, took eight hundred and fifty people hostage in a theater and made a number of political demands the Russians found unreasonable. After a two-and-a-half-day siege, Russian Spetsnaz forces secretly pumped some type of gas into the theater with the intention of knocking out both the captives and their attackers; the plan was to then swoop in and capture the unconscious Chechens. Unfortunately, the gas did more than knock folks out; a hundred and seventy people died, mostly hostages, because they were allergic to some element in the gas.

"I was wondering whether you might have something similar to the gas that was used in 2002," Mora said, and then explained what he needed.

"I don't know if we have anything like that," Leonid said. "When I was in the army, they gave me a rifle, not a chemistry set. But I'll make a few phone calls."

"We will pay very well for this," Mora said.

"I'm sure you will," Leonid said.

Three days later, Leonid called Mora. "It just so happens the wizards do have something similar to what you have in mind. But it's not a, oh, what do you call it? Ah. An off-the-shelf item. It will take about a month to get the quantity you need."

"I want someone who's knowledgeable to deliver it to me," Mora said. "I don't want a military instruction booklet translated from Russian to Spanish."

"I believe that can be arranged," Leonid said.

Now all Raphael Mora needed were two accomplices to execute his plan.

Mora found the actor he needed the same way movie directors find actors: through a casting agent. The man had only had a few small parts on Mexican television shows, which was a good thing as far as Mora was concerned. His primary qualification, other than his appearance, was that he was completely fluent in English.

Caesar decided he wanted to see the actor for himself, so Mora went with a couple of men to pick him up.

When the actor saw three men on his doorstep—two wearing guns in shoulder holsters—and Mora told him that Caesar Olivera, leader of the largest drug cartel in Mexico, wanted to talk to him, the actor was bright enough to know that it wasn't an invitation he could decline.

The actor met Caesar in the courtyard of Caesar's lavish home in Mexico City. It was the sort of courtyard most Mexicans only dream of having in their homes: soothing, burbling fountains, the floor paved with exotic handmade ceramic tiles, trellises laden with red begonia. It was an incredibly tranquil place—but Mora could tell the actor was so nervous that the only way he would be able to relax was if Mora gave him Valium.

Caesar Olivera introduced himself, although the introduction was hardly necessary. He personally poured the actor a glass of wine, but before he could take a sip, Caesar told him to stand, then turn around, then walk a few paces so he could see the way he moved.

"Good," Caesar said, but he was speaking to Mora, and the actor had no idea what was *good*.

"Okay, sit down," Caesar said, now impatient to be finished with the man. "I'm going to pay you five million dollars for the job you're going to do for me."

"Five million?" the actor said, but he noticed that Caesar had said, "I'll pay you for a job you're *going* to do for me" and not "I'll pay you for a job I *want* you to do for me."

"Yes, five million," Caesar repeated. "You need to look at this job in terms of your future. It's going to require some sacrifice on your part, and it may cost you ten years of your life."

"Ten years?" the actor said.

"That's right, but imagine only having to work ten more years and at the end of that time, you're set for life. How old are you?"

"Twenty-eight."

"So by the time you're thirty-eight, and maybe even sooner, you'll be able to retire and never have to work again. Also, by doing this job for me, you'll have earned my appreciation, and if you desire to continue to pursue your acting career, I will most certainly be able to help you."

"What do you want me to do, sir?"

Caesar Olivera told him.

Raphael Mora thought the actor might throw up on Caesar's handmade ceramic tiles. Fortunately, he waited until he was outside the house before he vomited.

22

Mike Figgins was trying to button a sport coat he hadn't worn in a year. He turned to his partner, Patterson, and said, "Ray, can you see my gun?" He sounded like a wife asking her husband *Honey, does this dress make my ass look fat?*

Patterson ignored the question. "If Hamilton finds out about this, she's going to kill us, Mike. I mean, we won't just get fired, we'll lose our pensions."

"She's not going to find out. It's one fucking night. If we don't do this, I'm gonna kill that little Mexican bitch. I can't take any more of her whining and screaming and all the rest of her shit. This will settle her down for at least a little while, and pretty soon the lawyers will start prepping her for the trial, and that'll give us another break. Plus, I need to get out of here, too."

"We can't drink," alcoholic Patterson said to alcoholic Figgins. "We gotta stay sharp. You're gonna have to stay glued to that broad like you're Siamese twins."

"Yeah, no drinking," Figgins said, but he was thinking there was no way he could go the whole day without a drink. He'd just have to pace himself.

Fortunately, María's mother had a cold and didn't

want to go. There was no landline in the house, she didn't have a cell phone, the nearest pay phone was ten miles away, and they'd be taking the only vehicle they had. Sofía would be okay.

An hour later, at ten in the morning, they all piled into the Explorer: Figgins, Patterson, and the Delgato siblings, who were acting like two kids on the last day of school.

The nearest major city to Neah Bay—and calling it a major city was a stretch—was Port Angeles, Washington, population nineteen thousand. It was eighty miles from Neah Bay. The first thing they did was have lunch at a place overlooking the ocean. Figgins and Patterson both winced when the Delgatos ordered steak and lobster and the most expensive bottle of wine on the menu. The agents were personally funding this little outing, because if they charged it to their DEA credit cards, Hamilton might catch them. They had figured it would cost them each five or six hundred bucks, but as they were making so much in per diem with nowhere to spend it, they could handle the money. Now they were both thinking that maybe they'd underestimated.

Figgins and Patterson both looked at the wine bottle when it arrived. "Aw, one glass ain't gonna kill us," Patterson said, and the four of them ended up drinking two bottles of wine.

The waiter was a handsome kid who looked like a

jock and was maybe twenty-two. María's eyes followed him around the restaurant like a hunter tracking game, and when he came to their table she batted her eyes at him. At one point, gazing at the young waiter, she said, "God, I'm horny. I'd screw a—"

"Jesus, María!" her brother said, cutting her off, embarrassed she'd say something like that in front of Figgins and Patterson.

"Well, aren't you?"

"Yeah, but—"

"Oh, pour me some more wine and quit acting like Mama."

T he next stop was a salon where María could get her hair cut and a manicure and a pedicure. Before they got out of the car, Figgins said to her, "I swear to Christ, María, if you start jabbering to anyone about where you're from or where you've been staying, I'm going to drag you out of this place so fuckin' fast, you'll get whiplash. You tell the hair gal you're from L.A., visiting a cousin, and then you basically keep your mouth shut. I'm going to be sitting as close to you as I can get and—"

"Yeah, yeah, I get it," María said. "But I gotta ask where I can buy some clothes."

"Fine. You stick to that. Where can I go shopping, take a little more off the top, that kind of shit. Because I'm telling you, María, anything you tell somebody about yourself, even the smallest thing, could come back to bite you on the ass, and by that I mean you could get killed. I'm taking a big risk with you and I'm doing you a favor, and—"

"Mike, I get it. I swear. And I appreciate what you're doing. I won't screw up."

Before Figgins and María went into the beauty parlor, Patterson said he and Miguel were going to stretch their legs, take a little walk around the neighborhood. Patterson *never* stretched his legs. Figgins bet they were going to walk as far as the nearest bar.

Miguel tried to tell María that the casino wasn't a fancy place, that most people who went there wore jeans. María said she didn't give a shit; she was dressing up. She'd been wearing baggy-assed jeans and sweatshirts for four goddamn months, and for just one night she was going to look good. She had wanted to find a Victoria's Secret but learned from the beauty parlor lady that there wasn't a Victoria's Secret in Port Angeles—or a Neiman Marcus or a Nordstrom or even a Macy's. To which Figgins said, "Thank God," since he was paying for María's outfit.

They finally ended up at a little boutique/consignment store, where she tried on one outfit after another. Figgins figured that Harry Truman spent less time deciding if he should drop the atom bomb on Japan than it took for her to decide which dress to buy. She finally settled on a skimpy red number that stopped about three inches below her crotch, had no back, and had barely enough material to contain her tits. She looked incredible—and Mike Figgins wished that he wasn't old and fat and that every vein in his nose wasn't broken.

But the dress was a problem. María was so damn good-looking that she could have worn bib overalls and still turned heads. The way she looked in the slinky dress, every man—and every woman—in the casino was going to stare at her. Plus, the casino had cameras; some security guy who was supposed to be looking for cheaters at the blackjack tables was going to zoom right in on her.

Figgins tried to talk her into buying something a little less flashy, but she went postal on him, telling him he'd *promised* her she could buy whatever she wanted, and he finally gave in because she was starting to make a scene. The good thing about the casino was that it wasn't a big place—it wasn't the Bellagio in Vegas—and most of the people who went there were locals. People from Seattle or Tacoma usually didn't go there because there were nicer, bigger casinos closer to the major cities. And someone from San Diego or Mexico sure as hell wouldn't go there unless they just happened to be in the area for some other reason, like salmon fishing.

Figgins figured the casino would be safe enough. They'd only be in the place a couple of hours and, unless María did something totally outrageous, the people there would only remember that they saw this good-looking Hispanic woman one night and then forget about her.

At least, he hoped that was the case.

The feeling that he and Patterson were making a big mistake was starting to vibrate through him.

* * *

The casino was called 7 Cedars. It was located at a speed bump in the road called Sequim, Washington, about twenty miles from Port Angeles and a hundred miles from Neah Bay. So it was a long way from where they were hiding out with the Delgatos, but it was a lot more crowded than Figgins had expected. For one thing, it was a Friday night and some shit-kicker band was playing; it looked as if half the people on the Olympic Peninsula were in the place. Then he thought maybe it was a good thing the place was crowded. The more people there were, the less noticeable María would be.

Yeah, right.

First they had dinner and two more bottles of wine. While they were eating, María had to go to the restroom—the one place Figgins couldn't follow her—not once but twice, and on her way there she swished her ass like a hula dancer to make sure every male standing at the bar noticed her.

Then it was time to gamble. But did María pick a nice, quiet blackjack table or a slot machine way in the back? Hell, no. She had to play craps, where there were fifteen men at the table, not counting the dealers, and where everyone walking by could see her butt every time she leaned forward to throw the dice.

Figgins had told her and Miguel that they'd spot them each two hundred dollars to gamble with but when the money was gone they wouldn't get any more. Figgins figured they'd lose the money in about twenty minutes. But María didn't. Whichever god it was who allowed a few players to beat the house odds and win decided to kiss María on the head that night. She won five hundred bucks, and while she was winning, there was a lot of shrieking and shouting and high-fiving the guys standing next to her. In case anybody hadn't noticed her earlier, they did by the time she was done.

Next, María wanted to dance. Figgins and Patterson had agreed that Patterson would watch Miguel and Figgins would stick with María. Miguel behaved himself; he was one of those guys who, the more he drank, the quieter he got. He didn't want to dance. He and Patterson took a seat at a blackjack table and sat there the rest of the night. And it looked like they were winning, too. Everybody was winning but Mike Figgins. He also noticed that Patterson was now drinking Jack Daniel's.

The evening was turning into a nightmare—and it was about to get worse.

Figgins sat with María on the edge of the dance floor, close enough for the shit-kicker band to rupture his eardrums. With his thinning gray hair, his tight-fitting sport coat, his gut slopping over his belt, he knew he looked like María's grandfather. It didn't take long at all for the young guys in the crowd to figure out that she was available.

She finally locked on to some tall, dark-haired guy wearing cowboy boots and started rubbing her boobs up against him. Why she'd picked him Figgins couldn't figure until she came back to the table where Figgins was sitting and said, "I'm taking that guy out to the parking lot and fucking him. He's got a camper."

"The hell you are!" Figgins said.

Then he noticed her eyes. Then he noticed the little smudge of white powder on her nostrils. She was higher than a kite. She'd been to the restroom half a dozen times since she'd finished playing craps; she must have used the cash she won to score coke from some gal in the ladies' room.

Figgins thought he should just take out his gun, right now, and eat it.

"The hell I'm not," María said. "I'm getting laid tonight. If you try to stop me, I'm gonna start screaming, tell everybody you're packing heat and you're trying to kidnap me. I'll scream my fuckin' head off. Now, I'm not gonna mess up, Mike. I've told the guy I'm from L.A. and just passing through. He thinks my name is Carrie. I'll be gone about an hour. You want to come out and look through the camper window like some kind of pervert, I don't give a shit, but you're not stopping me."

Two hours later, they were on their way back to Neah Bay. Figgins was the only one sober enough to drive, and he'd be in trouble if they got pulled over by a cop. María, Miguel, and Patterson were all passed out. Patterson was snoring like a hog, and María had a small smile on her face.

Please, please, God, Mike Figgins prayed, *don't let this night come back and bite me on the ass.*

S hirley Young woke up about two in the afternoon on Saturday, about the time she normally woke up, and the first thing she did was call her supplier.

"I was over at the casino last night," Shirley said.

"Oh, yeah," her supplier said. He sounded like he'd just woken up himself.

"There was this gal there, this good-looking Latina who bought some blow off me."

"Shirley, get to the fuckin' point, will you, please? I've got a hangover. Do you need more?"

"No. Remember a couple months ago when Ricky was up here from Seattle to go fishing and he talked about these hotshot Mexicans trying to find some woman? I think he gave you a picture of her. Do you still have it?"

"Hell, I don't know. I doubt it. Do you think this woman is the one you sold to?"

"I don't know. But she's the right age and Ricky said she was a friggin' knockout, which this chick was. He said the Mexicans were offering a lot of money for her, so why don't you call him, see if he's still got her picture, and have him e-mail it to me."

23

Move it, you asshole!" Kay screamed. She didn't have a siren in her Camry, but she did have a portable cherry—a flashing red light she could stick on the roof. She was thinking about using it when she finally caught a break in the stream of cars coming her way and was able to make a left-hand turn.

She was supposed to be at a parent-teacher conference at Jessica's school—forty minutes ago. She'd tell Jessica she got stuck at the office—or maybe taking down a meth lab, as that would sound more dramatic—but the plain truth was that she'd forgotten about the conference and didn't remember it until ten minutes ago. She found Jessica sitting on a bench just inside the main entrance to the school and she didn't see anyone else around; it looked as if the other kids and their parents had already left.

"I'm really sorry," she said. "I got stuck—"

Jessica just shook her head and said, "Come on. Mr. Adams is waiting."

The conference itself was anticlimactic. Adams—Kay couldn't remember if he was a guidance counselor or Jessica's homeroom teacher—was a sweet man in his sixties who wore a corduroy jacket with suede patches on the elbows; he was out of central casting for Mr. Chips. Adams said Jessica was doing great, an exemplary student, acing everything; the sky was the limit for her. After the conference, Kay asked Jessica if she'd like to go out to dinner to celebrate.

"Celebrate what? It was a mandatory parent-teacher conference."

"Well, would you like to go out to dinner anyway?" *Sheesh.*

Kay picked a nice place in La Jolla where they could see the beach. There were a dozen kids out on the water, dressed in wet suits, surfing in the fading light. Kay groped for something to say. She had been trying like crazy to talk to the girl, to get her to open up in some way, but so far . . . She figured the guys who ran North and South Korea had a warmer relationship than she and her daughter.

"Have you thought about what you want to take in college?" Kay asked. Adams—the teacher, guidance counselor, whoever the hell he was—had said that with her math and science grades, Jessica could probably get into any college in the country.

While watching the surfers, Jessica said, "I'm not sure yet, but most likely something that would get me a job with some high-tech company dealing with genetic research, microbiology, developing drugs, that sort of thing. I don't know. Maybe pre-med."

"Pre-med?"

"Yeah. Maybe."

Jesus. Her daughter, the doctor. When Kay was her age, all she'd thought about was being a cop like her dad—and screwing the guy who eventually knocked her up. How the hell could she possibly connect with this . . . this rocket scientist?

Noticing Jessica seemed to be mesmerized by the surfers, Kay asked, "Have you ever surfed?"

"Surfed? I was raised in Nebraska."

"Well, would you like to learn to surf?"

Jessica thought about the question for less than a second, and for the first time since Kay had known her, she let down her guard and grinned and said, "You know, that would be cool." Then, realizing what she'd done, she added, "I mean, if you're not too busy, if it wouldn't be an imposition."

Sheesh.

Kay had learned to surf in Miami—her ex-husband had introduced her to the sport. She'd started too late in life to ever be a truly stellar surfer, but she wasn't bad. The Saturday after having dinner with Jessica in La Jolla, Kay grabbed her board and they headed to Pacific Beach.

"We'll rent you a board and a wet suit at the beach," Kay said.

"That's cool," Jessica said. She didn't say anything else during the drive to the beach, but Kay could tell she was actually excited.

They spent three hours in the water. Jessica wasn't

afraid, she didn't ask about sharks, and she took her licks without whining when the surf pounded her into the sand. In general, she had the same kind of gritty determination that Kay had. She also got the hang of things quickly, and Kay liked to think that she'd inherited her athletic ability—if not her brains—from her.

They stripped off their wet suits and Kay got a blanket from her car and bought them hot dogs and Cokes from a stand on the beach. Kay was wearing a high-cut, one-piece black suit that maybe showed off a little more of her butt than it should. Jessica had on a red bikini and Kay thought she had a cute figure, although she wasn't as busty as Kay had been at her age—but maybe that was a good thing. Her legs were terrific.

"Would you be interested in taking lessons?" Kay said. "I mean, surfing's really a San Diego thing and a lot of kids your age are into it. It'll give you a chance to meet people outside of school, and it would be better if you learned from a pro than from me. I'll pay for the lessons."

Jessica thought about it for a moment and said, "Yeah, I think I'd like that, but you don't have to pay."

"I'll pay," Kay said. Sometimes she just wanted to smack her. She also knew she was too impatient to teach her more about surfing, and they'd be fighting if she tried. "Before we go, we'll stop at the surf shop and sign you up."

A few minutes later, two girls just a little older than Jessica walked by, both of them wearing bikinis that had less material than a Band-Aid. The little sluts.

Following the girls with her eyes, Jessica said, "Maybe I'll save up and get a boob job."

"Are you insane!" Kay shrieked.

"Easy for you to say. You got a rack on you like . . ." Then she started giggling. "Aw, lighten up. I'm kidding."

That was the first time Kay and her daughter ever laughed together.

24

"Is Tito allowed to have a barber and shave?" Mora asked Tito's lawyer.

"Yes," Prescott said, "but so far he's declined the barber and he shaves only occasionally. He looks like a hippie. Anyway, the marshals allow him to use an electric razor, and they watch him while he shaves."

"How often would he be allowed to see the barber if he decided to get his hair cut?" Mora asked.

"A barber goes to the brig once a week and all the marines in the brig get their hair trimmed. They're required to, but since Tito isn't a marine, he can refuse."

"Not anymore. I want you to go see Tito today and tell him he's to start shaving every day and he's to get his hair cut once a week. Tell him to cut it short. I want you to take a picture of him when he first has his hair cut and then go back a week later and take a second picture just before his hair is cut again."

"You know, it's really inconvenient for me to go see him at Pendleton," Prescott said.

"Would it be more convenient if I sent someone to cut your balls off before I hire Tito a new lawyer?"

* * *

The surgery performed on the actor wasn't extensive, which was the reason he'd been selected in the first place. A month later, all signs of the two small operations were gone. After that, Mora spent several days with the man, training him on what he would be required to do—or his *role,* as the actor thought of it. The actor's part was simple: If everything went as planned, he would have no dialogue and would just stand there.

Mora now had the first person he needed for Tito's escape.

It was time to recruit the second player.

Mora called the main house and asked to see Caesar. He was told his boss would meet him at the stables; he was looking at the new horse he'd bought for his younger daughter. She wasn't as confident as her older sister and she needed an animal that was more docile than the one she'd been riding. The horse had just been delivered from a ranch in Arizona, and although Caesar didn't really know anything about horses, he wanted to examine the animal.

Mora left the concrete operations center and walked the half-mile path to the stables. He found Caesar inside dressed in an expensive suit and tie, but wearing rubber boots on his feet. He was talking to a groom who was holding the reins of a golden palomino with a white mane and tail, and the groom was nodding his head like one of those little bobble-head figures. Very few people had the courage to do anything more than nod in agreement when Caesar Olivera was speaking.

Mora waited until the groom led the mare back to its stall before he approached Caesar. "I wanted to talk to you about the second person needed for the operation," he said. "The most logical choice would be a man named Kevin Walker, who is head of the Marshals Service in San Diego. The marshals guarding Tito at the Camp Pendleton brig would never question an order from him. The problem with Walker, according to our psychiatrists, is that he's guilt-ridden. He considers himself personally responsible for the deaths of the marshals in San Diego. He doesn't care if he dies, and in fact, our doctors say it's very likely he's suicidal.

"We could kidnap a member of Walker's family. He's divorced and has no children, but he does have a mother and a brother he's close to. But I'm afraid, in his depressed state, he might simply kill himself so that he can't be coerced and so his family will have no value as hostages. Finally, I'm worried about Walker because he's started to drink heavily and alcoholics are unreliable and unpredictable."

"So if you don't want to use Walker, who do you want to use? Someone who works for him?"

Mora could sense Caesar's impatience, but he didn't allow himself to be rushed. Raphael Mora wasn't a groom.

"No. I could use someone in Walker's chain of command, but I'm concerned that many of these people are the type who would call their superiors or the FBI. They are rule followers. I want a rule breaker. I want to use a DEA agent named Katherine Hamilton. She's the woman who directed Tito's arrest, and because of this, she would logically have some access to Tito. What I like about her is that she's a . . . a lone wolf. She's secretive even with her own people, she acts independently, and she's bent the rules in the past."

"How do you know all this?"

"I hired a woman to seduce a man who works for Hamilton, and when the man drinks, he complains about her. She's very unpopular with her subordinates. Until she arrested Tito, her most famous case was the fatal shooting of Marco Álvarez in Miami. Do you remember that? It happened four years ago."

"Vaguely, but refresh my memory."

Mora did.

"She slept with Álvarez for almost a year to get evidence against him?" Caesar said.

"Yes, and then she killed him and three of his men."

"How would you control her?"

"Approximately four months ago, Hamilton became the legal guardian of a fifteen-year-old girl. I'm still collecting information from a social organization in Cleveland, but it appears that Hamilton is the girl's birth mother and until recently the girl lived with her adoptive parents in Ohio. She now lives with Hamilton. I need a bit more time to analyze the situation, but I believe Hamilton can be controlled through her daughter."

"You've been analyzing for months. How long before Tito's trial?"

"Five months. As you know, Tito's lawyer tried to delay the trial until December but he wasn't successful. But there's plenty of time left for what I need to do."

"How's my brother holding up?"

"About as well as can be expected. He's frustrated, but he hasn't done anything to jeopardize his health— no hunger strikes, no suicidal behavior, nothing foolish like that. On the other hand, there's really nothing we can do to make his situation more comfortable."

"I don't want to make his situation more comfortable. I want him to experience what it's like when you make a serious mistake."

"The good news is that the longer he's in the brig, the more relaxed his jailers become. The general at Pendleton has stopped conducting weekly drills in case we attack the brig, and Tito's lawyer has told me the marines at the checkpoints aren't as cautious as they were in the beginning. The marshals, although they are more disciplined than the marines, have also become less vigilant. That's inevitable after guarding Tito for almost five months. I must warn you, however, that if an attempt is made to free him, I believe the marshals will do as Walker told Tito's lawyer: They will kill him immediately as payback for their dead friends, and then they will lie and say that he was killed during the escape attempt."

"Do you have the Russian chemical yet?"

"It will be here this week."

"Do you know if it will work?"

"No. I know what the Russians have told me and I

don't think they're lying, but I won't know for sure until I can test it myself."

"Okay," Caesar said. Then he looked at his watch and Mora knew one of his special guests was coming for dinner, which explained not only his impatience but also the suit. Caesar's . . . Mora didn't know what to call it. An appetite? A compulsion? Whatever the correct term, it was the only weakness his employer appeared to have, and Mora considered it a significant character flaw—and a significant security risk.

"What about the woman, the informant?" Caesar asked.

"Now, there I have some good news for you."

25

When Raphael Mora heard that a coke dealer had seen María Delgato in a casino, he called the private detective agency in Seattle he'd hired months before to find the woman.

The private detectives concocted a story that María had jumped bail and convinced casino personnel to allow them to look at security tapes. They found out that Miguel Delgato had been with his sister in the casino, and discovered two overweight white men in their fifties who looked like cops sitting with María and Miguel. Mora figured these were María's handlers, either DEA or federal marshals, but he couldn't imagine marshals showing such a lack of discipline as to bring María into a casino. He was betting the fat white men were DEA.

When shown María's picture, a casino cocktail waitress also remembered María and her little red dress; she'd even asked María where she bought the dress. María told her she bought it at a boutique in Port Angeles, and there were only a couple of boutiques in Port

Angeles. The owner of the boutique remembered María, too, and thinking she was talking to cops and not private detectives, she showed the detectives the credit-card record of María's purchases. The credit card was a VISA belonging to one Michael A. Figgins.

Then the trail ran cold. Mora's private detectives checked with real estate agents to see if Figgins had rented a house in the Port Angeles area. They visited other stores where María might shop if she was staying in Port Angeles. They did find the salon where she had her hair done the day she went to the casino, but the woman who did her hair couldn't tell them anything about where María might be. She said María had told her she was visiting from L.A.

A routine background check on Michael A. Figgins showed that he owned a home in Miami, so Mora sent men to Miami. They found out that Figgins had rented his house to a guy from the Dade County Sheriff's Office and had not been there in more than a year. His renter said he never talked to Figgins and dealt only with the property-management firm Figgins used.

One of Mora's people, an Anglo, cozied up to a retired DEA agent in a Miami bar. The retired agent had worked with Figgins in Miami. Mora's man claimed he was an NYPD detective on vacation and eventually steered the conversation around to Figgins, who he said he'd met when Figgins was working a case in New York. Three beers later, Mora's man learned one significant thing: Mike Figgins liked to fish.

*   *   *

Buzz Thomas was one of the Seattle-based private detectives sent to Port Angeles. He was also a fisherman—and he had an inspiration.

The area near Port Angeles is salmon-fishing paradise, particularly places like La Push, Sekiu, and Neah Bay. So Buzz started talking to fish checkers. Fish checkers are people employed by the Washington Department of Fish & Wildlife. They hang out at marinas, and when the fishermen come in for the day, the fish checkers make sure that what they've caught is legal. Using the same story they used for María, Buzz said Figgins was a bail jumper and he'd heard he was in the area. One fish checker, the one who worked the Neah Bay marina, recognized Figgins. He'd talked to him several times when Figgins and his two buddies—an older guy Figgins's age and a young Hispanic guy—brought in their fish. The fish checker was shocked to learn that a nice guy like Figgins was a criminal but said he hadn't seen him in several months. The last time the fish checker saw him, in fact, was about the time María Delgato disappeared from San Diego.

Buzz's boss told Raphael Mora that Figgins might be someplace near Neah Bay, which was all Indian reservation and little houses spaced miles apart up and down the coast. Mora looked at a map and Google Earth and he figured Neah Bay was the perfect place to stash María; it was as far from civilization as you could get.

Raphael Mora knew he was close, so close he could almost smell his prey.

Buzz figured that if the Delgatos were someplace near Neah Bay, they had to go out occasionally for supplies. There were no major stores in Neah Bay—no big Walmart or a Costco or anything like that. The detective figured they probably did their big shopping in Port Angeles, going once a month to buy in bulk the stuff they needed, but they wouldn't drive eighty miles to Port Angeles if they ran out of coffee or cigarettes. There were only two or three grocery stores near Neah Bay, and the best one was a place called the Sunsets West Co-op in Clallam Bay.

Buzz brought an RV over from Seattle—there aren't many motels near Neah Bay, either—and he and three other guys staked out all the small stores in the area, praying that Figgins would need something from one of them. Buzz staked out the store in Clallam Bay himself. It was a long shot, but he couldn't think of anything else to do and the Mexican who'd hired his firm didn't appear to give a damn about how much money he was spending.

A week later, Figgins drove into the parking lot near the store. He was wearing a baseball cap and sunglasses, but Buzz recognized him. He knew Figgins wouldn't be inside the place for long and he knew he couldn't follow Figgins, either. There wasn't much traffic on the roads near Neah Bay, and a DEA agent, trying not to be found, would spot a tail in no time. But Buzz was prepared for this.

As soon as Figgins walked into the store, Buzz took an object from his glove compartment, walked past Figgins's car, dropped his keys on the ground—and attached a GPS device to Mike Figgins's car.

As Raphael Mora had said, he had some very good news for Caesar Olivera.

26

Mike Figgins's cell phone rang, and he knew it was Kay Hamilton calling. Hamilton and her boss, Jim Davis, were the only people who had his number and Hamilton was the only one who ever called. She called every couple of weeks from a pay phone just to see how things were going—or maybe just to let Figgins and Patterson know that she hadn't forgotten about them.

A month earlier, two days after he took María to the casino, Hamilton called and Figgins's heart, which wasn't in the best of shape anyway, had started hammering in his chest. He knew—he just knew—that Hamilton had discovered the bone-headed thing that he and Patterson had done. He'd been ready to explain to Hamilton how that fuckin' girl had been driving everyone crazy and how they had to do something to settle her down. He'd also been ready for Hamilton to tell him that his fat ass was fired and she was sending someone with half a brain to replace him. But all Hamilton did on that phone call was ask how things were going, and she'd actually sounded—for Hamilton—fairly mellow.

This call was more of the same, Hamilton just asking if they needed anything, how things were going with the

Delgatos, and giving him an update on preparations for the trial. She concluded the call as she always did, asking if he'd heard of anyone sniffing around, looking for María.

"No," Figgins said. "Everything's fine up here."

It looked as if he and Patterson had gotten away with the stupid stunt they'd pulled.

Thank you, Jesus.

F iggins sounded funny, Kay thought. And he'd sounded funny the last time she talked to him, too. He sounded *nervous*—and Mike Figgins was the least nervous guy she knew. He was usually so laid-back she just wanted to smack him. But it seemed like everything was going okay up there, other than María being a pain in the ass, which was normal. Kay tried to make soothing noises, telling Figgins that he and his partner just needed to hang on a little bit longer. She ended the call as she always did, asking if he had noticed anyone strange hanging around Neah Bay. She knew it was a dumb question. If Figgins had even an inkling that somebody was in the area looking for María, he would have called Kay immediately. Mike Figgins was lazy—and sneaky— but he wasn't stupid. She hoped.

Kay was bored. She'd been spending way too much time in the office getting ready for the upcoming trials of the guys busted as a result of the Tito Olivera case, talking to Assistant U.S. Attorney Carol Maddox, and discussing security arrangements for getting María and Maddox together before the trial. Which made her think of poor Kevin Walker. He still hadn't recovered from the deaths of his men, and the last time Kay saw him she thought he might be hitting the sauce.

There were half a dozen other operations going on, but Kay's people were doing most of the fieldwork and Kay was playing supervisor. They'd picked up a rumor about another drug tunnel going from Mexico to an area near Calexico, California, but all they had so far was rumor. There was a mutt near Juanita who had a pot farm out in the woods they hadn't been able to find, and a couple of meth labs in Lemon Grove they had found but that Kay didn't want to bust until they identified whoever was supplying the chemicals. Then there was the Navy thing.

An informant in Turkey had given the DEA office in Ankara a tip that eventually led to some sailors on the USS *Ronald Reagan*. The Navy guys, as many as ten of them, including a couple of officers, were bringing duffel bags full of heroin back to the States, getting the dope when the carrier was deployed to the Middle East. The whole thing was a bureaucratic nightmare involving NCIS, JAG lawyers, and Pentagon PR weenies who didn't want to give the Navy a black eye when they finally arrested the yahoos. In other words, just the usual shit.

One thing making her job harder and less interesting was that she was spending a lot more time adjusting her people's work hours to accommodate their personal lives. She did this not because she really wanted to but because she was forced to now that she had a kid. The guys working for her appreciated this, but they also knew why she was doing it and made snide cracks. You just couldn't win with some people. She also made the effort to minimize weekend work as much as possible and delegated a lot of the backshift/nighttime duties to subordinates, which she really hated to do. She liked being in charge and she liked being out there prowling around at night, but she forced herself to back off because she didn't like leaving Jessica home alone too many nights.

She also realized that living with Jessica was changing her. She wasn't used to trying to act like a role model and she wasn't used to trying to accommodate another person, much less sacrifice for one. Hell, she'd never even made much of an effort to accommodate her husband when she'd been married. But she now felt a sense of obligation to another human being, which she'd never felt before, and it was like there was this . . . this *weight* on her. The weight of motherhood, she guessed. Whatever it was, it was there and she couldn't seem to get out from under it, and it was changing not just her personal behavior but her professional behavior as well—and she didn't like that.

Things with Jessica were going okay, though. She really didn't have anything to bitch about. The kid still kept pretty much to herself and she was still irritatingly self-sufficient, but she and Kay were talking more. They didn't exactly have mother-daughter chats—the kid never asked for advice—but she would occasionally gripe a bit about something happening at school or brag, just a little, about something that had gone well.

The other day, for example, when she got home from work, she could tell Jessica was excited about something, and when she asked how school went that day, instead of blowing her off with *Fine*, Jessica said, "You're not gonna believe it, but they fired Mr. Hancock."

"Who's Hancock?"

"My English teacher. You met him. Anyway, there's this rumor going around that he was hitting on one of the senior girls, and they fired him."

Kay started to say *Did this asshole ever hit on you?* In which case, she'd shoot the son of a bitch. She didn't say that, though. Instead, trying to act like the responsible adult, she said, "You gotta be careful with rumors."

"Yeah, well, it may be a rumor, but I've seen the way he touches some of the girls."

At which point Kay couldn't stop herself: "Did this asshole ever do anything to you?"

Which reminded her: They still hadn't had the discussion that Maddox told her to have with Jessica, about her getting pregnant when she was fifteen. Kay just wasn't ready for that.

Another good thing was that Jessica was still taking surfing lessons, and Kay went surfing with her whenever she could. That was the one activity they did together, and Kay actually enjoyed the time even if they didn't talk a whole lot. She also figured that in a few months Jessica was going to be a better surfer than her. Kay asked her why she didn't go out for a sport at school— softball, soccer, something like that. She was certainly athletic enough. Her daughter told her she really didn't like team sports but something like surfing, something she could do on her own without a whole lot of structure, appealed to her.

Her daughter. Kay knew she still hadn't really wrapped her mind around that fact. She didn't really think of Jessica as a daughter, more like a sister or like a young friend. But she wasn't a young friend—she was her *kid*—and at some point she was going to have to deal with motherhood as it related to her career. Now more than ever, she wanted Jim Davis's job when he retired. If she got the job, that would keep her in San Diego at least until Jessica graduated from high school, but she knew that Davis's job probably wasn't in the cards.

If she couldn't get Davis's job, then what she should be doing was maneuvering for an overseas assignment, someplace that would look good on her résumé. The Middle East would be ideal, someplace like Afghanistan, but she didn't think she'd get sent there because of her language skills. She was as fluent in Spanish as someone born south of the border, and she figured if the DEA sent her out of the country, it would most likely be to Colombia or Peru. They wouldn't send her to Mexico, that would just be too dangerous after having been personally responsible for putting Tito Olivera in jail for the rest of his life.

With Jessica still in high school, however, an overseas gig wouldn't be good. It had been hard enough to get her into a good school in San Diego; what the hell would she do in Kabul? In a couple of years, when Jessica was in college, an overseas assignment might be okay, but not now. So what should she do to advance? Just sit in San Diego and play nice for two years? She needed to talk to Barb. She really needed Barb's advice.

Barbara Reynolds was an assistant director back in D.C. She was also Kay's rabbi, her mentor. Barb, for whatever reason, took a shine to her even before she busted Marco Álvarez, and she liked her even more after that. Barb was the one who gave her career advice and looked out for her back at headquarters. Barb was also the one who'd flexed some muscle to get her the supervisor's job in San Diego.

Yeah, she was going to find some excuse to fly back to Washington so she could go out and get drunk with Barb and talk about how you juggled motherhood with a career in law enforcement. Barb had two boys, both out of college now, so she'd have something to say. The problem with Barb, though, was that she wasn't exactly the maternal type either, and as near as Kay could tell, it was Barb's husband who'd really raised her kids. Still, Barb could tell her . . .

The outer door opened and there was Wilson, striding toward her desk, looking like he was mad enough to shoot her. She noticed that the right side of his shaved head was covered with painful-looking, blistery red splotches.

"He wasn't there," Wilson said. "Just like I fuckin' told you."

She'd sent Wilson and three other guys out to the woods near San Carlos because she'd gotten a tip that a guy they'd been trying to nab for six months was hiding there in a broken-down trailer. The tip, however, had come from a really unreliable source and she knew it was pretty unlikely that it would pan out. Wilson, of course, had been adamant the tip wouldn't pan out—and it looked like he was right.

"What happened to your head?" she asked.

Wilson's lips moved a couple of times—like he was so angry he couldn't get the words out. "Poison oak."

Had it been anybody but Wilson she would have said *You need to get over to the emergency room right away and get something for it.* But since it was Wilson, she said, "I guess you should have worn a hat."

27

Caesar walked into the conference room in the operations center wearing a mud-splattered T-shirt, jeans, and scuffed cowboy boots. On his head was a blue, sweat-stained New York Yankees baseball cap. He'd been riding ATVs in the mountains near his Sinaloa estate with his daughters.

One of the things Mora had always admired about Caesar Olivera was that he didn't allow business to interfere with his personal life. Caesar would delegate a task, expect his people to perform, and he didn't—unlike Raphael Mora—pester them every few hours asking for progress reports.

The only ones sitting at the conference table were Mora and Juan Guzmán, the man who had been Tito's second-in-command in San Diego and who was now managing Caesar's U.S. operations. Guzmán was a heavyset, brutal-looking man about Caesar's age, and although he looked like a thug, he was quite intelligent. Mora was surprised, however, that Juan was still among the living; Caesar was still angry with the man for his failure to know about Tito's plan to kill Cadillac Washington.

Caesar took his seat at the head of the table and gestured for Mora to begin.

"We're ready," Mora said. "We have everything we need to know about the Hamilton woman and her daughter. We know where María Delgato is located, and I have a ten-man team in Washington State standing by for your command to proceed. The actor's ready and—"

"Are you sure he's ready?"

"Yes, sir. I've conducted numerous drills with him, so he's prepared to deal with a variety of scenarios. He's not a courageous man, but he knows what's at stake. And it's . . . I don't know how to describe it, but he's an *actor* and he really gets into the role during the drills. I believe he'll do fine, and, of course, if things go well he won't have to do anything but stand there."

Caesar nodded. "Continue," he said.

"The identity documents for the actor have been prepared. They're perfect. I have arranged for transportation to get Tito across the border and will have a team at the border to expedite the crossing and deal with any unforeseen issues we might encounter there."

Caesar wasn't worried about the border crossing. Moving people, drugs, and weapons back and forth across the Mexican border was something the Olivera cartel did every day. "Who's going to meet with Hamilton?"

"I am," Mora said. "That's not a job I feel comfortable delegating."

"Good," Caesar said. "How will you monitor the American response when Tito is freed?"

Caesar knew the American reaction to Tito's escape

would be massive, involving marines at Camp Pendleton, the California Highway Patrol, DEA agents, federal marshals, Homeland Security personnel at the border, and the police departments of every city between Camp Pendleton and the border.

Answering Caesar's question, Mora said, "We'll obviously be monitoring the American media. Our informants at Camp Pendleton and in the San Diego Police Department will provide intelligence updates, and Juan will have people in several locations monitoring radio traffic. The operation will begin at midnight, when there will be less chance of traffic congestion and delays at the border crossing. If everything goes as planned, Tito will arrive in Tijuana an hour and a half after he departs Pendleton."

"And the Russian chemical?" Caesar asked.

Mora smiled, a rare sight. "It works exactly as I was told it would. I've personally tested it on a dozen men." Then, knowing how Caesar felt about Juan Guzmán, he said, "If you'd like, I could give you a demonstration using Juan for a subject."

"I think I'd like that," Caesar said.

"Really, sir, is that necessary?" Juan Guzmán said, terrified of being used as Raphael Mora's guinea pig.

"Yes, it's necessary," Caesar said. It wasn't necessary, but he was going to enjoy the demonstration.

"Do you intend to carry out the operation on the Delgato woman before you free Tito?" Caesar asked Mora.

"No, sir. I believe that would be a mistake. If we kill her first, the marshals might change the security procedures at the brig, which is the last thing we want to happen at this point. The woman is of secondary importance to freeing Tito."

"No, she's not," Caesar said. "I want her to pay for what she did, and I don't want to wait any longer."

"I realize that, sir. I just believe it would be prudent to get Tito out of Camp Pendleton before we begin the operation against the woman. She'll be taken care of as soon as Tito is free."

Caesar sat for a moment, going through everything in his head one last time. He couldn't think of any more questions.

"Raphael, have you seen my condo in Tehuantepec?"

Mora frowned, not understanding the connection between the operations he was planning and Caesar Olivera's oceanside condo in southern Mexico. And Caesar knew that he'd seen the condo; he had been there a dozen times with Caesar. "Yes, sir," he said.

"If both operations are successful, it's yours."

Mora immediately said, "You don't need to do that, sir. I'm just doing my job, and you pay me very well."

"Consider the condo a well-deserved bonus," Caesar said. "Now, the demonstration. Are you ready, Juan?"

Caesar looked down at Juan Guzmán. He was lying on the floor of the conference room, sprawled on his back, an expression of shock frozen on his face. His eyes were open, and Caesar almost told Mora to close them, the way you'd do with a corpse. Caesar couldn't tell if the man was breathing or not.

"That was impressive," Caesar said.

"Yes," Mora said, "and the chemical could be useful in the future, but there are problems with it. About one person in ten thousand has an allergic reaction, and it's fatal."

Caesar kicked Guzmán's shoe; the man still didn't move. "But for this operation it doesn't matter if it's fatal, does it?" Caesar said.

"No, sir," Mora said.

28

Jessica walked toward the bus stop, thinking that it had been a pretty good day. She'd gotten a ninety-eight on a math test—the only one in the class who scored a hundred was that freak, Jacob Goldman—and she had been invited to a pool party at Taylor Campbell's place on Saturday. Taylor was a bit full of herself—probably because her dad owned half the real estate in downtown San Diego and she was the only kid who drove a Porsche to school—but Taylor was all right, and someone like Wolfgang Puck would probably cater.

The important thing about the party, however, was that Jessica had heard that Bobby McGuire was going, and he was going alone. She had a serious case of the hots for Bobby McGuire. Right now he was dating Judy Reeves, who was beautiful—and dumber than a box of rocks. But Bobby was her lab partner in chemistry, and Jessica could tell he liked talking to her and appreciated the fact that she had a brain in her head. Yeah, he'd eventually come around—and letting him see her in a bikini couldn't hurt.

She knew if she went to the party, Kay would grill her about Taylor's parents and check to make sure they were going to be there. Hell, knowing Kay, she'd probably look them up in some FBI database. She'd also give her the usual lecture about how she was going to kill her if she did any dope and, in her stumbling, mumbling way, Kay would tell her not to screw anybody at the party. Kay had a hard time talking about sex, and Jessica wondered if getting pregnant at such an early age had messed her up for life. Whatever the case, she hadn't had a date, as far as Jessica knew, since she'd moved in with her, which struck her as really strange.

It was possible that when Kay said she had to go out at night on stakeouts or to arrest someone she was really sneaking off to meet some guy. She didn't think so, however. For one thing, when Kay went out at night she was usually dressed all in black—black pullovers, black jeans, even black tennis shoes. One time she came back in the morning with camo paint on her face. And when she did have to work nights, she also usually called about two dozen times to make sure Jessica had set the alarm. Or maybe she called to make sure Jessica hadn't left the house. One other thing she noticed was that Kay always looked really happy when she was wearing her night stalker clothes and strapping on her Glock; she really seemed to get a kick out of what she did, like it was all a big game to her.

Thinking about Kay's midnight ninja outfit made Jessica wonder if she should get something new to wear for the party. She'd looked in Kay's closet one time when Kay was out of the house—maybe she shouldn't have, but she was just curious—and Kay had a lot of really neat, sexy clothes, most of them with Miami labels. None of Kay's clothes would fit her unless she grew four inches, but she could tell Kay had a sense of style and she knew that she didn't. Kay had offered to take her shopping a bunch of times, and now Jessica thought maybe she should take her up on the offer before the party.

There was something else she found in the closet that day. In a box on the top shelf were a bunch of old photos, mostly pictures of Kay at parties, or skiing, or dressed up in combat fatigues at one of those stupid paintball-shooting places. There were a lot of pictures of one guy in the box—a real stud—and Kay looked like she was in her early twenties when the pictures were taken. She wondered who the guy was. But there was one other picture in the box, way down at the bottom, in an envelope. The return address on the envelope was from a Marilyn Hamilton, who Jessica knew was Kay's mother, and it was postmarked fourteen years earlier. Inside the envelope was a faded snapshot of a chubby-cheeked blond baby who Jessica was certain was her. What hurt was that the picture was on the bottom of the box and Jessica could tell that Kay hadn't looked at it in years.

Aw, it was too nice a day to think about stuff like that.

The bus, for once, was on time, but the only seat she could find was next to an old guy who had to be at least sixty and whose breath smelled like he'd gargled with garlic. She was surprised when the old guy started playing a game on his smartphone. As the bus ride continued, she thought about summer. School would be out in a couple of days, and so far she hadn't made any plans other than surfing. There was a two-week DNA class at UCLA for high school kids who had the science prerequisites, and she'd applied and been accepted, but she hadn't talked to Kay about it. She was thinking it would be nice to spend some time on a college campus— and it would be good for both her and Kay to be apart for a while—but the class started just a couple weeks after the school year ended and she wanted to take a little break from studying.

She got off the bus, strolling to their house, wondering what she could have for dinner. She couldn't count on Kay for dinner. Some days she'd get home and fix something—spaghetti with Paul Newman marinara sauce was Kay's idea of a gourmet meal—but most of the time she'd just bring home something she'd picked up at a fast-food joint. And unless Jessica nagged her about it, there was never anything in the house to eat.

But Kay was . . . well, she was okay. Maybe she didn't want to be a mother, but Jessica could tell she was at least trying to make an effort to act like one. The problem was they really didn't have anything in common. When Kay was at home, she usually worked on the house, doing little carpentry projects, and when she wasn't doing that, she watched TV. Jessica had yet to see her crack open a book. She asked once if Jessica wanted to go to the firing range with her to shoot guns, and she could tell Kay was offended when she said she had absolutely no interest in learning how to kill. She probably should have been a little more diplomatic.

One thing she was really grateful to Kay for was introducing her to surfing. She just loved to surf. Which made her think about Randy Schommer. The guy was going to college next year, he was a hunk, and he should have been totally out of her league, but he spent more time with her than anyone else in the class. She also noticed Kay giving him the evil eye when she saw Randy talking to her after class the previous Saturday. For a woman who had never wanted anything to do with her since the day she was born, Kay was *way* overprotective.

The van stopped so fast its tires skidded. She turned to look at it—and then just stood there, paralyzed, when two Hispanic guys jumped out of the van and ran toward her. They were on her so fast she didn't even have time to scream before one of them clamped a hand over her mouth and muscled her into the van.

Oh, Jesus. She was going to be raped.

29

Kay got home at six, thinking she should have stopped along the way and picked up something for dinner. She just hoped there was something in the house to eat.

Kay opened the front door—and immediately smelled cigarette smoke.

I'm gonna kill that kid. "Jessica!" she yelled.

She stepped into the living room and saw a man sitting on her couch, looking completely relaxed, his legs crossed, smoking a brown cigarette. She whipped the Glock out of its holster and pointed it at his face. "You move and I'll blow your head off."

The man dropped the cigarette into a coffee cup he'd been using for an ashtray and showed Kay his hands, palms outward, a gesture to convince her he wasn't armed. He wasn't big, not much taller than Kay, and he probably didn't weigh more than a hundred and fifty pounds. He looked Hispanic, medium-dark complexion, short dark hair, a thin mustache. He was wearing a brown suit, a tan shirt, no tie.

Kay was about to tell him to stand so she could frisk him, when he said, "I'm sure you could blow my head off, Agent Hamilton, but if you do, your daughter will die."

"What?" Kay said.

"I'd suggest you put the pistol away and sit down so we can talk. We don't have much time."

Kay took two long strides toward him and pressed the muzzle of the Glock against his forehead. Just the way she'd done with Tito Olivera the day she arrested him. "What did you say about my daughter?"

"You heard what I said. If you don't cooperate, she'll die. Now, rather than waste more time, please open the laptop." He gestured to a white MacBook that Kay hadn't noticed sitting on the coffee table in front of him.

Kay backed away from him and, still pointing the gun at him, said, "You open it."

"Very well," the man said, as if she was being childish. He opened the laptop and turned it so Kay could see the screen. "Are you familiar with Skype?"

Kay nodded, feeling a knot begin to grow in her stomach.

He tapped the mouse and the screen came to life, and Kay could see Jessica sitting in a straight-backed wooden chair. She wasn't bound, but a man was standing behind her and holding a gun to her head. Kay couldn't see the man's face. Jessica looked all right; her hair was a bit mussed and her eyes were red from crying, but she wasn't bruised or bleeding. At least no place that was visible.

"Say something to your daughter, Agent Hamilton, so you'll know the transmission is live and that you're not looking at a recorded image."

"Jessica, have they hurt you?"

"Oh, God, Kay, help me."

She didn't think she'd get an answer to her next question, but she asked anyway. "Where are you, Jessica?"

"I don't know. Some guys threw me into a van when I got off the bus. I don't know where I am. I don't know what they want."

Jessica got off the bus almost three hours ago. She could be almost anywhere, and the wall behind her was a gray concrete surface, no windows, no pictures, nothing on it.

"Kay, what do they *want* with me?" Jessica said, and as soon as she said this the man sitting in Kay's living room closed the laptop.

"If anything happens to my daughter, I'm going to kill you," Kay said.

"Possibly," the man said. "Now, please sit down."

Kay took a seat, keeping the Glock in her hand.

"My name is Raphael Mora and I work for Caesar Olivera. I tell you this because I know my name and photo are in DEA and Mexican police databases and I don't want you wasting time trying to figure out who I am. You also need to know who I am and who I work for to understand the . . . the capabilities of the people you're dealing with."

Now that he'd said his name, Kay did remember him from the DEA's files. He was one of Caesar's top people and as smart as they come.

"You are going to assist Mr. Olivera by helping his brother escape from the brig at Camp Pendleton," Mora said. "If you don't do what Mr. Olivera wants, we won't kill your daughter. What we'll do is turn her into a heroin addict and place her in a whorehouse in a large city in Mexico or Central America. I imagine she'll die in a few years—heroin addicts tend to have short lives— but before she dies . . . well, you're an intelligent woman and I'm sure you can imagine what her life will be like."

Kay started to come out of the chair she was sitting in, intending to smash the Glock into Mora's smug face. She stopped when she was halfway up and settled back into the chair. If she knocked him unconscious, she'd have to wait until he recovered to question him.

Seeing her reaction, Mora said, "Good. I can see that you're starting to think instead of reacting emotionally. You need to be in control of your emotions to do what needs to be done."

"If you don't tell me where my daughter is, I'm going to start shooting you. I'll start with your kneecaps. I'll torture you until you tell me what I need to know."

"I'll be happy to tell you where she's being kept," Mora said. "She's in a house in Tijuana. But knowing where your daughter is won't do you any good, Agent Hamilton. The house is being protected by Caesar Olivera's men, and as you probably know, Mr. Olivera essentially controls the Mexican police as it relates to his business ventures. Assuming you could even mount an attack against the house, and assuming further that you could overwhelm Mr. Olivera's forces, your daughter would be killed. In fact, if I don't report back to Mr. Olivera in the next half hour and tell him that you've agreed to cooperate, then we're back to the scenario where your pretty young daughter joins a popular brothel."

"How do you expect me to get Tito out of Camp Pendleton? He's in a military brig, guarded by marines as well as federal marshals. There's no way to break him out of there."

"I know exactly how Tito is being guarded. I've had months to acquire that information. And you won't be breaking him out. You'll simply walk out with him."

"How would I do that?"

"I take it by that question that you've decided to help Mr. Olivera. Is that correct?"

"No. If I get Tito out of Pendleton, how would the exchange be made for my daughter?"

"An excellent question. Once Tito has been freed from the brig, you'll transport him to the San Diego border crossing in a specially designed vehicle we use for moving people in and out of the United States. I came here today in that vehicle, as a matter of fact. As soon as you and Tito are clear of Camp Pendleton, you'll meet the transport vehicle, Tito will be placed in a hidden compartment in the vehicle, and you will proceed to the border alone with Tito. In other words, you will have Tito and we will have your daughter; thus you'll be somewhat able to control the exchange."

"If I break Tito out of the brig, they're going to be looking for me at the border crossings."

"No, they won't. I'll explain why later. So, as I was saying, once you reach the border crossing you'll get into the far left-hand lane and you'll see your daughter accompanied by two men. There will actually be many men in the area to deal with any sort of trouble, but you'll see two of these men with your daughter. As you begin to cross the border, the men with her will let her go and she'll start walking toward the American side. You'll be able to see her walking. Your daughter is of no value to us—not even as a young whore—and we have no desire to keep her once we have Tito back. As your daughter walks into the United States, you will drive into Mexico with Tito. If you get out of the vehicle before you cross the border, or if anyone else attempts to interfere with the exchange, a sniper will shoot your daughter."

Kay tried to think of some way out of this. She knew Mora was right: There was no way to mount some sort of SWAT attack against a house in Tijuana to free her daughter—assuming she could even find the house. She also knew Caesar Olivera wouldn't exchange her daughter for Mora if she threatened to kill or arrest Mora. She knew Mora was a vital cog in the Olivera machine, but in the end, he was just an employee. She also suspected that she was Plan A. That if she didn't do what Olivera wanted, Mora's Plan B would be to kill her and her daughter and find somebody else to execute his plan. She figured that her being a federal agent was critical to Mora's plan, but there were a lot of other federal agents Mora could force to cooperate by kidnapping their spouses or children. She didn't immediately see a way out of the box she was in—and the thought of Jessica servicing men in a Mexican whorehouse was just too awful to contemplate.

Kay didn't bother to ask what would happen to her if she did what Mora wanted. She knew if she asked, Mora would lie. Kay knew she was going to be killed, and most likely in a very bad way, as soon as she handed Tito over.

She also knew, in that instant, and she was surprised by her certainty, that she was willing to sacrifice her life to save her daughter.

The only good news was that she'd have time to think of a way to screw up Mora's plan before she reached the border crossing. There was no way in hell she was going to make the exchange in the manner Mora had described.

"How do I get Tito out of the brig?" she finally asked.

30

Jessica came to in a small, windowless room with bare concrete walls. The only furniture in the room was a bed; there was a mattress on the bed, but no sheets or blankets. Her watch, her cell phone, and her shoes had been taken from her. She had a headache and her mouth was very dry.

She was still wearing her school clothes—the pink polo shirt and knee-length khaki shorts she'd worn to school. She didn't think they'd done anything to her. Yet.

She didn't understand why they'd kidnapped her. The guys who snatched her had been young, in their late teens or early twenties, with shaved heads and lots of tats; they looked like gangbangers, and Jessica initially thought that they were going to rape her. But as soon as they got her into the van, a woman who was older than the men, maybe thirty, gave her an injection while the gangsters held her still. Then she woke up in the windowless room, which she suspected was in the basement of some building.

She didn't think they'd kidnapped her for ransom. Kay wasn't rich; she worked for the government. Jessica wondered if they'd mistaken her for the daughter of some rich kid who went to her school. Another possibility occurred to her, one that made more sense than kidnapping her for money: Kay was a cop, and maybe this was somebody's way of getting back at her for someone she'd arrested.

No, this wasn't about money, and she didn't think it was about revenge. She thought it more likely that this was about sex. She'd read about young women in foreign countries being kidnapped and sold as sex slaves and turned into prostitutes. It happened all the time in places like Asia and South America and Mexico. She'd seen a movie a couple years earlier called *Taken*, in which Liam Neeson's daughter in the movie, a girl about her age, is kidnapped and sold for an enormous price to some pervert because she's a virgin. Jessica was still a virgin. But how would they know that? Had they done some kind of exam on her while she was unconscious? The thought made her want to throw up.

The fact that no one had worn masks really bothered her, too, neither the guys who grabbed her nor the woman who gave her the injection. They obviously didn't care that she'd seen their faces—and that meant that either they were going to kill her or send her someplace where they were sure no one would ever find her.

She started to cry.

Half an hour later, the door opened and she moved into a corner, her back up against the wall. There was nothing in the room to use for a weapon, but she was going to fight them with every ounce of strength she had.

The guy who opened the door was her worst night-

mare. He was about forty, Hispanic, a huge gross guy
with a beer belly, greasy hair hanging down to his shoulders, and a week's worth of black beard. Behind him was
a younger guy, in his twenties. He was short and wiry, a
weaselly little guy, also Hispanic. He had dark hair tied
into a ponytail, a sharp nose, and a stupid little strip of
hair under his lower lip.

She might be able to fight off the little guy—the
Weasel—but the big one was like a bear and weighed well
over two hundred pounds. This was not the way she'd ever
expected to lose her virginity.

Jessica knew several girls her age who had already had
sex, but she didn't feel ready for sex just yet. And now,
knowing how Kay had gotten pregnant at fifteen, she
felt even less ready. But she'd always figured that when
she did have sex for the first time, it would be with a nice
guy, someone a little older than her and someone she
really liked, even if she wasn't in love with him, and it
would occur in some romantic setting and not in the
backseat of a car. What she had never imagined was losing her virginity by being raped by two men like this.

The men didn't approach her, however. They stood
in the doorway, and the big one rattled off a bunch of
words in Spanish. Kay spoke Spanish like she'd been
raised in Mexico City, and Jessica was taking Spanish in
school at Kay's insistence. Kay said if you lived in California, speaking Spanish made sense, particularly when it
came to finding a job. But she couldn't follow the big
guy; he was talking too fast.

Seeing she didn't understand, the big one turned to

the Weasel and said, "Carlos," and the little one said, "My cousin asked if you are thirsty. Do you want some water?"

Hell, yes, she wanted some water. Her mouth was bone dry, probably from the drug they shot into her. But just like the men who kidnapped her not wearing masks, it bothered her that these two weren't wearing masks and that the big one had used the other one's name.

"Well?" Carlos said. "Do you want water or not?"

"Why am I here?" Jessica said. "Why did you kidnap me?"

"That will be explained to you later," he said.

"Yes," Jessica said, "I want some water." Then she added, "Please."

Carlos turned and left the room. The big one continued to look at her, his eyes showing nothing. He wasn't leering at her, nothing creepy like that; he was just staring at her in a dull sort of way, and Jessica got the impression he wasn't too bright. A moment later, Carlos returned and handed her a bottle of water.

"You can scream if you want," he said. "No one will hear you. If you need something, pound on the door. We'll feel the vibrations. But don't be a pest, or I'll hurt you."

And Jessica knew—even if she couldn't explain how she knew—that Carlos would enjoy hurting her. He might enjoy hurting her even more than having sex with her.

He closed the door, and she heard the lock being turned—and she was alone again to wonder what was going to happen to her.

* * *

Jessica drank the entire bottle of water and, half an hour later, wished she hadn't; now she needed to pee. She waited another ten minutes, then gave up and rapped on the door, softly at first, then harder, and Carlos finally opened the door.

"I have to go to the bathroom," she said.

"Come," he said, and stepped aside so she could get by him. He stunk from some kind of cheap cologne. "Down the hall," he said, and pointed.

She stepped out of the room and saw she was in a narrow corridor with concrete walls and overhead fluorescent lights and several closed doors along the corridor. She took a few more steps and came to an open door, the bathroom. There was a toilet and a small sink, and she was surprised to see they were clean. She started to close the door after she entered the bathroom, but Carlos said, "No. You must leave the door open."

"I'm not going to pee with you watching me," she said.

He shrugged. "Then go back to your room."

This couldn't be happening to her. She wasn't going to let this guy watch her pee. She'd pee on the floor of her room rather than allow that. She walked back to her room—her cell—and she heard Carlos laughing as he locked the door.

She didn't pee on the floor; she didn't want to have to live with the mess and the smell. She simply tried not to think about peeing, but she didn't know how long that was going to work. She tried to think of other things, pleasant things, good memories from the past. She tried to remember what her mother had looked like before the cancer had eaten her alive; her mother hadn't been pretty—not like Kay—but she had the kindest, sweetest face. She remembered a trip they all took to Yellowstone and how her father, who was the smartest man she knew, couldn't figure out how to pitch the tent and had to ask some guy camping next to them for help. But it didn't work. The only things she could think of were all the awful things that might happen to her.

Five years earlier she'd had a perfect life: good parents who loved her and protected her, a nice house, a nice school. Then it was almost as if God woke up one day and said *Let's see how this kid does when things aren't so nice.* Her father dying, her mother getting laid off, the move to Cleveland, her mother dying. And now she was living with a woman who may have been her biological mother but who didn't really want anything to do with her. Her family—her real family—had never been church-goers, and Jessica had always felt that it was hypocritical to pray only when you were in trouble. But she'd never been in this kind of trouble before; what could she do now but pray?

The door opened and both of them were there again, the big, gross one and Carlos. What did they want now? Were they going to rape her now?

"Come," Carlos said. "Señor Perez wants you."

Perez? Was he the one in charge? she wondered; Carlos had called him Señor. And what did he mean when he said Perez *wanted* her? Jessica didn't move.

The big one cursed in Spanish and stepped toward her, and she came off the bed swinging. She hit him in the left eye with her right fist. He cursed, grabbed her arm before she could hit him again, then got a one-handed grip on the nape of her neck, the way you'd grab a puppy, and dragged her out of the room, her bare feet skidding on the concrete floor. The big one was fat, but he was incredibly strong.

He took her down the hallway, past the bathroom she refused to use, and into another room, where there was a man sitting in a chair in front of a small table. On the table was a laptop and behind the table was a second chair. The Bear forced her to sit in the vacant chair and then held her in place by pushing down on her shoulders.

The man sitting across the table from her was in his thirties, clean-shaven, short hair, also Hispanic. There was something military about him. Maybe because he had a light green shirt with those little button-down flaps on the shoulders like epaulets. This must be Perez. And where Carlos and the Bear looked like they might be laborers, this guy looked like management.

In English, with only a slight Spanish accent, Perez said, "Sit there and be quiet or I'll slap the shit out of you. In a couple of minutes you're going to have a Skype conversation with your mother."

For five minutes they sat looking at each other, the

man smoking, flicking the ashes onto the floor, his eyes glancing frequently at the computer screen.

"I have to go to the bathroom," Jessica finally said. Her bladder felt like it was going to burst.

"Why didn't you go earlier?" he said.

Pointing at Carlos, she said, "Because he said he had to watch me go."

"He does. Those are his orders. We have to make sure you don't do something to harm yourself. He's not going to do anything to you, and as soon as we talk to your mother, you can go to the toilet. If you're too modest to pee in front of him, piss your pants. I don't care."

She'd just learned something really important: They needed her alive and uninjured—at least for the moment.

Then Jessica heard a man's voice, coming from the computer, say, "Are you familiar with Skype?"—and Perez turned the laptop so Jessica could see the screen. The time shown in the upper right-hand corner of the screen said it was six-fifteen p.m. She wondered if that was Pacific Standard Time; if it was, she'd been kidnapped about three hours before.

When Perez turned the laptop toward her, the Bear, keeping his left hand on her shoulder to keep her in the chair, pulled out a big black pistol and placed the muzzle of the gun against the right side of her head. Oh, Jesus, were they going to execute her? She thought they needed her alive.

The laptop screen flickered and she could see Kay.

She was sitting in the living room of their house in San Diego. Then she heard: "Say something to your daughter, Agent Hamilton, so you'll know the transmission is live and that you're not looking at a recorded image."

"Jessica, have they hurt you?" Kay said.

"Oh, God, Kay, help me."

"Where are you, Jessica?"

"I don't know. Some guys threw me into a van when I got off the bus. I don't know where I am. I don't know what they want. Kay, what do they *want* with me?"

Then the screen went dark and Kay was gone.

"What do you want with me?" Jessica asked Perez, struggling not to cry. She wasn't going to let these people see her cry.

"We want your mother to do something for us, and if she wants you back, she will. If she's successful, you'll be set free tomorrow. If she fails or refuses to co-operate . . . well, there's no need to burden you with what will happen next." To Carlos he said in English, "Take her back to her room. Bring her some food, no forks or spoons. And let her go to the bathroom, and don't be a creep about it."

In the bathroom, with Carlos staring at her, she pulled down her shorts as little as possible, giving him the barest glimpse of her thighs. She was embarrassed to hear her urine tinkling into the toilet, and he could tell she was embarrassed and he smiled. She finished urinating, pulled up her shorts, didn't bother to wash her hands, and Carlos grasped her upper arm to lead her back to her room. She noticed again that he wasn't much taller than she was and he didn't seem very strong; his hands were small. He said something to her in Spanish, something that he must have thought was funny, because he laughed. Then he locked the door.

She thought she might be able to take Carlos if she had the chance. After her dad died, and before her mom got breast cancer, her mom insisted they take a self-defense class together. Jessica didn't know if her mom was feeling vulnerable or just wanted to do something the two of them could do together. The main thing they were taught in the class was that if you couldn't just run away screaming your head off, then strike fast and hard and someplace where your attacker would feel a lot of pain: gouge his eyes, smash his nose, kick him in the nuts. Jessica had never had the opportunity to use what she'd been taught, but she figured she could do it if she had to. She was fast, she was pretty strong for her size, and the biggest thing she had going for her was that Carlos wasn't that big. The other guy, however, the Bear—she'd never stand a chance against him. But if it was just her against Carlos . . .

Now she also had some idea of what was going on. Kay was DEA, and these guys had kidnapped her to force her to do something, probably something involving drugs in Mexico. Maybe they wanted Kay to help them sneak heroin or grass into the U.S. Maybe they wanted Kay not to arrest somebody she was planning to arrest. The thing was, she didn't know if Kay would do what they wanted. She knew Kay liked her—but *like* wasn't the same as a mother's love.

She started to cry again, wishing more than anything that her real mom were still alive. Her real mom had loved her.

31

Mora explained to Kay how she was going to get Tito out of the brig—and Kay was impressed. She was impressed not only by the audacity of his idea but also by the fact that he had access to the type of materials she would be using. The reach of the Olivera cartel was clearly global. Whether or not Mora's plan would work, however, was something Kay couldn't be sure of until it was too late to back out.

"Your partner will be here at ten p.m.," Mora said. It was seven-thirty. "I'm leaving now. I need to get back to Tijuana. I would suggest you eat and sleep a bit if you can. You have a long night ahead of you. I realize that after I leave you might call the people you work with, the FBI, or the marshals. I can't stop you from doing that. But remember, I'll be with your daughter. If you don't follow my plan, you'll never see her again and she'll suffer incredibly."

After Mora left, Kay sat for a while thinking about how terrified Jessica must be, but she knew thinking about Jessica wasn't going to help. Instead she thought about her options. Should she call her boss or the FBI? The problem with getting either the DEA or the FBI involved was that these were federal agencies, and no way would they agree to exchange Tito for Jessica. The other thing was that Jessica was in Mexico and no federal agency was going to go into Mexico to attempt to free her without involving the Mexican government—and if the Mexican government got involved, Caesar Olivera, with his contacts, would know and her daughter would die. Kay finally concluded that she was on her own and the only option she had was to do what Mora wanted: break Tito out of the brig. But once she had Tito, things would be different. Then she'd have some leverage.

She thought about what she should take with her. She would need her passport to cross into Mexico—*if* she crossed into Mexico. She also had a second passport and a Florida driver's license issued in the name of Elle McDonald; McDonald had been her cover name in Miami when she was living with Marco Álvarez. She decided to take those documents, too, as much cash as she had in the house, and a pair of handcuffs.

She also decided to take one other item, a little surprise for Tito. She placed the item in the pocket on the driver's-side door of her Camry, the place where she usually stored a few CDs.

K ay left San Diego in her own car at ten-thirty p.m. It was about forty miles to Pendleton, and by the time she got through security, it would be close to midnight, and that's when Mora wanted the operation to begin.

Following Kay's car was a minivan driven by a Hispanic man wearing a white cowboy hat. The minivan was the specially designed vehicle that would be used for transporting Tito Olivera across the border. Mora had told Kay that she was to drive her own car to the brig, since it had government decals on it and in case the marines asked to see her registration and proof of insurance before allowing her onto the base. They sometimes did that.

Before they reached the town of Oceanside on I-5, Kay watched in the rearview mirror as the minivan took a right onto Highway 76 heading east. Kay was going to enter Camp Pendleton through the main gate off I-5. But when she had Tito—once she'd freed him from the brig—she was going to leave Pendleton via the San Luis Rey Gate, the southeast gate, and meet the minivan on a road called North River Road. The reason for this was that they didn't want to put Tito in the minivan near the Pendleton main gate or on the I-5 freeway, as these areas were too populated, even after midnight. North River Road, however, was a two-lane road passing through tracts of farmland—tomato and avocado farms and small orchards—and no one would see Tito slipping into the hidden compartment in the minivan.

Once Tito was in the van, Kay would drive to Escondido and take the I-15 freeway south forty-five miles to the San Diego border crossing. The minivan driver would take her car and drive north—in the opposite direction—for about fifty miles and abandon it. The idea was that once the various law-enforcement agencies began looking for Kay and Tito, if Kay's car was found north of Pendleton, it might confuse the searchers for a while.

Sitting in the passenger seat of Kay's car was her "partner"—a man with a full head of neatly trimmed blond hair, a blond mustache, and blue eyes. The minivan driver had dropped him off at Kay's house precisely at ten, as Mora had said. He wore black-framed glasses, a light-weight jacket over a blue polo shirt, khakis, and loafers. Like Kay, he was dressed casually but in a manner appropriate for their supposed assignment.

She didn't know the man's real name. When she met him, he introduced himself as Doug Kirk—DEA Agent Douglas Kirk. He spoke English without an accent—he sounded like any other Californian—and his DEA credentials, which he showed her, appeared to be identical to hers; if they were forgeries, they certainly would have fooled her.

Kay was wearing a blazer over a white T-shirt, jeans, and running shoes. She was dressed for running or fighting—but also appropriately for the mission. On her hip was her .40-caliber Glock in a holster. Mora had told her to dress as she normally would for a visit to Camp Pendleton, and he hadn't said anything about her taking or not taking her sidearm. Mora didn't care if she had a weapon; he knew she wasn't going to shoot anyone—not if she wanted Jessica back. Kay didn't know if Kirk was armed or not.

Kay and Kirk didn't speak during the drive—there was no reason for them to speak—until they were about a mile from Pendleton, when Kirk said, "Please pull over. Immediately."

"Why?" Kay said.

"Please. Pull over. I'm going to be sick."

Kay pulled her car onto the shoulder of the road and Kirk opened the door, spun sideways in his seat, and vomited. He sat there for several seconds with his head down between his legs, then closed the door.

Oh, great, Kay thought. Her daughter's life depended on this clown; he'd better get a grip on himself.

"Do you have any gum or breath mints?" Kirk asked.

"Fuck you," Kay said.

They passed through the main gate at Pendleton without any problem, showing the guards their DEA credentials and explaining where they were headed, then drove approximately seven miles until Kay saw the sign for the brig. She made a right-hand turn, passed a couple of barracks that looked like college dorms, a fitness center, and an enlisted men's club before reaching the second checkpoint, the one blocking the access road to the brig.

They showed their IDs again, and one of the marines at the checkpoint called the brig to let the guards there know that Kay was headed their way. As she passed through the checkpoint, Kay noticed the machine gun mounted on a tripod near the concrete vehicle barriers—and she couldn't help but think how their bright idea for putting Tito Olivera on a military base, surrounded by thousands of marines, had turned out to be no obstacle at all for Raphael Mora. It was like the Maginot Line in France during World War II: The Germans just waltzed right past the fortifications and fixed artillery.

The brig was at the top of a small hill about a quarter mile from the checkpoint: a two-story brick structure painted an off-white color with green trim and surrounded by a chain-link fence topped with concertina wire. Two of the four guard towers were visible from the lot where Kay parked.

Kay placed her Glock on the floor beneath the driver's seat. To Kirk she said, "If you have a gun, leave it in the car. They won't let you bring a weapon into the brig."

"I don't have a weapon," Kirk said.

Kay then took her badge case out of the inside breast pocket of her blazer, where she normally kept it, and put the case in the left outside pocket, where she could reach it with her left hand.

From this point forward, her right hand couldn't touch anything.

Kirk stepped out of the car, pulled latex gloves from a pocket of the jacket he was wearing, and pulled them on. He then went and stood on the driver's side of the car, in front of the driver's window, so anyone walking by the car would have a harder time seeing what Kay was doing.

Kay reached back and grabbed a plastic Walgreens bag sitting on the backseat and placed it in her lap. From the bag she took a surgical mask and placed it over her mouth and nose and inserted her left hand into a latex glove. Mora had said that cloth and latex were adequate barriers.

Next she took a four-ounce sky-blue aerosol can of Secret deodorant/antiperspirant from the Walgreens bag. As near as Kay could tell, the can was identical to cans of Secret she'd seen in stores. She took the cap off the can and sprayed her bare right hand, front and back, making sure every square inch of her hand and wrist was covered. She looked at her watch and waited for three minutes to pass; the three minutes felt like an eternity.

Using her left hand, she reached into the Walgreens bag again and took out a second aerosol can, this one labeled as VO5 hair spray for "hard-to-hold hair." Kay didn't use hair spray, but she was willing to bet the can matched an actual VO5 container. She popped the top off the hair spray can using her thumb, then placed her right hand deep inside the Walgreens bag and sprayed the palm of her right hand. The clock was now ticking. According to Mora, she had fifteen minutes. God help her if the marines inside the brig slowed her down.

Using her left hand, she rapped on the car window, and Kirk opened the driver's-side door for her. Kirk then removed the surgical mask from her face, stripped the latex glove off her hand, and pulled off the gloves he was wearing. He tossed the gloves and the mask into the car, onto the floor in front of the backseat. Acting like the perfect gentleman, he opened the door for her when they entered the brig.

* * *

The guys on duty, a couple of jarheads who were probably eighteen or nineteen years old, were at the desk.
Behind them was a sergeant in his thirties with a pros-
thesis for a left hand. *Iraq or Afghanistan?* Kay wondered. Using her left hand, she took her ID case from
the pocket of her blazer and flipped it open.

"Kay Hamilton, DEA," she said. "This is Agent Kirk,"
she added, jerking her thumb toward Kirk—or whoever
the hell he was. Kirk, just as she had done, flipped open
his badge case and showed it to the marines. She was relieved to see that he seemed okay, like he was just a little
bit bored, and not like he was going to puke again.

"We're here to see Tito Olivera," Kay said.

"At this time of night?" the one-handed sergeant
said.

"Hey, what can I tell you?" Kay said. "We work for
the fuckin' government."

This got a laugh out of everybody, even Kirk.

"I gotta call the marshals and let them know you're
coming," the sergeant said.

"So call," Kay said. She'd already wasted two minutes with these guys.

"Are you armed?" the sergeant asked.

"No, we left our weapons in the trunk of the car. We
knew we couldn't bring them into the brig."

The sergeant picked up a phone and told the marshal
who answered that DEA agents Hamilton and Kirk
were here to see Tito. There was a pause, and the marine

said, "Yeah, of course I checked their IDs," sounding irritated that the marshal would even ask.

The sergeant hung up the phone and said to Kay, "I'll escort you down to the corridor where they're keeping Olivera, so you don't get lost. When you're ready to leave, use the marshal's phone to call me and then return to the cage outside the control point."

Kay didn't know what he meant by *the cage*, but all she said was "Gotcha."

Her back and underarms were soaked with sweat. It was a good thing she was wearing the blazer.

Kay and Kirk passed through a metal detector without it alarming, then the sergeant walked her and Kirk through two sets of locked doors, the first door only about ten feet from the second. The two doors formed the cage the sergeant had mentioned, and prisoners and visitors would be trapped between the two locked doors until one of the marines at the control point hit the electronic lock-release, permitting them access to the guard station. Above the first door there was also a camera, so the guards could see who was in the cage before opening the door.

After they passed through the second door, the sergeant walked them down to a tee in the hallway, turned left, and pointed. "Tito's down there," he said, and turned to go back to the control point.

Kay could see a guy standing down at the end of the corridor dressed in civilian clothes: one of the two marshals guarding Tito. The marshals, the poor bastards, had been living in an unlocked cell next to Tito's, and

Kay figured they had to be going out of their minds with boredom.

As Kay walked past several empty cells toward the marshal, she noticed that there were no cameras in the corridor—just as Mora had said. When she was about ten feet away, the marshal, a powerfully built black guy—not a guy Kay would have wanted to arm wrestle—said, "Why in the hell did they send you two out here so late at night? Nobody told us you were coming."

By now Kay had reached the marshals' cell. The second marshal was inside the cell and lying on a cot, reading a paperback. He sat up when he saw Kay. He wasn't as big as his partner—he was a lanky guy who looked like he might run marathons—but Kay knew he'd also be a handful in a fight.

In the marshals' cell was a TV set, a stack of paperbacks about a foot high, and a bunch of magazines. There was also a microwave—Kay got just a whiff of popcorn—a laptop, a cribbage board, and some free weights for doing curls. The place looked like a college kid's dorm room—except for the two pistols sitting on top of the microwave.

Kay stuck out her right hand. "Kay Hamilton," she said. The marshal responded, saying, "Bill Lincoln," and shook Kay's hand. Kay held on to his hand just a bit longer than she normally did when shaking hands. Releasing Lincoln's hand, she pointed at Kirk and said, "My partner, Doug Kirk."

Kirk, as he'd been told to do, stayed outside the cell and far enough away from the marshal that the marshal made no attempt to shake his hand. Kirk just gave a little wave and said, "Hey."

Stepping forward, Kay said to the second marshal, "Kay Hamilton," and again stuck out her right hand, and the second marshal automatically took it.

"Cal Rivers," the marshal said. "Glad to meet you."

Now, Kay hoped, it was just a matter of time.

"The reason we're here is we need to talk to Tito," Kay said. "We executed a warrant this evening on one of his scumbags and found a file in a computer that we need to ask him about right away."

"Don't you have to have his lawyer here?" Lincoln asked.

"Screw his lawyer," Kay said. "And this whole thing is probably a waste of time, as I imagine Tito isn't going to tell us shit, but our boss told us to talk to him, so we're here."

Lincoln started to say something else, but then he closed his eyes for a moment and rocked back slightly on his heels, as if he suddenly was having a hard time maintaining his balance. When he opened his eyes, he said, "Whoa."

"You okay, Marshal?" Kay asked. Before he could answer, she said, "Oh. Do you guys have the key to Tito's cell, or do I have to call the MPs up front?"

"We have one," Rivers said. "It's, it's . . . shit, it's right there." He pointed to an electronic keycard with a lanyard hanging on a wire hook near the cell door, but the way he spoke, he was clearly having a hard time completing a simple sentence.

Kay already knew the marshals had a key to Tito's cell. Mora had told her. She just wanted to know where it was so she wouldn't have to hunt for it.

Rivers had been standing when he spoke to Kay, but now he sat down slowly on the cot where he'd been lying when Kay and Kirk arrived. "Jesus," he said. "Something's wrong."

He fell over onto his side and collapsed on the cot.

Lincoln looked down at his partner, but his eyes seemed unable to focus. "What the fu—"

Then he started to fall, and Kay caught him so he wouldn't hit the floor too hard.

Kay wondered if she'd just killed the two men. Mora had told her the chemical on her right palm was absorbed through the skin and would incapacitate the marshals for at least two hours. It wouldn't kill them, Mora said, unless they had some sort of allergic reaction to the drug. She hoped to God he hadn't lied to her. She checked both marshals' pulses; they felt strong.

Kay was also relieved to see that the drug wasn't affecting her. The first substance she'd sprayed on her right hand had been a thin, rubberlike coating that would keep the drug from being absorbed through her skin. Mora had said that fifteen minutes after the knockout chemical was exposed to air, it became ineffective and could be washed off with water. There was no sink in the room, but there was a toilet. Kay plunged her right hand into the toilet bowl, swirled it around, and then wiped her hand on Lincoln's shirt. She plunged her hand into the bowl a second time and wiped it dry. All she could do now was hope that the chemical was gone; she could just see herself scratching her nose and passing out.

She took the keycard off the hook and unlocked the door to Tito's cell. She knew that when the door opened the marines at the control point would see a light turn from green to red, indicating the cell door had been unlocked. That wouldn't be a problem, however, since the marines knew that Kay and Kirk had come to talk to Tito and because the marshals were guarding him.

Tito's cell had a solid steel door, not bars, and Tito was on his feet, apparently waiting for her, when she opened the door. Mora had said that Tito knew she was coming tonight, and Kay figured that Tito's lawyer was the one who had passed the word to him.

"Hola, bitch," Tito said, smiling broadly.

"Let's go," Kay said.

Back in the marshals' cell, Kirk had stripped off his blond wig and mustache, popped the blue contact lenses out of his eyes, and dropped the contacts into the toilet. He then handed Tito a contact lens case and a small vial of saline solution, and said, "Put the contacts in," then began stripping off his clothes.

Tito, being careful not to drop the contact lenses, put them in his eyes. While he was doing this, Kirk stripped down to his underwear. Tito also stripped and put on Kirk's clothes, which fit him perfectly. Kay couldn't believe how much Kirk looked like Tito. He looked *exactly* like him; an identical twin wouldn't have been a better match.

"Please sit on the cot," Kirk said to Tito, and then he

put the blond wig on Tito's head, adjusting it slightly until he was satisfied. Taking a small tube, he applied some sort of glue to Tito's upper lip and attached the mustache. Tito put on Kirk's glasses and said to Kay, "How do I look?"

"You look like an asshole," Kay said, and Tito laughed.

Kirk was now dressed in Tito's clothes. He took a breath, like a man about to plunge into a deep pool, and walked over to Tito's cell and stepped inside. As Kay closed the cell door, she could see the fear in his eyes and knew he was thinking about the years he would spend in prison for helping Tito escape.

In two hours, the marshals would wake up. They'd know they'd been drugged in some manner, and the first thing they would do was check to see if Tito was still in his cell, and they would probably think that Kirk was Tito—at least initially, and for a few precious moments afterward. But in *less* than two hours—before the marshals regained consciousness—Kay would be across the border with Tito.

Soon, however—how soon was anyone's guess—somebody would figure out that it didn't make sense for Kay Hamilton to render two federal marshals unconscious unless it was to free Tito Olivera, and they'd take a harder look at Kirk. Maybe Tito had an identifying scar or birthmark and they'd be able to tell that Kirk was an impostor. Or maybe they'd jump right to a fingerprint check. All Kay knew for sure was that the marshals would be groggy for a bit, confused, do a quick check to see if Tito was still in his cell, then start making a bunch of phone calls.

There was another possibility, according to Mora. He knew from reports passed on by Tito's lawyer that the marines, particularly on the night shift when things were quiet throughout the brig, liked to bullshit with the marshals. So a marine might go down to the marshals' cell in less than two hours and find them unconscious. They'd check Tito's cell, see Tito—or a guy they thought was Tito—sitting there, then call for the medics. The end result was the same: By the time they talked to the marshals and figured out that Kirk wasn't Tito, Kay would be over the border.

"You know what to do?" Kay asked Tito.

"Yeah, I just follow your sweet ass out of here and keep my mouth shut. Then we get in your car and go to the beaner machine."

"The what?" Kay said.

Tito laughed. He was in a great mood, and either too arrogant or too stupid to know he should be nervous. "The beaner machine. What we use to move us beaners across the border. Anyway, we get to the transport vehicle, I hop in the compartment, and off we go to ol' Mexico." He pronounced it *May-hay-ko*.

Their exit from Pendleton went smoothly. She called the marines at the control point from the marshals' cell, and when she and Tito arrived at the holding cage, Kay smiled up at the camera and gave a little wave. The door locks clicked open, and Kay and Tito passed into the control point area. Kay said, "Thanks, guys," to the marines, and out the door they went. At the vehicle checkpoint closest to the brig, a marine shined his flashlight into the car, directly onto Tito's face—blond-haired, blue-eyed Tito—and they held up their IDs and were on their way.

As they passed through the Pendleton San Luis Rey Gate, Tito said, "I hope I get to spend a little time with you, chica, before this is all over. I owe you." Then he laughed and said, "Hey, I'm kidding. The trouble you're gonna be in with your own government, I don't need to do a thing to you."

Kay knew Tito was lying—he'd do something to make her suffer if he got the chance—but she figured Mora had told him to be nice to her, to maintain the illusion that she'd be set free after she handed Tito over.

"Give me your cell phone," Tito said, and Kay handed him her phone. Great. Now there would be a record of her calling someone in Olivera's outfit down in Mexico, making it look as if Kay had connections with the cartel down there.

Tito punched a number into Kay's phone and said, "Raphael, I'm on my way. We just left Pendleton. The bitch done good. I owe you big-time."

As Kay was driving toward North River Road, she couldn't help but think that Tito was right about the trouble she was in with the U.S. government. If she somehow, miraculously, got out of this whole thing alive, not only was her career over but she would probably end up in jail. It was almost funny. Three days earlier, she'd been so worried about playing office politics to get a promotion; now that was the least of her concerns.

As the old saying goes: *Man plans, God laughs.*

Five minutes later, God laughed again.

32

When Tito called Mora to tell him the first part of the escape had gone smoothly, Mora was in the house in Tijuana where Jessica was being held captive. After speaking to Tito, Mora smoked a cigarette while sipping a cup of espresso—it was going to be a long night—then made a call.

"Take care of the woman," he said. "Don't waste any time on the brother or the mother. Just kill them." He looked at his watch. It was almost one a.m. both in Tijuana and Neah Bay, Washington. "I want her found tomorrow. I want them to be able to identify her by her fingerprints, not by her face."

"Yes, sir," the man said. He, too, was ex-military, although he hadn't been an officer like Raphael Mora. He was also the most sadistic human being that Mora had ever known: Nothing gave him greater pleasure than inflicting pain, and if he hadn't worked for the Olivera cartel, he most likely would have been a serial killer. Well, technically, considering the number of people he'd slain, he probably was a serial killer—but he killed for Mora and not for himself

* * *

Mike Figgins died well.

He and Patterson had never taken turns staying awake all night, guarding the Delgatos. They both agreed there was no point in doing that, because they knew if Caesar Olivera found out where María was hiding, he'd send in a team to kill them, more men than he and Patterson could possibly fight off.

They had installed motion detectors outside the house when they first moved in with Miguel, but the damn animals—coons, possum, and deer—were constantly setting them off, so they disabled them. The only thing they did was lock the front and back doors with dead bolts that required a key to open them, and they only did that to keep María *in* the house.

Olivera's men came in through the front and back doors simultaneously, using SWAT-style battering rams. The first person they killed was Patterson. Patterson had a hard time sleeping and was standing in front of the refrigerator, wearing boxer shorts, a bottle of Maalox in one hand, when the back door exploded. A man cut him down with rounds fired from a silenced M4 before he could take a step.

When the doors were smashed open, everyone in the house woke up. Figgins immediately realized what was happening, jumped out of bed, and reached for the Colt lying on the night table next to his bed. He glanced toward the bed where Patterson slept and saw it was empty. He figured that Patterson had been unable to sleep and was stuffing his face with a midnight snack when the assault team came through the doors. He figured his best friend was already dead.

As he stuck his head out the bedroom door, he heard the spitting sound of silenced M4 rounds coming from the other end of the house, where Miguel slept; he could also hear María screaming. María was behind him, in the last bedroom down the hall where she slept with her mother. Two guys dressed in jeans and black sweatshirts, no masks, both holding assault rifles, were coming down the hall. Figgins shot one of them immediately. He wasn't a particularly good shot and he didn't know the men were wearing bulletproof vests, but he got lucky and hit one of the attackers in the face, killing him instantly. Before he could get off a second shot, he was hit by four bullets—in the left arm, the left side, two in his left thigh. The shots didn't come from the attackers coming down the hall; they came from outside the house. They were fired through the window into the bedroom where he'd been sleeping. It was apparent that these guys had scoped out the house and knew where everyone slept.

Figgins collapsed to the floor, and he knew he was dying. His gun was a couple inches away from his outstretched hand, so he decided to play dead. He figured it would only be about a minute before one of the shooters came down the hallway and put a bullet into his head.

But they didn't. The two shooters stepped over him and burst into María's bedroom. He heard more shots being fired and figured that they had killed both María and her mother, but a moment later María was dragged out of the bedroom wearing a T-shirt and panties. The men pulled her down the hall toward the living room.

As near as Figgins could tell, there were six of them in the house, including the dead man lying in the hallway. They were speaking Spanish, so he didn't know what they were saying, but he could hear them whooping and laughing—and María screaming. There was the sound of a slap, and María stopped screaming.

He could see one guy in the doorway where the hallway entered the living room; the guy's back was to him. He was holding a rifle in his hand, the barrel pointing down at the floor. Figgins grabbed his gun and started crawling, dragging himself down the hallway, since he couldn't walk. When he was ten feet from the living room, he could see María through the legs of the guy standing with his back to him. María was on the floor, naked. Two men were holding her arms, and a third man was pulling down his pants.

Mike Figgins figured he had one shot. He could shoot the guy standing in the doorway, he could shoot one of the guys holding María, or he could shoot the guy about to rape her.

He also knew what was going to happen to María. She was going to be gang-raped until the men tired of that—or ran out of time—then she was going to be mutilated and tortured before they killed her.

He aimed the gun. Just before he pulled the trig-

ger he thought, *Should never have gone to that fuckin'
casino.*

Then Figgins made the best shot of his life. He got
María Delgato in the head.

Five seconds later, DEA Agent Michael Figgins was
dead, too.

33

Kay knew that within a couple of hours, every law-enforcement agency in California was going to be looking for her car. In fifteen minutes, however, she'd be out of her car and in the "beaner" minivan waiting on North River Road, then she'd head south and take Tito across the border. That is, she'd be in the minivan if she followed Mora's plan—and she had no intention of following Mora's plan.

Mora had needed Kay to get Tito out of Camp Pendleton, but once Tito was out, Mora wouldn't need her. So although Mora may have been telling the truth about letting her take Tito across the border to exchange him for Jessica, Kay thought it more likely he was lying. What he'd probably do was have the minivan driver—the guy with the cowboy hat—try to kill her, and then who knows what might happen to Jessica: a whorehouse or a grave? It also occurred to Kay that the real reason Mora wanted her to meet the minivan on North River Road was that it was so dark and isolated, and thus a better spot for the driver to ambush her.

So Kay had a little surprise for Mora and Tito. The object she'd placed in the pocket in the driver's-side door was a Taser. At the right moment, she'd reach down, pull up the Taser, and shoot across her lap. Then she'd zap the son of a bitch until he was unconscious and dump him in the trunk.

After that, she'd swap her license plates with plates from some parked car. And then she would call Mora. She'd tell him that if he wanted Tito back, they'd make the exchange in the U.S. and Kay would pick the spot. If Mora threatened to hurt Jessica, she'd threaten to hurt Tito. If Mora threatened to kill Jessica, she'd threaten to kill Tito. She was going to force Mora to bring her daughter across the border and make the exchange in some place and in some manner where she and Jessica might both survive.

Tito, sitting next to her, still wearing the blond wig and the blond mustache, interrupted her thoughts. "Drive faster," he said.

"No," she said. "The van is only a few miles away, and it's going to be at least two hours before they know you've escaped. We don't need to get stopped by a cop for speeding."

"Huh," Tito said, which Kay took for his agreement.

"Where's your gun?" he asked next.

She wished he'd just shut up so she could think.

"It's in the trunk. I couldn't take it into the brig, so I left it there." Actually, her gun was on the floor of the car, beneath the front seat.

It was time to put Tito in the trunk. She reached down with her left hand for the Taser . . .

And that's when God laughed.

Coming toward Kay's car was another car, and for some reason the idiot driving had his brights on and they were blinding her. Then the other car swerved into her lane and was coming directly at her.

Kay reacted without thinking and did the only thing she could do: She cranked the steering wheel hard to the right to avoid a head-on collision—and sent her car into a drainage ditch. Kay and Tito both screamed as the car flipped over onto its roof.

Kay didn't move immediately, but it didn't feel like anything was broken and she didn't seem to be bleeding. She did a physical inventory, moving fingers, arms, legs, and neck. Everything seemed functional. The seat belt and air bag had apparently worked as advertised. She looked over at Tito; like her, he was upside down—but he wasn't moving and his head was at an odd angle. Oh, shit. Then it registered in her mind that there was no air bag deployed around him, and no seat belt holding him in place. Kay's 2004 Camry sounded an alarm when you started the car to tell you the seat belts were unfastened, but it stopped after about ten seconds, figuring it had given you enough warning. And with her mind focused only on escaping from Pendleton, she hadn't even noticed he wasn't wearing his seat belt. She had no idea why the air bag didn't deploy, but considering the age of the car, maybe that wasn't a mystery, either.

Before she could free herself from the overturned car, someone rapped on the driver's-side window. It was a young guy, maybe twenty, dressed in civilian clothes, but he had a short military-style haircut and Kay guessed he was a marine stationed at Pendleton.

He was screaming, "Are you okay? Are you okay?"

Kay nodded.

The guy tried to open her door, but it was stuck. A moment later, he came back with a tire iron and yelled, "Close your eyes." He broke the window, cleared away the glass, reached inside, and cut Kay's seat belt with a jackknife. When he leaned over her, she could smell the beer on his breath. "I got you," he said as he pulled her from the vehicle, but she was thinking, *I was almost killed by a fuckin' drunken marine.*

As the one marine was dragging Kay out of the car, his buddy—another young guy with a boot camp haircut—was on the other side of the car. He didn't have to break the window to get at Tito; the passenger-side door opened and Tito fell out of the car. The marine looked down at Tito, then knelt down and touched his throat. "Oh, God," he said. "Ken, I think this guy's dead."

Kay ran around to Tito's side of the car and, like the marine, knelt down next to Tito and felt for a pulse in his throat. There was no pulse. Tito was dead.

But Tito couldn't be dead.

"He's alive," Kay said. "He's just unconscious. Is your car okay to drive?" she said to the marine named Ken.

"Yeah."

"Then carry him over to your car and put him on the backseat."

The other marine said, "I'm sorry, lady, but I don't

think he's alive. And if he is alive, he shouldn't be moved. His neck looks funny. I'm calling 911."

The marine speaking was as drunk as his buddy, Ken, and he, too, smelled like the inside of a beer keg and his words were slurred. He reached for his cell phone, fumbled it, dropped it on the ground, and it went under Kay's overturned car. While he was on the ground, trying to locate his phone in the dark, Kay ran to the driver's side of her car and groped for her gun. She found it, and just as the marine started to punch numbers into his cell phone, she pointed the gun at him and said, "Give me the phone."

"Jesus, lady, are you nuts?" the young marine said.

"Yeah, I am nuts. You have no idea what's at stake here. So you and your buddy pick him up and put him in your car like I told you." Then she added, "And be careful with him."

The marines looked at each other, not sure what to do.

Kay said, "Guys, I'm not screwing around here. You don't do what I tell you, I'll shoot you both."

The marines picked up Tito, and while they were carrying him over to Ken's car, the other marine said, "I'm telling you, lady, this guy's dead. I've seen a lot of dead guys."

"He's not dead!" Kay said. "And if he is, you and your buddy are guilty of vehicular homicide. You're both shitfaced."

After they put Tito down on the backseat of Ken's car, Kay said, "Now give me your car keys."

"Hey, fuck that," Ken said—and Kay fired a round that went right between him and the other marine's head.

"Jesus Christ!" Ken screamed.

"Give me the keys," Kay said.

"Give her the damn keys, Ken," the other marine said. "She's crazy."

Ken flipped her his keys, and Kay said, "Now your cell phones. Toss them in the car."

Still aiming her gun at the marines, Kay moved around to the driver's-side door. As she was moving, she said, "Think about this, Ken. If my friend dies, you go to jail for vehicular homicide like I said. So you could call the cops and tell them I stole your car, and if they catch me, I'll tell them how your drunken ass ran me off the road and how I was just trying to get my friend to a hospital. Choice number two is, you go back to your barracks, sleep until the booze is out of your system, then call the cops and tell them someone stole your car. If you do it my way, I'll ditch your car somewhere close by, you'll get it back in a couple of days, and you won't get in trouble for hurting a guy, maybe crippling him or killing him. Give it some thought."

Kay knew the two marines were basically good guys, the type inclined to do the right thing even if it meant getting in trouble themselves. She just hoped they wouldn't do the right thing this time.

Kay started Ken's car, planning to drive away, then shut off the engine and got out. The two marines, now thirty yards down the road toward Pendleton, stopped and looked as she returned to the wreck. She reached inside the Camry and grabbed the Taser and the Walgreens bag containing the chemical she'd used on the marshals.

She didn't have a clue what she was going to do next, but the chemical and the Taser were extra weapons. She returned to the marines' car, started the engine, then waved at the guys as she drove past them; Ken gave her the finger. Kay couldn't help but smile and think *Semper Fi*. She stepped on the gas and headed toward the I-5 freeway—away from the minivan waiting for her on North River Road.

Now what in the hell was she going to do?

How was she going to exchange a dead man for her daughter?

If she had followed Mora's plan and not been in an accident, by now Kay and Tito should have reached the minivan. She wondered how long the minivan driver would wait before he called Mora to tell him that Kay had not shown up.

Mora wouldn't be too worried—or at least not immediately—because he knew that as long as he had Jessica, Kay would contact him. No, Mora wasn't the primary threat at this point. The threat was the law-enforcement agencies who would soon be hunting for her, and who might prevent her from freeing her daughter.

As she drove, Kay tried to figure out how much time she had before the cops began chasing her. The accident had used up twenty minutes; the marshals should be unconscious for another hour and a half. It would take the marines at least an hour to walk back to Pendleton; as drunk as they were, she didn't think they'd run. Hopefully, they'd take Kay's suggestion, go to their barracks, and report Ken's car stolen in the morning and say nothing about Kay and Tito. But she couldn't count on that. If they reported the accident as soon as they reached the base, the highway patrol would start looking for Ken's car and a woman who had fled the scene of an accident within the hour. The worst scenario would be if the marines found a pay phone before they reached the base and started making calls.

So. She had to assume that in less than sixty minutes, every person with a badge in Southern California was going to be on her tail—which meant that she had less than an hour to figure out a way to evade her pursuers.

Then there was the larger problem: Tito was dead, and when Mora discovered this, her daughter would die.

Kay exited I-5 at the town of Carlsbad and pulled off onto a quiet side street to think. She needed a plan. As she stepped out of the car, she glanced at Tito's body lying on the backseat. *You useless son of a bitch.*

The first thing she had to do was get a new car. She couldn't keep using Ken's car, because at some point it would be reported stolen. She might be able to steal a car, but only if someone had left the keys in it; one thing the DEA had not taught her was how to hot-wire a car, and she didn't have time to wander around trying to find an unlocked car with the keys conveniently dangling from the ignition. Then she came up with an easier way to steal a car.

Stealing a car, however, wasn't her biggest problem.

How was she going to get Jessica back now that Tito was dead? And even if she could come up with a plan, how could she give herself enough time to execute the plan? It wouldn't be long before the minivan driver called Mora and told him that Kay hadn't arrived with Tito—and when that happened, Mora was going to know that something had gone wrong.

She rested her butt against the hood of Ken's car, closed her eyes, and thought—and came up with a plan, or if not a plan, *half* a plan. Half a plan was the best she could do for the moment. To give herself the time she needed to execute her half-assed plan, she was going to call Raphael Mora and tell him the truth.

Well, almost the truth.

Kay's next stop was at a twenty-four-hour supermarket in Encinitas. Tito was still lying on the backseat, but if anybody walking by saw him, they would most likely think he was just sleeping or a drunk who'd passed out. She ran into the store, to the toothpaste aisle, and found the thickest dental floss they carried. She would have preferred clear monofilament fishing line, but she didn't have time to drive around and find a place that sold fishing equipment at one in the morning.

Back in the car, she drove as fast as she could to Del Mar—meaning five miles over the speed limit. If a co stopped her, she was screwed. As she was driving, her cell phone rang. She looked at the caller ID and didn't recognize the number, but she figured it was Mora calling. She let the call go to voice mail.

Kay pulled over at an unlighted spot behind a building that looked like a warehouse. She dragged Tito out of the backseat and put him in the front passenger seat, sitting up. It wasn't easy moving his deadweight, and she was sweating by the time she was done. She put the seat belt across Tito's chest to hold him in a sitting position and turned on the dome light in the car.

She turned Tito's head so it was facing toward the driver's seat and then noticed that his eyes were open. His eyes made him look *dead*. She pushed down on his eyelids and just prayed they'd stay down. Next, she tied the dental floss to his left wrist, looping the floss over the rearview mirror. The floss was pale green, but you could see it in the light provided by the dome light. That wasn't good. She took her cell phone, put it in video mode, and framed the picture. Okay. If she held the phone just right, the dental floss couldn't be seen clearly. She should be able to pull it off.

She took a breath and called Mora.

Mora answered immediately, saying: "What's going on, Agent Hamilton? Why aren't you where you're supposed to be? Why didn't you meet up with the transport vehicle?"

"We've got a major problem," Kay said. "I got Tito of Pendleton without a hitch, just like he told you e called. Then, a couple minutes later, we got in a wreck with two marines who were driving back to Pendleton. My car—"

"Agent Hamilton, you do not want to play games with me. I wasn't bluffing about what would happen to your daughter if you—"

"Listen to me!" Kay screamed. "I'm not lying. I'm not playing games. You can verify everything I'm trying to tell you." When Mora didn't interrupt, Kay continued. "Like I said, we got in a wreck. My car turned over in a ditch on North River Road about five miles from where I was supposed to meet the minivan. Tell the minivan driver to go look; he'll see it. Anyway, I had the marines put Tito in their car and I took their car, but—"

"What do you mean, you had the marines *put* him in the car?"

"I'm getting to that. Quit interrupting me. I had the marines put him in their car because Tito was hurt in the accident. The idiot wasn't wearing his seat belt. His right shoulder is dislocated for sure, and he's got a concussion, a bad one. He really smacked his head, and I need to get him to a doctor."

"I don't believe you."

"I didn't think you would. I'm going to take a video with my cell phone. I'll send it to you in one minute."

Kay put her cell phone in video mode, then she panned Tito's corpse sitting in the seat next to her. As she videoed, she started talking. "You can see him, Mora, he's just sitting here. Tito, say something. Tell Mora you're hurt. Tito! Tito! Say something!"

Kay gave a low groan, hoping Mora would think the

sound came from Tito, then pulled on the dental floss and dead Tito slowly raised his left hand. Kay immediately stopped recording and sent the video to Mora's phone, waited thirty seconds, then called him back.

"You can verify the car wreck," Kay said again, "and you can see that he's hurt. But pretty soon the marine is going to report that I stole his car, so I need to get a clean car."

"You don't need another car. I'll call the transport driver and have him meet you. Give me your location."

"No! I'm not going to give your guy a chance to kill me and take Tito. What I'm going to do is take Tito to a doctor right away so he doesn't die on me, and then I'll get a clean car."

"You can't take him to a hospital," Mora said.

"I know that. I'm taking him to a doc I know."

"I'll give you the name of a doctor we use, one you can trust not to call the authorities."

"No. I'm taking him to my doc, not yours. If I take him to yours, you'll just send in a bunch of your goons to take him from me. I don't trust you, Mora. We're going to do this my way."

"I won't—"

"I'm not going to debate this with you. I know a doctor, a good one, and he's close to my current location. He got his ass in trouble selling OxyContin to addicts a couple years ago, and I did him a favor so he wouldn't lose his license. When Tito's stable, we'll make the exchange."

"How? How will we make the exchange?"

"I don't know. I can't think about that right now.

You figure something out. But things have changed. By the time I get Tito to the doctor, the marshals at Pendleton are going to be conscious. Not long after that, every cop in California is going to be looking for me, and they'll definitely be checking the border crossings. In other words, it's not going to be as simple as me just driving Tito across the border anymore. So you figure something out, genius. You come up with a way to make the exchange in California or Arizona. And it has to be like you said before: I have to be able to confirm that my daughter's free before I give you Tito."

Mora didn't say anything for a long time, then he said, "I think you're lying to me, Agent Hamilton. Maybe I'll have a dozen of my men rape your daughter to give her a taste of her future."

"You do anything to my daughter—*anything*—and I swear I'll cut the balls off this piece of shit sitting next to me. So you'll get him back, but he won't be happy about his condition."

Again Mora went silent. "I want you to call me every hour."

"I'll call you when I'm ready to call you. By the way, I'm also getting rid of my cell phone. I'll get a clean one from the doctor. If I don't ditch this phone, the marshals will be able to track me. Now, I'll talk to you later. I've got to get Tito to the doctor before he goes into a coma or something."

Kay knew that Mora didn't necessarily believe everything she'd told him—but he had to *act* like he did. He had no choice.

* * *

The next thing Kay needed to do was dump her cell phone and the marines' cell phones. She dropped the marines' phones into a curbside waste container, but she placed hers on a bus stop bench. She was hoping someone would pick up the phone and then start moving around Del Mar—and the marshals would waste some time tracking that person. She hoped.

It was now time to go get her new car, after which she'd put Tito's body someplace where it wouldn't be found for a couple days. She looked at her watch. The marshals at Pendleton would be regaining consciousness very soon. She was running out of time. She wanted to be across the border by five a.m.

34

A ringing cell phone lying on the coffee table next to his Heckler & Koch .45 woke Marshal Kevin Walker a little after two a.m. For the second night in a row, he'd passed out on the couch and never made it to bed. And for the second night in a row, he considered putting the .45 in his mouth and pulling the trigger. His head ached, his mouth was dry, and his back hurt from lying on the couch.

He knew he had to stop drinking. Either that or swallow the gun. He should go to his boss, tell him he was a drunk, and ask for time to go into rehab. Or maybe just resign and go into rehab. Or maybe just resign and forget rehab. Whatever he did, he couldn't continue doing what he was doing. He was either going to end up as a bum in a gutter or, worse yet, do something stupid that could end up killing more people who worked for him.

The heavy drinking really started after the fifth funeral. He'd made it through the first four about as well as anyone could, telling the survivors how sorry he was, how they'd get the animals responsible, handing the folded-up flag to the widows, their small hands trembling as they took it. But at the fifth funeral . . .

Walker barely knew the guy they were burying. He'd just been transferred out from Kansas City. He was young, in his twenties, and had a wife and twin daughters, beautiful little blond girls, only three years old. The little girls didn't know what was going on, just that there were a lot of people around and their mother was crying, but one of them saw Walker looking at her and she gave him a shy smile and a little wave. It was the smile that did it. Something shattered inside him.

He'd go to work during the day and do his job, but at night he'd come home and start sipping whiskey. It was like there was a video loop playing in his head. He'd sit there, seeing everything he'd done the day of the massacre, thinking he should have done this, he should have done that . . . He just couldn't stop thinking about it. And he could see, as clear as the day it happened, the burned-out SUV that contained four of his men. He could still smell their flesh burning.

The damn cell phone kept ringing. He finally answered it on the sixth ring, just before it went to voice mail. "Walker," he croaked.

"Sir, this is Lincoln, up here at Pendleton."

Walker didn't really know Lincoln either; he was one of the new guys he'd been given to replace the guys he'd lost. The guys he'd killed.

"Yeah, Lincoln, what's going on?"

Lincoln told him: Two DEA agents, Hamilton and Kirk, came to Pendleton about midnight with orders to interview Tito Olivera about some ongoing DEA operation. The next thing Lincoln and his partner knew, they were waking up two hours later.

"I don't understand," Walker said. "Were you knocked out, drugged, what?"

"I don't know. All I know is one minute we were talking to Hamilton and, two hours later, we're waking up."

"Have you checked on Tito?"

"Yeah. It's the first thing I did when I woke up. He's still in his cell."

"This doesn't make any sense," Walker said. "Did anyone else in the brig pass out? I mean, was there a carbon monoxide leak, a gas leak, something like that?"

"No. We checked with the marines. Everybody's fine. We were the only ones affected."

"What about Tito?"

"He was sleeping when I looked in on him, so I don't know if he passed out like we did or not."

"I'm going to call Hamilton's boss and see what he knows. I'll get back to you."

Walker woke up Jim Davis two minutes later and repeated the story. "What the hell was Hamilton doing up at Pendleton?" Walker asked.

"I don't know what you're talking about," Davis said. "I didn't send her there, and the only DEA agent I know named Kirk is stationed in Colombia."

"Well, you need to contact Hamilton and see what's going on. If my guys are right about the timing, they passed out while she was with them. Why wouldn't she have called the medics or something?"

"I don't know. Maybe . . . I don't know. I'll call her right now and—"

"Oh, shit," Walker said. "I'll call you back." He disconnected the call with Davis and called Lincoln. "Lincoln, I want you to take Tito's fingerprints. Right away. Then call Daniels, You know Daniels? He's my admin guy. Anyway, tell Daniels to get his ass down to the office and you fax him the fingerprints. Move!"

Half an hour later, Kevin Walker had showered and tried to disguise the smell of booze on his breath with mints and toothpaste. He'd also received two phone calls. One was from Jim Davis saying that Hamilton wasn't answering her cell phone, that there was no DEA agent named Kirk in California, and there was no operation under way that would have required Hamilton to interview Tito Olivera. The second call was from Daniels, who'd checked the fingerprints Lincoln had sent him; he told Walker that the man in Tito Olivera's cell was not Tito and, whoever he was, he had no fingerprints on file in the United States.

By four a.m., the head of virtually every law-enforcement agency in Southern California and a dozen people in Washington, D.C., had been notified that Tito Olivera had escaped from Camp Pendleton aided by DEA Agent Kay Hamilton. FBI agents, DEA agents, U.S. marshals, the California Highway Patrol, and cops in every town between Pendleton and the Mexican border were looking for Hamilton and her car. Border patrol agents were looking for her and Tito at the California and Arizona border crossings. Hamilton's cell phone provider was also cooperating, trying to locate her via her phone. In the morning, Hamilton's and Tito's photographs would be plastered all over the news.

And Kevin Walker knew that everything they were doing was futile. Hamilton had left Camp Pendleton at twelve-thirty a.m. She was already in Mexico.

At five a.m., Walker was informed that Hamilton's cell phone had been found on a bus stop bench in Del Mar. Ten minutes later, he was informed that Hamilton's car had been found lying on its roof in a drainage ditch. Did that mean Hamilton was on foot somewhere in the Camp Pendleton area? No. If that was the case, her phone wouldn't have been found in Del Mar. She'd found another car, and they had no idea what she was driving.

Since Walker started boozing, he never drank in the morning or during the day while he was working. Now he was wondering where he could buy a bottle at five a.m.

35

About the time Kevin Walker found out that the marshals at Camp Pendleton had lost two hours of their lives, Raphael Mora was wondering if he should wake up his boss and tell him the news about Tito, or if he should wait until morning. There wasn't anything Caesar would be able to do at two a.m.—Mora was already doing what needed to be done—but Caesar always said that he wanted to receive bad news right away. According to Caesar, good news delivered late was just a pleasure delayed, but he needed bad news immediately so he could make decisions to quickly address whatever the problem might be. That bit about good news being a "pleasure delayed" was something Caesar had read in a management book.

Mora decided to wake up his boss.

"Do you think she's lying?" Caesar asked after Mora told him Kay's story.

"I don't think so," Mora said. "She didn't lie about the accident. Her car was in a ditch, just like she said. I had the transport van driver verify that. And Tito certainly looked hurt in the video she sent me, and I believe she's doing everything she can to make sure he stays alive. She knows she can't exchange a dead man for her daughter.

"I have my people trying to find the doctor. She said he got in trouble selling meds illegally a couple years ago, so I have them looking at arrest records, court appearances, anything that might give us a lead tying Hamilton to a doctor. She told me she was going to dump her cell phone, so I can't track her that way." Mora paused before he added, "And we have another problem. Hamilton wants to make the exchange in the U.S."

"What do you mean? I thought you were going to have her drive Tito across the border in one of the transport vehicles."

"Sir, by now the marshals most likely know that Tito has escaped from the brig. They probably think he's already across the border, but for the next several hours they're going to be looking for him and Hamilton at the border crossings. So Hamilton is afraid she'll be caught crossing into Mexico and wants to make the exchange in the U.S."

"You *can't* make the exchange in the U.S.," Caesar said. "As soon as she has her daughter, she'll call someone and they'll arrest Tito again when he tries to cross."

"I realize that," Mora said, making no attempt to hide his exasperation. "I'll have to convince Hamilton that if she wants her daughter back, the exchange must be made on this side of the border, and she'll have no choice but to do it my way. What I'm trying to tell you is that I can't finalize the details of the exchange until I hear back from the damn woman."

"Son of a bitch," Caesar muttered.

"Sir, don't worry. I'll get Tito back. I promise."

Caesar went silent, apparently pondering everything Mora had told him, and Mora could imagine him trying to contain his rage. He did.

"Very well," Caesar finally said. Then he added, "And I won't forget the promise you just made."

36

Getting a new car would be simple. Hiding Tito's corpse, not so simple.

Kay drove to a run-down apartment building in Del Mar. Inside one of the units lived a surfer—at least a guy who used to surf before he decided he liked dope better than the perfect wave. He was a minor snitch, and Kay had used him a couple of times; the main thing was, she could put him in jail anytime she wanted and the surfer knew this.

She parked her car in the small lot behind the apartment building. Tito would be okay sitting in the front seat; in this neighborhood, a guy sleeping off a binge in a car wasn't a novel sight. At one time, the apartment building's front door was always locked and you had to buzz a tenant to get in, but the lock had been broken and no longer functioned. Kay walked right up to a unit on the second floor and started pounding on the door.

Two long minutes later, the ex-surfer yelled from the other side of the door: "Who the hell is it? What do you want?"

"It's Kay Hamilton, Rodney. Open the door or I'll kick it down."

Rodney, who liked to be called Rod-Man, opened the door wearing only dirty white boxer shorts. He had long blond hair, touching his shoulders, and a tanned but booze- and drug-ravaged face. His once finely toned body was wasting away, and his toenails looked like talons.

"Jesus, Hamilton," he said, "it's almost three in the morning. What the hell do you want?"

Kay pushed past him and into his filthy apartment. The place smelled like rotting garbage and spilled beer. "I want your car and your cell phone. I don't have a lot of time, we've got something big going on, and I need a clean car and a clean cell. You give me any shit, I'll have your skinny ass hauled off to jail."

"My car and my cell?"

"Rodney! Wake up! I'm telling you, I don't have time to screw around here."

"Yeah, sure, I'll get the keys. But when will I get my car back? I need my car."

"Later today, I'll call you and tell you where it is. The phone will be in it."

"But how can you call me if you have my phone?"

Good question, and one that Kay should have been ready for. She wondered how many other things she was failing to think about.

"Give me a phone number for somebody who lives around here," Kay said, "and I'll call that person. But if for some reason I need the car and the phone longer, you just sit and wait for my call, no matter how long it takes. If you don't, if you call anybody and tell them I have your car, I swear to Christ, Rodney, I'll ship your ass off to Victorville."

Rodney came back with his keys and the phone, then seemed to take forever to write down a phone number on the back of an envelope. "Call Trixie. She lives downstairs and she has a thing for me."

Kay was thinking that Trixie must be one desperate woman to have a thing for Rodney, but didn't say so. Instead, she decided to give Rodney a little carrot to compensate for all the stick. "If everything works out okay, I'll mail you five hundred bucks for helping me out."

"Seriously, Kay?"

"Yeah, seriously, Rodney."

Rodney was most likely never going to see his car or his phone again.

Or Kay, for that matter.

N ow for Tito's body.

Kay found Rodney's dusty, dented Ford Focus in the parking lot, started it up—and noticed the gas gauge was almost on empty. Great. She backed up Rodney's car directly behind the marine's car and, after sweeping all the shit off Rodney's backseat onto the floor—fast-food wrappers, a dozen empty beer cans, a couple of baseball caps, a beach towel, and some nasty-looking swimming trunks that were as stiff as cardboard—she transferred Tito's corpse to Rodney's car. She was really getting tired of moving Tito around, and when rigor mortis set in, it was going to be even harder to move. She tossed the beach towel over the body, then wasted fifteen minutes driving around Del Mar, praying she wouldn't run out of gas before she found an open gas station. She filled up the tank, paid with cash, and then headed toward La Mesa.

It was now three a.m.

Kay didn't have a garage at her San Diego house—just a carport—and when she moved from Miami she rented a unit at a public storage place. She kept a mountain bike there she rarely used, skis she would use again one day if she ever found time to go skiing, some camping equipment—a tent and sleeping bag and a little propane stove—and a couple of old surfboards. It was all stuff she didn't want cluttering up her house but didn't want to throw away.

The good thing about public storage places was that customers had access twenty-four hours a day. There was a chain-link fence surrounding it and a gate, but the gate opened by punching a code number into a keypad, and all the customers were given the number. The bad news was that it was located in La Mesa, half an hour northeast of San Diego, which was out of her way since she wanted to go south, across the border. The other thing was, she paid for the storage unit with an automatic withdrawal against her checking account, and if somebody, like the marshals, decided to look at her financial records—and she knew they would—they might go check out her unit.

So she was going to stash Tito's body at the storage place—just not in her unit.

On the way to La Mesa, she stopped at an all-night Vons and ran inside, praying they'd have what she needed. They did. A padlock. Ten minutes later, she arrived at the storage place, punched in the security code, and drove through the gate.

The storage units were made of sheet metal, had roll-up doors, and varied in size. Some were as big as one-car garages. The small units, like the one she had, were six-foot cubes. Some were heated; the last thing she wanted was one with heat. A lot of the storage units were empty—maybe more than normal since the economy had tanked in 2008—and the units closest to the office and the main gate were usually rented first. The farther back you went there were more empty units, and what Kay wanted was a row where at least half the units already had locks on the doors.

Six rows in from the gate, she found a row that had several unlocked, unrented units and some that were padlocked. She opened one of the unlocked units, dragged Tito's body inside, and put her new padlock on the door. She didn't bother to memorize the combination.

If she got lucky—it seemed like too much of what she was doing relied on luck—nobody would rent this particular unit and the guys who managed the place wouldn't even notice a lock on an unrented unit. In a few days, of course, Tito's corpse was going to start to stink, but that didn't matter. Jessica had to be rescued long before Tito started to rot.

Now, finally, it was time to cross the border.

PART III

37

Jessica didn't know how long she'd been in the room. She knew she'd been kidnapped at three p.m. and talked to Kay about six, but hours had passed since she'd spoken to Kay. Without a watch and in a windowless room, she had no idea just how many hours; she was guessing ten or twelve, but she was anything but certain.

She'd slept for a while, but not much, and she was tired. She couldn't sleep thinking that if Kay couldn't—or wouldn't—do what these drug people wanted, she might not be alive tomorrow. She was also thirsty. Really thirsty. A few hours before, Carlos had given her two pork-filled tacos and two bottles of water. She didn't know if it was the salt in the pork or the drug she'd been given when she was kidnapped, but she couldn't seem to get enough to drink and she finished both bottles. Which meant she needed to pee again, but the thought of Carlos leering at her—staring at her thighs, hoping to get a glimpse of her crotch—had made her put off peeing as long as possible. But she couldn't wait any more.

She pounded on the door, and when no one came after three or four minutes, she pounded on it again.

* * *

Carlos Núñez felt his wife prodding him with her elbow. "Get up," she said, "the girl is hitting the door."

"She can wait," Carlos muttered, and burrowed under the covers.

His wife poked him again. "Get up. She's going to wake the baby," his wife said—and at that moment the baby in the crib next to the wall began to wail.

Carlos cursed and threw back the covers. If it wasn't for Mora's man, Perez, he would have lashed the little gringa bitch with his belt until she bled. His wife was now out of bed with the baby, and he said, "Go make breakfast." If he couldn't sleep, neither would she.

Mora had told Perez to take the girl to Carlos's house because it had rooms in the basement where the cartel stored marijuana and heroin before shipping the drugs north. The surrounding houses in the neighborhood were occupied by more cartel men—men like Carlos who barely made any money and who were treated like pack animals. So Perez came to Carlos's house—*his* house—and ordered Carlos and his wife to move down to the basement and take care of the girl like they were zoo-keepers, while Perez and his girlfriend settled in Carlos's bedroom. All this when the house was already crowded with Carlos's two other children and his oaf of a cousin, a man who bathed only if his wife screamed at him.

Carlos Núñez wasn't the only one suffering, either. Perez had garrisoned two dozen men in nearby houses, men he could call on if someone tried to get the girl back; Carlos's wife and the neighbors' wives had to cook for all of them.

But what else could they do?

The door finally opened, and Jessica stepped back as Carlos entered the room. It looked as if he'd been sleeping, and he was angry that she'd woken him. He was wearing a sleeveless T-shirt, exposing his scrawny arms, and lightweight sweatpants.

"What time is it?" she asked.

"You woke me up to ask the time?"

"No. I . . . I need to pee. And I'm thirsty. But what time is it?"

"Never mind what time it is." He yawned, then unconsciously scratched his butt. Gross. "Well, come on," he said. "I want to get back to bed."

Jessica stepped past him, this time smelling not his cheap cologne but the stale beer on his breath. He walked behind her to the small bathroom and, as she had done before, she lowered her shorts as little as possible and peed. And, as he had done before, Carlos stared at her thighs. He made her sick. She got off the toilet, pulling her shorts up simultaneously.

"Can I have some water?" she asked. She was still in the bathroom, and he was still standing in the doorway.

"Yeah, yeah. I'll bring you some in a minute. Now back to your room."

He moved aside so she could leave the bathroom, and as she stepped past him, he pinched her butt—really hard, hard enough to leave a bruise—and Jessica shrieked. His intent hadn't seemed sexual; he just wanted to hurt her. Impulsively, she placed her hand on his chest and pushed him away from her. Carlos staggered backward, then raised his hand to slap her, but as he was about to strike, a door opened down the hall and Carlos's head spun in that direction.

Jessica saw Perez and another man step out of the room where Jessica had been taken to Skype with Kay. The man with Perez was older than Perez but looked cut from the same mold: slim, neat, dark-haired, something vaguely military about him.

"Carlos, what are you doing?" Perez asked in Spanish.

"I'm just taking her back to her room, sir," Carlos said. "She had to go to the bathroom again."

Jessica didn't know what they were saying, but she could tell that Perez sensed something had happened between her Carlos. And then Perez said to her in English, "Are you all right?"

Jessica hesitated, thinking about ratting Carlos out, but decided not to. "Yeah. I'm okay."

Perez stared at Carlos intently for another moment, then he and the other man proceeded to a door at the other end of the hallway.

Jessica watched as Perez held the door for the older man and let him pass through the door first. Perez acted deferential toward the other man and Jessica thought that this might be Perez's boss, the big honcho in charge. And when Perez opened the door, Jessica noticed two other things: the door at the end of the hallway wasn't locked, and there were steps going up on the other side of the door.

Carlos gave her a push to get her moving, and Jessica walked back to her room. Just before he shut the door, she said to him, "Don't forget the water. And if you touch me again, I'm going to tell Perez."

He gave her a look of pure hatred, and she could imagine that all his life he'd been pushed around by men like Perez, men bigger and smarter and tougher than him.

"I'll bring you the water when I feel like it, you little—"

Carlos uttered something in Spanish that Jessica didn't understand, probably a swearword, but she could see that he was definitely afraid of Perez.

Jessica hoped Carlos would take his time bringing the water. She had to make a decision, and she had to make it quickly—before he returned.

They were forcing Kay to do something. And after Kay did whatever she was supposed to do, Jessica was certain that they were going to kill her. No matter what Perez had told her, they couldn't let her go after she'd seen their faces and knew some of their names. And before they killed her, they were probably going to rape her, and if Carlos got the chance, he was going to do something even more awful to her. She didn't know exactly what, but she could tell he was the kind of sick little man who enjoyed causing pain and he would make her suffer. So she figured she had two choices: She could sit in her cell and hope and pray that Kay would somehow manage to free her before they killed her, or she could try to escape.

She knew Kay was good at her job; everything she'd read about her said she was. And she'd watched Kay as she prepared to go out at night sometimes, dressed in those black combat fatigues, strapping on the bulletproof vest, the eager look on her face as she put the black Glock in her shoulder holster. Kay was a hunter and she was fearless—but even as good as she was, how would Kay ever find her? The guys who'd kidnapped her wouldn't have been so stupid as to have put her in some place where she'd be easy to find.

But Jessica figured she had one big thing going for her: She knew they needed her alive and unhurt, at least for the time being. And Kay was probably checking periodically to see if she was okay, so they wouldn't kill her until Kay did whatever she was being forced to do. This meant that if she tried to escape now and they caught her, they probably wouldn't kill her immediately. But what would they do? How would she be punished? Would they just beat her, or would they do something worse?

She thought about what she'd seen in the hallway: the unlocked door and the flight of stairs. But she didn't know where the stairs went. Just up. She didn't know what kind of building she was in—if it was a house, a warehouse, or an office building. She didn't know how many people were in the building. And she decided that none of that mattered.

She wasn't going to rely on hope and prayer.

* * *

Carlos, probably just to get back at her for waking him up, waited fifteen minutes before bringing the water. So for fifteen minutes Jessica stood in front of the door, hands clenched into fists, ready to strike the minute the door opened. She knew he wouldn't knock before he opened the door.

She heard the key turn in the lock and took a breath. The door swung open.

"Here's your wa—"

He was completely unprepared when she kicked him in the groin. She just wished she were wearing shoes. He bent over and dropped the water bottle on the floor, and she kicked him again, in the face, and she thought she heard something crunch, maybe his nose. He fell back against the wall opposite her door, and when he did she ran for the door at the end of the hallway.

She heard Carlos yell but ignored him, flung the door open, and ran up the stairs, where there was another door at the top. *Oh, Lord, please don't let the door at the top of the stairs be locked.* It wasn't.

She saw that she was now in a kitchen, and that two women were there. One was at the stove, stirring a pot, and the other was sitting at a table, feeding a baby a bottle. The woman with the baby shrieked when she saw Jessica.

Jessica looked about frantically for another exit—and there it was, a door that led outside. Through the window in the door, she could see a building next door to the building she was in. She ran to the door, yanked it open, and as she did, she could hear someone pounding up the stairs.

She saw she was in a narrow alley between two small houses. She looked to her right and saw cars going by on a street. Lots of cars. A busy street. She ran toward the street. She figured it was still early morning, because Carlos had been sleeping, but there were vehicles moving down both sides of the road in slow processions, bicycles whizzing by, cars honking, people walking. She didn't know where she was—obviously some big city—and she didn't know which way to go. She picked a direction—left—and started running.

She glanced behind her and saw Perez coming after her. Jessica was fast—she could have been a sprinter at school if she'd wanted to go out for track—but Perez was fast, too, and his legs were longer than hers.

As she ran, dodging pedestrians, her bare feet slapping the pavement hard, she looked for someplace to hide, for a building to duck into. She wondered if anybody in a car would stop and let her in, but she figured by the time she stopped a car and convinced a driver to let her in, Perez would be on her. She glanced behind her; Perez was gaining. Then she saw her salvation: a Mexican cop directing traffic at an intersection, only fifty yards away. He was wearing a uniform, a baseball hat on his head with some sort of insignia on it, and dirty white gloves on his hands. Jessica ran directly at him, screaming, "Help! Help! Help me!"

The cop looked over at her, puzzled by the barefoot young girl heading toward him, screaming. Most likely, he could see Perez behind her, too. Jessica ran into the street, oblivious to the traffic, and heard a driver slam on his brakes and the angry toot of a horn, and then Jessica was right in front of the cop.

She noticed the cop was armed. Thank God. She grabbed his arm, pointed at Perez, and said, "He kidnapped me! Help me!"

God, she wished she could speak Spanish. She could tell the cop didn't understand her.

A moment later, Perez, breathing heavily, was standing in front of the cop. He spoke to the cop in Spanish, pointing at Jessica, pointing back up the street at the house she'd fled from. She heard him say the word *Olivera* several times. The cop, instead of questioning Perez or drawing his gun, just stood there listening as Perez talked. Then the cop said something, and it looked to Jessica like he was apologizing to Perez. What the hell was going on?

By now Carlos had caught up with Perez. He was bleeding from the nose, and there was blood all down the front of his shirt. Perez reached out and grabbed Jessica's left arm and started dragging her back to the house. She turned and yelled at the cop, "Do something! Help me! He's kidnapping me!"

She struggled to break Perez's grip on her arm, and yanked free of him for a moment, but when she did, Perez backhanded her across the face, knocking her to the ground. People on the sidewalk had stopped to watch, and they saw Perez slap her, but none of them did anything. *What was wrong with these people?*

Perez pulled her to her feet, and Carlos grabbed her other arm and helped drag her back toward the house. As they pulled her along, Jessica screamed again that she was being kidnapped—some of these people *must* speak English—but at the same time Perez made soothing sounds in Spanish to the people they passed, probably explaining to the onlookers that Jessica was simply crazy or something.

The damn cop just stood there. Then, after a moment, he started directing traffic again, making a point of not looking in Jessica's direction.

Inside the house, they took her down to the basement. Standing in the hallway was the Bear, the big, gross-looking, unshaven man she'd seen when she first arrived.

"You must think this is some kind of game," Perez said to her.

Jessica didn't say anything. She was terrified now, wondering what they were going to do to her.

"I'm going to show you it's not a game," Perez said.

He pulled a weapon from behind his back, a stubby, black automatic. It must have been tucked into his belt.

Oh, God, he's going to kill me.

But he didn't. He shot Carlos—right in the center of the forehead. The shot was so loud in the concrete hallway that for a moment Jessica couldn't hear.

Jessica looked down at the body, at the red-black hole in Carlos's forehead, at the blood seeping out. He was twitching a little—his fingers were twitching. He wasn't dead yet, but he soon would be.

"It's not a game," Perez said, then he gestured to the Bear, and the Bear grabbed her arm and led her back to her room. She was so shocked by what had just happened that she didn't resist.

Jessica sat on the bed and leaned her back against the wall. Her mouth hurt where Perez had slapped her; her lower lip had been cut and it was starting to get puffy. She couldn't believe the way Perez had executed Carlos. It was like he was stepping on a bug. He'd probably show just as much emotion when he killed her.

She'd failed to escape, but maybe something good would come from the attempt. A lot of people had seen her, and they'd seen Perez slap her and drag her back to the house. Maybe one of those people would call the cops—and maybe talk to an honest cop.

And maybe pigs would fly.

The door opened and Perez came into the room, followed by the Bear and a woman. Jessica realized it was the woman she had seen in the kitchen feeding the baby. She also realized it was the same woman who had injected her with the knockout drug when she was kidnapped.

Perez said something in Spanish and the Bear lunged forward, jerked her off the bed, and then wrapped his big arms around her. He stunk to high heaven, as if he hadn't bathed in days, and she could feel his big, soft gut pressed up against her back. He was so strong she couldn't move her arms at all.

The woman stepped forward. She had a hypodermic in her hand, and she plunged the needle hard into Jessica's upper left arm. She just jammed it in.

"Because of your foolishness," Perez said in English, "we have to move you."

A minute later, Jessica's world faded to black.

38

Kay arrived at the border at five a.m., as she'd planned, but decided not to cross immediately. She wanted more time to elapse since Tito's escape from the brig, and she wanted more people crossing. At six a.m., she joined the queue of cars crossing into Mexico. Six was also good because it was about the time the border security personnel changed shifts, the day shift replacing the graveyard shift, and a shift change often resulted in people milling around talking to their replacements and not being where they were supposed to be.

Crossing into Mexico was normally easy. The Mexicans *wanted* Americans and their money in Mexico, and the Mexican border guards barely glanced at the IDs; they would have allowed a guy with TERRORIST tattooed on his forehead to cross. As far as Kay could tell, the Mexican guards appeared to be behaving as usual, and cars were moving south at the usual rate of speed. This time, however, Kay could see uniformed men walking up the lanes of traffic moving toward Mexico. The men were California Highway Patrol officers—and they were looking at the license plates and into the windows of the cars heading south.

Kay had her long blond hair tucked up under one of the baseball caps she'd found in Surfer Rodney's car, and she was wearing sunglasses with large frames. That was the best she could do for a disguise. If anyone asked to see her ID—which the Mexican border guards would do—she'd show her Miami credentials made out in the name of Elle McDonald. She didn't want there to be a record of Kay Hamilton crossing into Mexico.

Kay figured she had three things working in her favor. If the cops were looking for a particular car, it would be the marine's car, which she'd ditched in Del Mar, and not Rodney's. They would also be expecting Kay to be accompanied by a blond-haired, blue-eyed version of Tito Olivera. But the biggest advantage she had was that the cops would be thinking that if she'd left Camp Pendleton just after midnight, she would have crossed into Mexico long ago, and by now they would be less vigilant.

At least she hoped so—because one of the California cops was just approaching her car.

Kay had one of Rodney's CDs playing, a rap song, the volume way up, a guy screaming bitches this and bitches that, and she was bobbing her head to the music, tapping the beat on the steering wheel with her hands. The cop checked the license plate on her car, then looked at her—and as he did, she gave him a smile and a friendly wave, like she didn't have a worry in the world, and then went back to playing steering wheel bongos. The cop barely glanced at her and moved on.

Thank you, Jesus.

A mile into Mexico, Kay pulled to the side of the road and called Colonel Roman Quinterez of the Policía Federal.

Mexican law-enforcement personnel have a reputation for being extremely corrupt, especially when it comes to the cartels, and such corruption was somewhat understandable. Cops in Mexico earn as little as three hundred dollars a month—about the price of an eighth of an ounce of cocaine.

There was also the violence. The cartels had demonstrated too many times that they would kill anyone: cops, politicians, judges, journalists. No one was safe. And they didn't just kill the people they had some issue with; they sometimes killed their families as well, and the killings were often incredibly gruesome. This didn't mean, however, that there weren't honest men and women in Mexico, men and women brave enough to take on the *narcotraficantes*. One of those people was Roman Quinterez.

The cartels couldn't buy Roman, because he was already rich. They couldn't get to him through his family, because his family was dead. His mother and father had died of natural causes, but his wife and twelve-year-old daughter were killed when they were caught in a cross fire between two gangs in Mexico City. One of the gangs worked for Caesar Olivera; the other worked for a rival cartel that was now extinct. Roman knew his beautiful wife and daughter were not killed intentionally, but that didn't mean that he held Caesar Olivera any less responsible.

Roman was a brave man but not a fool. Kay knew he rarely stayed in the same place for more than two nights in a row. His bodyguards were federal police officers, but they were men he had handpicked, and he paid them out of his own pocket and paid them well. They were also men who had their own reasons for hating the cartels: brothers who had been killed, sisters who had been raped, friends who were collateral damage in the constant warfare.

Roman had spent ten years—the decade following the deaths of his wife and daughter—trying to bring down Caesar Olivera, and he told Kay one time that he had come to a sad conclusion: He was nothing more than an angry bee buzzing around the head of a grizzly bear. The bee would sting whenever it could, but it had no more chance of killing the bear than . . . well, than a bee. But Roman continued to try. He disrupted cartel drug shipments leaving Mexico and seized weapons coming in. He passed information to the DEA because he wanted the cartel's men arrested in the U.S., where they were much more likely to go to prison. Kay had also heard—she'd heard this from several sources—that when Roman did succeed in tracking down cartel gunmen on his native soil, he didn't arrest them. Arresting them would be pointless. He killed them.

Roman was a pragmatist.

But Caesar Olivera was too well protected to kill, and

at this point in his life, he was too far removed from the crimes he committed to be arrested. If he was arrested, there was no way he'd ever be convicted. Not in a Mexican court. So Roman did what he could: He jabbed his small stinger into Olivera's operations as often as possible, and he would continue to do so as long as he lived.

Roman Quinterez was the DEA's most powerful ally in Mexico.

Kay had met with Roman three times in San Diego when she was building a case against Tito Olivera. Roman liked her and wanted to go to bed with her, and Kay had considered taking him into her bed. Roman was only ten years older than her, very handsome and very charming, but the circumstances had never been quite right. For one thing, she was seeing Robert Meyer at the time, but she also wanted her relationship with Roman to remain professional, at least until after she had dealt with Tito.

Now she wished she had gone to bed with him.

Roman Quinterez was the only person on earth who could help Kay save her daughter.

When Roman answered the phone, he sounded as if he'd been sleeping—and knowing Roman, he wasn't sleeping alone.

"Roman, it's Kay Hamilton. I need to see you."

Roman didn't say anything for a long time. "I've been told that you've done a very bad thing, Kay. I hope what I've been told is not true."

"It's true, Roman. I helped Tito Olivera escape. But

that's only half the story. Caesar Olivera kidnapped my daughter, and I—"

"Your daughter?"

The last time she'd seen Roman, she didn't have a daughter.

"It's a long story, and I don't want to tell it to you over the phone. I need to see you. Right away."

Roman paused again, a pause so long that Kay knew he was debating whether or not he should meet with her. Or maybe he was thinking he should meet with her— then arrest her and turn her over to the Americans.

"Roman," Kay said, "my daughter is going to die if you don't help me. Just meet me and listen to what I have to say."

"All right, Kay. But God help you if you're lying to me. Where are you now?"

"I just crossed the border."

Roman gave her directions to a Laundromat in Tijuana.

"A Laundromat?" she said.

"Yes," he said. "Go inside and wait for me. I'll be there in less than an hour."

"You're in Tijuana?" she said. She thought he'd be in Mexico City, and it would take three or four hours for him to get to Tijuana.

"Yes. I came up here a couple days ago. A personal thing."

Like maybe the woman he was with?

"Anyway, go to the Laundromat," Roman said. "I'll be there as soon as I can."

* * *

The Laundromat contained two dozen fairly new washers and dryers, but at six-thirty in the morning only four of the machines were being used. There were two women sitting in plastic chairs, drinking coffee and chatting when Kay walked in, and they looked over at her, probably wondering why an American woman was here at this time of day. She took a seat away from the windows where she was almost hidden by one of the washing machines.

Kay could hear the two women talking; they probably didn't think she could speak Spanish. They were going on and on about some guy named Paulo who was apparently a rat and cheating on one of the women's daughters. They kept giving her darting glances, and Kay wished that she had something to launder so she wouldn't look so out of place.

Roman arrived forty minutes later. He walked over and spoke to the women, and Kay wondered why. Did the women work for Roman? Were they really lookouts and not two middle-aged women doing the weekly wash?

Roman made a gesture for Kay to follow him. He opened a side door with a key and they went up a flight of stairs. On the upper floor of the Laundromat were an office and two bedrooms—making Kay wonder if the Laundromat was some sort of safe house used by the Policía Federal.

The office had a battered wooden desk, an old but

comfortable-looking leather chair behind the desk, two wooden chairs in front of the desk, a file cabinet, and several large maps of Mexico on the walls. Behind the desk was a brightly colored Gauguin print, one showing women washing clothes in a stream. Roman's idea of irony?

Normally, when Roman saw Kay, he hugged her tightly, kissed her on the cheek, and complimented her on her looks. This time he just took a seat behind the desk and pointed her to one of the wooden chairs. He was treating her the way a cop would treat a suspect.

"What is this place?" she asked.

Roman shrugged. "It's a Laundromat. I own it."

Roman wore a gorgeous gray suit and a bright blue shirt with his initials monogrammed on the pocket. She had never seen him when he wasn't dressed like a model ready to pose for the cover of *GQ*. He had a full head of curly dark hair and a perfectly shaped Vandyke beard. There was not a gray strand in his hair or beard, and knowing how vain he was, Kay suspected that he used dye.

"Your boss called me at four this morning and told me that you helped Tito Olivera escape from Camp Pendleton and you were probably already in Mexico with him. Mr. Davis asked for my help in finding you and sending you back to the United States."

"Tito Olivera is dead," Kay said. "And like I told you, Caesar Olivera kidnapped my daughter."

Then Kay told him the whole story.

"Mora told me that Jessica is here in Tijuana," Kay said. "I don't think he was lying, because he'd probably want her someplace close to the border so he could exchange her for Tito. I need you to help me find out where they're keeping her, and I need to find her fast, before Mora figures out that I don't have Tito."

Roman shook his head. "What you're asking is impossible, Kay. This is a big city. There are almost two million people in the metropolitan area. If I called out a thousand men to look for her, which I could, Caesar Olivera would immediately be informed. And how would I find her? I can't search every house in Tijuana."

"Jessica has a cell phone. You can find her using that."

Roman shook his head again. "Raphael Mora is an intelligent man, and he's not ignorant when it comes to technology. He's already dumped her cell phone." He saw Kay start to object, and he held up his hand. "Give me the number and the name of the provider, and I'll get someone to see if your daughter's cell phone is still working."

Roman made a call and asked whoever he was talking to see if he could locate Jessica's cell phone. While they waited, Roman went out for coffee and sweet rolls. He had just returned to the Laundromat when he received a call back: Jessica's cell phone had either been destroyed or the battery had been removed, so the GPS chip wasn't active.

"Goddamn it," Kay muttered. She thought for a moment, then said, "Maybe we can find the place where she's being kept through property records."

"Kay, it would take months to identify all the property Caesar owns in Mexico, and a lot of his property is held by companies he owns and not by him personally. Or he could be keeping her in a place owned by one of his men. I'm telling you: There is no way to find your daughter, not in just a few hours."

"What about your snitches? You must have snitches in his organization. Contact them and see if they've heard anything."

"Kay, I don't have snitches in his organization. You need to understand that it's not like in the United States. Caesar's people aren't afraid of being arrested, so I can't threaten them with jail if they refuse to talk to me. And they all know Caesar will kill them and their families if they ever do talk to me."

"But there *must* be a way to find her," Kay said again. "There has to be."

Roman shook his head. "I'm sorry."

Kay felt herself on the verge of tears—and she couldn't remember the last time she'd cried, probably ten years before when her folks died. She immediately clamped down hard on the sudden surge of emotion. There was no time for tears.

"Then I need to find some way to get to Caesar," she said. "I'll force him to release my daughter."

Roman shook his head, as if he felt sorry for her. "Kay, Caesar Olivera is protected as well as the president of the United States."

"I have to try," Kay said. "Mora said they're going to put Jessica in a whorehouse if they don't kill her. She's fifteen years old, Roman. So do you know where Caesar is?"

"Of course. I always know where Caesar is, and right now he's at his place in Rosarito Beach."

Kay knew that Caesar Olivera had homes all over Mexico. She also knew his primary residence was in the state of Sinaloa and it was a virtual palace containing every luxury a man with Caesar's vast wealth might desire. His place in Rosarito Beach in the northern Baja wasn't quite so grand, but it was still a multimillion-dollar home. It was surrounded by a high wall and had expansive views of the Pacific Ocean. Roman had once told her that Caesar bought out—or forced out—three neighbors and razed their homes so he could have more space. Kay figured that Caesar had come to Rosarito Beach because it was only twenty miles from the U.S. border, and he was waiting there now for Tito.

"I want you to take me to his place in Rosarito so I can see his security for myself," Kay said.

"What do you think you're going to do? Break in?"

"I don't know. Maybe I can find a way to make him invite me in."

Roman cocked his head to the side and repeated, "Invite you in. Maybe there is a way." Then Roman looked at her, his eyes moving up and down her body as if he was making some sort of appraisal. "Yes, there might be a way," he said again. Then he smiled and added, "But not looking the way you do."

Kay was still wearing the blazer, T-shirt, and jeans she wore when she visited Camp Pendleton—and she looked exactly like a woman who'd been up all night

moving a corpse around. She didn't understand, however, what her appearance had to do with invading Caesar's home.

Roman took out his cell phone, and when someone
answered, he said, "This is Colonel Quinterez. I need to
speak to Claudio." There was a brief pause, then Roman
interrupted whoever was speaking and said, "I know
what time it is. You find that pimp and tell him to call
me. If I don't hear from him in the next fifteen minutes,
I'm going to put him in a cell with two diseased queers
and let them play with him for a couple of days."

"Who's Claudio?" Kay asked.

"Just what you heard me say: He's a pimp. Now let
me tell you a little secret about Caesar Olivera, although
it's not much of a secret since so many people know. I
suspect even his lovely wife knows."

Caesar Olivera," Roman said, "has a strong sexual
appetite." Roman laughed. "In fact, he may be the
horniest man in Mexico, present company not included,
of course."

"You mean he likes hookers," Kay said, thinking of
Claudio the pimp.

Roman made a Latin gesture with his right hand that
Kay interpreted as *Not exactly.* "I'm not sure *hooker* is the
appropriate term. Caesar has a, ah, *fantasy* he likes to reen-
act. Or maybe fantasy isn't even correct. It's more of—"

"Goddamn it, Roman, just spit it out! What does he

do? Tie them up? Whip them? Does he like twosomes, threesomes, sex with ten-year-olds? Just tell me."

Roman laughed. "No, no. You misunderstand. Caesar likes to have a *date*. An agreeable *encounter*. The women he sleeps with are sophisticated, intelligent, quite often university educated—"

"You mean young coeds?"

"Please, Kay, let me finish. He likes, as I was saying, beautiful, sophisticated women. These women are sometimes married; some are professionals, like lawyers or teachers. Most are high-class call girls who can pass themselves off as belonging to some other profession.

"At any rate, the woman is invited to his home, or wherever Caesar might be at the time—his yacht, a hotel, wherever. They are introduced, they have dinner together. They converse. Caesar insists on a woman who is capable of carrying on a conversation. After dinner, they go to bed and, from what I've been told, Caesar acts in a normal manner. No sadism, no kinkiness, just enthusiastic sex.

"After they're finished, the woman—never Caesar— says I'm so sorry but I have to leave now. I'm catching a plane to Paris in the morning, or I must fly to L.A. for an audition. In other words, the sort of excuse a desirable, sophisticated woman might give her lover if she's unable to spend the night. The woman leaves, money is sent to an account or mailed to her, and Caesar never sees her again. He likes variety.

"I suspect that most of these women go to bed with Caesar for the money, but some of them must think that

Caesar might become so smitten that he'll leave his wife—which Caesar would never do."

"But *why* does he do it?" Kay asked. "If he wants to get laid, why not just call an escort service, get his rocks off, and get back to work?"

"I think it's because Caesar wants to be thought of as a man who wants more than sex from a woman. He wants to do more than 'get his rocks off,' as you put it. I think he wants a lover, even if it's only for the night. I also think he would consider visiting a brothel or calling out for a hooker beneath him. It would make him feel crass, shallow . . . ordinary. But I don't really know. I'm not a psychiatrist."

"How often does he do this?"

Roman shrugged. "Not every night, and never when his wife or his daughters are with him. But frequently. And since his wife was with him for almost a month down in Sinaloa, I would say he's overdue."

"And this Claudio person can tell you if he's ordered a girl for tonight?"

"Yes. But you need to understand something, Kay. You might be able to get into the house posing as one of Caesar's dates—you're certainly attractive enough—but you won't get in there with a weapon, and you won't get out if you do something to Caesar."

"I'll figure it out," Kay said. A plan was already beginning to form in her head.

Ten minutes later, Claudio called Roman back and Roman ordered him to come to the Laundromat. When

Claudio knocked on the office door, Roman gestured for Kay to go into a closet. She'd be able to see and hear if she left the closet door cracked open.

Claudio was a large, soft man who was dressed as fashionably as Roman. His head was shaved and he had no eyebrows; Kay thought he looked like one of Cleopatra's eunuchs. He was wearing a double-breasted black suit with pinstripes, a bright white shirt, a cravat, and ankle-high black boots. The first thing Roman said to him was: "Where did you get those boots, Claudio?"

"England," Claudio said. "Would you like the shoemaker's name? But you should know that you have to go to London so he can personally measure your feet. It's the only way he works."

"Yes, give me his name," Roman said—which infuriated Kay, as Roman took the time to write down the name of the shoemaker.

"Sit down, Claudio," Roman said, and Claudio took a seat on one of the wooden chairs while Roman remained standing, resting his butt against the desk. "I want to know if Caesar Olivera has ordered a woman for tonight."

"Really, Colonel. Would you expect me to tell you if he did? My clients rely on my discretion."

Roman took out his gun, a nine-millimeter Beretta.

"You're going to shoot me?" Claudio said, smiling, obviously thinking Roman was bluffing.

"No," Roman said, and hit Claudio in the face with the Beretta, knocking him off the chair.

"Get up," Roman said.

Claudio struggled to his feet, holding his hand against the left side of his face. Roman hadn't drawn blood, but Claudio was going to have one hell of a bruise tomorrow.

"Listen to me, pimp," Roman said. "I won't shoot you but I will hurt you until you tell me what I need to know. So does Caesar have a woman coming tonight?"

"Yes," Claudio said. "What's wrong with you? Why are you acting this way? I think you've broken my cheekbone."

"Who is the woman?"

Claudio said she worked for an escort service in L.A., but before that she attended UCLA.

"What did she take in school?"

"Art history. Film. Drama classes. That sort of thing. She wants to be an actress. They all do."

"Where is she now?"

"She's still in Los Angeles. She'll be flying down this evening."

"What's her name?

"Sandra. Sandra Whitman. But really, Colonel, if this is another one of your schemes to get recording equipment into Mr. Olivera's house—"

"How old is the woman?"

"Twenty-nine. Or so she says. She's probably in her early thirties."

"What have you told Caesar about her?"

Claudio's fingers gently probed the spot where Roman had hit him. "Do you have any ibuprofen? I'm really in a lot of pain."

"Answer my question. What have you told Caesar about the woman?"

"Nothing. He doesn't want to know anything. He relies on my judgment to find him suitable companions, but he likes to learn about them himself. All he knows is that she's a beautiful young woman from Los Angeles."

"Is she white?"

"Yes, but Caesar doesn't care about their ethnicity. He prefers, however, that they speak Spanish."

"What time does he expect the woman?"

"Eight p.m. As usual."

"Call the woman, Claudio, and tell her that Caesar has changed his mind about seeing her this evening."

"I can't do that," Claudio said.

Roman pointed the Beretta at Claudio's left foot. "Claudio, would you have to go back to London for another fitting if I shot off some of your toes?"

Claudio took out his cell phone and made the call.

"Thank you, Claudio," Roman said, then he raised the Beretta and shot Claudio in the heart. Kay immediately came out of the closet. "Jesus, Roman! What did you do?"

"It was necessary, my dear. If I had let him leave here, he would have called Caesar and told him about this meeting. He was always more afraid of Caesar than he was of me." Roman looked down at Claudio's boots and muttered, "I wish he didn't have such small feet."

"Forget the damn boots, Roman. Goddamn it! Why didn't you ask him about Caesar's security before you killed him?"

"I didn't need to ask him. I already know everything

there is to know about Caesar's security. Which is why I know that whatever you're planning is suicidal."

R oman went to one of the bedrooms down the hall from the office, pulled a blanket off a bed, and tossed the blanket over Claudio's corpse. He took out his cell phone and said to whoever answered, "I have an item to be disposed of. I'm at the Laundromat."

He hung up and said to Kay, "Now, when you arrive at Caesar's house . . . Please, Kay, sit down and quit pacing. Try to relax. So, as I was saying, when you arrive at Caesar's house, your handbag will be searched and you will be patted down by a woman."

"Will they ask to see ID?"

"Yes, but that's not a problem. You have your passport and driver's license with you, don't you?"

"Yes. I needed ID to get across the border."

"Give me your driver's license, and I'll have a California license made for you in the name of Sandra Whitman with a Los Angeles address. The ID check performed by Caesar's security people is perfunctory. They'll simply confirm that your ID matches the name Claudio has given them. Claudio has provided many, many women for Caesar over the years, and Caesar's security people trust him. They don't do background checks on the women. But has Caesar ever seen you?"

"I don't know. I'm assuming Mora researched me before he kidnapped Jessica, and maybe he showed my picture to Caesar. I was also on TV when Tito was arrested, but that was five months ago. The only one who's seen me up close recently is Mora."

"Your boss told me they're going to put your picture on television this morning. I don't know how many people here watch American news stations, but—"

Kay didn't want to hear it. "I'll cut my hair shorter, I'll dye it. I'll wear glasses. That's the best I can do. If my hair color doesn't match the color on my ID, Caesar's security people won't think twice about that. Women dye their hair all the time."

"I don't know if that will be good enough," Roman said. "You're taking an incredible risk that someone won't recognize you. If Mora is at Rosarito Beach—"

"I don't have a *choice*, Roman!" Kay shouted. "Don't you understand? They have my daughter. How long will it take for you to get the ID made?"

"Just a couple of hours. As you might expect, we have several people here in Tijuana who provide identification for Mexicans going to the United States. You might say it's a growth industry."

"You said a woman will pat me down. Will she do a cavity search?"

"No. Caesar would never treat a guest that way, any more than your president would treat one of his guests that way. His security people will, however, pass devices over you and everything in your handbag, looking for weapons and surveillance equipment, anything with a power source or a transmission source. If you have a cell phone, it will be taken from you and given back when you leave. So don't even bother to take a phone.

"But, Kay, you will never get a weapon into the house, and without a weapon, I don't know how you will be able to convince Caesar to release your daughter. He's a powerfully built man, Kay, and no matter how well trained you are, you'll never be able to overcome him without a weapon. And his security will be nearby."

"I understand, Roman. How do I get to his house? Does he send a car for the women?"

"It depends on where he's staying. When he's at Rosarito Beach, the women usually take a cab or Claudio's driver takes them. If you like, I could take you in a cab."

"Let me think about that. Now I need a couple of things."

"Yes?"

"First, a hairdresser, a good one, and one that will come here to fix my hair. Then I'll need the name of a place where I can order clothes and shoes appropriate for dining with Caesar Olivera, a shop that will deliver the clothes. I'm sorry, but I'll also need one of your credit cards to pay for everything. It would be too risky to use my own credit cards."

"Don't worry about the money. And leave the clothes to me," Roman said. "I know how the women who visit Caesar dress, and I have excellent taste. I'll just need your sizes." This made Kay pause. She couldn't imagine letting a man buy clothes for her, but her instincts told her that Roman probably did have excellent taste; in fact, when it came to clothes, his taste was probably better than hers.

"Okay," she said. "Have the hairdresser come at four-thirty and have the clothes here no later than six."

Roman nodded.

"I need one other thing, Roman. I need a specialist."

"What sort of specialist?"

Kay told him what her plan was. The whole time she was speaking, Roman kept shaking his head—but Kay wasn't going to be deterred and he could tell.

"It's a good idea, Kay, assuming you can get Caesar out of his house, but—"

Kay cut him off. "Do you know someone who can get me what I need? Someone local?"

"Yes."

"Then call him."

"Okay," Roman said. "Let's just hope that God is on your side."

Kay had never been too sure how God chose sides.

Roman made another phone call, vouched for Kay, then put her on the phone so she could explain what she needed. The man asked a couple of short questions—he didn't ask why she needed what she needed—and told her everything would be ready at one p.m.

"I hope this guy's good," Kay said.

"He's one of the best."

There wasn't anything Kay could do but trust Roman.

She gave him her sizes so he could order clothes for her and also told him the kind of makeup she needed.

He jiggled his eyebrows like Groucho Marx when she told him her bra size, and Kay couldn't help but laugh.

Kay looked at her watch. Ten a.m. "I need to get a couple hours of sleep. I've been up all night. Please wake me at noon."

Kay wasn't sure she'd be able to sleep, her mind spinning, thinking about what she was about to do, but she had to try. She needed to be as well rested as possible before facing off against Caesar Olivera in his own home.

39

Kay's new ID was ready by the time she awoke from her nap.

The California driver's license made out in the name of Sandra Whitman was flawless. It looked exactly like Kay's California license, and although she'd never noticed it before, the picture on the ID, which was the same as the one on her legitimate ID, wasn't a very good one. She had it taken on a day when she was tired, her hair tied back in a sloppy ponytail, and the DMV picture was washed out, making her skin look as if it had been bleached. In this case, however, a bad picture was probably a bonus in case anyone had seen her face recently on television.

Claudio's body had also been removed from the office while she slept, and Roman had a chicken salad waiting for Kay's lunch. He was a very thoughtful man. When she finished eating, she decided to call Mora. She had to give him an update on Tito's "medical" status. More important, she had to tell him something to keep him believing that everything was on track.

She used Surfer Rodney's cell phone to call Mora so Mora would see the California area code on his caller ID and think she was calling from California. The other reason she used Rodney's phone was that it was old and cheap and she doubted it had a GPS microchip. But even if Mora tried to find her by triangulating cell phone towers, and since Tijuana was so close to San Diego, he might not be able to tell which side of the border she was on. She hoped.

"It's Kay Hamilton," she said when Mora answered. "Is my daughter okay?"

She didn't ask to speak to her daughter because Mora might ask to speak to Tito.

"Yes, she's fine. For now. What's Tito's status?"

"Better. The concussion is bad, like I told you, but he'll be okay to travel by tonight. Right now he's completely out of it because of the drugs the doctor's given him for the pain in his shoulder. His shoulder is going to require surgery eventually. Anyway, tell me the plan for making the exchange."

Mora told her it was basically the same as before. He'd give Kay an address where she would meet a man driving a specially designed transport vehicle. The driver would call Mora to confirm that Tito was with Kay and would stash Tito in the hidden compartment in the transport vehicle. The driver would then leave, and Kay would drive the transport vehicle to the border crossing. As soon as Kay arrived, Jessica would be sent across the border and Kay would be able to see that Jessica was free.

"No way!" Kay said. She couldn't agree too easily to

whatever Mora proposed. "I told you, I want the exchange to take place in the U.S."

"That's not going to happen," Mora said. "If we make the exchange in the U.S., as soon as you have your daughter, you might call the marshals and they'll arrest Tito before he crosses the border. If you want your daughter back, the exchange must be made in Mexico."

"But they're looking for me at the border crossings," Kay said.

"No, they're not," Mora insisted. "I know from my own sources that the marshals believe you're already in Mexico with Tito. If it will make you feel more comfortable, disguise yourself—wear a wig or something—to make it harder for the border guards to identify you. I don't believe you'll need to take such precautions, but I don't care if you do."

"If they're not looking for me at the border crossings, then why do we need to use a special vehicle for getting Tito across?"

"It's just a precaution I prefer to take," Mora said.

Kay didn't understand why Mora wanted to use the transport vehicle to get Tito across the border. Maybe he was thinking that if Kay was driving the transport van and she was arrested Tito wouldn't be found hidden inside the vehicle. Then, when the van was later towed to an impound lot, Mora's men might be able to free Tito. Or maybe Mora was thinking that if his people had to fight the American border personnel, Tito would be safe from all the flying bullets if he was inside the van. But since Tito was dead, and since Kay had no intention of driving the transport vehicle across the border anyway, it didn't really matter why Mora wanted to use the van and there certainly wasn't any point in arguing with him about it. Kay switched the subject.

"But if we make the exchange in Mexico, then you'll be able to take me," she said.

"I'm afraid that is a risk you must take," Mora said, "but I wish I could get you to trust me, Agent Hamilton. All we want is to get Tito back. We don't care about you or your daughter. We have no desire to kill you. Once you're back in the U.S., you'll be arrested for breaking Tito out of jail, and as far as Mr. Olivera is concerned, that's punishment enough for having arrested his brother in the first place."

"You're right, I don't trust you. How do I know the guy driving the transport vehicle won't try to kill me and just take Tito across the border himself?"

"Ms. Hamilton, the driver won't be armed, and I know you have a weapon. If he tries anything, you have my permission to shoot him. We don't care about the driver."

After a long pause, Kay said, "Okay. We'll do it your way, but I'll pick the place where I'll meet the transport."

"Fine," Mora said, sounding as if he thought Kay was being silly.

"And I'm not going to identify the place until the last minute. I'm not going to give you time to get a bunch of your goons there first."

"That, too, is fine," Mora said. "Let's make the exchange at nine p.m. Rush hour will be over, and there will be fewer people crossing the border. You should be able to drive into Mexico without any delays."

If Kay's plan worked, she'd be meeting Caesar at eight. Nine p.m. was too early.

"No," Kay said, "nine's too early. Make it midnight. By then the drugs the doctor's given Tito will have worn off and he'll be able to function. And it'll give me a chance to scope out the border before we cross. I want to see for myself that no extra precautions are being taken to find me."

"I don't want to wait until midnight," Mora said.

"I don't give a shit what you want. And remember, Mora, I'm going to want to speak to my daughter before she comes across. And if you've hurt her, if you've done anything to her, I'm going to give Tito a permanent injury. I'll call you around eleven, maybe a little later, to let you know everything's still a go. Then I'll also give you the address where I'll meet the transport van. It will be somewhere south of San Diego, close to the border crossing."

Kay wanted to make sure that Mora kept Jessica in Tijuana.

When she was done with Mora, something occurred to Kay: Mora had most likely captured Rodney's cell phone number—which meant that Mora would soon have Surfer Rodney's name and address. The human race would not be greatly diminished by Rodney's absence, but Kay preferred not to see him tortured.

The deal she'd made with Rodney for getting his car and phone back was that she would call a woman named Trixie who lived in Rodney's building, a woman who had the hots for him, and she would tell Trixie where Rodney's car was so he could retrieve it. Kay called the woman, who was either high or stupid or both, but was finally able to make her understand that she needed to tell Rodney that they both had to leave their apartments and not come back for a while. When Trixie asked why, Kay said that if they didn't disappear, somebody might kill them. "Wow!" Trixie said. *Wow?* Kay could only hope that Rodney's gal pal could retain the message long enough to pass it on.

Roman drove Kay to a busy shopping district in Tijuana, parked illegally, and they entered a shop that reminded Kay of a RadioShack: electronic equipment all over the place, computers, cell phones, audio equipment, iPods, iPads, televisions. There were three geeky-looking salesmen in the store, dressed in white shirts and skinny black ties, and one of them came rushing over to help as soon as she and Roman stepped across the threshold.

"We have an appointment with Mr. Durant," Roman said.

"Oh," the geek said, disappointed, knowing now that Roman and Kay weren't looking for a smartphone. "Please wait right here."

The salesman walked behind a maroon curtain at the back of the store and a moment later returned followed by a man who wasn't the least bit geeklike: six foot three, a hundred and ninety rock-hard pounds, long dark hair down to his shoulders. He looked the way Kay thought an Apache might have looked back in the days when Geronimo was operating. He was wearing cowboy boots, black jeans, and a white sleeveless T-shirt to show off his muscles. Instead of a pocket protector, he had a large, black, semiautomatic pistol shoved into his belt. He took a long look at Roman and Kay, then gestured for them to come to him.

On the other side of the curtain, sitting behind a worktable cluttered with electronic parts, wire, and a couple of soldering irons, was a dark-skinned, white-haired man in a wheelchair. He looked like he was in his seventies, and Kay noticed the last two fingers on his left hand were missing.

"Mr. Durant," Roman said, nodding to the old man.

The old man said nothing in return, but he stared at Kay for a moment. He had the lifeless, unblinking, black eyes of a bird of prey. He used his right forearm to sweep aside the clutter on the worktable to clear a small space, then spun the wheelchair around and picked up a cardboard box on a shelf behind him; he slapped it down on the worktable.

"Ten thousand U.S.," he said.

Roman reached into the inside pocket of his suit coat and placed an envelope on the table. The old man picked up the envelope and, without opening it, held it out to the muscle-bound thug with the gun. The thug opened the envelope, counted the money, and nodded to the old man.

Thank God Roman was rich, Kay thought. But if she lived through this, she was going to owe him a bundle.

There was no place for Kay and Roman to sit, so they stood in front of the worktable as Durant opened the cardboard box and showed Kay the three items it contained. Two of the items appeared to be identical, but they weren't.

"Which is the real one?" Kay asked.

Durant pointed at the one in her left hand, and she saw it had a small dab of white paint on it, whereas the one in her right hand didn't.

She examined each item carefully; they were exactly what she had ordered—and she had no idea if they would work. She was just going to have to trust the old man's craftsmanship. Durant still didn't ask why she wanted the items; he obviously didn't care what his customers did with his products.

"What's the range?" Kay asked in Spanish.

"A kilometer with good sight lines, nothing to interfere with the signal," Durant said. "That's the best I could do on short notice."

A kilometer was six tenths of a mile, a little over a thousand yards.

"Then I guess a kilometer will have to do," Kay said. "Thank you."

As they were walking back to Roman's car, Kay said,

"I hope that guy doesn't know folks who work for al-Qaeda."

"He might," Roman said. "Mr. Durant is not political; he only cares about money. He's a very greedy old man."

She and Roman returned to the Laundromat. Roman wasted a little time again telling Kay that the likelihood of success was nil, then, seeing that he wasn't going to change her mind, he applied himself to helping her figure out all the details. When they were finished, she said, "I need to see this place. I mean, it looks fine on Google Earth, but I need to see it."

Roman looked at his watch. "Sure. We have time."

They got into Roman's Mercedes and headed toward Rosarito Beach.

Rosarito Beach is a city approximately half an hour from central Tijuana and about twenty minutes from the San Diego border crossing. It has beachfront resort hotels, upscale retail shops, golf courses, and gated communities. Wealthy Americans—and wealthy Mexicans like Caesar Olivera—buy fabulous homes there with glorious views of the Pacific. Many of the houses are surrounded by high stone walls to increase the owners' sense of security—in other words, to protect themselves from the drug cartels run by men like Caesar. Parts of Rosarito Beach are to Tijuana what Bel Air or Hollywood is to South-Central L.A.

As they passed Caesar's mansion, Kay told Roman to

slow down so she could look at the place, but all she could see was an eight-foot white wall. They continued on to Mex 1D—the major north-south highway along the coast of Baja, Mexico—and half an hour later came to the spot that Kay had selected in Roman's office using Google Earth. She and Roman got out of the car, and she looked around.

What Kay saw was a barren strip of land approximately a mile long and half a mile wide between the Mex ID Highway and the ocean. Whatever structures had once occupied the land were now gone and something large was being constructed, maybe another hotel. There was earthmoving equipment on the site—graders and backhoes—and mounds of dirt piled in a few spots, but the foundation for whatever was being built had not been laid. To the south of the construction site was a golf course, and she could see a foursome playing, and to the north was a gated community, the houses all with red Spanish-tile roofs. The gated community was entirely surrounded by a six-foot ocher-colored stucco wall, which was also good from Kay's perspective, as the occupants couldn't easily see the construction site.

"I hope the surf's not that rough tomorrow morning," she muttered, looking at the waves crashing onto the beach.

Roman noticed a couple walking their dog on the beach about a quarter mile away. "At five in the morning, there won't be many people around. Certainly no one will be golfing."

Kay didn't really care if there were people around.

"Yeah, this will work," she said. But just like the items provided by the greedy Mr. Durant, she really had no idea if the place she'd picked to make the exchange would work.

"When does the tide go out tomorrow morning?" she asked.

"About dawn."

"Good."

Roman recorded the GPS location of the spot using his smartphone.

Back at the Laundromat, Kay borrowed a bathrobe from Roman and showered. Half an hour later, the hairdresser arrived, a short woman in her fifties who was Asian and not Mexican, as Kay had expected.

"All my girlfriends in Tijuana use Mrs. Tanaka," Roman said.

"*All* your girlfriends?" Kay said.

Roman smiled.

Kay told the hairdresser what she wanted, and an hour later she was transformed. The little woman was a magician. Kay's hair was now more red than blond, and it was cut in an asymmetrical pattern that went down just past her ears. She put on glasses with clear lenses and large black frames and studied herself in the mirror. The sexy secretary. She was still recognizable as Kay Hamilton, but she looked significantly different—and significantly better—than she had an hour before.

Five minutes after the hairdresser left, there was a knock on the door.

"I believe your new wardrobe has arrived," Roman said.

In spite of her stress, Kay was excited to see what Roman had bought her to wear for her dinner with Caesar Olivera.

40

Roman had borrowed—or commandeered—a taxicab to take her to Caesar's place in Rosarito Beach. He was wearing a red baseball cap pulled down low on his forehead, and in place of his expensive suit, he had on faded blue jeans and a white T-shirt emblazoned with the word XOLOS in large red letters. Xolos, Roman informed Kay, stood for Club Tijuana Xoloitzcuintles de Caliente, Tijuana's professional soccer team.

Caesar's house stood alone on a bluff overlooking the Pacific, and for Caesar the place was relatively small, only four thousand square feet, sitting on about an acre. As Kay had seen earlier, an eight-foot wall surrounded the grounds, and Roman had told her there were cameras and motion detectors monitoring every possible way in and out. Double wrought-iron gates barred the driveway to the house. Next to the large gates was a small door.

As soon as Kay exited the taxicab, a man holding a MAC-10 machine pistol stepped through the small door in the wall. He was dressed in jeans and a short-sleeved white shirt that hung outside his pants. Kay assumed that his shirttails concealed a sidearm. The man then stepped aside and a slim woman in her forties, wearing a dark blue pantsuit, looking like an executive secretary for a CEO, approached Kay. "Please come with me," she said.

Kay assumed the woman knew that she was Caesar's whore for the night, but she acted as if Kay was just a guest expected for dinner, which, in a way, she was.

Kay was dressed in a simple but very expensive aquamarine Christian Dior dress that left one shoulder bare, stopped two inches above her knees, and clung to every curve she had. She figured the dress had cost three or four grand. Underneath the dress, the only thing she had on was a sheer, white thong. Her shoes matched the color of the dress, had three-inch stiletto heels, and had straps that went around her ankles. The shoes were gorgeous, the most expensive pair she'd ever worn. Her purse, although made by Coach, was unfashionably large for her stylish outfit. Kay was packing a lot of crap inside the purse.

There was one other article of clothing that made up Kay's ensemble—a long silk shawl that she could drape over her bare shoulders if she was chilly. The shawl was about six feet long, a slightly darker green than her dress, and was the most important thing she was wearing. She needed the dress to seduce Caesar. She needed the shawl to capture him.

Kay followed the woman to a golf cart. The golf cart was useful, as the main house was about a quarter mile away, up a fairly steep driveway, and Kay didn't want to walk that far in stilettos. As beautiful as the shoes were, she wished she were wearing shoes she could run in, but she figured Reeboks wouldn't look too good with Christian Dior.

The woman stopped the golf cart at the main entrance to the house, and just as Kay and her escort were going up the steps, the door opened and Raphael Mora stepped out onto the porch, holding a cell phone to his ear, speaking quietly to someone. Kay guessed that he might be at the Rosarito Beach house to give Caesar an update on the situation with Tito.

If Mora recognized her, her entire elaborate plan was going to disintegrate—and she and her daughter were going to die.

Mora started down the steps, still talking on the phone. He glanced over at Kay—at red-haired Kay with the large-framed glasses—and frowned. Kay didn't know if the frown was because she looked vaguely familiar to him or because he didn't approve of Caesar bringing hookers to his home. Suddenly, he raised his voice—as if whoever he was talking to had said something to annoy him—and glanced away from her and continued down the steps.

Kay and her escort continued up the steps, and Kay felt like telling the escort, "Hurry up!" If Mora had shouted *Stop!* she was sure her knees would have buckled. But he didn't; Mora kept walking, still berating whoever he was speaking to, and Kay's heart rate slowed.

Inside the house, the woman led her to a small room off the foyer. "I'm sorry," she said, "but we have certain security precautions we must take regarding Mr. Olivera's visitors."

Apparently, Olivera didn't care if the whores knew his name; Caesar Olivera was not a person you blackmailed.

"Yes, Claudio told me," Kay said.

"May I see your ID, please?"

Kay reached into her purse, groped through all the clutter, and extracted the driver's license made out in the name of Sandra Whitman. The woman examined the picture on the license and compared it to Kay's face.

"Yeah, I know, not a good picture," Kay said. She didn't bother to comment on the fact that her current hair color didn't match the ID photo, and the woman didn't say anything. Apparently, she was used to Caesar's visitors having hairstyles that didn't match their photos.

The woman then patted Kay down very thoroughly, taking her time, running her hands down the length of her body, cupping her breasts, sliding her hands up her bare legs, touching her crotch. She was as intimate as a lover, and Kay wondered if the woman was turned on by the frisk. She probed Kay's hair with her fingers, and Kay, as might be expected, said, "Please don't mess up my hair."

"I'm being careful," the woman said.

She then looked inside Kay's handbag, which was just *full* of shit: Kleenex, three lipstick tubes, condoms, tampons, two combs, a hairbrush, a toothbrush, toothpaste, breath mints, enough makeup for a drag queen, perfume, and a small can of VO5 hair spray. At the bottom of the purse was a pair of long white gloves, gloves that would be appropriate with a ball gown and that would almost reach Kay's elbows if she was wearing

them. The way the gloves looked—wrinkled and somewhat soiled—it appeared as if Kay had worn them on
some past occasion and had just forgotten they were inside the purse.

"Do you have a cell phone?" the woman asked.

"Yes, but Claudio told me not to bring it," Kay said.

The woman pulled each item from the purse and
examined it carefully. She took the tops off the lipstick
tubes, squeezed the tampons to make sure they felt as
they should, and did the same thing with the condoms.
She then picked up the perfume dispenser, spritzed a little
perfume into the air, wafted it back toward her nose with
her hand—and Kay thought: *Please, please, God, don't let
her spray the hair spray.*

The woman put the top back on the perfume dispenser and picked up the small can of hair spray, and
Kay prepared to launch herself at the woman. She'd get a
choke hold on her and . . . and she didn't know what
she'd do next. But all the woman did was glance at the
label on the hair spray can, then place it down on the
table with everything else. It seemed like she had sprayed
the perfume only because she was curious as to what
sort of scent Kay might favor.

Next the woman passed two electronic wands over
Kay's body. She assumed one was a metal detector and
the other was seeking eavesdropping devices. She passed
one of the devices over all the items she'd removed from
Kay's purse, and then the woman made her take off her
glasses and spent more time testing them. Kay was glad
the woman didn't look through the glasses; if she had,

she would have discovered that the lenses were plain glass.

Kay said nothing while all this was going on. The expression on her face, however, made it clear that she thought the whole process was rather silly but she was too well-mannered to make a fuss.

"Thank you," the woman said, finally finished, and put everything back into Kay's oversized purse. "I'll escort you to Mr. Olivera now."

"Do you mind if I use the restroom first?" Kay asked. "To check my hair," she added. Kay figured that the woman she was supposed to be would demand to check a mirror after being pawed at and before meeting a lover.

"Of course," the woman said, and she took Kay to a small, beautifully appointed powder room down the hall.

Kay stepped inside, closed the door, and stood in front of the mirror. She had just wanted to take a moment to center herself, to prepare for what was ahead.

Her hair looked fine.

"It's showtime," she said to the woman in the mirror.

41

The woman who frisked Kay led her to a room on the second floor of the house that appeared to be a combination library and den. There were comfortable-looking red leather chairs, Tiffany-style lamps, hardback books in floor-to-ceiling shelves, pottery Kay thought might be Mayan, and a large globe in a stand that appeared to be very old—like Christopher Columbus old.

Caesar Olivera was sitting behind a desk made from some expensive, gleaming hardwood, talking on the phone. When he saw Kay, he said good-bye to whoever he was speaking to and stood to greet her.

"Ms. Whitman," he said in excellent English, "I'm Caesar Olivera."

Kay responded in Spanish, saying, "Please, call me Sandra. And thank you for inviting me to your home." Kay figured that Caesar would want a Sandra, not a Sandy, and she could tell he was pleased that she spoke Spanish.

He was dressed in a black sport jacket, an open-collared light gray shirt, dark gray slacks, and black loafers. He looked better than the pictures Kay had seen of him. In the surveillance photos he looked brutal, his face cruel and hard, his eyes intense, focused on whatever he was looking at or thinking about when the photo was taken. Tonight, he looked relaxed.

He was clean shaven and his thick hair was combed straight back from his forehead without a part. He was a handsome man and powerfully built, with a deep chest and broad shoulders. His hands were large, the knuckles lumpy, and Kay wondered if he'd ever boxed. Then she thought: Well, he probably never boxed for sport, but he probably has beaten a few men to death.

"Would you like a drink?" he asked.

"Thank you," Kay said. "I'll have whatever you're having."

He poured her a glass of white wine, something very good and very smooth and, Kay was sure, very expensive.

"Would you like to see my home?" he asked.

She wondered if he was going to be so formal all evening.

"I was hoping you'd offer to show it to me," Kay said. And she was. The more she knew about the layout of the house, the better.

As he walked her through the house, he touched her occasionally, but not in an inappropriate way. He'd place a hand on her upper arm or lightly touch her back as he guided her into a room. She thought he might paw her just a bit, fondling the merchandise, as it were, but he didn't. Caesar was a perfect gentleman.

Kay couldn't do what she planned to do until after

dinner, because she was sure dinner would be served by someone—a chef, a maid, a waiter—and she didn't want any interruptions. So until dinner was finished, she would have to continue to play her role. And if Caesar decided to take her to bed before dinner . . . then she'd go to bed with Caesar.

The house, as one would expect of a man with Caesar Olivera's wealth, was truly magnificent. Kay didn't know anything about Persian rugs, tapestries, art, or high-end furniture, but she could tell that she was looking at quality and was impressed. The Pacific Ocean could be seen from almost every room, and with the sun setting on a bloodred horizon, the view was breathtaking.

Talking with Caesar was surprisingly easy. He was a marvelous host, and he acted as if he was genuinely interested in learning about her. When he asked about her family, she invented one: a grade-school teacher for a mother, a real estate agent for a father, and a big brother she adored who was an engineer in Boise. When he asked what she did for a living, she didn't tell him that she was an L.A. call girl; she knew that wouldn't suit Caesar's fantasy. She told him instead that she was going to college—to law school—and that it was taking her longer than normal to graduate because she'd switched majors a couple of times and had to work to earn money to pay her tuition. Her day job, she said, was working as a part-time paralegal and researcher in a law firm.

If Caesar suspected she was lying, he didn't act like it. Instead, he asked what type of law she planned to practice when she graduated.

"Entertainment law," she said.

She picked entertainment law because her ex-lover, Robert Meyer, the Assistant U.S. Attorney, had talked to her several times about the complexities of intellectual property laws, particularly in today's electronic world, and she could pretend some expertise in these areas. She didn't pick criminal law because she figured Caesar might be more knowledgeable than she was when it came to that subject.

As any good courtesan would do, Kay turned the conversation to him as quickly as possible, and she was surprised that he spoke quite truthfully about himself. Kay knew he was speaking the truth because over the years, she'd read everything that had been written about him. He didn't say he ran a drug cartel, of course. He spoke only of being a very successful businessman, and when Kay asked about his businesses, he mentioned real estate and communications firms and other industries that she knew he legitimately owned. He complained about the sour economy, which he blamed on the Americans.

Had Kay not been thinking about Jessica and what lay ahead the whole time they were talking, and if she'd been able to forget what a monster Caesar Olivera could be, it would have actually been a very pleasant evening; it reminded her of similar evenings with Marco

Álvarez, her drug-dealing lover in Miami who she had shot dead.

Dinner was served at eight forty-five in a small, informal dining room, also on the second floor of the house. It consisted of a salad containing pears and oranges that Caesar said came from his own orchards, an incredible mushroom soup, boneless quail, vegetables from a farm he owned, and a tart decorated with swirls of raspberry like a work of art. Two different kinds of wine were served with dinner, though neither she nor Caesar drank very much.

Two young women cleared the table when they finished dessert, and Caesar asked if she would like a brandy. She said no, maybe later, giving him a look that made it clear she was ready for bed and thinking that by now Caesar must be eager to get her into bed. She did ask if she could use the restroom, and he told her it was just down the hall. She took her purse with her when she went to the restroom. She put one of the long white gloves on her right hand, pulling the material up as high as it would go on her arm, and removed the can of hair spray from her purse.

When she returned to the dining room, Caesar was standing, his back to her, looking out at the ocean and the stars. He must have heard her enter the room, the way her high heels struck the hardwood floor, but he didn't turn to face her. She walked toward him rapidly, the hair spray in her gloved right hand, and when she said, "Caesar," her voice low and sultry, he turned to look at her, a small smile on his face—and she sprayed him directly in the face with the same drug she used to incapacitate the marshals at Pendleton.

Kay had no idea how much of the chemical was left in the can. Enough, she hoped.

She had no idea if the spray had lost its potency. She hoped not.

She prayed that the long glove on her right hand and arm would protect her from any droplets that might blow back and hit her own skin.

Caesar said, "What did you do?"

He started toward her, then stopped and shut his eyes for a moment, as if he was feeling dizzy—and then swung his right fist at her face. She was able to get her left forearm up in time to block the blow, but it was a hard punch and it struck the bone in her forearm and made her stagger backward. If the punch had hit her face it might have knocked her out. She felt her backside hit the dining room table, turned quickly, and picked up one of the heavy candleholders on the table.

If he started to yell for his guards she was going to hit him with the candleholder. She didn't want to do that, but she'd have no choice. But he didn't yell. He just shook his head as if he was trying to toss off the effect of the chemical, which appeared to be working on him faster than it had on the marshals at Pendleton, probably because she'd sprayed it not only on his skin but directly into his mouth and nostrils. He took another step toward her, saying, "You—"

Then he fell, and she rushed to catch him and let him down gently because she didn't want his security people to hear the thump of a body hitting the floor. If the drug worked as it had on the marshals, he would be unconscious for two hours. Unless the drug killed him because he was allergic to it.

As far as Kay had been able to determine, all of Caesar's security people and other staff members were either outside the house or on the first floor; she and Caesar had the second floor to themselves. She didn't think his servants would come upstairs, now that dinner was finished, unless he called for them. The servants and his security people were all expecting Caesar to take Kay to his bedroom and make love to her for the next few hours.

Now she needed a weapon—a gun—and this was the weakest part of her plan. This was the part of her plan that she had absolutely no control over.

She was betting a man like Caesar Olivera—a man whose life had been filled with violence and defending himself against his enemies—would have weapons in his house where he could reach them easily. But she didn't know for sure. Caesar also had young children, and it was very possible that because of them, if he did have guns, the guns could be in a lockbox—in which case Kay was probably going to die.

She took a glance at Caesar to make sure he wasn't moving, then went to the door of the dining room and looked down the hallway. It was empty. She slipped off her high heels and ran down the hall in the direction of his den, the room where he met her when she arrived at the house.

She figured one logical place for him to have a weapon would be in his desk, and she found one immediately, in the uppermost right-hand drawer—but it wouldn't do. The gun was an enormous nickel-plated .45 with a barrel that was at least eight inches long. She had to find a smaller weapon; she'd never be able to pull off Caesar's capture with a .45-caliber hand cannon. She rummaged through the rest of the drawers in Caesar's desk and searched end tables and cabinets that were in the room, but she didn't find another weapon.

The only other rooms on the second floor of the house, besides Caesar's den/library and the room where they had dined, were two bathrooms and a media room with a massive television set and eight theater-type seats. There were no weapons in the bathrooms. In the media room there was a wet bar and floor-to-ceiling shelves stocked with DVDs, but again no weapons. She even looked under the seats in the media room to see if there might be a pistol taped beneath one of them, but there wasn't.

She looked at her watch. She had wasted thirty-five minutes. She ascended the stairs to the third floor.

Up there were bedrooms and more bathrooms. The first two bedrooms, judging by the décor and the posters on the walls, were clearly used by young girls. One of Caesar's daughters appeared to be a horse lover, as photos of horses dominated one room. She didn't bother to search these rooms.

She entered the master bedroom. There was a large walk-in closet, filled with men's and women's clothes, which would take her an hour to search. The bed was a king-size model with an elaborate headboard—the bed where Caesar had most likely been planning to make love to her. On each side of the bed were nightstands, and she immediately went to the one on the right-hand side of the bed.

This was the one place she was sure Caesar would have another gun—next to his bed so he could reach it quickly and defend himself if his home was attacked at night. As soon as she opened the drawer in the nightstand, she could see it was the one used by Caesar and not his wife—and her heart sank. There was no gun in the nightstand. There was a management book written by the guy currently running GE, a pair of reading glasses, a bottle of chewable antacid tablets, and a box of condoms. It looked as if Kay was going to have to use the huge .45 she'd found in Caesar's desk, even though she knew that probably wasn't going to work.

Not expecting to find anything, she went to the other side of the bed, where she suspected Caesar's wife slept when she was at Rosarito Beach. The drawer contained a tube of lubricant and three paperback Spanish romance novels. Under the novels was a small, pearl-handled .32. Kay let out a sigh of relief. The gun was perfect. Kay wondered if philandering Caesar knew his wife kept a loaded pistol next to her bed.

She ran back to the dining room holding the little .32. Caesar still hadn't moved. The next thing she needed was a cell phone—Caesar's cell phone. She wanted a phone with a number that Mora might recognize on his caller ID when he saw it. Finding the phone was easy. It was on Caesar's belt. She removed the phone and turned it off, then placed it back on Caesar's belt. It would be fine there until she needed it.

Now all she could do was wait for Caesar to regain consciousness—and pray that none of his servants or guards would need to see him.

42

It was eleven-thirty p.m., and Raphael Mora's instincts were telling him that something was wrong.

After the girl tried to escape, he had Perez move her from the house in central Tijuana to another house on the west side of town, closer to the border. The house belonged to another man who worked for Caesar. The girl was upstairs in a locked bedroom and apparently behaving herself.

For the last two hours, Mora had been sitting alone in the living room, chain-smoking. He had turned all the lights off so he could think, and also so he wouldn't have to look at the absurd religious pictures on the walls. He wondered why poor Mexicans always seemed to have a picture of Jesus or Mary in their living rooms. Was it a matter of taste or something they felt compelled to do, as if God would be offended if there wasn't at least one picture of the Virgin prominently displayed? But what he was really wondering was why he hadn't heard from Kay Hamilton.

She was supposed to have called him at eleven to give him the address where she would meet the transport vehicle in San Diego, but she hadn't called and he couldn't reach her to find out what she was doing. He'd called the number of the phone she used the last time she'd called him—a phone registered to a man named Rodney Sheppard in Del Mar—but she didn't answer and Sheppard, whoever he was, was not in his apartment building. Mora knew this because he'd sent men to the apartment to question him—then kill him.

Mora stubbed out a cigarette and immediately lit another. All he could do was wait, but he knew that she'd call him eventually. She had no choice, not if she wanted to get her daughter back. But why was she delaying? What was she up to?

There was something else, something he couldn't put his finger on, and it was something he heard or saw at Caesar's house. He'd gone to see Caesar about seven-thirty to give him an update on where things stood with Tito. Caesar was waiting for another one of his whores to arrive, and he'd been getting dressed and talking to his cook the whole time Mora was trying to brief him. Mora left the house just as the whore was arriving, a beautiful redhead wearing glasses.

But what had he seen or heard? Everything about the Rosarito Beach house looked normal, Caesar's security people all seemed to be doing their jobs, and his household staff was behaving as they usually did preparing for one of Caesar's "guests"—but something felt wrong. He just couldn't figure out what it was.

Mora knew he had to stop trying to pry the information from his brain. If he thought about other things, whatever he'd seen or heard would hit him eventually. He left the living room, walked into the kitchen, turned on the lights, and poured a cup of strong black coffee. It was going to be a long night.

43

An hour and forty-five minutes after Kay sprayed him with the gas, Caesar stirred. He'd been lying face-down, but he rolled over onto his side. Finally, he sat up, still disoriented, then he saw Kay, standing and pointing the .32 at his face. He shook his head—as if he was trying to get his mind to start working—and started to rise to his feet.

"Just sit there," Kay said. His eyes were a bit red from the spray; that wasn't ideal, but there wasn't anything that could be done about it. Kay was now dressed as she'd been when she entered the house—the gorgeous high heels on her feet, the long silk shawl thrown over her shoulders.

"Are you insane?" he said. "Do you understand who I am and what I could do to you?"

"Yeah, I know exactly who you are," she said. "My name's Kay Hamilton."

"Ah," he said, as if that explained everything.

"That's right. You have my daughter, and I'm going to exchange her for you."

"What?" he said.

"Tito is dead. It wasn't my fault; he died in the car

accident outside Pendleton. So the only thing I can exchange for my daughter is you. Now, you and I are going to leave this house together and—"

"Tito's dead?" It was as if it had taken a moment for the idea of his brother's death to sink in, and then she saw the rage bloom in his eyes and he started to rise, seemingly oblivious to the gun she was holding.

"Don't!" she said. "I swear to Christ, I'll put a bullet in your head."

He stopped halfway to his feet, poised to spring at her, then took a breath, and she could see his muscles relax.

"I don't want to kill you," she said. "Like I said, I'm going to exchange you for my daughter. But if you resist, if you fight me, I'll have no choice."

"If you shoot that gun, you'll never get out of this house alive. I have fifteen men here."

"I know that," Kay said. "So the best thing for you to do is to leave this house with me, then I'll contact Mora and we'll make the exchange, and everybody will live. But if you try to alert your guards, I'll kill you. I know I can't fight off all your men and I know they'll kill me eventually, but I'll have the satisfaction of knowing you're dead."

Caesar simply nodded. Roman had said that Caesar wasn't the type to get emotional on her, and it looked as if he'd gotten over the shock of his brother's death and was suppressing whatever grief and anger he might be feeling.

"My men won't let me leave the house alone," he said. "I always travel with security."

"You're the boss. You better convince them that you want to leave alone. If you don't—"

Caesar shook his head, but she kept talking.

"Well, there's no point in me repeating myself. Now I want you to call whoever you need to call and tell them to bring a car to the front of the house. An open-topped car. A convertible. Not a sedan or an SUV. I need to be able to shoot you while we're getting into the car.

"What we're going to do is go downstairs, and I'm going to be hanging on to your arm. This little .32 is going to be pressed against your left side, so the first shot will hit your heart. You're going to tell your security people that you're taking me to the marina to see your yacht. I know the yacht's there. I saw it today. You'll insist on driving yourself, and you don't want anyone coming with us. You'll get in the car first. You'll drive. And while you're getting in the car, I'm going to be ready to kill you if you try to run or if you say something to your guards. And I'm a good shot, Caesar. Take my word on that.

"If you do this my way, we'll meet Raphael Mora in a couple of hours and I'll exchange you for my daughter. If you don't do it my way, we'll both be dead, but you'll die first."

She knew what he was now thinking: If he played along with her, he'd kill her and her daughter later. With his wealth and the resources he commanded, he had no doubt that he'd be able to find her.

"Very well," he said. He was so calm that Kay found it disconcerting.

* * *

Leaving the house with Caesar went well.

He made a phone call, telling someone to bring his Jeep to the door. Five minutes later, they walked out of the house and down the front stairs, with Kay clutching Caesar's left arm and the small .32 pressed against his side. The shawl was draped in such manner that it covered her hand so the gun couldn't be seen. That's why the shawl had been the most important part of her ensemble—it hid the gun.

Walking next to Caesar, Kay smiled and giggled like a girl who was just a bit drunk and had just gotten laid. When Caesar told his men he was driving down to the marina alone, he got a brief argument from the woman who had frisked Kay, saying some of his men should accompany them, but Caesar gruffly overruled her.

They walked down the steps and, just before they separated to get into the Jeep, Kay checked to make sure the shawl was still concealing the gun and whispered into Caesar's ear, "I'm not bluffing. I'll put a bullet into your brain if you try anything." Then she laughed for the benefit of his guards. Caesar got into the Jeep and started it; if he was nervous or afraid, he didn't show it.

It occurred to Kay that he really wasn't nervous. It could have simply been his ego; a man like Caesar Olivera would never believe that a woman, even a trained agent like herself, could kill him. Most likely, however, Caesar understood that he was no good to her dead, and the sooner she had her daughter, the sooner he would be able to send his men to kill them both. She also knew her death would be very painful, not only because Tito was dead but also because she had humiliated Caesar.

The gates at the bottom of the driveway were open and Caesar drove through them, not even looking at the gate guards.

"Where are we going?" he asked.

"Drive toward the marina," Kay said.

A mile from Caesar's house, Kay said, "Pull over and stop behind that blue Ford." The Ford was just where Roman had said it would be.

Caesar stopped the Jeep behind the Ford, and Kay pointed the .32 at him and said, "Get out."

Keeping the weapon aimed at Caesar, she reached down and found the keys for the Ford on top of the right rear tire. She used the remote to open the trunk and took out an olive green duffel bag and placed it on the ground. "Turn around," Kay said.

Caesar just stood there staring at her.

"Caesar, I need you alive, but if you're injured, that's okay. Now, turn around or I'll put a bullet into one of your knees. You don't want to fuck with me, not in the mood I'm in."

Caesar turned, and Kay took handcuffs from the duffel bag and cuffed Caesar's hands behind his back while holding the .32 against his spine. Next, she pulled Caesar's cell phone off his belt.

"Get in the trunk."

"No," Caesar said. "With my hands cuffed, there's no reason why I can't just sit in the car with you."

Kay placed the pistol against his left buttock and said, "Do you think I'm bluffing about shooting you? You kidnapped my daughter, you arrogant prick. Now, if you don't do what I say, I'm going to put a slug in your ass. I don't think you'll die from a .32-caliber bullet, but you never know. You just might bleed to death."

Caesar, with some difficulty because his hands were cuffed behind his back, lowered himself into the trunk and Kay slammed the lid shut. The last thing she saw was the hate in his black eyes as he glared at her—and she imagined she was looking into the eyes of an animal peering out of a cave.

Kay got into the Ford and drove a couple of miles. She wanted to put some more distance between herself and Caesar's estate. She saw a FedEx place that was closed for the day, pulled off the road, and drove behind the building where the trucks were parked. She stepped out of the car and took off her lovely aquamarine Christian Dior dress and her beautiful shoes and, wearing nothing but her sheer thong underwear, she tossed the dress and the shoes onto the backseat of the Ford.

From the duffel bag that she'd removed from the trunk, she pulled out the tennis shoes, jeans, and T-shirt she'd worn to Camp Pendleton, her Glock, her badge, and her real passport. Lastly, she removed two orange vests from the duffel bag, which she tossed onto the backseat of the Ford. She got dressed, then put her badge and passport in the back pocket of her jeans, and tucked the Glock into the waistband. She looked at the little .32 she'd taken from Caesar's place, wondering if she should keep it on her person as a backup piece. If things went well, she wouldn't need a gun, so she certainly didn't need two guns, and if things didn't go well, it wouldn't matter how many guns she had. She tossed the .32 into the duffel bag.

She checked her watch. It was midnight. She was right on schedule. She called Roman using Caesar's cell phone.

"I've got him," Kay said.

"Mother of God," Roman said. "I really didn't think I'd ever hear from you again."

"Well, you know what they say: It's better to be lucky than good. Are you ready to go?"

"Yes," Roman said.

"Okay, then I'll be there in a few hours, just like we discussed. And thank you, Roman. I know I owe you more than I can ever repay you."

She called Mora next, and when he answered he said, "Yes, sir."

Mora had recognized Caesar Olivera's number on his caller ID and he thought it was Caesar calling.

"It's Kay Hamilton," Kay said.

"What?"

"Yeah, I'm using Caesar's cell phone. I've got Caesar."

"What?"

"You gotta quit saying *What*? Raphael. It makes you

sound like a dumb shit. I said I've got Caesar. He's in the trunk of my car."

"You're lying."

"I thought you'd say that. Hang on."

Kay popped the trunk lid open and said to Caesar, "Talk to Mora. Tell him he'd better do what I say."

Kay placed the cell phone near Caesar's mouth, and he said, "It's me, Raphael. She took me from my house. I'm in the trunk of a car, and my hands are cuffed. Do what she says."

Kay slammed the trunk lid shut and said, "Okay, Mora, are we on the same page now? I'll give you Caesar if you give me my daughter. You hurt my daughter, I hurt Caesar. You kill my daughter, I kill Caesar."

"Why are you doing this? Why aren't you exchanging Tito for your daughter?"

"Because Tito's dead."

"What?"

"There you go again. Stop saying *What*? Tito's dead. He was killed when my car overturned near Pendleton, and that's why I had to kidnap your boss. Now, I'm going to call you again just before dawn and tell you where to meet me to exchange Caesar for my daughter. I'm picking a place where I'll be able to see if you have people with you or if you bring a shooter. You be ready to move when I call."

"Wait a minute," Mora said, but Kay hung up. Then she took the battery out of Caesar's cell phone so one of Mora's wizards wouldn't be able to track her using the GPS chip in the phone.

44

Mora had known something was wrong when Hamilton didn't call when she should have, but this was the last thing he'd expected. He also now knew what he'd seen at Caesar's, the thing he had been trying to drag from the recesses of his brain for the last four and a half hours. He'd seen Kay Hamilton and hadn't recognized her.

Although he was certain that Hamilton had told him the truth about having kidnapped Caesar, he had to make sure. He'd feel like an even bigger fool if Hamilton was lying and her phone call was part of some elaborate ruse. He called the house at Rosarito Beach and asked to speak to Carmen Vega, the woman who had been responsible for frisking Caesar's whore.

"Where's Caesar?" he asked when Carmen came to the phone.

"He's on his yacht with the woman who came here tonight," Carmen said. Carmen disapproved of the prostitutes as much as Mora did.

"How do you know he's on the yacht?" Mora asked.

"Because that's where he said he was going."

"You didn't send men with him?" Mora said. It wasn't really a question; he already knew the answer.

"No. He insisted on going alone."

"Well, he's been kidnapped, Carmen. The whore wasn't a whore. She was a DEA agent."

"Madre de Dios," Carmen said in a whisper. Carmen Vega was an intelligent woman. She knew what happened when you made a serious mistake working for Caesar Olivera—and she couldn't have made a more serious mistake.

But Mora surprised her. "Don't worry," he said. "This isn't your fault."

Mora meant what he said—it really wasn't Carmen's fault. He had always known that Caesar's sexual escapades posed a security problem; he just hadn't anticipated this particular problem.

Since Mora knew he couldn't stop Caesar from seeing the women, he took precautions to make sure the whores weren't armed and to make sure they didn't try to slip listening devices into Caesar's house. His biggest fear had always been that one of the whores might be someone who wanted revenge against Caesar, some woman whose family had been harmed by him, some woman so overcome by the need for vengeance that she'd be willing to sacrifice herself to kill Caesar. Since the women weren't armed when they met with Caesar, the best they might be able to do was grab a steak knife and try to stab him or use some heavy object and try to crush his skull, but he couldn't imagine a woman being able to overcome a man as physically powerful as Caesar Olivera. The one thing he had warned Caesar about repeatedly was to never fall asleep after he finished having sex with the women.

The other thing was, Claudio hired the whores and recruited them from a wide variety of places. He rarely used the same escort service more than once, and any woman who approached Claudio and volunteered to be Caesar's guest for the night, Claudio instantly rejected. That was the only way to make sure that some woman didn't try to use Claudio to get near Caesar.

But somehow Hamilton had found a way to replace the whore Claudio had planned to send to Caesar tonight. Mora remembered looking at the woman as he was walking down the steps at Caesar's house, thinking something about her looked familiar, but he'd been talking to Perez at the time and the phone call distracted him. And it was somewhat understandable that he didn't recognize her. He'd only seen Hamilton in the flesh one time, when he'd met her in her home in San Diego, and her hair had been blond and not very stylish, and although she was an attractive woman, he wouldn't have described her as *gorgeous*. But with makeup on, the sea-green dress clinging to her figure, the red hair . . . she just didn't look like the same woman.

So he could understand how she had managed to get into Caesar's house, but what he couldn't understand was how Hamilton had managed to convince Caesar to leave the house with her. She must have found some way to get a weapon into the house, although that seemed unlikely. Or maybe she'd compromised one of Caesar's servants, and the servant left a weapon in the house someplace where she could get to it easily after she passed through the security checkpoint. No, that didn't make sense. Hamilton would not have had time to re-cruit one of Caesar's people after her daughter was kid-napped, nor would she have known that Caesar would be staying at Rosarito Beach. Well, however it happened, she had been able to find a gun and force Caesar to leave the house with her.

"What was Caesar driving when he left the house?" Mora asked Carmen.

"A Jeep. A red one."

"Send men to the marina to see if by some chance Caesar is there, and get them looking for the Jeep."

Mora was fairly certain, however, that Kay Hamilton didn't have Caesar in the Jeep. Caesar said something about being in the trunk of a car.

"Find Claudio, too, and question him. Question him hard." Mora almost felt sorry for the pimp. "Call Alberto as well. Tell him to try to locate Caesar's cell phone using the GPS system. I imagine Hamilton has disabled the phone, but I want him constantly monitoring to see if he can locate it."

"Yes, sir," Carmen said. Mora could tell she was weeping.

Mora hung up and closed his eyes.

What would Hamilton do? What was her next move in this little game of chess they were now playing?

She would probably make the exchange in Mexico. It would be very hard for her to cross into the United States with Caesar as her prisoner. The American border guards would find a man hiding in the trunk of a car. Hamilton must also be worried about her own people arresting her when she tried to cross the border.

Yes, that was logical. She'd make the exchange in Mexico but someplace close to the border, and then she'd scurry across the border as soon as she had her daughter. She would also want to make the exchange in some area where she could see if he had brought men with him, someplace where she could see in all directions for a fairly long distance.

The most logical place, he concluded, would be east of Tijuana, in a barren desert area near the border fence line. But he knew he was missing something. Something huge.

He tried to visualize the exchange: Hamilton arrives at the exchange point first with Caesar. She looks around for places where a team of men or a sniper might hide. She calls him, giving him her location but little time to reconnoiter the area. He drives to the exchange point with Hamilton's daughter. He stops his car fifty yards from Hamilton, maybe less, maybe more. Hamilton has a weapon, most likely a pistol. She tells him to send the girl to her, and at the same time she tells Caesar to start walking. She keeps her weapon aimed at Caesar; she'll kill him if Mora tries anything. She probably hides behind her vehicle to make her less of a target for a sniper. So Caesar and the girl walk toward each other, they pass each other on the road, the girl reaches Hamilton and . . .

And what? Did Hamilton think she'd just jump into her car with her daughter and run for the nearest border crossing? No. She couldn't be that stupid. She would know that the moment he had Caesar, he'd send men after her to catch her and stop her from crossing the border. So what would she do to get away?

A helicopter. Yes, that made sense. Hamilton would have someone waiting on the U.S. side with a helicopter, and as soon as she had her daughter, the helicopter would swoop in, pick up Hamilton and the girl, and fly back into the U.S.

Hmmm. Maybe, but he still felt like he was missing something.

Mora woke up Perez. Like Mora, Perez was ex-military, a former officer, and Mora's second-in-command. He told Perez to pick four good men, men with brains, not thugs. One of the men would be the sniper Mora had taken with him to San Diego the day they killed the marshals. Although he expected the exchange would be made during daylight hours, he told Perez to make sure the sniper had a night vision scope. He also told him to bring rocket-propelled grenades and the .50-caliber rifle he used in San Diego. He didn't have time to acquire a shoulder-launched surface-to-air missile.

Mora knew Caesar Olivera would want Hamilton to suffer before she died, and he would want to make her watch her daughter suffer—but rather than let Hamilton escape by helicopter, he would blow her out of the sky.

45

After speaking to Mora, Kay drove east, through Tijuana, and stopped near the eastern edge of the sprawling city. She checked her watch. Two a.m. Right on time.

Kay had wanted to exchange her daughter for Caesar Olivera in the U.S. and not on Caesar's turf in Mexico. The problem was that she couldn't easily bring Caesar across the border because, unlike the Olivera cartel, she didn't have specially designed vehicles and tunnels for smuggling people into the U.S.

Going from the United States *into* Mexico was relatively easy. The Mexican border guards checked to see if you had a passport, asked if you had anything to declare, and rarely searched cars. And unless it was the rush hour with hordes of Mexican workers going back into Mexico at the end of the workday, the border crossing was usually fairly quick.

Going from Mexico into the U.S. was a whole different story. It could take anywhere from an hour to four hours to cross the border. Some cars were funneled through enclosures, where they were X-rayed and dogs were used to sniff for contraband. Vehicles were frequently searched, including vehicles driven by people who were obviously American. The searches sometimes seemed arbitrarily random, and probably were. So Kay couldn't drive across the border with Caesar in the trunk, and she couldn't drive across with him sitting next to her as a passenger with no passport and his hands cuffed behind his back.

As much as she hated to do it, she was going to have to make the exchange in Mexico, and she knew as soon as Mora had Caesar he would try to kill her. But she was prepared for that.

She put the battery back into Caesar's cell phone. She was counting on Mora using Caesar's phone to track her and that's why she'd driven east of Tijuana—far away from the place where she planned to exchange Caesar for her daughter. She wanted to confuse the shit out of Raphael Mora.

She called U.S. Marshal Kevin Walker.

Kay figured a Las Vegas bookie would put the odds of her and Jessica making it to the United States at about a hundred to one. Even if her plan for getting out of Mexico worked, she would need help to enter the U.S. and, more important, she would need someone to protect her daughter. She knew the minute she set foot on U.S. soil she would be arrested for helping Tito Olivera escape, and then Jessica would be on her own.

She figured the best person to help her was Kevin Walker. For one thing, Walker was in the protection business. The other thing was, she needed a man who could make up his mind in a hurry and wasn't afraid to act independently.

She could have called Jim Davis, her boss at the DEA, but Davis was too much of a bureaucrat, too much of a team player, and too close to retirement. He wasn't going to put his pension on the line to save Kay Hamilton's bacon, and she didn't blame him. Whether it would be to cover his ass or because he felt it was the correct thing to do, Davis would call back to D.C. for permission and probably contact a couple of other federal agencies, too. At a minimum, he'd alert Homeland Security, who owned the customs agents at the border. The FBI might be included as well. And somebody, most likely somebody back in D.C., might even decide it would be a good idea to call someone in the Mexican government to let them know what was going on—and the last thing Kay wanted was the Mexican government involved in any part of her plan.

Walker's phone rang six times and went to voice mail. Shit. Since it was two in the morning, there was a pretty good chance that he was sleeping and didn't hear the phone ring. She called the number again, and this time, on the fourth ring, Walker answered.

"What?" he said. "Who the hell is this?"

It didn't sound like he'd been sleeping. He sounded drunk. Great.

"Marshal, it's Kay Hamilton. I need your help."

Walker started laughing. He was definitely drunk.

"Listen to me!" Kay said. "Caesar Olivera kidnapped my daughter, so I had to break Tito out of the brig. I was going to exchange Tito for my daughter, but he's dead. Did you hear me? Tito's dead. He died in a car accident right outside Pendleton. But I've got Caesar and—"

"You what?"

"I said I've got Caesar Olivera. I'm going to exchange him for my daughter in three hours, then I'm going to make a run for the U.S. I need you to meet me, to help me get into the U.S., and then take my daughter into protective custody."

"Jesus," Walker said, then he added, "hang on a minute."

Kay heard the sound a bottle makes when it hits the lip of a glass. "Are you drunk?" she asked.

Walker laughed again. "Yep. I'm about as drunk as a man can get and still be vertical. Let me tell you something else, Hamilton. Thanks to you, I'm out of a job. They were thinking about firing me when my men were massacred, but decided not to. They decided because I'm such a good guy, they'd give me another chance. But after you got Tito out of the brig, they shitcanned me, and I don't blame 'em. Right now, I'm officially on administrative leave, which means I'll be on leave until the paperwork goes through to permanently remove my ass from the U.S. Marshals Service. So I'm sorry to hear about your daughter, but you called the wrong guy."

Kay didn't say anything for a moment. "Look, I can't make a dozen calls from this cell phone. If I do, Olivera's guys are going to locate me, and I don't have time to call ten other people. So sober up for five fuckin' minutes and listen to me! Please. In three hours . . ."

Kay told him her plan, concluding with, "Now I need you to call the right person and send some help my way. Will you do that for me, Kevin? Please. Will you do that for my daughter?"

She heard the bottle strike the rim of the glass again as Walker thought about the question.

She wondered what odds the Vegas bookies would give her now.

M ora's cell phone rang. It was Alberto, the technician monitoring Caesar's cell phone.

"She just made a seven-minute call," Alberto said. "She was east of Tijuana when she made it, and I have the GPS coordinates if you want them."

This was just what Mora had predicted: Hamilton was planning to make the exchange out in the barren area along the border fence line.

"Is she still in that location?" Mora asked.

"I don't know. As soon as she made the call, she disabled the phone."

"Thank you," Mora said. "Keep monitoring the phone."

He could send men out to find her. He could send fifty men, a hundred men, two hundred men. He would tell them to look for a white woman driving alone at two in the morning. How many could there possibly be? But if they located her, there could be problems, the biggest one being that she might kill Caesar if they attempted to capture her. If they attempted to follow her, she would probably see them, because the traffic would be sparse at this time of night. Then there was the problem that the people who would be looking for her weren't the brightest people in the world, and who knew what one of them might do.

No. The best thing would be to let the exchange proceed and kill her after he had Caesar.

Then another thought occurred to him, a thought that he realized had been in the back of his mind for some time. What if Caesar was killed? With Tito dead, who would replace Caesar Olivera? He knew half a dozen men who would try to fill the power vacuum—but none of those men was as bright as he was.

Jessica didn't have any idea what time it was or where she was. She knew it had been early morning when she tried to escape and it was dark outside now, so at least a day had passed. But she didn't know how long she'd been unconscious after she was injected with that knockout drug. All she knew was that she was hungry, really thirsty, and her left arm ached where that woman had injected her.

The room she was in was similar to the room in the other place—just a bed, no other furniture, nothing she could use for a weapon. Someone had even taken the clothes rod out of the closet. The one difference was that instead of being in a basement, she was on the top floor of the place. She knew this because there was a cheap skylight in the ceiling, one that appeared to be made of plastic, not glass. There was no way for her to reach the skylight without a ladder.

She thought about banging on the door to see if someone would bring her some food and water, but decided not to. She didn't want to annoy these people. She could still see Carlos lying on the floor, the blood seeping from the hole in his head, his fingers twitching as he died. It was the twitching fingers she couldn't forget. And until Carlos had been killed, all her fears had been in her head—*imagining* what they might do to her—but Carlos's death had been real, and now that she'd seen what Perez was willing to do, she was even more afraid. No, she wasn't going to bang on the door; she figured that if they still cared about keeping her alive, they'd bring her something to eat and drink eventually.

She looked up and could see a few stars through the skylight, which made her realize that the only constellation she could identify was the Big Dipper. She'd always found astronomy fascinating, but Jessica had always been more interested in the smaller universe of the human body and had never really learned anything about the stars. There were so many things she didn't know, and so many things she would never know if she didn't survive this. She'd never attend college, or see Paris or Rome. She'd never become a doctor or have a lover or become a mother. Her life would end before she had lived at all.

No! That wasn't going to happen. She was going to live. Kay was going to save her.

At least, she hoped Kay would do what these drug

people wanted—which made her feel guilty. She'd never really made much of an effort to become close to Kay— or to reciprocate when Kay tried to get closer to her— and now she was hoping the woman would do something illegal to save her.

She couldn't help but wonder how far Kay would go for her.

She couldn't help but wonder if this would be the last time she'd see the stars.

46

There were several reasons why Kay had picked the construction site on Mex 1D as the place to exchange Caesar Olivera for Jessica: it was accessible from the ocean, it was only twenty minutes from Caesar's place in Rosarito Beach, and it was close to the U.S. border. It was also relatively isolated, with the golf course to the south—no one would be playing golf at five a.m.—and it couldn't be seen clearly from the walled-in gated community to the north. And at five in the morning, it would be too early for the construction workers to show up to continue building whatever they were building. If a few people did happen to be there while the exchange was taking place—such as the dog walkers she and Roman had seen the preceding afternoon on the beach—that wouldn't interfere with her plan. It might, however, put those people at risk, but there wasn't anything she could do about that. Kay's only concern was her daughter.

The downside to the location was that she knew Mora would bring people with him and try to capture or kill her after the exchange was made. Those people could sneak onto the construction site, slithering on the ground, and hide behind the earthmoving equipment.

She also suspected Mora would bring a sniper—but she wasn't worried about a sniper.

On the western edge of the construction site where it abutted the beach, there was an embankment that was four or five feet high. You could walk down the embankment to get to the beach, but you couldn't actually drive down onto the beach unless you had an ATV or dune buggy. Well, that wasn't exactly accurate: You could drive down the embankment in a regular car, like the Ford that Kay was driving, but you'd never be able to get the car back *up* the embankment again.

But Kay didn't care about getting her car up the embankment.

Kay had no intention of driving away.

Kay drove the Ford through the construction site, bouncing over the rough ground, knowing Caesar Olivera was being tossed all around in the trunk. Poor Caesar. As she neared the embankment, she pressed down on the accelerator and drove her car directly off its crest. Kay's head hit the roof of the Ford when the tires hit the beach and she bit her tongue. She had no idea if she'd broken the axles on the Ford—nor did she know if Caesar Olivera had survived the crash without breaking any bones.

She stepped on the gas pedal, and to her amazement, the car was still drivable. Thank God Ford still made a good car. She drove fifty yards down the beach and parked the car so the passenger side faced the construction site. If she stayed on the driver's side of the vehicle, she'd have cover.

She got out of the car and hammered on the trunk. "You okay in there, Caesar?"

Caesar responded by kicking the trunk lid and growling a litany of muffled curses. Good. It sounded like he was okay—but he probably had bruises everywhere.

Kay looked at her watch. Four a.m. It was time to call Mora. She didn't know exactly where Mora was, but she knew he had to be somewhere near the San Diego border crossing. She also knew that Mora wouldn't have a problem exceeding the speed limit to get to Rosarito Beach.

She reached into the green duffel bag and pulled out Rodney's cell phone. She wanted to confuse whoever Mora had monitoring phone calls.

"Where are you?" she said when Mora answered.

"Tijuana," Mora said.

"Okay. You have thirty minutes to bring my daughter to Caesar's house in Rosarito Beach."

"We're going to meet at Caesar's house?" Mora said.

"No. How stupid do you think I am? I'll call you again in thirty minutes and give you the exact location for the exchange." Then she hung up before Mora could say anything.

She was going to give Mora as little time as possible to reconnoiter her location and put people in positions where they could kill her. When Mora reached Caesar's house, she would call him again and finally tell him where she was; Mora then would have only twenty minutes to deploy his men or interfere with her plan.

As she waited, she wondered briefly how Caesar Olivera was doing. He'd been in the trunk since midnight. She thought maybe she should give him some water. Then she thought: Fuck him.

M ora had been wrong. Hamilton wasn't going to make the exchange along the border fence line, as he'd originally thought. She was going to make it someplace near Rosarito Beach. The closest border crossing to Rosarito Beach was the San Diego crossing, but he still didn't think she'd try to cross into the States via a border crossing. That made no sense. She had to know he would stop her before she crossed the border.

The idea of her bringing in a helicopter to escape still seemed like the most viable option. Then another thought occurred to him. Maybe she would make the exchange at the Rosarito Beach marina and use Caesar's yacht to escape, or maybe some other boat that was smaller and more maneuverable. If she tried that, he'd blow Caesar's expensive yacht out of the water. Caesar would be less annoyed at losing a three-million-dollar boat than he would be if Hamilton escaped.

The one thing Mora knew for sure was that the damn woman was running him around so he'd have less time to counteract her plan—and right now he needed to get the girl to Rosarito Beach.

* * *

He walked up the stairs to the bedroom where the girl was being held. She was sitting on the bed when he opened the door, and she stood up when he walked into the room. Her small hands were clenched into fists. This was the first time Mora had seen her up close. She was only five foot four, and she couldn't have weighed more than a hundred pounds. She must be terrified—but she looked defiant. Like her mother, she was a fighter.

He almost smiled, thinking about her beating the shit out of Perez's man.

"I'm taking you to meet your mother," he said. "Let's go. We need to move quickly."

He walked the girl down the stairs and out of the house. There was a black SUV waiting on the street and a second black SUV parked behind it, containing Perez and four other men. He opened the passenger-side door of the first SUV and said to Jessica, "Get in and buckle your seat belt. I'm not going to handcuff you, but if you give me any sort of problem, I'm going to pistol-whip you. I'll turn your face into a Halloween mask. Do you understand?"

The girl nodded, but he guessed that if she got the chance, she'd fight him.

He got into the driver's seat and took off, with Perez following right on his bumper.

Jessica didn't know who the guy was, just that she'd seen him before with Perez. She sensed that he was the big boss. He drove like a maniac. There were times she was certain they were going more than a hundred miles an hour. He was going to kill them both if he had an accident.

She had no idea what was going on. All he'd said was that he was taking her to meet Kay. She wondered if Kay knew that this guy had a car filled with a bunch of other guys coming with him.

About twenty minutes later, they stopped in front of a big, fancy house with a high wall and double wrought-iron gates. Near the gates were a bunch of men holding machine guns. Jesus! Kay was taking on an army.

Kay checked her watch. Mora should be at Caesar's house by now. She called him again, and this time gave him the GPS coordinates of the exchange location. "Park on the highway," she said, "and walk across the construction site and down onto the beach. I'll be there with Caesar. If you're not here in twenty minutes, then I'll know that you're trying to pull something and I'll take off with Caesar.

"Now, I know what you're thinking, Mora. You're thinking you can take as long as you want because I'll just have to wait for you if I want my daughter back. But I won't wait. I won't give you time to surround me or block me in. I'll take off and I'll set up another location for making the exchange, and if I have enough time, I'll call in reinforcements from the U.S to help me."

She closed the phone and looked out at the water.

There was a single boat about three hundred yards off the beach and two men were fishing from it. She opened the trunk, and Caesar Olivera immediately started cursing her. She could smell urine; Caesar had pissed his pants. He was still wearing the black sports jacket, gray shirt, and dark gray pants he had on when Kay met him earlier in the evening—an evening that now seemed like days, not hours, ago—and his beautiful clothes were wrinkled and stained and one of his loafers was missing. He'd knocked off the shoe somehow while moving around in the trunk. He had a livid bruise on his forehead—probably from when the car went over the embankment—and his hair was disheveled.

For some reason, probably the hair, Kay was reminded of the pictures she'd seen of Saddam Hussein when they caught him in that hole in Iraq. That was another guy who thought he'd live forever.

Caesar Olivera had been in power for almost twenty-five years, and Kay was willing to bet that during that time no one had ever abused him the way she had. If he got his hands on her after this night was over, she couldn't even imagine the things he'd do to her. She didn't *want* to imagine the things he'd do to her.

Kay was holding in her hand one of the items she'd obtained from old Mr. Durant. "I want you to hold still," she said. "I'm going to put this around your neck."

The object she held was a section of fire hose about an inch and a half in diameter, and it was shaped into the form of a ring approximately eighteen inches in diameter. A flexible metal strip had been inserted through the hose and holes were drilled in the metal strip at each end so a padlock could be inserted into the holes after the ring was put around Caesar's neck.

"The hell you are," Caesar said. Caesar's hands were still handcuffed behind his back, but when she tried to put the ring around his neck, he snapped at her forearms with his teeth, nipping her once, and he kept shaking his head from side to side so she couldn't get the device on him.

"I don't have time for this," Kay said. She pulled the Glock from the waistband of her jeans and hit him on the head with it, not hard enough to knock him unconscious, but hard enough to stun him. She placed the fire-hose ring around his neck, put the padlock through the holes in the metal strip, and snapped the padlock shut. By the time she finished, Caesar had recovered enough from the blow to his head to say, "What is that thing?"

"Get out of the trunk," Kay said. She actually had to help him out, as his legs had cramped up from being bent for so long. When he was standing on the sand, she said, "Now I'll tell you what you're wearing around your neck."

When she finished speaking, she showed Caesar the object she was holding in her left hand, then went behind him so he couldn't see her and raised her right hand over her head—and the collar on Caesar's neck began to emit a beeping sound, one beep every three seconds.

"You better hope Mora doesn't do something stupid, Caesar. If he does, you're gonna die."

* * *

Mora turned to the girl and said, "Your mother's a smart woman. It's going to be a pleasure to kill her."

To this the girl responded, "You're the one who's gonna die."

Mora couldn't help but smile; the little gringa had guts. "Don't get out of the car or I'll shoot you," he said, then he exited the SUV and walked back to talk to Perez, who was parked behind him with his four men. He told Perez where they were going—about twenty minutes south on Mex 1D—and gave him the GPS coordinates for the exchange location, which Hamilton had said was a beachfront construction site.

It then occurred to Mora that it was more likely Hamilton would use a boat to escape instead of a helicopter, as he'd originally thought, and if that was the case, and if by some chance she got away before he could kill her, maybe his men could intercept her after he had Caesar. The problem was that she had given him only twenty minutes to reach the exchange point—he didn't think she was bluffing about taking off if he didn't arrive on time—and it would take much longer than twenty minutes for his men to drive to the marina, steal a boat, and then sail the boat to the exchange point. After thinking about all that for a few seconds, he decided to get some of his men headed toward the exchange site in a boat, even if the chance of them arriving in time to intercept Hamilton was small. Yes, that seemed prudent, and it was maybe the only thing he could do to keep her from escaping if he failed to kill her. If Hamilton escaped, after what she had done to Caesar . . . Well, Mora didn't even want to think about what Caesar might do to him.

"I want you to send three of your men to the marina," he told Perez, "and have them get a boat, the fastest one they can find."

"What about Caesar's yacht?" Perez said.

"It's too big and too slow. They need to get a boat that's very fast and easy to maneuver. Like a cigarette boat. After they have the boat—and I don't care who they have to kill to get one—tell them to proceed to the exchange point.

"I want you and the sniper to follow me in your car. As soon as I start walking toward the beach with the girl, you and the sniper belly-crawl into the area. Find a place where you can see the beach and not be seen. The sniper brings his rifle, you take the grenade launcher. When Hamilton tries to get away after the exchange, whether she tries to drive away or fly away in a chopper or escape by boat—use the grenades. Kill her and the girl. But don't do anything before the exchange is made unless you receive a direct order from me. Do you understand?"

"Yes, sir," Perez said.

Mora got back into the SUV with Jessica and drove as fast as he could to the exchange point.

"Get out," he said to Jessica. "Your mother's waiting on the beach."

Mora took Jessica by the arm and guided her through the construction site. He turned once and saw Perez and the sniper exiting the second SUV. Just before Mora and Jessica reached the embankment, his cell phone rang. He could see a car on the beach about a hundred yards away. Caesar was standing next to the car and his hands were behind his back—as if they were cuffed or tied—but Hamilton wasn't visible.

Kay was inside the car, holding Caesar's cell phone to her mouth, lying on the backseat. She wasn't going to let Mora's men shoot her before she had a chance to explain the situation to Mora. She wasn't worried about Caesar running away.

Mora answered her call on the first ring. "Now what?" he said.

"I want you to listen carefully, Raphael. Caesar has a collar locked around his neck, and the collar is filled with plastic explosive. And I'm holding a dead man's switch in my left hand. Do you understand what this means?"

"Yes," Mora said.

"I'm gonna explain things to you anyway, just to make sure there are no mistakes. If my thumb comes off the button on the dead man's switch, an electronic signal is going to be transmitted to a detonator in the collar and Caesar's head is going to be blown off his shoulders. The collar and the detonator were manufactured by one of your fine Mexican craftsmen in Tijuana. So if I fall down and my thumb comes off the button, Caesar dies. If I'm shot and my thumb comes off the button, Caesar dies. Do you understand?"

"Yes," Mora said.

"There's one other thing. The transmitter in the dead man's switch has a range of two kilometers. This means that after I exchange Caesar for my daughter, if you try to kill me, you and Caesar had better be at least two kilometers away. And if you're standing next to Caesar when the bomb goes off, you'll die, too. Do you understand?"

"Yes," Mora said.

"Good. I've already explained the situation to Caesar, which is the reason he's standing outside the car like his feet are buried in the sand. Now, I know you've brought people here with you, so I'm going to give you two minutes to call your guys and explain the situation to them. Then, as soon as I step out of the car, you and my daughter come down to the beach. You send my daughter to me, and I'll send Caesar to you."

Kay hung up, and then a horrifying thought occurred to her. What if Mora wanted Caesar dead? With Tito gone, who would be a better man to assume control of Caesar's empire? Caesar had come to power by killing his boss. Raphael Mora could come to power the same way—but without actually pulling the trigger himself.

Well, there was nothing she could do about that.

Mora closed the phone.

This was the piece of Hamilton's plan that he'd missed. If Caesar was rigged so Hamilton could blow his head off like she said, he couldn't kill her until he and Caesar were at least two kilometers away. Which meant if a helicopter came in to pick her up off the beach, Perez couldn't shoot down the helicopter until the distance between the helicopter and Caesar was two kilometers— too far away to make an accurate shot. But was she lying to him?

He didn't think she was lying about the explosive charge. He did think, however, that she might be bluffing about the range of the transmitter. Two kilometers seemed unlikely. And if he was off the beach, a signal from the transmitter might be affected by the contours of the land. He mulled all that over for a moment but finally decided he really couldn't afford to take the chance that she wasn't telling the truth. As she said, not only would Caesar die, he would, too.

He still had the option of having Perez's sniper shoot her as soon as she exposed herself; Hamilton and Cesar would die, and then he could try and take over the cartel. He had come to the realization in the last hour, however, that he didn't want to become the new Caesar Olivera. If Caesar was killed, a struggle would follow and a lot of people would die—and he could be one of those people. He had a comfortable job with Caesar Olivera; he'd made a lot of money, certainly more money than he could ever spend in his lifetime. Why risk everything to earn more money he wouldn't have time to spend? There were some people whose egos demanded that they be the top dog. Caesar was one of those people; so was his idiot brother, the late, unlamented Tito Olivera.

Raphael Mora was not one of those people.

So Caesar would live, and not far in the future, Mora would track down Hamilton and present the woman to him so Caesar could exact a horrible revenge.

He called Perez, speaking in Spanish so Jessica wouldn't understand, and explained the situation with the explosive collar and the dead man's switch.

"I still want you to get into a position where you can look down at the beach," Mora said, "but don't kill the woman unless I give you a direct order."

He closed the cell phone and gave Jessica a little push. "Let's go. Walk down to the beach."

Kay got out of the car. In her left hand was a black tube with a red button on the top—the dead man's switch—and her left thumb was depressing the button. She went and stood next to Caesar. She watched as Jessica and Mora slid down the embankment, and when they were standing on the beach, she called Mora again.

"Send Jessica to me," she said, and when she saw Jessica begin to walk toward her, she said to Caesar, "Go."

Caesar was no longer raging the way he'd been in the trunk of the car. He seemed to have regained the self-control he was known for. His head was bleeding slightly where she'd struck him with the Glock, and his face was smudged with dirt. He was still missing one shoe. He now looked more like a guy you'd find sleeping in a doorway in Tijuana than the head of the most powerful drug cartel in the Americas.

The collar around his neck continued to emit a beep every three seconds.

"If it takes the rest of my life," he said, turning to look Kay in the eye, "I'll find you. There is no place on this planet where you will be safe. If you were smart, you would kill yourself and your daughter right now to save yourselves the pain."

Kay knew he was right. She knew she and Jessica would be running from Caesar Olivera for the rest of their lives. He'd never stop hunting for the woman who had killed his brother. But she'd worry about that later, after she had Jessica back.

"Go," she said to Caesar a second time.

J essica wanted to run to Kay, but she didn't. She didn't understand exactly how the exchange was set up, so she forced herself to walk slowly. She passed the man who had been with her mother, a big guy, not that tall, but broad. His hands were behind his back and he was wearing some kind of collar around his neck. It looked like those inflatable rings that people wore on long airplane flights, except it seemed to be made of canvas. The guy was a mess—and he looked pissed off—but as she passed him, he smiled at her and said, "Until we meet again."

Jessica went cold thinking about meeting any of these monsters again, but she didn't say anything and kept on walking.

47

Kay didn't have a helicopter coming for her.

The dead man's switch in her hand was a fake.

What she had was Roman Quinterez and one of his men heading toward the beach in a Boston Whaler with a two-hundred-and-fifty-horsepower outboard motor. Roman had been anchored off the beach posing as a fisherman. He picked the Whaler because it had a deep, V-shaped bottom—a place where Jessica could lie down and be out of sight—and the hull was made of fiberglass. Kay would have preferred a metal hull—a material better able to stop a bullet—but fiberglass was still better than an inflatable boat like a Zodiac. Boston Whalers, because of their double-hulled construction, were also unsinkable. Supposedly.

Roman had the *real* dead man's switch. Kay knew she wouldn't be able to swim holding the dead man's switch, and she thought the water might damage the electronics in it. At the same time, she wanted Caesar Olivera to die if he killed her or her daughter. So Roman was holding the real dead man's switch, and when Kay had raised her right hand after putting the explosive collar on Caesar, Roman, watching everything unfold with binoculars, had activated the bomb. Roman would kill Caesar if Kay and Jessica didn't make it.

As soon as Jessica reached her, Kay gave her a brief hug—they didn't have time for an emotional reunion—and took one of the two orange vests she had in the car and tossed it to Jessica. It wasn't a bulletproof vest; it was a life vest.

"Put that on," Kay said as she donned her own vest. "We gotta hurry. You see that boat coming toward the beach? Head out in the water right now and swim to it. As soon as you get on board, get down on the bottom of the boat so you're out of sight. Now, go. Go!"

Kay looked down the beach as she ran into the surf after her daughter. Caesar had reached Mora.

G et this goddamn thing off me!" Caesar said.

Mora touched the padlock binding the collar to Caesar's throat. "I can't. I don't have anything to cut through metal, and I'm afraid if I tamper with the collar or cut through the hose, it will explode. We need to get out of range; we need to get as far away from this place as fast as we can."

Mora looked back and saw the Boston Whaler making its way toward the shore and the girl and her mother running into the water. He also looked up the coast, hoping to see Perez's men in a boat they'd commandeered from the Rosarito Beach marina, but they were nowhere in sight. He had known they most likely wouldn't make it on time.

Mora wanted to get off the beach immediately. He wasn't worried about Hamilton deliberately killing Caesar at this point. Hamilton knew he'd brought men with him, and she knew if she killed Caesar, Mora's men would kill her and her daughter. So he wasn't worried about her intentionally killing Caesar—but he was worried about her accidentally killing him. If her thumb slipped off the dead man's switch while she was swimming or getting into the boat, then he and Caesar would die.

He grabbed one of Caesar's arms and started running with him, but Caesar was having a hard time running with his hands cuffed behind his back; he stumbled once and fell. Mora jerked him to his feet and said, "Hurry. We need to get off this beach."

They reached the steep embankment, but with his hands behind his back, Caesar was struggling to get up. Mora began tugging at him, doing his best to pull a two-hundred-pound man up a steep hillside, the sand caving beneath their feet as they climbed.

"Slow down!" Caesar said.

"Hurry!" Mora said.

Roman Quinterez watched Caesar and Mora start up the embankment.

He knew the transmitter in the dead man's switch didn't have a two-kilometer range, only one kilometer—a thousand yards. Old Mr. Durant, the man who built the collar bomb, also said there needed to be a clear line of sight between the transmitter in the dead man's switch and the receiver in the detonator. Once Mora and Caesar reached the top of the embankment, Roman would lose sight of them.

Roman had been hunting Caesar Olivera for ten years, ever since his wife and daughter were killed, and he knew he'd never be able to arrest Caesar. He also knew that if Caesar lived, he would hunt down Kay Hamilton and her daughter and kill them in the most gruesome manner he could devise.

Roman took his thumb off the button on the dead man's switch.

In addition to the plastic explosive in the collar, there were more than a hundred small ball bearings. When Roman released the button, Caesar's head disintegrated into a red mist of blood and brains. The ball bearings in the collar shredded Raphael Mora's face and chest, and he was dead before his body hit the ground.

Jessica was ten yards from the Boston Whaler when she heard the explosion on the beach. She turned her head to see what had happened, but a handsome man with a Vandyke beard called out, "Hurry, sweetie. You need to get in the boat." When Jessica reached the boat, he reached down and pulled her over the side, and said, "Lie down on the bottom of the boat."

A moment later, Kay reached the boat and the man with the Vandyke began to pull her on board. Jessica went over to help, and Kay screamed, "Jessica! Get down!"

Jessica dropped to the bottom of the boat, but before she did she looked back at the beach. There was a small cloud of smoke and two bodies lying on the embankment.

As soon as Kay was on board, she said, "Jesus, Roman, what did you do?"

Roman smiled at her. He had a beautiful smile. "I couldn't let him live, Kay."

Kay shook her head, not sure if she should be mad or grateful, then said, "Roman, tell the guy driving to make the boat zigzag. He's got to make us a harder target. Don't head straight out to sea."

Two seconds later, a grenade exploded off the port side of the Whaler.

It took Perez a few seconds to understand what had happened.

He and his sniper had crawled through the construction site and taken positions behind a mound of earth. He watched the exchange take place, saw the boat heading toward shore, and saw the girl and her mother running through the waves to meet the boat. He figured the boat would be the sniper's target when Mora gave the command.

When he turned his head to see what Caesar and Mora were doing, he saw them trying to scramble up an embankment, but he couldn't understand why they were moving so frantically.

And that's when the explosion occurred.

Perez's first reaction was to run to help Caesar Olivera, but he could see that neither Caesar nor Mora was moving. He took out his binoculars and trained them on the two men lying on the beach. Caesar didn't have a head; Raphael Mora didn't have a face. For a moment he didn't know what to do, then he made up his mind.

He looked back out to sea and watched Hamilton being pulled into the boat.

"Kill them," he said to the sniper. "Use the RPGs."

The sniper lived for moments like this.

He was the man who'd shot the armored-car driver in San Diego with the .50-caliber round. There wasn't a weapon he couldn't shoot, and that he couldn't shoot well. His dream—a dream he'd only told his boyfriend—was to one day assassinate someone really important, like the U.S. president or the president of Mexico. He picked up the grenade launcher and took aim at the Boston Whaler.

In San Diego he had been shooting at a moving vehicle, but the vehicle had been traveling on a smooth surface and going in a straight line. The Whaler was being tossed around in the surf, and when he fired the first shot, the boat had just made a hard starboard turn. He missed the boat by ten yards with the first grenade.

He calmly inserted the second grenade into the launcher, while Perez yammered in his ear for him to hurry. Now the boat was moving fast and zigzagging at the same time. He sighted again, tried to anticipate the next turn the boat would make, took a breath, and fired—and missed a second time, the grenade exploding in the water behind the boat.

He heard Perez cursing, but he ignored him and picked up the .50-caliber rifle. He was much better with a rifle than the RPGs. The boat was now about four hundred yards away—not far at all for a man with the sniper's ability. He sighted in on the man driving the Whaler. He was exposed, sitting at a console in the middle of the boat, steering the boat with an automobile-like steering wheel. He aimed at the back of the driver's seat and fired.

The .50-caliber round went through the seat back like it was paper, went through the driver's back and chest like they were paper, too, and embedded itself in the boat's instrument console. The driver fell forward and collapsed on the steering wheel, and the boat began to turn in a long arc back toward the beach.

The sniper couldn't see Hamilton or her daughter. They were lying on the bottom of the boat. But he could see the shoulders and head of the other man in the boat. He took aim at the man's head—he could see the man's beard through the scope as if it were a foot away—but with the boat turning and bouncing up and down in the waves, it wasn't going to be an easy shot. Then he had an idea.

A .50-caliber bullet has enough power to penetrate the cast-iron engine block of an automobile—and the shroud protecting the outboard motor on the Boston Whaler was not made of cast iron. It was made of sheet metal and was considerably larger than a man's head.

The sniper shot the engine. Black smoke poured out of the motor and the boat stopped. Now the sniper could kill everyone in the boat and he wouldn't even need to be able to see them. He'd just keep shooting .50-caliber rounds into the fiberglass hull of the Whaler until they were all dead.

Kay saw the man driving the boat get hit and fall over the steering wheel. She had no idea who the poor man was, just that he was one of Roman's friends. The boat begin to turn in a circle, and Roman started to get up to grab the steering wheel, but then Kay heard a loud twang and the motor began to billow smoke and the boat stopped dead in the water.

"Jesus," Roman said. "What the hell is that guy shooting?"

Kay didn't know what they were going to do next. Before she could think of anything, bullets started to penetrate the sides of the Boston Whaler, going in one side of the boat's hull and out the other. Kay realized the bullets were hitting the boat in a systematic manner, starting at the stern and moving toward the bow. The shooter was marching his shots up the hull, spacing them about a foot apart.

Kay and Jessica were lying in the bottom of the boat, just behind the steering console, which was in the middle of the boat. And when Kay saw bullets punch through the fiberglass hull like it was made of soft cheese, she threw herself on top of her daughter.

A moment later, Roman cried out in agony. He was near the stern, just a few feet away from Kay and Jessica, and was hit in the right thigh. The .50-caliber bullet certainly broke his femur.

Then another shot penetrated the hull and blew a hole in his chest.

Oh, God, Roman. I'm so sorry.

"Move to the stern! Move to the stern!" Kay yelled at Jessica, and the two of them scrambled over Roman's body, keeping their heads down, looking for cover in the part of the boat that the shooter had already hit. As they were moving, one shot grazed the rubber sole of Kay's right tennis shoe, making her whole leg tingle. If the bullet had hit her foot, it would have blown it off.

As the sniper continued to march bullets toward the bow of the Whaler, Kay said to Jessica, "We have to get out of this boat. I want you to go over the starboard side, then—"

The sniper had reached the bow of the boat, and after a brief pause where Kay assumed he was reloading his rifle, he begin to march his shots back toward the stern where she and Jessica were huddled.

"—as soon as you're in the water, take off your life jacket. If you don't, you'll be bobbing in the water and that guy will kill you."

Bullets continued to punch through the hull; the last shot fired was about three feet from Kay's outstretched legs.

"Do you understand?" Kay screamed.

"Yes," Jessica said. Her eyes were the size of saucers.

"I'll go first to distract the guy. I'll go over the port side . . ."

A bullet passed over Kay's legs. "Christ!" she screamed.

There was no more time to talk. Kay jumped up and dove over the side of the boat, just praying that Jessica would move quickly. If Jessica did as Kay had instructed, she would be on the side of the boat not visible to the beach. Kay, however, would be a target.

Kay struggled to get the life vest off. The damn thing was an orange neon sign and keeping her head above the water. The shooter fired at her, and the bullet struck the hull of the boat that was now behind her, missing her head by no more than an inch. Thank God she was bobbing around in the water. She finally got the vest off and dove under the boat.

Jessica was in the water and her vest was already off. Kay swam next to her daughter and said, "Start swimming out to sea. Stay underwater as long as possible and don't travel in a straight line. Go."

"What are you going to do?" Jessica said.

"Just do what I'm telling you. Go!"

"But, Kay, look," Jessica said, and pointed over Kay's shoulder, away from the beach.

Kay didn't have time to look. "Just go!" she screamed at Jessica.

Jessica dove and started swimming out to sea. Thank God she'd been taking surfing lessons and was a strong swimmer. But Kay didn't know how long she'd be able to last.

Kay didn't follow Jessica out to sea. She was going to

continue to distract the sniper to protect Jessica, and instead of swimming away from the beach, she swam parallel to it and kept her head above water. She zigzagged as best she could, but she knew the shooter was good and if he took enough shots at her, he was going to kill her. And her wonderful daughter was probably going to drown.

Then Kay heard the sound of a heavy-caliber machine gun firing—and the sound was coming from *behind* her. *Oh, God help us.* Mora must have sent some of his people to the exchange point by boat, and now she and Jessica would be dodging bullets coming from two directions. But when Kay turned to see who was firing, she saw the most beautiful thing she'd ever seen: a U.S. Coast Guard cutter. It was moving toward the beach at about forty knots, and the man on the bow of the cutter wasn't firing his machine gun at her—he was firing at the sniper. That's what Jessica had been trying to tell her, that she'd seen the Coast Guard cutter.

Kevin Walker had come through after all.

Bullets hit the ground in front of the sniper, and he dropped his rifle and scrambled as fast as he could over to a backhoe that was parked about ten feet away. As he was crawling, he heard Perez cry out in pain. Once he was safely hidden behind the backhoe, he turned to look at Perez. He'd been hit in the stomach and the sniper could see his intestines. Perez was going to die.

The sniper began crawling toward the highway, keeping the backhoe between him and the machine gunner. He heard Perez call to him, but he ignored him. As he crawled he realized his bosses were all dead or dying: Caesar Olivera, Mora, and Perez. Oh, well. He'd find employment with some other organization. A man with his talents was always in demand. He would live and maybe one day have a chance to fulfill his dream and shoot someone who really mattered, not some little girl and her mother.

48

As the machine gunner continued to fire, the crew of the Coast Guard cutter pulled Kay and Jessica out of the water. The cutter then made a wide turn and headed west—and north—back toward the United States.

The machine gunner, a kid from Iowa who had never seen an ocean until two years before, saw a cigarette boat moving toward the cutter at about fifty knots. Two of the men in the cigarette boat were armed with what looked like AK-47s.

The kid from Iowa fired a short burst over the cigarette boat, deliberately aiming high—and laughed when the boat made a turn so tight it almost capsized as it headed back to wherever it had come from.

A white-haired chief, a lifer in his fifties, led Kay and Jessica to the galley and gave them blankets to throw around their shoulders and cups of hot coffee. Kay asked if Kevin Walker was on board, but instead of answering her question, the chief just laughed and said, "The lieutenant will be down in a minute to talk to you."

"Are you okay, Jessica?" Kay asked. The girl's hair was

plastered to her scalp, her lips were blue, and her teeth were chattering from the cold water. Her current physical condition wasn't what worried Kay, however.

"Yeah, I guess," Jessica said.

"Did they hurt you? Did they . . . did they do anything to you?"

"No, they didn't do anything. I'm fine. Really." Jessica decided she wouldn't tell Kay how Perez had slapped her; Kay might decide to go back to Mexico and shoot him. "But why'd they kidnap me?"

Before Kay could answer, a woman wearing a blue Coast Guard jumpsuit came into the galley. The woman was slim, had a narrow face and short dark hair. She looked bright, competent—and tough.

"Agent Hamilton," she said, "I'm Lieutenant Janet Stevenson, and I'm . . ."

"Thank you for saving our lives, Lieutenant," Kay said.

"Yeah, well, I just fired a machine gun into Mexico and I'm fairly certain I've committed an act of war."

"Those men belonged to a drug cartel," Kay said.

"I'll be sure to mention that at my court-martial."

"I'm sorry," Kay said, "I didn't know Marshal Walker was going to involve the Coast Guard."

Kay had asked Walker to get a boat and head toward Rosarito Beach. She assumed he'd borrow some civilian's boat, one belonging to a friend or someone who worked for the Marshals Service. Kay had told him that Roman Quinterez was going to bring her and Jessica out of Mexico, and all Walker had to do was meet them off the Mexican coast, escort Kay back to the United States to face the music, and take Jessica into protective custody.

If Roman hadn't decided to kill Caesar Olivera, everything would have worked out just the way she planned, Roman would still be alive, and Kay and her daughter would have escaped—except Kay and Jessica would have been on the run from Caesar Olivera for the rest of their lives. Yes, Roman did the right thing, even though what he did put Jessica in danger. Kay owed him so much for everything—and now would never be able to repay him.

"Why did you help Walker, Lieutenant?" Kay asked.

"If I had known I was going to have to drive my boat onto a Mexican beach, I wouldn't have."

Kay wondered if Walker had some sort of personal relationship with the lieutenant and that's why she helped him. She was a good-looking woman, and Walker was—or used to be—a desirable man. Most likely, though, Walker had simply told her that she'd be helping the marshals with a conventional rescue mission in international waters. But when Roman's boat was disabled and the lieutenant saw people being shot, she was forced to take action. Whatever the case, Kay was grateful to her and sorry about the trouble she was in now.

"Is Walker here?" Kay asked.

"Yeah, he's in a bunk up forward. He was drunk when he came on board, and he started puking the minute we left the pier. Now, I'm not going to put cuffs on you, but you're under arrest for helping Tito Olivera escape."

Jessica jumped up and said, "What!"

"It's okay, Jessica," Kay said. "She's only doing what she has to do, and she's right."

"I've already radioed San Diego that you're on board. Someone will be meeting us when we dock. FBI or U.S. Marshals, I imagine, but I don't know who has jurisdiction over you."

"What will happen to Jessica?"

"I don't know, and she's not my problem. She's not under arrest, so you can probably call a friend to take care of her."

Kay didn't have any friends to call—well, maybe Maddox—but there was no point in bringing that up.

"Can you tell me where Tito Olivera is?" the lieutenant asked. "The guys in San Diego want to know."

"Yeah," Kay said. "He's dead. His body is in a storage locker in La Mesa."

"Jesus, Kay," Jessica muttered.

"Give me the address of the storage place," the lieutenant said, "and I'll radio that information to San Diego. Did you kill him?"

Before Kay could answer, the lieutenant said, "Wait! You don't have to answer that. You have the right to an attorney."

Before the lieutenant could complete the Miranda warning, Kay told the lieutenant where Tito's corpse was hidden. As soon as she left, Jessica said, "Kay, tell me what's going on. Why are you being arrested?"

Kay told her the whole story.

When she finished, Jessica said, "I don't know what to say, Kay. I mean, I can't believe you did all this for me."

Now, that pissed Kay off. "What the hell did you think I was going to do? You're my *daughter*, for Christ's sake. Did you think I was going to let those guys kill you?"

Before Jessica could respond, Kevin Walker lurched into the galley. He looked awful. He hadn't shaved in a couple of days, his eyes were bloodshot, and he was as pale as a sheet.

"I guess you made it," he said to Kay. "I was sort of out of it when all the shooting started."

"Thanks, Kevin. I owe you big-time."

Walker started to say something, then he clamped his hand over his mouth, turned, and ran out of the galley. Kay wondered if anyone had ever died from seasickness.

"Do you think they'll actually send you to jail?" Jessica asked.

"I don't know," Kay said. "I do know my career with the DEA is over."

"What are you going to do?"

"I don't have the slightest idea. Maybe I'll become a stay-at-home mom after I get out of jail." Then she started laughing, and Jessica joined in, and they couldn't seem to stop.

49

Kay and Jessica disembarked the Coast Guard cutter in San Diego to find Jim Davis standing tall on the pier. With his white hair and white mustache, he looked like somebody's grandfather—somebody's very pissed-off grandfather.

"If you're here to put cuffs on me, Jim," Kay said, "I want my daughter—"

"Shut up, Hamilton. I don't want to hear a word from you. The marshals are going to escort you and your daughter to your home so you can pack some clothes, then you'll be taken to a hotel here in town and the marshals will provide protection until we can assess the threat against you. This afternoon, someone from the U.S. Attorney's Office will be over to take a statement from you, and tomorrow you'll be taken to a meeting to discuss this whole mess."

"A meeting? So I'm not going to be arrested?"

Davis ignored the question. "Give me your gun and your badge and your passport."

"My passport? You think I'm a flight risk?"

"Hamilton, give me your gun, your badge, and your passport."

"I lost the gun in Mexico," Kay said. "It's in fifty feet of water off Rosarito Beach." She pulled her badge and her passport out of the back pocket of her jeans and handed them to Davis.

"There's something else, Hamilton. María Delgato, her mother, her brother, Figgins, and Patterson were slaughtered in Neah Bay. They're all dead."

"Oh, God," Kay said. Now *she* felt like throwing up.

"Did you tell Olivera's people where María was being kept?" Davis asked.

"No!" Kay said. "I would never do that. You know I wouldn't."

Davis looked at her for a long time, then said, "Yeah, I didn't think so. But somehow Olivera found out where they were staying."

Kay remembered how nervous Figgins had sounded the last two times she spoke with him and wondered if he'd made a mistake or withheld something from her. Whatever the case, she felt just sick about him, his partner, and the Delgatos having been killed. Her only satisfaction was knowing the people responsible were also dead.

"So what's going to happen to me, Jim?" she asked.

"I don't know," Davis said. Then he paused and added, "You should have called me before you decided to bust Tito out of jail, Kay."

"Oh, yeah? What would you have done?"

"I don't know, but—"

"Well, I know. You would have called a dozen people, then a big meeting would have been held with a lot of bureaucrats, and they would have decided that the United States government doesn't negotiate with drug cartels. Then my daughter would have died."

"I'm not going to argue with you, Hamilton. Just go with the marshals."

Kay still thought Jim Davis was a pretty good guy.

The marshals took Kay and Jessica to an Embassy Suites in La Jolla. She'd been expecting some fleabag motel. After they showered, they ordered an expensive dinner from room service and celebrated that they were still alive. If she hadn't been with her daughter, Kay would have downed half a dozen of those little bottles in the minibar.

"I like your hair, by the way," Jessica said.

"I can't get used to myself as a redhead," Kay said, "but I like the style. If I don't go to jail, I'll get the dye taken out and go back to my own color, but maybe I'll wear it this way for a while."

"You really think you'll go to jail?" Jessica had asked this before, and Kay imagined the girl was not only concerned for her but also concerned that she'd be on her own again.

"I don't know. There's a rule they teach you when you work for the government. It says: *It's better to ask for permission first than have to beg for forgiveness later.* I didn't ask permission. If things had gone wrong, Tito could have gotten away." She didn't bother to add: And you would have been killed. "Then there's the small problem that I knocked out two federal marshals, helped kill a couple Mexican citizens, and—"

"They were drug dealers."

"—and, thanks to me, the U.S. Coast Guard invaded Mexico. So, will I go to jail? Maybe. Will I get fired? No doubt about it."

That afternoon, a wooden-faced lawyer from the U.S. Attorney's Office showed up with a tape recorder. He read Kay her Miranda rights, then just sat there as Kay told him everything she did after Jessica was kidnapped. Kay thought about lying about whose idea it was to build the explosive collar that killed Caesar Olivera—she thought about blaming that on Roman—but she didn't.

The lawyer turned off the recorder when Kay was finished and said, "You might want to hire your own attorney."

Jim Davis called Kay the next morning and told her the meeting had been postponed for a day. Apparently, the big dogs were still arguing over what to do with her. The marshals wouldn't let Kay and Jessica leave their hotel room, so they spent the day watching pay-per-view movies on TV that cost about fifteen bucks a pop.

At one point Jessica looked over at Kay, and feeling eyes on her, Kay said, "What?"

"I still can't believe what you did for me."

"Does this mean you're going to start calling me Mom now?" Kay said.

Jessica looked at her for a moment, then said, "Nah, I don't think so."

They both started laughing again, but when they stopped, Jessica grew serious and said, "Why did you decide to give me up for adoption?"

Kay nodded her head. "Yeah, let's talk about that. And about what I did in Miami."

50

The meeting to determine Kay's fate was being held in the Federal Building on Front Street and the U.S. Attorney for the Southern District of California, a man named Callahan, was personally chairing the session. With Callahan was Assistant U.S. Attorney Robert Meyer, Kay's old lover, and Kay wasn't sure why he was there. Maybe he was responsible for prosecuting some of the crimes she'd committed.

Also attending was Kay's boss, Jim Davis; Assistant U.S. Attorney Carol Maddox, the lawyer who would have prosecuted Tito if Tito had lived; U.S. Marshal Harlan Declan, the man who had replaced Kevin Walker after Walker was fired; a gray-haired lady from the State Department who wasn't introduced by name and who was wearing a blue-green pantsuit that might have been borrowed from Hillary Clinton's closet; and a dork with a bow tie who was responsible for the U.S. Attorney's PR—in other words, the guy they stuck behind the podium to deliver carefully drafted obfuscations.

There was one other person there who Kay hadn't expected but was delighted to see: Barb Reynolds, her friend and mentor, and the one person in the DEA who had always looked out for her back in Washington.

Kay was pretty sure, however, that not even Barb could save her.

Kay sat down at the end of the long conference table. Barb winked at her—which Kay took as a good sign— and when she looked at Robert Meyer, he managed a small smile, which disappeared when his boss started talking.

Callahan, the U.S. Attorney, was a florid-faced, balding man who reminded Kay of a TV actor whose name she couldn't remember. He began the meeting by saying: "Agent Hamilton, you're in a lot of trouble."

No shit, Kay almost said, but didn't. Instead she said, "Then maybe I should have a lawyer here." But she already knew that she didn't need a lawyer.

"I suggest that you just sit there and be quiet and not interrupt when I'm talking," Callahan said. "Right now you're facing federal prosecution for helping Tito Olivera escape, and two counts of reckless endangerment for exposing two U.S. marshals to a chemical agent that could have killed them. In addition to these federal charges, the State of California can convict you for leaving the scene of the accident that killed Tito Olivera and for double counts of grand-theft auto."

"Oh, bullshit," Kay said.

"What did you say?" Callahan shouted, half rising from his chair, his red face becoming even redder. Kay hoped the guy didn't have a stroke.

"I said *bullshit*. You're not going to prosecute me for

anything. I'm a mother who saved her daughter from a Mexican drug cartel. You couldn't find a jury in this country who'd convict me." Looking at Carol Maddox, Kay said, "What do they call it when the jury says to hell with the law and lets the defendant go?"

"Jury nullification," Maddox said. Maddox seemed amused by the whole proceeding—and before the meeting started, she was the only one who had asked Kay how her daughter was doing. Kay figured she'd gone a couple of steps up the motherhood ladder in Maddox's eyes. Maybe not Mother of the Year material, but at least now she was part of the sisterhood.

"Yeah, that's it," Kay said. "Jury nullification. And if you think I won't talk to the media, you're crazy. I'm the movie of the week. I'll get an agent and I'll go on talk shows and tell the whole world how I saved my daughter and how Caesar Olivera was killed. I know you don't want that to happen, so why are we really here?"

Kay noticed that Barb Reynolds was struggling not to smile, but then Barb said, "Settle down, Kay. Mr. Callahan wasn't threatening you, he was just explaining what the government *could* do if it chose to."

The hell it wasn't a threat.

"So, like I said, what are we all doing here?"

Seeing that his boss was too angry to speak without spitting, Robert Meyer answered her question.

"Ms. Hamilton," he said, "we have a couple of problems here."

The impersonal *Ms. Hamilton* was to remind her that although he might have slept with her a few times, his

primary allegiance was to the Department of Justice—
and his career. But Kay knew that Robert Meyer was on
her side.

"First," Meyer said, "the media is aware that you
helped Tito Olivera escape. They're aware because we told
them when we released your picture to keep you from
crossing the border with Tito. The story, of course, immediately went national. 'DEA Agent Helps Drug Czar
Escape,' that sort of thing. Right now the media doesn't
know that Tito's dead, nor do they know what happened
in Mexico, but we can't contain this whole thing. There
are going to be leaks, because too many people know
most of what happened. So we're going to have to tell the
truth." Meyer paused, then added, "Well, sort of the
truth."

The nameless lady from the State Department jumped
in. "The headless body of Caesar Olivera and the bodies
of two of his top people were found by the Mexican police at Rosarito Beach. Fortunately—although I suppose
fortunately isn't the right word—the bodies of Colonel
Roman Quinterez of the Policía Federal and one of his
men were also found in a bullet-riddled boat right off the
beach. I've told the Mexican foreign ministry that Caesar
Olivera kidnapped your daughter and that Colonel Quinterez helped you get her away from the Olivera cartel. And
that's *all* we know.

"The State Department's biggest concern is the action
taken by the Coast Guard to rescue you. The Mexican
government doesn't really care that Caesar's dead, particularly as it appears, as you have told us, that it was a

Mexican police officer who killed him. The Mexicans do care, however, about United States military forces entering their territorial waters. Countries are rather sensitive toward that sort of thing.

"The good news is that Mexico isn't like the U.S. When the locals hear gunshots down there, they don't rush outside with their video cameras and they don't call the media—they're afraid the cartels might kill them if they do. What all this means is that so far no one has reported seeing a U.S. Coast Guard vessel off Rosarito Beach at dawn three days ago firing a machine gun."

"What if somebody does report it?" Kay asked.

"Then I'll probably lie my ass off," the State Department lady said. Kay was beginning to like her.

"What we're going to do is tell an abridged version of the truth," Robert Meyer said. "Stanley"—Meyer pointed at the dork with the bow tie—"is going to hold a short press conference tomorrow. He's going to say that your daughter was kidnapped by the Olivera cartel and you took unauthorized action to free her, which included removing Tito from the brig at Pendleton. We'll say that Tito was subsequently killed in an automobile accident but that your daughter was eventually freed thanks to the Mexican federal police, and that you're no longer employed by the DEA. Stanley will also say that we have no *direct* knowledge of what happened in Mexico, that the U.S. government had absolutely no involvement with the death of Caesar Olivera, and that we can't comment further as additional comments could affect ongoing DEA operations and put DEA personnel at risk. When the press starts to bombard Stanley with questions, he'll repeat: I cannot comment further because blah, blah, blah, and then we'll hope that some sort of financial or political or natural disaster occurs to give the press something else to think about. Fortunately, the press has the attention span of a flock of hummingbirds—and Stanley is very good at using a whole lot of words without actually saying anything."

Stanley smiled modestly at this remark.

"What all this means," Callahan said to Kay, finally resuming control of the meeting, "is that you keep your damn mouth shut. You don't talk to the press. You don't hire an agent. You don't write your memoirs. If you do, I'm going to press charges against you, and my lawyers are good enough that there won't be any goddamn jury nullification."

Callahan didn't seem to like her.

"I can live with that," Kay said, "but why can't I keep my job, get transferred to some other part of the country, maybe overseas? I mean, I know I—"

Barb Reynolds shook her head. "Sorry, Kay, you're gone. If you keep your mouth shut like Mr. Callahan says, you'll be allowed to resign. If you don't resign, then I'll fire you and you'll have a hard time getting a job anywhere in law enforcement."

"Okay," Kay said. She'd known that keeping her job was a long shot. This was the best deal she was going to get.

Barb slid a couple pieces of paper across the table at her and said, "Sign those. Don't bother reading them, because we're not going to change the wording. I'll get you copies later."

Kay signed the papers and Barb passed them to Jim Davis; as the lowest-ranking bureaucrat in the room, he would make the copies. Everybody else stood up to leave. Robert Meyer's eyes met hers and he smiled at her before he left, a sad sort of smile, the smile of an old lover saying he missed her—and Barb Reynolds noticed.

Barb turned to Kay and said, "Now, you and I need to go have a couple of cocktails."

"What?" Kay said. "We're celebrating?"

"Not exactly. Or maybe we are. Whatever the case, we've got a few other things to talk about. And I want a drink."

They went to a bar a couple of blocks from the Federal Building, and Barb ordered them both Grey Goose martinis.

Barb looked great. She had short dark hair, the kind of cheekbones you saw on models, and green eyes that promised mystery, sex, and mischief. She was wearing a red St. John suit with a hemline that stopped an inch above her knees and clung to her butt. She was almost fifty, but she had the body of a thirty-year-old. Thanks to a face-lift and maybe a little Botox, she had the face of a forty-year-old.

When they sat down at the table, Kay noticed a good-looking, gray-haired guy at the bar—one of those California guys with a George Hamilton tan who probably drove a Porsche and considered eighteen holes a full day's work. He was looking at Barb, and Barb noticed him looking, and gave him a smile Kay could only describe as seductive. She had always wondered if Barb was faithful to her marriage vows, but when it came to sex and morals, Kay was anything but sanctimonious.

Barb took a sip from her martini and said, "God, that tastes good. I might have to have a couple more of these." She glanced over at the guy at the bar.

"What's going to happen to that Coast Guard lieutenant?" Kay asked. "Is her career over, too?"

"Oh, hell no. The lieutenant didn't tell you, but her mother happens to be a congresswoman from Maine, and Mama sits on the House Defense Appropriations Committee. The lieutenant's going to get a very vague, very mildly worded official reprimand stuck in her file for what she did—and, simultaneously, pats on the back from a couple of admirals for saving your bacon. That lieutenant will be the Commandant of the Coast Guard one of these days."

"How 'bout the marines? The guys whose car I stole? Are they going to end up doing time for a DUI homicide?"

"Again, the answer is: Hell, no. You gotta learn to have some faith in your government, Hamilton, and your government doesn't want the marines in a courtroom talking about what happened. As your friend Mr. Meyer said, we want this whole thing to just fade away. Those marines, God protect 'em, will shortly be in Afghanistan.

"And speaking of Meyer, he's the guy you have to thank for everything. He was the one able to talk some sense into Callahan. Do you have some sort of special relationship with Meyer?"

"Uh, no," Kay said. "I just worked with him on a couple of cases when I first got here, but I don't know him all that well."

"Hmm," Barb said, and Kay figured she was thinking, *Liar, liar, pants on fire.*

To change the subject, Kay said, "Did the marines ever get their car back?"

"Yeah, they found it in Del Mar."

"That's good," Kay said. "I'll send them some money for new cell phones, and I've got to get some money to Rodney, too, because he's never going to be getting his car back."

"Rodney?"

"The other guy whose car I stole. I left it in Mexico."

"Jesus. You're a veritable one-woman crime wave." Barb finished her first martini. Kay's was only half gone, but Barb waved at the bartender and held up two fingers. She again glanced over at the gray-haired guy at the bar, and again they smiled at each other.

"I've tried to get ahold of Kevin Walker," Kay said, "to thank him again and to see how he's doing, but I can't find him."

"Walker is in a rehab place up north, near Sacramento. He's doing fine. He's also going to land on his feet. After he's sober, he'll be moving to Wyoming."

"Wyoming?"

"Yeah. Walker has an uncle who's been the sheriff of Sweetwater County for twenty-two years and is planning to retire in three years. The smart money is on Walker replacing his uncle."

Kay could see the Marlboro Man as a county sheriff. "So everybody ends up okay but me," she said. "Maybe Walker will offer me a job as a deputy in Shitwater County."

"That's *Sweetwater*, and quit feeling sorry for yourself. You're lucky you're not dead or in jail. And face it, Kay, you really weren't going to go any higher in the DEA, even before this happened."

"What do you mean? I was a great agent."

"That's the point. You were a great *agent*. But you were a lousy supervisor and a lousy bureaucrat."

Kay started to object, but Barb said, "How's your daughter doing?"

"She's okay. She's a tough kid. Smart as a whip, too."

"Are you worried about Caesar's guys coming after you and her?"

"Yeah, but I don't think that'll happen. They're all too busy fighting over Caesar's empire."

"Still, it might be a good thing if you moved away from here."

"My daughter still has two years to go in high school, and she's in a good school right now."

"They have good schools in Washington. In fact, I'm sure I can get Jessica into the school my boys went to."

"Washington?"

"You see, even though you're not supervisor material, you—"

"I don't agree with that."

"—you have other qualities. You're quick on your feet, you're brave, you're tough, and you have a facility for languages. Well, there's a certain organization in Washington who needs people with your talents, and I have some pull with this organization."

"What are you talking about? CIA?"

"Not exactly. But I'm thinking by the time you go through training and get a couple more languages under your belt, Jessica will be out of high school and off to college."

"Does this unnamed organization know what I did in Mexico?"

"You bet. I told them all about Mexico, and they love what you did down there. As far as they're concerned, that was your job interview. They can hardly wait to meet you."

Barb finished her second martini. Kay was still on her first.

"Now, I'd suggest you go home and tell your daughter you're going to be moving to D.C., and in a day or two, you'll get a phone call."

Kay just sat there for a moment, unable to move, unable to believe how lucky she was. She hoped Jessica wouldn't be too upset by having to move to Washington—she knew her daughter liked living in Southern

California—but she also knew Jessica would understand and would want what was best for Kay's career. Furthermore, it sounded like this unnamed agency that wasn't "exactly" CIA could even be more fun than the DEA. She wondered if—

Barb gave her a tap on the hand. "Go on, honey. Get moving. Go home to your daughter." Barb looked over at the gray-haired guy at the bar—he really was a hunk—showed him that her martini glass was empty, and made a little pout. "The grown-ups have things to do."

ACKNOWLEDGMENTS

I want to thank the following people for their help on this novel:

Kaaren Netwig, Jessie Kanallakan, and Owen Kelly for helping me with and taking the time to read some of the Mexico scenes in the book. Any errors relating to Mexico, border crossings, Rosarito Beach, et cetera, are mine alone.

Linda Kirk for educating me on the nature of fifteen-year-old girls. I don't have a daughter and never spent any time with teenage girls, and Linda spent over an hour talking to me about her daughter, Jessica, when her Jessica was fifteen. The Jessica in this novel is based—very loosely—on Linda's real-life daughter, who is now a brilliant doctor.

Rodger Brown for letting me play with a real .32-caliber automatic like Kay uses in this book.

Judge James P. Donohue for taking so much time to educate me on federal warrants, the Patriot Act, and other legal matters. Any errors in the legal stuff also are mine alone.

George Steffen for introducing me to Steve Wolfe, and to Steve, who was a huge help in so far as educating me on Camp Pendleton when I made a research trip to San Diego.

James Barber, a friend and former boss. There's a line in the book attributed to Caesar Olivera about good news delivered late just being a "pleasure delayed." I paraphrased that line from a 1986 training paper Jim wrote regarding principles for managing Navy nuclear work. The paper is still in circulation today, twenty-eight years later.

Phoebe Pickering, Peter Grennen, Tony Davis, Aileen Boyle, and everyone else at Penguin/Blue Rider Press who participated in the production of this book. I particularly want to thank David Rosenthal, President of Blue Rider Press, for the wonderful job he did editing and improving the book, and especially for being willing to take a chance on this novel.

Finally, David Gernert, for all the effort he put into finding a home for this book. David, I don't know what I'd do without you.

Read on for an excerpt from
M. A. Lawson's novel

VIKING BAY

Coming in January 2015 in hardcover
from Blue Rider Press.

I t began with a text message.

Alpha texted Bravo and the burner phone in Bravo's pocket vibrated. Bravo looked at the message: *Transfer complete.*

Bravo punched numbers into the same phone, calling Charlie. He let the receiving phone ring twice, then disconnected the call. No words were necessary.

The man designated as Charlie removed his phone from a leg pocket in his cargo pants, punched in five digits, and hit CALL—and a transformer at a substation half a kilometer away disintegrated, sending bolts of white light a hundred feet into the sky. Witnesses later said that lightning—on a clear, cloudless night—had struck the transformer.

Delta didn't need a text message or a call to tell him to perform his task: the power going out in the compound was his signal. He put on night-vision goggles and slipped into the house. He caught the old man just as he was coming out of his bedroom to investigate the power outage, and Delta slit his throat as if the old man were a newborn lamb. He dragged the body into a closet and left the house.

Delta called Bravo's phone and it vibrated twice. Again no words were needed to tell Bravo that Delta had completed his mission.

Bravo didn't use the burner phone for his next call. He used his personal phone, because it didn't matter if his next call could be traced. He dialed a number and spoke for less than ten seconds. Then he counted slowly to sixty—sixty seconds should be plenty of time. If he was wrong, a man Bravo needed to live was going to die. At the count of sixty, he reached into his pocket and, without looking, punched the # key five times.

The package erupted inside the house. Stainless-steel ball bearings and roofing nails spread outward faster than the speed of sound, and an odorless flammable gel inside the package ignited. The people in the room, some sitting no more than two feet from the bomb, were ripped asunder in an instant. Their flesh was burning seconds after that.

Bravo was confident that no one had survived; nothing made of flesh and bone could have survived.

Bravo was wrong.

Bowman struck faster than a rattlesnake and his right hand darted out and grabbed Kay's sweatshirt, his big hand clutching the material between her breasts. As he jerked her off balance, she slashed downward with her right hand to break his grip, but all that did was hurt her hand; hitting Bowman's forearm was like hitting a baseball bat.

Bowman quickly shifted his grip and started to turn to his left—the move a precursor to his tossing her over his shoulder—again—and as she began to counter the move, she realized, too late, the move was a feint. Bowman's right leg snaked behind her left calf and he simply smacked his hand into her chest, knocking her down, and then he belly-flopped onto her, knocking the wind out of her. His forearm—the baseball bat—slammed across her throat and started to crush her larynx.

"Stop!" Simmons said.

Simmons was a tough little nut in his fifties, about five-foot-six, built like a pint-sized version of Superman. He was an ex–Marine master sergeant and in charge of the hand-to-hand combat course. For some reason, he'd matched Kay up with Bowman, who was six-foot-four—eight inches taller than she was—and weighed two hundred thirty pounds—almost exactly a hundred pounds more than she did. On top of that, Kay sensed that Bowman liked to knock women around—his way of demonstrating that they shouldn't be on the same playing field with the boys—and he was just beating the shit out of her. She already had a mouse developing under her left eye where he'd "accidentally" hit her with his elbow and she knew tomorrow there would be a bruise the size of Bowman's big paw in the center of her chest.

"Hamilton," Simmons said, "how many times do I have to tell you? You can't let him get ahold of you first. You gotta be quicker than him."

Kay just shook her head; she didn't bother to say that she wasn't *intentionally* letting Bowman maul her.

"Okay, let's try it again. This time, Hamilton, circle to his left. He's right-handed. And when he reaches for you—"

"Yeah, I got it," Kay said, but she was thinking that this whole thing was total bullshit. It was only in movies that women beat up men who outweighed them by a hundred pounds. For that matter, that was why they had weight divisions in boxing, because, in general, big guys beat little guys. If a monster like Bowman had attacked her on the street—out in the real world—she would have pulled out a gun and shot him or hit him with anything that would dent his thick skull. Or she'd kick him in the nuts—a move not permitted in this particular course.

Bowman came toward her again, and Kay circled to his left as Simmons had told her. Then, when Bowman's back was to Simmons so Simmons couldn't see his face, Bowman made a smooching gesture with his lips.

And Kay kicked him in the nuts. As hard as she could.

Bowman fell to the mat, grasping his crotch, and Simmons started screaming at her. Well, fuck them both.

"Are you okay, Bowman?" Simmons asked.

"I think she crushed my testicle," Bowman said. At least that's what Kay thought he said. It was hard to understand him with his teeth all clenched.

Simmons turned to one of the other students—there were only four people in the class, and Kay was the only woman—and said, "Connors, go get the medic. And Hamilton, you get your ass to my office and wait for me there."

Simmons's office, just down the hall from the gymnasium, looked like a high school coach's office and not a coach who taught at one of the better schools. There was a battered metal desk, a wooden chair behind the desk that swiveled and could be tilted back, and a couple of straight-backed chairs in front of the desk. On the walls were charts showing photos of men in various judo and karate positions. In one corner was a set of weights for doing curls, which explained Simmons's hard little arms. Kay shut the door and noticed a small mirror on the back of the door.

She looked into the mirror and touched the blooming mouse under her eye. It wasn't too bad and could be covered with makeup. She was lucky her eye wasn't swollen shut. She was also lucky Bowman hadn't broken her nose. She'd had her nose broken once before and it had really hurt.

She didn't know what she was going to say to Simmons. She knew he was going to chew her out, but she also knew that's all he was going to do. They weren't going to fire her for kicking Bowman; she was more valuable than Bowman to the Group.

Bowman was muscle, pure and simple. He was good with his fists, okay with a pistol—although he wasn't any better than Kay with a pistol—but he was exceptional with a rifle. She wondered if Callahan was grooming Bowman to be his designated sniper. Bowman, however, didn't have her language skills; in fact, he had an accent like the guys who hawked the beer at Fenway and was barely understandable in English. Kay could speak Spanish like a native, and in a few months would be passable in Farsi. Bowman was also slow when it came to the technical stuff—alarms, computers, listening devices, GPS systems—anything with a microchip—and Kay outscored him in those classes.

The door opened and Simmons stepped into the room and slammed the door shut behind him. "Hamilton," he said, "I don't know what I'm gonna do with you."

Kay almost smiled. She remembered her last boss saying the same thing to her—right before she was fired.

Three and a half months earlier, Kay had been an agent with the Drug Enforcement Administration. She'd enjoyed the work and had been a good agent; she made a name for herself in Miami after she killed a major player there named Marco Alvarez and three of his men. Marco was the one who broke her nose when he tried to beat her to death after he found out she was an undercover cop who'd penetrated his organization.

After Miami, she was transferred to San Diego, placed in a vacant supervisor's spot, and put in charge of her own team—and she immediately set her sights on the brother of Caesar Olivera. Caesar was the leader of the most powerful drug cartel in Mexico, and his little brother, a moron named Tito, ran his North American operations. Kay eventually arrested Tito for murdering another San Diego drug dealer—a murder she could have prevented, had she chosen to. Unfortunately, it didn't end there.

Caesar Olivera kidnapped Kay's daughter, Jessica, and forced Kay to break his brother out of jail in return for her daughter. By the time it was all over, Tito Olivera had died in car accident, Kay had killed Caesar Olivera and one of his top guys down in Mexico, and a colonel in the Policía Federal had died assisting her. Then the United States Coast Guard virtually committed an act of war by sailing into Mexican territorial waters and killing more of Caesar's people to help Kay and Jessica escape.

Kay could have been prosecuted for breaking Tito Olivera out of jail, but the DEA wanted to keep what she had done in Mexico under wraps as much as possible and didn't want the publicity that would accompany a trial. On the other hand, the DEA at that point didn't want Kay Hamilton anymore, either.

Kay had made the mistake of not informing anyone in her chain of command that Caesar had kidnapped her daughter, and she didn't get permission to go into Mexico on her own to save her. She'd already had a reputation for being insubordinate and playing loose with the rules before she killed Caesar, and killing Caesar the way she did was the last straw: The DEA fired her.

Ironically, the person who fired her was the best friend she had in the DEA, a woman named Barb Reynolds, who was a deputy director back in D.C. and who had been Kay's mentor. After Barb fired her, she took Kay out for a drink. While Kay was sulking, wondering what she was going to do for a living and how she was going to support her daughter, Barb told her that she might be able to get Kay into a certain organization in Washington who valued her talents.

"Do they know what I did in Mexico?" Kay had asked, and Barb had responded by smiling and saying, "As far as this particular organization is concerned, Mexico was your job interview. Believe me, they want you."

When Kay had asked if the unnamed organization was the CIA, Barb had said, "Not exactly."

Not exactly turned out to be one hell of an understatement.

Simmons chewed her out as expected, essentially giving her a lecture on fair play and sportsmanship as if she and Bowman were a couple of five-year-olds on a T-ball team. Kay pretended to be contrite and Simmons pretended to believe her. After Simmons finished, Kay showered and had just exited the gym when her phone rang. It was Anna Mercer, Callahan's deputy.

"Drop whatever you're doing and come to my office," Mercer said.

"I'm down at the gym in Alexandria," Kay said. "I just finished with that stupid hand-to-hand combat course you're making me take."

"Yeah, well, drive fast."